The Agreements

Other Books by Wendy Jo Cerna

The Baby-Catcher Gate (2017)

The Agreements

A Novel
by
Wendy Jo Cerna

The Agreements

Copyright © 2020 Wendy Jo Cerna

All rights reserved.

This is a work of fiction. Any similarity to persons, living or dead, is not intended by the author. The places, incidences and circumstances portrayed are the product of the author's imagination.

Cover design: Julie M. McKnight

ISBN: 979-8647510952

For my parents
Arnold & Doris
And for their parents before them
I am eternally grateful

As for us, we have all of these great witnesses who encircle us like clouds. So, we must let go of every wound that has pierced us and the sin we so easily fall into. Then we will be able to run life's marathon race with passion and determination, for the path has been already marked out before us.

We look away from the natural realm and we fasten our gaze onto Jesus who birthed faith within us and who leads us forward into faith's perfection. His example is this: Because his heart was focused on the joy of knowing that you would be his, he endured the agony of the cross and conquered its humiliation, and now sits exalted at the right hand of the throne of God!

Hebrews 12:1-2
(The Passion Translation)

Prologue

There was a time, before time, when time hung suspended in plans and hopes and dreams. Where beginnings were not yet begun and endings not yet ended. Where scrolls were composed and blueprints drawn up. Where lives were imagined, gifts wrapped, genealogies conceived, and nations invented. It was a time that to even describe in terms of time is impossible. But for now, for the purposes of stuffing the infinite into the finite, the impossible must be. For it is in this irreconcilable moment of non-time that agreements are being made and were made and will be fulfilled. Agreements unfathomably complex and fearfully deep that were entered into willingly with no guarantees save one—that love will prevail.

Chapter 1 – The Agreement

The bundle of energy that swept into the agreement chamber on a robust exhale of wind was gorgeous. Before the agreement facilitator assigned to the case could greet the newcomer, however, the being began to spin, casting out a dizzying array of flashes. When it finally came to a halt, it had divided and formed into two human beings. Two females, to be exact. Tall and willowy with flowing black hair and amethyst-colored eyes and garbed from head to toe in glowing light, they were identical but separate. Not unheard of, of course, but unusual. For the facilitator, it was not only a first but, in fact, the first appointment of his entire career, having just been called over from the far side of eternity to participate in this, the latest creation of the Designer's hand.

The facilitator's name was Carlyle the Caretaker, for he was immensely gifted in his ability to care for even the finest of details in all matters of administration. His résumé included the census of cosmic beings, the surveyance of heavenly bodies, and the oversight of superstructure multiverse planning. But this, his latest assignment, involved direct interaction with a race he had never before encountered, the race that was identified among the heavenly beings as the apple of the Designer's eye—the human race.

Made in the Designer's own image, these people were his response to the angelic revolt that had shaken the cosmos. People whose purpose was to carry the heart of the Designer into the rebellion, overcome the darkness, and restore peace to this slice of eternity. But, in infusing this godlike race with free will, something had gone awry.

So, the Designer had recalled many angelic forces from far-flung stretches of creation to focus attention on this decidedly complicated disarray. Word was that a plan was already in place to work this all together for good. It was also widely rumored that he didn't so much need the additional help from the angelic hosts as he wanted them to participate in something they had never participated in before—redemption.

A polite "Ahem" from the twins standing in front of him returned Carlyle's attention to the task at hand. Having no experience in agreement signings, he wondered for the briefest of moments how he should proceed. For there was only one scroll, one pen, and one stamp on the stone table that he had meticulously arranged next to the all-important document of authorization.

He leaned his slender frame back into the velvety softness of his chair behind the table, smoothed out the folds of his navy uniform, and pondered his predicament. As he did, the scroll lifted off the table of its own accord, spiraled upward, and unfurled around the three of them in a perfect circular wall. The girls clapped their hands in delight. Carlyle nodded nonchalantly at them as though he had been expecting this all along.

"I, uh, welcome both of you to this momentous occasion," he said. "I was not anticipating two of you at once, but I'm certain there is a plan. There is always a plan, as I'm sure you are aware, having come from your planning sessions so very recently."

Carlyle knew he was rambling, but he truly did not know how to proceed. His trainer, the highly respected Madeline of the High Plains, had told him to be prepared for the marvelous, unique, and sometimes strange, but she had left open the particulars of procedures.

"You must allow the humans to lead the way," she had told him. "For they are a race that has been designated for exact times and places agreed upon between their spirits and the One who holds all things together. And though they know the way, they know not

The Agreements

how they know. They may need some encouragement to lean into their knowings. This is your job: to guide and facilitate and follow."

Life exuded from the twins. A pulsing, weighty vibration. Yet they did not move.

"So, the scroll has been opened, as you can see," Carlyle said. "Please begin as you see fit."

He settled back, hoping this small prodding would be enough. Long moments expanded and breathed. He waited, remembering Madeline's instructions to never hurry and always hope.

Finally, just as he was about to try a different tactic, the two girls turned toward each other and embraced. The colorful lights from their garments merged and flowed from one to the other, unimpeded by any barrier. But then, in a twinkling, they pulled back, with one girl drawing nearly all the deep shades of blue and purple into herself while the other drew nearly all the yellows and reds into herself. Only a concentrated circle of the opposite shadings remained in the center of the heart of each twin. And the two that had been seeming duplicates became distinctly unique.

The dark-toned twin turned to the left and the bright-toned twin to the right, and they slowly began to read the scroll, one moving in one direction and the other in the opposite. The words before them illuminated as they passed. Though their backs were to each other and each seemed unaware of the other's pace, they moved in perfect synchronicity until at last they met at the far side of the circle. There they stood, side by side, and read and read and read until the purple-toned twin turned back to Carlyle and sped toward the table. She grabbed the pen, signed the document of authorization without hesitation, and turned back to the brighter twin, who still stood before the scroll, unmoving. Finally, she, too, slowly progressed back to the table and carefully added her signature to the bottom of the same form.

Carlyle pulled the paperwork toward himself. Evidently, the destiny of these two beings was so inextricably woven together that only one document was required. He verified both signatures—Julia Jolicoeur and Nellie Jolicoeur. Then he folded the form into thirds and slid it into its envelope.

"Thank you both. Just one more step," he said. "I need you to stamp and seal right here with the official crest of authority, if you would."

In unison, the twins reached out and lifted the stamp. As they impressed the golden crest on the paper, their eyes met and locked. An arc of deep indigo and orange shot between them, and it seemed to Carlyle that in this moment another agreement was made. One uniquely confined to the twin girls. One that was perhaps even deeper than the legal binding of the written words on the page.

An agreement between two hearts knit together as one.

After the twins left his presence, Carlyle tucked the sealed envelope into the pouch that hung from the back of his chair and zipped it shut. He slung its long strap over his head until it rested on one shoulder. Only then did he consider what was to be done about the scroll. It remained in its circular open position. He knew it must be rolled up and taken to the library of unsealed scrolls. But again, he was uncertain of how to proceed.

Madeline's words rang in his head once more: "The scroll will tell you. It is a living document designed for destinies. It has a way as unique as the being it represents."

Carlyle stroked his trimmed brown beard, stepped from behind the desk, stretching fully upright into his eight-foot frame. He ventured toward one end of the scroll and stood with his hands clasped behind his back.

"Perhaps you stand open so I, too, may read your contents," he said, and the letters all around him began to glow. "Excellent. I will do just that."

Though he started at one end, he somehow was able to read both sides of the scroll at once. The stories intertwined in chronological fashion from conception to final graduation. At the far side, where the conclusion was written, a thin, intense line of light divided one story from the other. It was here that the twins had stood and stood and stood. When he reached it, he peered deeply into it, sensing that something more, something important, was contained in the light. But no matter how he strained to see, he could not ascertain the contents. He shook his head and blinked away the brilliant reflection.

"My, my, my," he shuddered.

Without warning, Madeline of the High Plains stood next to him, her head even in height with his own. Glimmering, jewel-encrusted medals adorning the shoulders of her navy livery were the only thing that differentiated it from his own. The jewels' inner glow reflected off her tawny skin and danced like shooting stars across her brown eyes. Her signature black braid hung all the way down her back, nearly to her feet.

"Ah, I see you are beginning to ponder the depths of the human spirit," she said.

"Well, I have, of course, read about their capacities, but this," he said, "but this is . . . quite something."

"Indeed."

Suddenly the scroll began to roll itself back up from both ends into the middle until it hung elevated in the air in front of Carlyle.

"Take it. Let's journey to the library of unsealed scrolls," Madeline said.

"You'll go with me?" he said, taking hold of the sturdy leather straps that ran the length of each side of the scroll.

"As far as the library, yes." She nodded and led the way off to their right, past thousands and ten thousands of agreement chambers and toward the front exit.

"And after that?" he asked.

"We shall see what the Scrollmaster recommends."

"I have another appointment after this one."

She only nodded.

Carlyle was perplexed and growing a bit agitated as he hurried after her. He was not the sort to let his schedule slip, but the source of his distress went deeper than that. He was shaken by what he'd read. Who were these human beings that they would agree to such things? And why would the Designer require it of them?

***

"Climb aboard," Madeline said as she mounted the front seat of a spectacular two-wheeled vehicle that materialized in ribbons of light at the bottom of the entrance ramp of his building.

"And what is this?" he asked.

"The humans call it a *motorcycle*. They pulled it from the blueprints in the century of time called the 1800s and made many improvements over the years. But this model here," she said, stroking the gleaming handlebars, "is the model they have not yet imagined."

"I see. Well, it appears to be quite powerful."

Madeline laughed.

"You have no idea. Take a seat," she said, wrapping her braid around her neck and tucking it securely into itself.

Carlyle slung one leg over the back seat, strapped the scroll on his back like a pack, and set his boots on the golden footrests.

"Now what?"

"Wrap your arms around my waist and hold on," she said.

Although Carlyle was noted for his caretaking abilities, he also had a streak of risk-taking in him that had rarely been tested in his previous job. And so, it was with a tremble of excitement that he did as instructed.

Before he could blink, they were off. They raced through the highways and byways of the administration city until they reached the edge of the high plains. Here Madeline accelerated even more, and though he could not hear it over the roar of the wind and the engine, he suspected she was laughing, for her belly was shaking. A broad smile stretched over his face.

This was awesome.

All too soon, the motorcycle slowed as they reached the massive white edifice of the library of unsealed scrolls. Madeline steered them to a spot along the far-west wing and parked. Still vibrating with excitement, Carlyle dismounted, stifling the urge to break into applause.

"What a magnificent machine!"

The Agreements

"That it is," Madeline said as she came to stand beside him. She briefly reached out to caress the finely upholstered seat. "It has served me well, and I shall miss it."

"Miss it?"

She turned to him and placed a golden key in his hand. "I am giving it to you."

"But I couldn't possibly accept such a gift."

"Oh, you mustn't refuse. You will need it." She folded his fingers over the key. With that, she turned and headed toward the library's entrance.

Carlyle stared at the light machine, hardly daring to believe that it was his. He tucked the key into the pouch alongside the legal form and zipped it shut. He ran his hand along the chrome handlebars and a smile lifted up the edges of his moustache. He was beginning to warm up to this new career.

He trotted off to catch up with Madeline, who stood at the top of a marble stairway before a set of enormous bronze doors. Sentries garbed in burnished armor clicked their heels and saluted Madeline before seizing the immense handles and pulling the doors open for the pair to enter the building.

Inside, all was intensely quiet. Not even their own footsteps made noise as they walked past rows and rows of shelves that reached as far as he could see. As they passed a dimly lit corridor to their left, a chilling wind blew across Carlyle's face, arresting him in his tracks. He stared into the dusky passageway. A gate of bronze bars stood between him and the sconces that flickered on the walls. At the far end of the hallway, an iron door was securely shut with heavy steel chains and locks. A large guardian stood beside the door with a flaming sword.

"Carlyle, what are you doing?" Madeline whispered, coming back to retrieve her trainee.

"Is this the exit you told us about?"

Madeline sighed and stood beside him, peering into the gloom. "Yes, this is where the rebels were ushered out."

"And are the shadow scrolls kept behind that door?"

"They are," she replied.

"What's on them?"

Madeline turned to face him, and her eyes blazed. "At this present juncture in your new job, you would do well to focus on what is true, lovely, just, fair, and of noble report."

Carlyle accepted the correction with a dip of his chin.

"Good. Now, let's go," Madeline said.

Carlyle ventured one last glance toward the vigilant sentinel, and a cold shudder ran up and down his spine. It was with no small effort that he shook off its effects and hurried away to fall in behind his trainer.

After what seemed like an eon of walking, they came to a narrow door where the words *Office of the Scrollmaster* were carved. Madeline pressed the button next to the entry. A deep reverberation sounded behind the door.

A tiny shaft of light shot through the door and a voice asked, "Who has arrived?"

"Madeline of the High Plains and Carlyle the Caretaker," Madeline replied.

"And what scroll do you carry?" the voice asked.

Madeline nudged Carlyle and he unstrapped the scroll from his back.

"The Jolicoeur twins," he said.

"Excellent," said the voice as the thin door suddenly split open. "Come in, come in."

The tumult of sound that exploded from the opening was overwhelming. The interior of the Scrollmaster's office was immense. Rank upon rank of long stone tables stretched for acres. They were surrounded by tall, winged creatures animatedly talking and gesturing over opened scrolls. The doorkeeper who had let them in smiled up at them from his compact, four-foot frame as they entered. He was dressed from head to toe in a slightly rumpled three-piece, white suit that matched his slightly rumpled white hair and mustache.

"Welcome. We've been expecting you," he said in a surprisingly strong voice that cut through the commotion around

The Agreements

them. Stretching his hand up to Carlyle, he added, "And you must be the new recruit. I'm Grammateus. Follow me."

As they walked past the tables, Carlyle strained to hear the conversations passing among the winged creatures.

". . . if she sees that . . ."
"The next step is . . ."
". . . then he chose to . . ."
"She's wandered, but . . ."

Grammateus moved so quickly, Carlyle heard only snippets. They followed him past all the tables down a long corridor paneled in mahogany. At the far end, Grammateus pressed on one of the panels and it slid back to reveal a small but well-appointed office.

"Come in. Take a seat," Grammateus said, indicating two petite chairs that sat in front of an ornately carved desk. "And don't worry," he laughed, "much larger ones than you have sat in those seats."

Grammateus walked around to the back of the desk. Bookshelves lined every wall on every side of the room. They were crammed willy-nilly with books at odd angles and in precarious stacks, so much so that Carlyle marveled they didn't simply tumble to the floor.

Madeline took a seat in one of the small chairs, her knees drawn up to her chest, and Carlyle did the same, tucking the scroll across his lap. Grammateus busied himself sorting through an enormous stack of papers on the desktop.

"Will the Scrollmaster meet us here?" Carlyle whispered to Madeline as he slipped his hands under his thighs, stifling the urge to tidy up the place.

"Yes."

After shifting documents to one side to create a clean space on the desk before him and removing a stack of books from his chair, Grammateus sat down and looked at Carlyle.

"Now then, let's take a look at the documents you've brought," he said, pulling a pair of spectacles out of a drawer and placing them on the end of his nose. His deep hazel-green eyes magnified behind the lenses looked like worlds all their own. For a moment,

Carlyle felt engulfed by their depth and had to give his head a quick shake to pull himself back into the present.

"I'm sorry sir, but in our training course, we were instructed to give the completed documents to the Scrollmaster and him alone," Carlyle said.

Madeline stifled a chuckle.

"Oh, do forgive me," Grammateus said, reaching under a file folder and pulling out a brass name plaque. "I keep meaning to put this back on the door, but . . ." He brushed off the plate with his sleeve, turned it around, and leaned it up against the folder. It read "Kyrios Grammateus: The Scrollmaster."

"You're the Scrollmaster?" gulped Carlyle.

Grammateus and Madeline shared a laugh.

"They're always so surprised, aren't they?" Grammateus said.

"They are, indeed," she nodded.

"I'm sorry, sir," Carlyle said. "I guess I just expected . . . I don't know . . . someone, well . . . I mean . . ."

"Larger?" Grammateus asked.

"Yes, sir. I suppose that about sums it up."

"You are new to this sphere, and you will learn that at the core of it are small beginnings. Seeds are never as big as what grows from them."

"Yes, sir. I have read that seeds are the way of this world. But does that apply here as well?"

Grammateus pulled his glasses off and sat back in his chair.

"You have many questions. Some I will answer and some I will not. For now, I will tell you that the connections between this realm and the earthly realm are far-reaching. I'm sure Madeline explained much of this to you in your training, but much of it must be experienced." He leaned forward on his desk and his eyes sparked as he spoke. "The Designer is deeply invested in this creation. Never before has a race of beings been created in his own image. The stakes are high."

"Yes, sir, I am aware of the stakes," Carlyle replied. "At least, I think I am."

The Agreements

"Hand me the scroll and the authorization document, please," Grammateus said, reaching across the desk.

Carlyle complied.

"Very good," Grammateus said, breaking the seal on the envelope and extracting the signed document. He replaced his spectacles and carefully perused the paperwork before setting it atop a pile of forms in a wooden box marked "Outgoing." He then picked up the scroll, and as he began to unroll it, he returned his gaze to Carlyle. "You've read this, I presume?"

"Yes sir, I have."

"And what do you think about what you read?"

Carlyle dropped his head and tapped his fingers on his knees.

"Is every scroll like theirs?" he asked.

"What do you mean by 'like'?"

"Are they . . . well . . . I know the Designer is all-wise, but sir, is it possible? I mean, has it ever happened?" He took a deep breath. "What the twins agreed to is so . . . so risky . . . and the options . . . do they all have so many options?"

Grammateus nodded and rolled the scroll back up. He leaned back in his chair and stared at his new agreement facilitator. Carlyle averted his eyes to avoid the scrutiny. It wasn't that the gaze was angry or demeaning in any way; it was just penetrating in the extreme.

"You are aware, I'm sure, that love can only triumph over darkness in an atmosphere of choice," Grammateus said.

"Of course, sir," Carlyle replied. "It just seems like the Designer is expecting an awful lot from people. Wouldn't it be wiser of him to set a few limits here and there? Or maybe insert some of his power into the equation?"

"And who says he hasn't?"

"Excuse me?"

"Who says the Designer has left the humans without his power or love or wisdom or any other resource they might need?"

Carlyle remained silent under the Scrollmaster's gaze.

Madeline cleared her throat.

"I know we usually wait to send our new recruits into the field until they have a few cases under their belts, but I'm wondering," she said, "if perhaps we should make an exception."

Grammateus sat back in his chair and closed his eyes. Silence filled the small office space. Carlyle glanced at Madeline. She, too, sat with eyes closed. Not knowing what else to do, he bowed his head and did likewise. Suddenly a weighty presence permeated the room and fell like a thick blanket over Carlyle, causing him to double over in his chair. And then, without any forewarning, he was enclosed in a blue tube of light and sucked up out of the room.

The two remaining occupants of the room opened their eyes and smiled. Grammateus pulled a golden watch from his vest pocket and flipped open the engraved cover.

"Good call," he said. "Their hour in time has arrived. I will take this scroll to the reading room. You keep an eye on him."

Chapter 2 – The Nativity

The Jolicoeur twins were not only born on separate days, months, and years but also separate millenniums: one just before midnight on December 31, 1999, and the other just after, on January 1, 2000. And the timing was not the only peculiar fact about their delivery. The firstborn girl presented in a footling breech position, with one hand reaching back up into the womb. The second born followed ten minutes later, not headfirst but hand first, as if seeking to find the one who had gone out into the world before her.

The attending doctor at NewYork-Presbyterian Brooklyn Methodist Hospital said, "I've delivered a lot of babies in my time, but I've never seen a birth like this one."

"But they're healthy?" the mother asked.

"And whole?" the father added.

"Every finger and toe accounted for," the doctor reassured. "They're small, of course, but for twins, I'd say they couldn't have asked for a better start in life."

For the parents, Ryan and Beth Jolicoeur, it was more than a start—it was an end. An end of nine long years of trying to start a family. Years filled with disappointment month after month. Followed by tiny hopes. Ending in multiple miscarriages. An end to the feelings of despair and humiliation engendered by the fact that this supposedly most natural thing in the world did not come naturally to them at all. An end to expensive fertility treatments and highly regimented intimacy. And they were relieved beyond any sense of the word that their girls had finally arrived, healthy and whole.

They were, in fact, elated.

Except for one thing.

There was no one to share the joy with them except the doctors and nurses, for they were each an only child. And, being new to the area, they had yet to find the type of friends they would want to include in this intimate family celebration.

"If only our moms could've seen these two . . .," Beth whispered to her husband over the bundle she held in her arms.

"They'd have loved each having a namesake," Ryan said. "Julia Junior and Nellie the Second."

Beth nodded and smiled as big tear droplets rolled down her cheeks.

"Hey now, no sad tears today," he said, handing her a tissue.

"I know, it's just . . . maybe if this all could've happened sooner . . ." She choked on her thought. "Daddy might have . . ."

"Might've held on a little longer."

"I think he'd have been a wonderful grandpa," Beth said, peering into her daughters' open eyes. "I so wish you could have met him, my little ones."

A moment of silence settled before Ryan commented under his breath, "Yeah, well, I hope they never, ever meet their other grandpa."

Beth kept her eyes averted from his, not wanting to see the anger that inevitably flashed across her spouse's face whenever he mentioned his estranged father. She didn't want to allow even an inkling of that unresolved tension into this glorious day.

"I think as soon as we get home and get settled into some kind of routine, I'm going to join that support group the nurse suggested for mothers of multiples," Beth said.

"I think that's a great idea, babe," he said, knowing how lonely his wife had been since their move from Toronto to New York City. She'd given up a lot in order for him to take his new position at the

The Agreements

law firm in Manhattan: her own career as an event planner, her friends, the city she loved. But he sometimes wondered if the shift in environment and all the distraction the move had entailed had allowed the emotional space she had needed to make room for the miracles they now held in their arms.

Upon returning to their two-bedroom apartment in Brooklyn, the new parents relied on the identification bracelets wrapped around the babies' wrists to keep the girls straight, for they had no distinguishing birthmarks or physical traits to make it readily apparent who was who. Both heads were covered in thick caps of wavy, black hair like their father's. Both full faces were punctuated with rosy cheeks and eyes the color of deep sapphire, like their mother's. For a full week after leaving the hospital, the bracelets were not removed for fear of accidently attributing the wrong name to the wrong baby.

But as the days progressed, Ryan and Beth came to realize that although their daughters were identical physically, they were nearly the opposite emotionally. Julia was quiet and pensive. She didn't cry or fuss about anything. And when she was held, she peered at the face of the holder with an unremitting stare. It was a bit disconcerting to the parents, for it was difficult to know what she needed. But they need not have feared, for Nellie seemed to speak for both of them. If the babies were hungry, she cried. If they needed changing, she bellowed. If they wanted attention, she fussed until they were picked up. And then, unlike her sister, who only sighed as if to say, "Finally," Nellie cooed and gurgled with delight. She smiled a full-blown smile when she was only ten days old. From that day forward, the plastic identifiers were snipped and removed.

Ryan went back to work at his position at the law firm in Manhattan, leaving early every morning and returning late in the evening. But no matter how weary he was at the end of his day, he ran up the two flights of stairs, barged through the door of apartment 2A, and asked, "Where's my girls?" before sweeping the twins up in his arms and kissing them lightly on the tips of their noses.

"My Nellie," he said with one kiss, and "My Julia," he said with the other.

Beth adored his enthusiasm and welcomed the assistance for at least a few hours. She was, of course, exhausted past any exhaustion she had ever felt before by her new role but adamantly refused to complain, for this is what she had begged God to give her for years on end. And so, the Jolicoeur family bravely and merrily slogged their way through the first year of the twins' lives.

It wasn't until the girls' first birthdays approached that Beth began to wonder if something might be wrong, not with her girls, but with herself. The birthday party was to be small. Besides she and her husband, only Fiona Flanagan, the widow from apartment 2B, and Beth's new friends Hector and Maria Gomez, along with their twin boys Albert and Alfred, were invited. It wasn't like she didn't know how to put a party together. In her former career, she could throw together a corporate seminar weekend for 500 without breaking a sweat or a wedding reception at a high-end hotel practically in her sleep. But for some reason, she struggled greatly to pull together the simple elements for this tiny party.

"It feels like my brain is in a perpetual fog," she told Ryan.

"Sleep deprivation will do that to ya, babe. I wouldn't be too worried. By the time the girls are ten or eleven, you'll probably feel just fine," he teased.

Maybe he was right. Maybe it was just fatigue.

The party was planned for the first Saturday after New Year's. On that day, while the twins napped, Ryan went to pick up the cupcakes from the bakery down the street and Beth set out the pink paper plates atop her favorite lace tablecloth. The wall behind the small kitchen table was festooned with pictures from the past year clipped on strings of twine with miniature clothespins. She sat and stared at them for a moment, marveling at the richness of the blur of their lives. And although she had always imagined a much grander first birthday party for the children she had pictured having one day, she was surprised to find herself quite content with the simplicity of her reality. It wasn't until Ryan gently shook her shoulders that she realized she was fast asleep with her head on the table.

"Hey, our guests will be here soon. You okay?" he asked.

"The girls. Did you check on the girls?"

"I just walked through the door," he said. "But I don't hear any squawking."

Beth brushed her long, sandy hair back from her face as she headed toward the nursery. But halfway down the hall, she stopped and summoned Ryan with her finger. They stepped quietly together toward the nursery door. The girls were awake and talking, or at least trying to talk. Although there were no discernible English words in the babbling, it was clear they were carrying on quite a conversation. Ryan and Beth stood on either side of the threshold, hidden from view, and listened, barely able to contain the urge to laugh.

It was easy to tell which twin was talking without having a visual on them, for Nellie's voice was far more animated then Julia's, and her speech was punctuated with spurts of laughter. She loved to laugh and did so often. But Julia, who seemed content to simply enjoy her sister's antics, was far more reticent. In fact, they had never heard her laugh, and they had begun to wonder if perhaps they should be concerned. But in that moment, on that day of celebration, a sound burst forth from the nursery so pure and blissful that the parents popped their heads around the doorframe to see what had happened. And there, standing in her crib, holding onto the side rails, and quaking with laughter, was Julia, as Nellie pointed to the ceiling and said quite clearly, "Car, car, car."

Like a dam that had burst, the laughter gushed from Julia for several minutes until she flopped backward into her blankets and gasped for air.

The three other Jolicoeurs stood in stunned silence until Nellie began to clap and shout. Ryan scooped Julia up and held her close, her little arms wrapped around his neck, while Beth picked up Nellie, who reached out to pat her sister on the back.

The entry buzzer buzzed. It was time to party.

Chapter 3 – The Secrets

Weeks later, Beth's mind was still in a fog. And though she spoke to very few people save the twins throughout her day, her voice was nearly gone by the time she lay her head on the pillow each night. Thinking that she was simply worn out by the epic demands of raising twins, Beth upped her vitamins and watched her diet more closely. She asked Fiona Flanagan if she could watch the twins one hour a day just so she could sneak in an uninterrupted nap.

"Would be my delight," her neighbor replied. "And you'll not be paying me a penny to watch the wee angels. I won't have it. I should be paying you for the joy they bring to my lonely heart."

Fiona and her husband had immigrated from Dublin, Ireland, to the United States in the 1960s. Both her son Jimmy and her daughter Irene had been born in Brooklyn, but her son now lived with his family in Seattle and her daughter had moved back to Ireland, where she had married and settled. After Fiona's husband had retired, they'd planned to travel back and forth between the two children, but all that was permanently interrupted when her husband was diagnosed with early-onset Alzheimer's. She cared for him faithfully until his passing in 1999.

As far as Beth could tell, Fiona's family clearly loved their mother, based on the phone calls, letters, and gifts they sent, but

The Agreements

they rarely visited. From time to time, Fiona did venture east or west to spend a week or two with each family, but she had firmly refused all offers to move in with either one of them.

"I'm equal distance between the two, and I'll not pick a favorite," she had declared to Beth over a cup of tea one day. "But it sure leaves my heart longing for company some days."

So, it worked out for both the Jolicoeurs and the widow Flanagan to adopt one another as next of kin.

"Why don't I just pop over to your place and you can come rest in my bed over here. Not a soul will disturb ya here, and we won't have to move a thing," Fiona suggested. It was the best idea Beth had heard in ages.

But even with the attention to self-care, Beth could not shake the nearly debilitating fatigue or the persistent cough she had developed. Finally, at the urging of Maria and others at her parents-of-multiples support group, she made an appointment to see the doctor.

At the neighborhood clinic, Dr. Lara listened intently to Beth's explanation of her symptoms, typing notes into her laptop as they talked. After performing a routine examination, she ran her hands up and down Beth's neck.

"Hmm," the young Latina doctor said as she gently manipulated the area several times. "I think you may have a small goiter around your thyroid. Not a huge cause for concern but something we should look into." She turned and washed her hands in the small sink set in the weary-looking cabinetry of the room. "I suspect that blood tests may reveal a condition called *hypothyroidism*, in which your thyroid is failing to produce enough hormones. It's a fairly common condition among women."

She crumpled up the paper towels she had used to dry her hands and stashed them through a plastic flap before turning around to face her patient.

"The good news is that, though we don't have a real cure for the condition, there is a very effective medication you can take to alleviate the symptoms. Occasionally we find a goiter or enlarged area of the thyroid, too, and we may have to pay some attention to that. It may explain the sore throat and hoarse voice. Rarely, a goiter may be cancerous, but only very rarely. So, let's not get too worried about that."

Beth didn't hear anything else after that. The mere mention of cancer sent her brain into a panic.

She left the clinic in a stupor.

When she came to her senses, she realized she was walking back to their apartment instead of to the Gomezes', where she had dropped off the girls. She turned around and retraced her steps. Along the way she decided that she would only tell Ryan about the hypothyroidism part of the diagnosis.

No need for him to worry about something that was probably nothing.

The sun was warm on her back as she climbed the stairs to press the buzzer for Maria's apartment. A promise of spring was in the March air, and she breathed deeply of the hope it held.

"Bueno," Maria's mother's voice came over the intercom speaker.

"Hello, Lupe. It's Beth."

The front doors unlocked with a click and she stepped over the threshold, across the lobby, and into the elevator. She was slightly envious of this simple luxury, for she was weary of the gyrations it took to get her two babies and a diaper bag down two flights of stairs to the stroller they stashed in the foyer of their apartment building. But Ryan had reminded her that morning, "Hang in there. When Jake and I close this big case, Larry is promising a hefty bonus. We'll look for another place after that."

Beth stepped off the elevator into the long, narrow hallway on the third floor. Maria flung open the door to her apartment before Beth could knock but offered no greeting.

"Freddy, let Nellie have it mijo," she yelled into the living room over Nellie's screams as she chased Albert down the hallway. "Beto, no! You bring that back right now."

Beth shook her head and marveled at the speed of Beto's little two-year-old legs. He was the pudgy, low-to-the-ground model of the Gomez twins, while Freddy took after his father—thick and tall.

The Agreements

These twin boys were as different from one another in looks as her girls were alike.

The smell of refried beans and chile verde wafted from the kitchen where Maria's mother, Lupe Hernandez, stood next to the stove with Julia on her hip. She was a small, round woman with thick, silver hair and remarkably wrinkle-free caramel-toned skin. Telltale signs of tortilla making lay strewn on the counter. Julia gnawed on a strip of fresh tortilla that stuck out from the top of her fist.

"She likes it," said Lupe as Beth passed by on her way to mediate whatever was happening in the living room.

Nellie sat next to the scattered pieces of a farm set and smiled at her mother as Beth entered the room.

"Mine," she proclaimed, holding a tractor close to her chest.

Freddy, who was nearly a full year older and at least ten pounds heavier, sat beside Nellie with tears streaming down his cheeks. Beth was continually astonished by Nellie's strength and agility. Both girls were over the 100th percentile on the height charts for their age. Their pediatrician had, in fact, begun to call them his little twin towers. But while Julia was soft and willowy, Nellie was taut, wiry, and tough as nails.

Beth got on her knees beside the distraught Freddy and tried to interest him in a truck. Nellie grabbed it, too, from her hand.

"Mine," she said, stashing the truck next to the tractor.

Freddy reached over and tried to rip the prized pieces from her grasp. Beth was astounded at the ferocity of the wrestling match that ensued. Julia always acquiesced to Nellie's every demand, but Freddy was clearly of a different mindset. As odd as it seemed, she sort of enjoyed the fact that her daughter had met her match. But when Nellie leaned in to take a bite out of Freddy's arm, Beth snatched her off the carpet.

"No, Nellie! We do not bite," she said, ripping the tractor and truck from her clutches.

Maria marched into the room with Albert, who they called Beto, in one hand and a flour-covered rolling pin in the other.

"Sorry about this," Beth began. "Nellie seems to have a thing about vehicles."

"No worries, Beth. Honestly, up until about a minute before you got here, they were all fine. And then, all of a sudden, all hell broke loose," she said. "Freddy you're okay, mijo. That's enough fussing."

Beto broke free from his mom's grip and walked over to Beth. "Please?" he said.

"See, Nellie, this is how you should ask for a toy," Beth said. "Here ya go, Beto."

Beto accepted the toys and then took them to his brother, who grabbed them and immediately stopped crying.

"Well, that's a first," Maria said as she rubbed her hand over her protruding belly. She was one of those women who glowed when pregnant. Her soft brown cheeks glowed. Her wavy, shoulder-length, black hair glowed. Even her lovely brown eyes seemed to have an extra measure of light. "Usually these two are the ones in the wrestling match. But maybe having a common enemy puts them on the same team."

"I have no idea how you're going to manage with a newborn in the midst of all this," Beth said.

"Well, it helps to have a live-in grandmother. But we are definitely on the lookout for a bigger place."

"Stop it, Nellie," Beth said to her wriggling toddler. "You are behaving badly. Sometimes I wish you would take a lesson from your sister and just mellow out."

Lupe entered the room, holding Julia.

"Come," she said to Beth. "You eat."

"Oh, no," Beth said. "I need to get home and put these two down for a nap."

"You have to eat something, mija," Lupe insisted before she turned and went back to the kitchen.

"She isn't going to let you out that door without feeding you," Maria said. "Go sit for a minute. I'll be right there after I change a diaper or two."

Beth checked her watch. She had a few minutes.

The Agreements

In the kitchen, Julia sat in one of the boys' high chairs, chasing beans across the tray and stuffing them in her mouth one by one.

"Sit," Lupe ordered, grabbing Nellie from Beth's arms and settling her in the other high chair with her own serving of beans.

Beth sighed as she sat at the table that was snugged up against the wall to make room for the bulky high chairs. A sudden pang of longing struck her heart. Beth's mother, Nellie, had died of breast cancer fifteen years before, when Beth was still in college. She thought she had put the years of grieving behind her until the twins were born. And then suddenly, the ache for her mom's presence was intense and constant.

Watching Lupe shuffle around the kitchen in her house slippers and apron, fixing a generous plateful of food for her, Beth struggled to keep the tears from spilling out and true jealousy from rising up. The envy over having an elevator didn't even come close to the envy she felt over Maria still having a mom around to help her raise her kids.

Lupe set the plate before Beth with a warm tortilla folded up on the edge. After several such visits, Beth had learned that no utensils were forthcoming. She had become quite adept at scooping up her meal with a tortilla. In fact, she enjoyed it immensely, and she tucked into the meal with pleasure.

"Ba, ba, ba," Julia said, patting the tray before her.

"Okay, mija. Just a minute," Lupe said with a laugh. "She likes frijoles."

Lupe scooped up another measure of beans and set them on Julia's tray, which led Nellie to squawk "Ba, ba, ba," too, although she still had plenty of beans in front of her.

Lupe shook her head.

"Muy, muy differentes," she said.

Beth nodded and swallowed.

"Yeah, I know. They are very different. Muy differentes."

Lupe patted Nellie's head as she placated her demands by moving a bean or two from Julia's tray to hers.

"This one, un río feroz. And this one," she said, moving to stroke Julia's head, "un río profundo."

"Do you understand what she's saying?" Maria asked, entering the room.

Beth lifted her hand and swung it back and forth like a teeter-totter.

"Kind of."

"She says Nellie is like a raging river and Julia is like a deep river."

"She certainly has that right," Beth replied.

"Now, you eat. Todo," Lupe commanded.

Beth did as she was told.

Across the East River in his thirty-second-story office, Ryan sat staring out the window at the wall of glass on the building next door. Some days, the sterile view bothered him and he longed for the day when he might be promoted to a coveted corner office with a real view. But on that March day, his mind was occupied with weightier matters.

The letter lay open on his desk atop a stack of papers he needed to get ready for court the next day. The information the papers contained was vital to their case, and he knew every word had to be precise. But he could not focus.

Not yet.

Not until he had processed the letter.

How that man had tracked him down again, he didn't know. Sometimes he wished he had followed through with the impulse to change his name all those years ago. But *why* the man had tracked him down bothered him even more. Somehow Claude Jolicoeur had discovered that he was a grandfather. He knew about the twins and he wanted to meet them.

"Over my dead body," Ryan declared to the air.

Eleven years old. That was how old Ryan had been the day his dad walked out the door and never came back. And Ryan had been elated to see him go. No more excuses for not showing up for anything. No more hiding loose change from his addictive hands.

The Agreements

No more late-night fights and beatings for his mom. No more puke on the floorboards of the car. No more bursts of pathetic repentant tears. No more.

For twenty years, he and his mother hadn't heard a word from his father. And then one day a letter arrived from some tiny town in North Dakota. His father claimed he was sober and he wanted to make amends. Ryan didn't buy it, and he begged his mother to burn the damn thing. His dad was a liar. Always had been. Always would be. Besides, they didn't need him. They had done just fine without him. Ryan had graduated top of his class from law school and was an attorney making decent money. He was committed to taking care of his mom. When he'd married Beth, she, too, had agreed to that commitment. His dad had no right to stick his nose in their business.

But his mom, Julia Jolicoeur, believed for some insane reason that she was obligated to at least hear out her ex-husband. She said it was the Christian thing to do and there wasn't anything Ryan could say to talk her out of that. So, against his wishes, his mother made the phone call his father requested. Ryan sat in the other room and listened and stewed, praying to a God he didn't even know if he believed in anymore that somehow his mother would lose her cool and cuss out the liar on the other end of the line.

She did not.

It was only months later that she told him about the diagnosis. She hadn't wanted to worry him or Beth, since she knew of Beth's history with her mother. He would never forget the words that fell from her mouth.

Non-Hodgkin's lymphoma. Stage four. Six to twelve months. She was dying.

"I will not leave this planet with regrets or anger," his mother told them. "So, I am thankful your father reached out when he did. My heart is at peace and I am praying every day that you will find that same peace."

Miraculously, she held on for two years. Never again, that he knew of, did she speak to her former husband. But somehow, Claude got word of Julia's passing and showed up unexpectedly at her memorial service. Ryan would never forget the moment his father walked through the back doors of the church sanctuary. It was right in the middle of the eulogy Ryan had so painstakingly crafted the night before. He had been nervous about delivering it in front of his mother's friends and pastors. But Beth had propped him up with lots of encouragement and sat in the front row with shining eyes, allowing him to believe he was giving a speech his mother would truly have been proud of.

All that flew out the stained-glass windows when Ryan realized the late-arriving man in the suit and tie slipping into the back row of the church was his father. The words on the page sitting before him on the wooden lectern seemed to disappear as a surge of rage flooded his system. He nearly came unglued and abandoned his duties altogether. Beth, who had swiveled around to see what was causing his sudden consternation, mouthed, "Is that your dad?" Ryan had nodded slowly, his eyes fixed like a laser on the man he loathed. Beth grabbed his attention with a clearing of her throat and a don't-you-dare-lose-your-cool stare. And somehow, he had continued with the eulogy, keeping his eyes averted from anyone but his wife.

At the end of the service, Ryan wanted nothing more than to run down the aisle, grab his old man by his starched collar, and toss him from the premises. But his mother's friends delayed him with their hugs and condolences, and by the time he was free, his dad had disappeared.

That was the last he had seen or heard from him.

Until the letter.

He opened his laptop and began to type furiously. In just a few minutes, his reply was printing out on company letterhead.

It was firm. It was concise.

It was attorney-like.

He signed it, addressed the envelope to the return address in Grace, ND, and stuck it in his out-box for his assistant Melanie to mail. He blew out a long, slow breath, folded up the unwelcome correspondence from his father into as small of a square as he could and stuffed it in the inner pocket of his suit coat.

He would not tell Beth.

The Agreements

There was no need to worry her about something that would probably never happen.

Chapter 4 – The Realities

It was quite a shock, Carlyle recalled. One moment he was sitting in the office of the Scrollmaster and the next he was observing the birth of twin girls on the planet. Carlyle had never seen anything like it. Amazingly intense. Wonderfully strange. Extraordinarily fulfilling.

He had realized soon after his arrival that he was invisible to the humans in the room and quite small. He hadn't felt any different, but he definitely was different—by about seven and a half feet. It had been unsettling at first, but eventually, he had come to embrace the flexibility it allowed him. He could float up and situate himself in small nooks and crannies: on shelves and frames and mantlepieces, inside strollers, between car seats, atop the diaper bag—anywhere he needed to be to watch his two subjects.

He had also found out that though he could easily maneuver in flight anywhere around the girls, he could not fly freely too far beyond their immediate environs. He absentmindedly rubbed the spot on his forehead where he had encountered the invisible but firm boundary set for him the one time he had decided to explore farther afield.

It had also come as a shock to realize that try as he might, he was unable to recall the details of the Jolicoeur twins' scroll. He had feelings about certain events and circumstances at times, like they were things he'd experienced before. But by and large, it was as if he'd been allowed to see a movie and then had all but the overall sense of the plot erased from his mind.

It might have been nice to get a bit of forewarning about some of these things before being whisked away and plopped down in the middle of humanity. But he was learning that part of his experience was just that: to learn. Even as the humans he had come to observe needed to learn, so did he.

He sighed and leaned forward onto his crisscrossed legs. Carlyle enjoyed the view from the shelf on the wall. And though he would admit it to no one, the teddy bear beside him that had been Beth's as a child had become something of a silent companion to him in the night hours as he watched the twins sleep. Carlyle asked him questions that arose from observing the ins and outs of the everyday existence of the Jolicoeur household. Although the bear was obviously unable to reply, it helped Carlyle to hear his own thoughts.

He knew that he was not the only spirit being in and around the family, but upon arrival on the planet, his vision of that realm had been blinded. The only thing he was allowed to see beyond what the humans themselves seemed able to see was the light of life at the core of every individual person—their heart light. He was amazed by the array of colors and the different levels of brightness he had seen in these lights among the throngs of New York. But what truly astonished him was how obtuse the general population was to them and to the fact that they had been fashioned in the image of their luminous Designer to be the light of the world.

Why this basic element of information should be a point of discovery for the human race and not just general knowledge was a mystery to Carlyle. There was much he did not yet understand about the Designer's intentions for humanity. But the months he had spent in the field were beginning to shed some illumination on his questions.

He looked down at the two cribs that filled the room. Nellie slept soundly, with her knees scrunched under her and her little bottom up in the air—not a position he felt could be remotely comfortable, but she had a gift for sleeping however she landed. She played hard and she slept hard. Her amber heart light always vibrant and on display. Staring back at him from the crib on the south wall was Julia, her purple heart light pulsing softly. Unlike her twin, who babbled at him whenever she spied his presence, Julia just stared. At first, he had been quite uncomfortable with her penetrating gaze, but he had learned that behind her intensity lay a tender heart—one her sister protected carefully. Although Nellie was the younger of the two, she played the role of defender for her older sister with ferocious skill.

Carlyle waved from his perch, even though *The Guidelines for Suitable Observations* he had studied in his training course discouraged such interaction. Previous generations of watchers had wantonly breached the boundaries set between the earthly and the divine, wreaking all manner of havoc that had required a deluge of rectification. Since then, the spectrum of interactive abilities of the observers had been curtailed.

But the girls were just so cute.

A little wave here and there surely couldn't hurt.

Julia smiled ever so slightly and waved back.

"Car," she whispered as she rolled over onto her side and hummed herself back to sleep.

It tickled him that the girls seemed to know his name without him ever having to tell them and that they could see him even though their parents could not—a fact he found a bit puzzling. Ryan and Beth were, after all, more mature and learned than their daughters.

He thought back to the various teachings Madeline had given about the growth and development of humans. She had said that babies were born with full spiritual awareness and ability to converse in heavenly languages. But as they matured physically and gained their earthly language, instead of getting wiser in the ways of the spirit, this awareness diminished for most. In fact, the vast majority of the race suffered from a syndrome known as *infantile amnesia*, in which memories from conception to age three or four were lost, the most profound of which was the memory of their primordial identity.

They simply seemed to forget who they had agreed to be.

Carlyle gazed at the girls as they slept. He often wondered how long it would be before the girls lost sight of him.

And, more importantly, of themselves.

It was a Friday afternoon in April when Beth opened the door to the apartment and found Ryan sitting on the sofa. He was in his shirtsleeves, his tie undone and his long legs stretched out, with his stocking feet on the coffee table.

"Hey, hon," she said. "You're home early."

"Hey," he replied.

The twins ran to him as quickly as their little legs could manage, shrieking, "Dada, dada, dada," in stereo. He opened his arms and accepted their adoration.

"My girls. My girls. Where have you been?" he asked with a kiss for each nose.

Beth disencumbered herself of diaper bag and jackets on the bench by the door.

"We've been to the park with Maria and the boys." She sat down across from her family in the love seat, happy to have her reinforcement home so early. "She is amazing. I wouldn't be out and about with those boys in her condition. I think she's hoping some exercise will get things rolling and get this baby out. What are you doing home?"

"Finished up early," Ryan said.

"Cool," she said, surprised by the brusqueness in his tone. He was probably just tired. "Wish you could have joined us at the park. The girls had a ball. Only one mishap when some boy pushed Julia away from the ladder to the slide and Nellie decked him."

"Decked him?"

"Oh yeah. One swift bop to the side of the head. Thankfully, his mama didn't see that part and the kid had a thick skull."

"What are we going to do with you, Miss Ali?" Ryan asked Nellie, who squirmed away from his arms, slid off the couch, and headed toward the diaper bag.

"Car," she said as she ransacked the contents of the bag.

"Nellie, don't throw everything out," Beth said, dragging herself from the comfort of the plaid cushions. Her energy levels were much better, thanks to the marvels of modern medicine. She was beginning to feel like herself again, but life as the mother of twins still took every ounce of strength she could muster.

"Stay put," Ryan said as he stood and handed Julia to her.

"She's digging for a little motorcycle the boys gave her today. She's obsessed with it," Beth said.

"Car!" Nellie lifted the new toy exultantly over her head and vroomed it across the hardwood floors.

Ryan lay down on the floor next to her and joined her play. He had always told Beth that, as a kid, the only good memory he had of his dad was riding dirt bikes together. Evidently, his father was quite the mechanic and quite the rider—at least when he was sober.

Beth sighed as Julia leaned back against her and relaxed. In just a few minutes, the soft whiffling noises she emitted told Beth she had fallen asleep. And less than ten minutes later, both Nellie and her dad had joined Julia in la-la land on the area rug in the living room. Beth smiled to herself. She was right.

He was just tired.

With skill developed over the course of the past months, Beth stood stealthily to her feet without waking Julia. She took her to the nursery and settled her in her crib before successfully retrieving Nellie, who clung to the new toy even in her sleep, and tucked her in as well. Ryan remained passed out on the floor. Beth arranged the striped afghan Mrs. Flanagan had crocheted for them over his back and let him sleep.

She picked up Ryan's briefcase, shoes, and suit coat from the pile on the floor where they had been shed helter-skelter.

"Sometimes you're as bad as your daughters," she muttered on her way down the hallway.

The Agreements

In their bedroom, she placed the briefcase on the upholstered bench at the end of the bed and deposited the shoes on the shoe rack in the closet. As she opened the suit coat to hang it up, she detected a lump of something stuffed in the inner pocket. She reached in and pulled out a piece of paper folded into a small, condensed square. Normally she took his receipts or spare change or whatever remains of his day she discovered in his pockets and placed them on top of the dresser in a bowl without much interest. But as she hung the suit coat on the rod, something in her gut urged her to take a peep at this particular parcel.

As she unfolded the paper, she repressed the sudden suspicious thoughts that tried to bombard her brain. It was probably nothing. But when she saw the greeting "Dear Son" at the top of the page, her chest constricted and she backed out of the closet to take a seat next to Ryan's briefcase on the bench. She wasn't sure how long she had been sitting there digesting the handwritten words or how long Ryan had been standing in the doorway before she looked up.

"Were you going to tell me about this?" she asked.

He leaned his solid, six-foot-four frame against the doorframe and remained silent.

"Well, were you?" she repeated.

Ryan reached into his back pocket and pulled out another piece of paper. He unfolded it and held it open so she could see it.

"Were you going to tell me about this?" he asked.

The letterhead was clearly visible. It was from the hospital. She had been waiting for it. The results of her biopsy.

"The doctor was supposed to call first," she whispered.

"The doctor? What doctor, Beth?"

"Dr. Hazeem."

"Dr. Hazeem? Who is Dr. Hazeem? I thought you were seeing Dr. Lara down at the clinic. What the hell is going on, Beth?"

"What does it say, Ryan?"

"Read it yourself," he said, stepping toward her with the document.

She pulled it from his hand and quickly scanned its contents. Her hand clamped over her mouth, and she began to shake. Ryan quickly moved the briefcase and sat beside her. He pulled her into his arms and held her as she wept.

"He said it was rare," she sobbed.

They held each other until the initial shock subsided. Ryan grabbed a box of tissues off the dresser and handed it to his wife. A strained calm settled as they turned to face each other.

"I should have told you. I just didn't want to worry you over nothing. It was supposed to be nothing," Beth said at last. "I'm sorry."

Ryan nodded.

"And I should have told you about the letter. I don't know how he found us. I'm sorry too," Ryan replied.

He leaned forward with his forearms on his knees.

Beth leaned back against the bed.

They both stared straight ahead through the open door to the girls' room across the hallway.

"Guess we have some realities to face," Ryan said.

"Guess so."

Chapter 5 – The Gift

As the elevator doors opened, the sound of music and chatter spilled down the hallway from the celebration going on in the Gomez apartment. Ryan and Beth approached the Gomezes' door with their arms full, Ryan's with twin girls and Beth's with a pan of pastries in one hand and a gift bag in the other. She juggled her load and knocked on the door.

No answer.

She knocked louder. The door swung open.

"Hey, you guys!" Hector Gomez greeted them. "Pasense. Come in. The party is just getting started. I'll get these to the kitchen and maybe I'll leave a few for somebody else," he said, relieving Beth of the pan of pastries.

Ryan and Beth stood in the doorway, scanning the crowded apartment. Nellie squealed as Beto and Freddy went zipping by with several other children behind them.

"Down," Nellie demanded.

Her dad obeyed and she joined the fray.

Julia clung to her daddy's shoulder until Lupe showed up.

"Lita," she said, leaning out and reaching for her.

"Ay, corazón," Lupe said as she scooped her up, kissed her on the forehead, and vanished toward the kitchen.

"Lita? I thought Maria's mom's name was Lupe," Ryan said.

"It is. But Lita is short for abuelita—little grandmother. It's what the boys call her."

"You'd think she was Julia's grandma," Ryan said. "What about an abuelito? Is Maria's dad around too?"

"No. Left the family and went back to Mexico a long time ago. Maria says she barely remembers him."

"Hmm, guess I'm not the only one with a deadbeat dad."

Beth swatted him in the gut. "Shh."

"Jeez. Take it easy. Not like anyone can hear me over all this racket."

"Just mind your manners," Beth replied. "I'm going to try to find Maria. Give her this gift."

"Not without me," Ryan said, grabbing her elbow as they snaked their way through the crowd. "Who are all these people?"

Beth shrugged. They surveyed the living room but didn't see Maria in the mass of bodies gathered there. A young man sat on a stool by the far wall, playing a guitar and singing. Many joined with him in full-voiced harmonies. In the midst of it all, baby Rosie slept soundly in the arms of someone who looked a lot like Maria.

"That's her sister, Carmen," Beth said, waving to the woman before going back toward the kitchen.

The countertops were stuffed with platters of meat, bowls of rice, kettles of beans, pans of roasted veggies, and accoutrements from salsa to sour cream. Lupe had already strapped Julia into one of the high chairs.

"You eat." Lupe handed them each a plate before turning back to the stove to flip a tortilla on the hot cast-iron placa.

"Sounds good to me," Ryan said.

"Everything looks great, Lupe. Gracias," Beth said.

With plate heaped high, Ryan turned to find a place to sit or even stand while he ate.

Lupe placed a warm, folded tortilla on his plate and strode to the table. She took the dish towel off her shoulder and used it to swat a young man seated at the table.

"Mijo, get up. We have guests."

The Agreements

The teenager raised his hands in defense and began to rise at once.

"Okay, okay, Lita. I'm moving." He laughed and nudged the guy next to him. "Come on Tavo, let's find the dessert tray."

"Thanks," Ryan said as he and his wife took their vacated chairs.

"These are all mine," Lupe said, indicating the six others crammed around the small table. "Ernesto, Juan, Josephina, Eustolia, Jorge, y Gustavo."

"Hi. We're Ryan and Beth. And that one," Ryan pointed to the high chair, "is Julia, one of our twins. Not quite sure where the other one is."

"Mucho gusto," Ernesto said, holding out his hand to Ryan. "Welcome to the family."

"Don't worry. There won't be a pop quiz to remember names," Maria said as she entered the kitchen.

"These are all your siblings?" Ryan asked.

"Not exactly," she said, bending to hug Beth. "Ernesto, Gustavo, and Eustolia are, but Josie is my cousin. Juan is my uncle. Jorge is my brother-in-law, and those two that just got chased out are my nephews. Carmen and Carlos, my two other siblings, are around here somewhere."

"Yeah, I saw Carmen in the living room with Rosie. Here," Beth said, lifting the gift bag from off the floor, "this is for you. Well, for Rosalinda Maria Josefa. Did I say that right?"

"Perfecto! But you didn't need to get anything. You've already done too much with the beautiful decorations you made," Maria said, indicating the bright bouquets of crepe paper flowers and garlands gracing the tables and doorways.

"It was my pleasure to make them. Sort of like therapy for me."

"Next time, invite me to your therapy session," Eustolia said. "It looks like way more fun than mine."

"And probably cheaper," added Jorge.

Maria lifted the tissue out of the pink chintz bag before pulling out a small velvet box.

"It's what my mom always gave to babies baptized in the church I went to as a kid," Beth said. "I know your church does dedications and not baptisms, but I thought it was still appropriate."

Maria lifted a silver necklace from the box. A cross hung at the end with a small diamond at its center.

"Her initials and the date are engraved on the back," Beth said. "It's for when she's older, so she can remember this day."

"It's beautiful. Thank you so much." Maria said, bending over and hugging Beth again. "I'm so glad you came to the service, and I'm so glad you're here."

"Who would want to miss this?" Ryan said over a mouthful of carne asada.

"It's your reward for sitting through church," Josie said with a smile. "Pastor Armando gets so excited about baby dedications, he tends to get a little long-winded."

"Oh, I really enjoyed it," Beth said. "And the girls loved the music and the dancing. I've never been to a church with so much . . . I don't know . . . so much spirit."

"You should come on a Sunday night," said Gustavo. "Things really get spirited then."

"Stop scaring them and let them eat," Eustolia scolded.

"What did you think of that word from Hermano Raymond?" Jorge asked, and the conversation around the table turned to a lively discussion of the happenings at the church service.

The Jolicoeurs sat quietly and ate, nodding politely from time to time. Occasionally someone would interpret a Spanglish phrase, noting the perplexed looks on their faces. By the time Ryan and Beth had cleaned their plates, drunk the coffee served to them, and consumed several types of desserts, they truly were beginning to feel like part of the family.

It was nice to be distracted by the fullness of the day's events. Nice to not think about what tomorrow held.

***

The Agreements

From his vantage point over the refrigerator, Carlyle watched the fiesta in the Gomez apartment. Even as it wound down, the place pulsated with color and light. In all his time as an observer, he had not seen such strong heart lights from so many. It was fascinating to see how the lights blended and morphed as individuals interacted one with another and how brilliant flashes, almost explosions, ignited with the laughter and hugs and music. Not for the first time, he wished they could see what he saw. But for the first time, he suspected that perhaps a few of them actually did.

Across the hallway in the living room, the crowd had thinned considerably. Baby Rosie began to fuss. Cousin Josie, who held her, got up to find Maria, who alone could meet the need of her baby girl. As she did, Carlyle was surprised to see a small spirit follow her. When the handoff of the infant was made from Josie to Maria, the spirit followed mother and child toward the back bedroom. Carlyle's curiosity was piqued. Who was this spirit, and why could he see her? He checked on the twins. Julia and her daddy were taking a siesta on the couch. Nellie was seated on the carpet in front of the television with Beto and Freddy. Carlyle flew to the back bedroom.

There, on top of the dresser, sat the spirit watching Rosie, who was nursing at Maria's breast. The rocking chair mother and babe sat in squeaked rhythmically as they rocked. The spirit was dressed in a navy linen uniform like Carlyle's, except she had a shiny medal attached on each shoulder. As he entered the airspace, she looked up, a bit startled by his appearance. He lifted up a friendly hand as he approached.

"Hey, I'm Carlyle the Caretaker," he said.

"Ardith the Ardent," she said, shaking his hand briskly. "I'm here as an observer."

"Yeah, I guessed as much. Me too. The uniform, you know," he said, "sort of gives us both away."

"Yes, I suppose it does."

"Besides, you're the first spirit I've seen since I've been here. All the rest have been blocked from view for some reason."

"Focus," she said.

"Excuse me?"

"Our vision is limited so that we will focus on our mission," she said, her eyes trained on Rosie, whose pink heart light had blended with her mother's crimson to form a fuchsia aura around the two.

"Oh, yes, of course. I knew that," he said. "Mind if I join you?"

"Be my guest."

Carlyle settled beside his newfound companion.

"Is Rosie your mission?" he asked.

"Yes. My first time in the field. You?"

"My first time for everything," he replied.

"Really?" Ardith turned to look directly at him. "They sent you here on your first agreement?"

He nodded.

"Must be a doozy," she said.

"You've seen the twin girls, Julia and Nellie?"

"You have both of them?"

He nodded again.

"That is quite unusual," she said, returning her gaze to the mother and child.

"Well, the entire case is peculiar, from what I gather. Although I'm pretty sure every case has its interesting ins and outs."

"This is most certainly true. I've facilitated two other agreements, and they were beyond the scope of what I had been prepared for in training."

"Really? How so?"

"Um, you know I can't talk about the particulars, don't you? Client confidentiality?"

They sat quietly for several minutes. Carlyle was happy to have someone to talk to who actually talked back.

"If you don't mind my asking," Ardith said, "where are the twins now?"

"In the living room."

"And you're in here?"

The Agreements

"One is asleep and the other is engaged with the boys. I did check before I came," he said.

Rosie became fussy. Maria lifted her up and placed her belly down atop the burp cloth on her shoulder and patted the infant's back. As Rosie lay her head on her mother's shoulder, she blinked and blinked as if she were trying to focus on Ardith and Carlyle.

"I think she sees us," Ardith said.

"Oh yeah, babies see practically everything. It isn't until later they start to forget," Carlyle replied.

"I am aware," his fellow observer said.

A small burp erupted from Rosie's lips, and Maria moved her back to feed on the other breast. Just then, Beth opened the bedroom door.

"Can I come in?" she whispered.

Maria nodded and pointed to the bed.

Beth sat on the bed's edge next to the mom and baby. Carlyle noted that the seafoam green of her inner light was more subdued than usual.

"We're gonna head out soon," Beth said. "Just wanted to say thanks for everything. You guys know how to throw a party."

"Don't leave yet," Maria said. "I wanted to see how you're doing with . . . you know. With tomorrow."

Beth shrugged.

"Is Mrs. Flanagan okay with both girls? We can help, you know," Maria said.

"You've got your hands full," Beth said. "Ryan took the day off. The surgery is scheduled for 8:00 a.m., so we have to be at the hospital really early. Mrs. Flanagan is just gonna come over and stay at our place."

"I can send my mom over if anything goes, well, not like expected. Not that it will. But, you know, just in case. I'm serious, Beth. We are here for you no matter what."

Beth's eyes filled with tears.

Lupe and Carmen entered the room and Beth wiped at her nose and eyes.

"Um, Beth," Carmen said, "my mother is wondering if it would be okay if she prayed for you?"

"Yes," Lupe nodded. "May I pray?"

"Mamá, she might not . . . ," Maria began to protest.

"No, it's okay," Beth said. "I think I would like that . . . a lot."

"Come," Lupe said, reaching her hands out to Beth.

Beth stood and Lupe pulled her close as she spoke in Spanish to Carmen.

"When she prays, she likes to do it in Spanish. It's just more comfortable for her. But I'll translate. Is that okay?" Carmen asked.

"Sure," Beth said as Lupe placed her hands gently along Beth's neck.

"Don't be afraid," Lupe said, looking into Beth's eyes. "Maybe you feel something. Maybe not. Just believe. Okay?"

Beth nodded.

"Wait for me." Maria swaddled a sleeping Rosie and placed her in the center of the bed. She adjusted her top and came and stood next to Beth with one hand on her friend's shoulder. "If we're gonna do this, I want in."

Ardith and Carlyle stood to attention as the burgundy heart light coming from Lupe flamed up and encompassed the entire room.

"First time I've seen this," Carlyle whispered.

"Well, say what you want about forgetting, but I think that woman remembers something," she said.

Carmen placed a hand on Beth's other shoulder as Lupe began to pray.

"En el nombre sobre cada nombre, el nombre de Jesucristo . . ."

Carmen translated over the top of her mother's words.

"She says, 'In the name above every name, the name of Christ Jesus, I command this cancer to be removed and sent back to the pit of hell from which it came. It will not have its way in this precious daughter of the King. She will be free from disease. Healthy, whole, and strong. Go! And do not return!"

Lupe's hands glowed on Beth's neck, and to the observers' eyes, the entire group began to emit a brilliant white light.

The Agreements

As Lupe commanded the cancer to go, Carlyle saw a glob of darkness fall from Beth's neck and land on the rug. Lupe alone among the women seemed to see the vile thing.

"Your feet. Do this," she said to Beth as she demonstrated a fierce stomp. "Do. Now. Ahorita. You do."

Beth stomped her feet several times tentatively.

"Otra vez," Lupe instructed.

"Again," Maria translated.

Beth stomped again with more conviction.

"Gloria a Dios," Lupe said, clapping her hands. "Gloria a Dios."

"Is that it?" Beth asked. "Is it gone?"

Lupe placed her hands back on Beth's neck and felt for the lump.

"Yes," Lupe nodded and hugged her. "It's gone."

"She's usually right about this stuff," Maria added.

Beth felt for herself.

"I can't feel it anymore," she said.

"He is a healer," Lupe said, pointing heavenward.

Beth looked past her circle of intercessors to the doorway. Ryan stood holding Nellie's hand with Julia's armed draped around his neck as she rode on his back. The girls' eyes were as big as saucers.

"Uh, what's going on here?" he asked.

Lupe turned to him.

"We pray," she said. "She is healed."

"Huh?" Ryan replied.

Beth went and stood in front of him.

"I felt the warmth, Ryan. Something really happened. Feel it," she said, grabbing his free hand and placing it where the lump had been.

"Okay . . . well, that's interesting but, I don't know . . . maybe it just sunk back or something," he said quietly. "But we should get home. You've got a big day tomorrow."

A shadowy veil slid across Beth's heart light.

Ardith grabbed Carlyle's hand without even realizing it.

"Come on, Beth. Stand your ground," she whispered.

Carlyle nodded in agreement.

"Well, you can think what you want, but I'm gonna ask the doctor for another ultrasound before they cut me open," Beth said, and the shadow disappeared.

Ryan sighed.

"Fine," he said. "It's your neck."

It was 8:10 on Monday morning and Beth was not on the operating table. She was sitting next to her husband in Dr. Hazeem's office in the Brooklyn Hospital Center. The doctor sat with both elbows on his desk and his chin resting on his crossed fingers.

"I don't know what to tell you," he said to the Jolicoeurs. "It would appear that some mistake was made, perhaps in the previous tests. But as of this morning, I can find no goiter on Beth's thyroid."

"Seriously? That's your explanation?" Ryan said. "You made a *mistake*? Did you not see it or feel it yourself? What about the biopsy? Was that a mistake too?"

The doctor shrugged and sat back in his leather office chair.

"I don't know what happened, Mr. Jolicoeur. This is as surprising to me as it is to you. I will certainly be making some inquiries about the process we have been through. And I will want Beth to come in, say, in two weeks, and we will check again just to make sure." He spread his hands out before him in the air. "But for now, go home. I would say I'm sorry, but it isn't often that I get to deliver such good news."

Ryan sat forward on the edge of his chair.

"Do you have any idea what kind of hell we have been living through the past weeks? And all you can say is 'Go home'?"

Beth put a hand on her husband's back.

"Honey, it's okay. I told you it was gone after Lupe prayed," she said. "Now we know. It worked. God healed me."

Ryan blew out a frustrated breath.

The Agreements

"Young man, I have seen many things in my days in the medical field," Dr. Hazeem said. "I am a man of science, not faith. But I have come to suspect that at times, based on my experiences with my patients, faith can be more powerful than science."

Beth leaned over and picked up her purse.

"Thank you, Dr. Hazeem, for honoring my request for the ultrasound. I'm not sure every doctor would have done that, and I am most grateful," she said. "Come on, Ryan. Let's go home. You've got the day off. We can do something fun with the girls." She stood up and zipped her coat. "But first, let's get breakfast. Just the two of us. Then I need to call Maria."

Ryan stood and seized his jacket off the back of his chair. He pulled a business card out of the pocket and flung it on the desk.

"If this 'nothing' turns into 'something' when you check again, you'll be hearing from me," he said.

"Make an appointment on the way out," Dr. Hazeem said to Beth, who had gripped Ryan's hand and was pulling him out the door.

Chapter 6 – The Shadows

The second checkup showed no signs of anything amiss in Beth's thyroid. Neither did the third or the fourth. By August, Ryan grudgingly admitted that something miraculous had happened to his wife. Either that or, as Dr. Hazeem had said, the initial diagnosis had been a mistake. But Ryan had seen the lump. He had felt it. And it simply wasn't there anymore. Not only that, but Beth had weaned herself from the medication and her blood tests showed her hormone levels were completely normal.

As Ryan sat at the kitchen table with his laptop open finishing some emails, he decided that perhaps it was time to relax and accept the good news. It was Saturday. The sun was shining. Beth was getting the girls ready to go to the park. The case he and Jake were working on was nearing the finish line. He could almost see the bonus check in his hand. His world was looking pretty rosy. Maybe he should just embrace it.

A knock sounded at the apartment door.

"I'll get it," he yelled to Beth.

He opened the door to find Mrs. Flanagan.

"Come on in," he said. "Beth will be right out. She's getting the girls changed. We're taking an expedition to the park."

"A lovely day for it," she said. "But it's not your wife I've come for."

The Agreements

She reached into her front apron pocket and retrieved a blank envelope.

"This was under my door when I got home from the market last night. I didn't open it 'til just now. Thought it was the super bothering me about some wee thing or another." She handed the envelope to Ryan. "But it would appear it's for you. Must've got our apartments mixed up."

Ryan slipped the contents of the envelope out, unfolded it, and began to read.

"Why don't ya sit, lad?" Mrs. Flanagan suggested. "Ya don't look so good."

She grasped his elbow and guided him to the couch.

"I wasn't aware your da was even alive," she said from her spot on the armrest. "I didn't mean to snoop, but, like I said, I thought it was for me."

"Who is it?" Beth hollered from the back bedroom.

"Only me, love," Mrs. Flanagan yelled back. "Does she know? About your da?" She said quietly to Ryan.

He nodded.

"That's good. It's better if she knows," Mrs. Flanagan said, smoothing a stray gray strand back into the hairnet she wore whenever she was baking.

Just then, the girls came running down the hallway, jostling for position to be the first to get to Nana, as they called their favorite neighbor.

"Well hello, my angels," she said, bending down to accept their enthusiastic hugs.

"Ookie," Nellie said.

"Ookie," Julia echoed.

"Is that all I am to you?" she laughed. "A cookie factory?"

"Girls, be nice to Nana," Beth said, entering the room.

"Oh no, 'tis fine. I anticipated the demand," she said, pulling two shortbread cookies from her apron. "Fresh from the oven. Can they have them now?"

"Pease," the girls begged in unison. "Pease."

Beth laughed.

"Oh, okay."

Mrs. Flanagan handed the cookies out simultaneously in order to avoid conflict. The girls snatched them from her hands and took them to their little table and chairs set behind the couch where all snacks or juice were to be consumed.

"So, is that it? You've just come to distribute cookies?" Beth asked.

"Well, no," Mrs. Flanagan said, tipping her head toward Ryan, who remained like a statue on the couch.

Beth came around the sofa, moved a stuffed puppy, and sat down next to him. She leaned in to read whatever it was he held in his hands.

"Oh my gosh," she said. "Where did this come from?"

Ryan looked up at their neighbor.

"She had it. He made a mistake and slipped it under her door."

"What? Here? In our building? Your dad—here?" Beth sat back. "I don't get it. How did he get in? How does he even know where we live?"

Ryan ran a hand through his coarse black hair.

"I'm getting a restraining order."

"I know it's none of my business, but do you think that's even possible? He's not made a threat. It doesn't sound like he means any harm," Mrs. Flanagan offered as she moved to sit on the loveseat. "Maybe you should hear him out. They are his granddaughters, after all."

Ryan crumpled the paper and threw it on the coffee table.

"You're right. It is none of your business," he sputtered.

"Ryan," Beth said. "She's just trying to be helpful. She doesn't know what he's like."

"Okay. Okay. You're right. I'm sorry," he said. "You have no way of knowing what kind of man my father is. So, let me fill you in."

For the next twenty minutes he proceeded to do just that as Beth distracted the girls with a DVD.

"Jesus, Mary, and Joseph," Mrs. Flanagan said when he at last wound down. "I'm sorry ya had to live with all that. Do you want me to ask the super to beef up the security around here? For I'll not stand for it. Your da won't be getting anywhere near my angels."

"Thanks, but I'll handle it," Ryan said. "He won't even know what hit him when I get done with him."

Beth watched the tension flare through her husband from head to toe. Though she had never known him to be violent, she was concerned that he might be thinking about something more than just legal retribution.

Two weeks later, on a Monday morning in September, Beth was back at the park with the girls. Carlyle was enjoying the vantage point he had from the padded handle of the double stroller. The girls were playing in plain sight in front of him, and he had a clear view of the grass sports fields and strolling paths stretching out around them. It was a glorious, blue-skied day, but Carlyle kept noticing shadowy swirls gathering over the trees.

They weren't clouds. He was sure of that. They gave off a frequency like a mounting storm, but they weren't weather related. He wished Maria and her kids were with them so he could consult with Ardith. He'd seen umbras drop across individuals' heart lights before, but this was the first time he had seen a shadow move over an entire city.

A cold shudder ran up and down his spine, eliciting a vague memory from the time outside of time. He looked from human to human in the park. They all seemed oblivious to what he sensed. It was one of those moments when he wished he could interfere. Send up a warning flag. Whisper in ears. But that was not his role. His role was to observe, and that was just what he was doing on that fall morning.

School-aged children were back in their classrooms and the play structure was less busy than it had been over the summer months. Julia used the opportunity to climb up the five rungs of the ladder and go down the slide over and over again to her heart's content. Her sister sat astride a plastic duck that was attached to the ground by a massive spring. Whenever Julia emerged from the short tunnel of the slide, Nellie yelled, "Again," as she rocked back and forth. Julia gladly obliged.

It was a good thing the girls were so content that day by themselves, for Carlyle could see that Beth was having a hard time staying engaged in their play. She sat alone on the green wooden bench, staring off at the azure expanse overhead with only an occasional glance back at her daughters. He guessed she was probably processing all that had been said the night before. In all the time Carlyle had lived with the Jolicoeurs, he had never seen the level of anger displayed between husband and wife as he had seen in those moments.

Marriage was certainly one of the most fascinating and complicated elements of humanity he had yet encountered. Carlyle remembered Madeline's teaching on the subject. She had said that though the two long to be one and, in fact, do become one, there is a constant war against this oneness, for out of unity comes life and light.

Why was this so hard for them to see? Evidently, in the human heart it was all too easy to confuse the issue. To the married couple, the enemy of oneness too often seemed to be flesh and blood rather than the shadowy powers of darkness who greatly feared the powers of human unity. He shook his head as he thought about the preceding hours and the words they held.

It had all started out with the phone call.

"We did it!" Ryan said as he put the phone back on its charger. "Beth, baby, we did it!"

He slid down the hallway in his stocking feet, looking for her.

"Shh," Beth said, coming out of the girls' room and closing the door behind her. "I just got them both asleep."

Ryan picked her up and swung her around.

"Ryan," she protested between giggles.

The Agreements

He kissed her soundly, set her down, and, grabbing her hand, pulled her to the living room.

Hearing all the commotion, Carlyle left his sleeping charges and followed the activity. Ryan sat on the couch with Beth on his lap. He was smiling from ear to ear.

"Are you going to tell me what this is all about?" Beth said.

"One more kiss, I think, and then I'll tell ya."

"Well, that seems to be a pretty small price," she said, turning her head to pay the piper.

"Oh, this is just a down payment on the full price," he said.

Carlyle smiled as he settled on the mantelpiece, enjoying the sudden burst of joy.

"That was Larry on the phone," said Ryan.

"And?"

"And . . . we did it! We closed the case, and he's got bonus checks waiting for me and Jake tomorrow morning."

Beth threw her arms around Ryan's neck and began to cry.

"Hey, hey, hey," Ryan said. "This is happy news."

"I know," Beth said. "These are happy tears."

"Well, hold, on 'cause there's more."

"More? More what? Money?"

"Well, no, not money. At least not immediately, although Larry says closing this case is a big deal and will only mean more lucrative cases will be funneled our way. So, yes, in that sense, more money. But for now, the more is something else. Something you and I have always wanted to do."

"What?"

"It's sort of short notice, but we can make it work. Larry is leaving town Tuesday evening, and he wanted to do something special for me and Jake and our wives before he leaves. Something really special."

"Ryan, just tell me," she said, punching his chest.

"Okay, okay," he laughed. "He is taking us and Jake and Lisa to . . . drumroll please . . . Windows on the World! For breakfast on Tuesday."

Beth gasped.

"Seriously?"
Ryan nodded.
"Seriously."
"But how? How did he get reservations so quickly?"
"Oh, he's been doing 'power breakfasts' up there for years. He has a standing Tuesday-morning reservation for clients and whoever he wants to reward. And this week, that's you and me, babe."

Beth slipped off his lap to the couch and leaned back into the cushions.

"What? Aren't you excited?" Ryan asked.

Beth pulled her sandy locks back from her face and swirled them into a bun.

"Don't do that," Ryan said.
"Do what?"
"Play with your hair. Whenever you want to avoid a topic, you play with your hair."
"What? I do not."
"You do."

She pulled the bun out and crossed her arms over her chest.
"Happy?" she said.
Ryan rolled his eyes and sighed.
"Don't do that," Beth said.
"What?"
"Roll your eyes."

"Oh my god, Beth." He stood up from the couch and turned to look down on her. "The biggest moment of my career and you can't seem to find it within yourself to just be excited."

Beth scooted to the edge of the sofa and grabbed his hands.

"Keep your voice down, please," she said. "I'm sorry. Really, I'm so happy for you . . . for us. You've worked so hard. And this is so great."

Carlyle let his legs dangle over the edge of the mantle and leaned forward. He was hoping for the best, just like Madeline had instructed. "Wait and hope." Usually it was an apology that made the way for reconciliation. He'd seen it before between these two and he was hoping it would be enough again.

The Agreements

"It's just that . . . ," Beth started.

Ryan ripped his hands from hers and stuck them deep in his pockets.

"Okay, here we go," he said and spun away from his wife.

"Ryan, that's not fair. I'm just trying to think of the girls. It's really short notice, just like you said."

"Mrs. Flanagan will take them. She always does," he said from the perch he had taken up on a kitchen stool.

Beth turned around to face him over the back of the couch.

"Her son Jimmy is in town and I am not going to ask her to interrupt that time. She sees him so seldom."

"Well, then ask Maria."

Beth shook her head.

"It's just too much for her right now."

"Lupe's there to help. Come on Beth, at least just ask."

"Lupe works at the soup kitchen every Tuesday."

Ryan threw his hands in the air.

"You know what? Forget I even asked you to come along. I'll go by myself. I'm tired of taking last place, Beth. Ever since the twins came, that's where you put me."

"Well pardon the heck out of me. Why don't you try staying home with these two and seeing how much energy you have left at the end of the day?"

"Oh, and my job doesn't have any stresses? I am breaking my back trying to get a career off the ground so you can stay home and live out your dream of being a mom. You would think that might earn me a little, I don't know, gratitude at the very least."

"I am doing the best I can! You get to run out the door every day all by yourself. You get to talk to adults and get a paycheck and go out to lunch. And I'm stuck here with toddlers and diapers and tantrums and . . . and I am exhausted."

Ryan stood up and marched toward his wife.

"You're not so tired that you can't go out the door with two toddlers on Sunday morning to that crazy church. Sunday, Beth! One day I could help, when we could be together, you leave me here."

Beth got on her knees on the couch.

"You're here by yourself because you choose to be."

Carlyle flew up to the top of the bookshelf. It was not fun to watch them quarrel. In fact, it was disturbing, but he couldn't seem to look away. The angrier they became, the darker the light that was within them grew, until it was almost undetectable.

"Because I'm not as gullible as you," Ryan whispered as he walked away.

"Gullible!" Beth sprung from the couch. "Just because I believe in God doesn't mean I'm stupid. It means I have faith. Faith in someone bigger than myself."

Ryan stopped and stared at his advancing wife.

"One little bump on your neck is gone. I'm not impressed. If God is so big, why didn't he heal my mom? Or your mom, for that matter?"

Beth let her hands fall to her side as tears erupted in her eyes.

"Why didn't he keep my dad from beating my mom? Or your dad from shooting himself in the head?" Ryan continued his attack.

A thick shadow grew between husband and wife. So thick that, as Carlyle looked through it from his vantage point behind Ryan, the light in Beth was completely imperceptible.

Beth squared her shoulders and drew in a jagged breath.

"He died of a broken heart," she whispered.

"No, Beth." Ryan bent forward to get within two inches of Beth's face. "He killed himself. My dad may be a brute, a liar, and a drunk, but your dad was a coward."

Ryan spun around and tramped down the hall, slamming the bedroom door behind him.

Beth leaned against the wall and slid to the floor. She drew her knees to her chest, buried her head in them, and sobbed.

As Carlyle watched the girls play on that beautiful Monday morning, he was glad they had not been privy to the things he had seen transpire between their parents. He shook his head to clear it from the images of the night's conflict and focused on his charges. Julia squealed with delight on yet another trip down the slide and Nellie urged her on yet again. Try as he might to enjoy the simple pleasures of the moment, he could not get rid of the sense of impending darkness that swirled around them.

Chapter 7 – The Threat

It was the smell of tobacco that first drew Beth's attention away from the replaying of the previous night's argument in her head back to the present. Few people smoked cigarettes in the park anymore. Fewer still cigars or pipes. Although the nutty aroma was almost pleasant, she was not a fan of smoke of any kind near her children. She scanned the horizon, looking for the culprit.

About forty feet away, under a maple tree whose leaves had just begun to brighten into their autumn reds, stood a tall, lanky man. Older but not old. He wore blue jeans, a denim jacket, and a baseball cap. Not the trendy sort. No, his clothes looked more like the type Beth associated with farmers or blue-collar workers. He was leaning against the trunk of the tree with one hand in his jacket pocket and one hand on the pipe jutting from his mouth. As odd as this farmer type looked in the middle of Brooklyn, this was not what caused Beth's breath to catch and her heart to constrict. It was not *how* he looked but *where* he looked. He was staring straight at her girls.

Beth jumped from the bench and ran toward Nellie. She scooped her off the duck. Momentarily stunned by her mother's abrupt interruption, Nellie was silent. But only momentarily. Then, as Beth sprinted the remaining feet to the end of the slide where Julia was just emerging, Nellie found her voice.

The Agreements

"No, no, no!" she screamed as her legs kicked and her arms flailed.

Beth nearly dropped her.

"Nellie, stop it. Stop it now!"

Nellie's feet ceased kicking. But her eyes still flamed. She went limp like a dead fish in her mother's arms. Julia sat on the edge of the slide with a perplexed look on her face.

"Nel, no. Mama, no," she said, raising one hand in reprimand.

Beth slung the limp Nellie onto one hip as best she could and grabbed Julia's upraised fingers.

"Come. Now," she ordered, dragging a startled Julia back to the stroller that stood by the bench. Beth glanced back over her shoulder to the man. He was still under the tree, but he wasn't leaning back any longer. The pipe was out of his mouth and he looked right at her as if to say something. Beth wasn't waiting around to find out what that might be. She stuffed Nellie into the back seat of the stroller, where her kicking and screaming resumed. She rammed Julia into the front seat with such force, her daughter stared at her with something very close to terror.

"I'm sorry, honey," Beth said with a quick stroke of her cheeks. "Mommy is in a hurry. Mommy didn't mean to hurt you."

Then she whisked the diaper bag, the container of fish crackers, and the juice boxes off the bench and flung them into the bottom rack of the stroller. As she pushed the cumbersome apparatus onto the paved path toward the park exit, she risked one more glance. The man had begun to move toward her.

She picked up her pace.

It was him.

She was sure of it.

She had only ever seen him the one time—at her mother-in-law's funeral. And that was just a distant glance. But she knew that build and that face. It was aged and worn, and she had not seen it up close. But it was familiar. It was the same as her husband's.

At the park exit, Beth turned north, away from their apartment. Maria's place was closer. And not only that, she needed her friend. She needed a safe place. The light for the crosswalk was about to change, but Beth ran into the intersection, extending her arm like a traffic cop toward the cars and taxis that were just about to careen forward.

Horns blared.

Fingers flew.

But she didn't care.

She needed every second.

Every obstacle.

Reaching the far sidewalk, she peeked back over her shoulder.

Claude Jolicoeur had just reached the park exit. His head swung back and forth. Just when she thought they might have escaped detection, he spotted her and ran toward the intersection. But he was too late. The light had changed and he had to stop. The thick traffic had become her friend.

Beth charged ahead.

"Move. Behind you. To your left," she cried, nearly running over an elderly couple who either couldn't hear her warnings or couldn't respond quickly enough.

Sweat sprung from her pores.

Nellie switched gears from screaming to squealing as if on a roller coaster.

Julia gripped the front rail with white knuckles.

They were making a spectacle of themselves. But Beth couldn't stop. Maria's building was only a block away.

Ryan had been unable to get a restraining order. His father "didn't pose harm," according to the judge. Claude had not made any further attempts to contact them. And they had hoped that maybe he had gone back to North Dakota, that maybe he had given up.

But clearly, they were wrong.

At the stairs leading to the Gomez apartment, Beth swung the stroller to one side and parked it.

"Let's see Lita," she said to a wide-eyed Julia. The words seemed to calm her daughter and she lifted her arms. Beth deposited her on the sidewalk. "Wait for mommy to get Nellie," she ordered, all the while scanning the oncoming pedestrians.

Nellie was already scrambling from her seat.

"Go, Nel go."

"Yes, Nel go," Beth seized both girls by the hand and launched up the steps.

She pressed the buzzer.

No response.

"Come on, come on."

She pressed again. Three times in a row.

"Bueno?" came Lupe's voice over the intercom.

"It's me, Lupe. Beth and the girls," she said.

The front door clicked. She dropped Nellie's hand and swept the door open.

"In, in, in," she said, pressing Nellie's back and following her inside with Julia.

She pulled the entry door shut behind them with a satisfying click and rushed the girls to the elevator.

She pushed the button, her fingers tapping on the metal square around it.

Nellie pounded on the elevator door.

"Nel go," she demanded.

As if it could not resist her power, the elevator's scuffed silver doors slid back. The girls needed no prompting to enter the familiar box. Each lifted a finger toward the floor buttons and said, "Me, me, me."

"Not today, girls," Beth said, ignoring their pleas and pushing number three.

As the doors closed, she looked back across the lobby to the front door.

Claude was there.

He was watching.

The shaking had stopped, but Beth was still having a hard time breathing. She gripped the phone in Maria's kitchen with a sweaty palm. Lupe had the two sets of twins settled in the living room with a snack. Rosie was down for a nap. Maria sat across the table from her friend with one arm stretched out to hold her hand.

"Did you call the police?" Ryan asked on the other end of the phone.

"No, I, uh, I just . . . I just needed to hear your voice," Beth said as tears sprung fresh in her eyes.

"Are you sure it was him?"

"It had to be him. He looks just like you. And he was smoking a pipe . . . just like you told me he did. Who smokes a pipe around here, Ryan? Who wears a John Deere hat?"

"Okay, listen. You're okay. The girls are okay. That's all that matters. We'll figure this out."

Beth nodded, knowing he couldn't see her response but unable to reply.

"I'm gonna ask around and see what we can do legally. He's not gonna hurt my family. No way. I'm not gonna let him. Do you hear me, babe?"

"Yes," she managed to say. "I hear you."

Quiet settled over the phone line.

Hector reentered the apartment from his tour around the exterior of the building and came into the kitchen.

"No sign of him anywhere. I went clear around the block. Didn't see anyone matching your description," he reported.

"Did you hear that?" Beth said into the phone

"Yeah, I heard. Tell Hector thanks. Glad he was home," Ryan replied. "But now we know. He's not giving up and he's not going away. Not without a fight. If that's what he wants, that's what he'll get. Listen, I've gotta go. But I'm gonna leave early. Can you stay there until I get home? Just so I can make sure he's not hanging around our place? I'll call you if the coast is clear."

Maria and Hector both nodded, having heard the request.

"Yeah, I'll stay here until I hear from you," Beth replied. "And Ryan . . ."

"Yeah?"

Beth swallowed and blew out a quick breath.

"I'm sorry about last night," she whispered.

The Agreements

A moment of silence dangled.
"Yeah," came Ryan's reply. "Me too.

Carlyle didn't know if it was the scare of the day or the regrets of the night, but something had caused Ryan and Beth to set aside all the ugly words and be reconciled. He was relieved to see their heart lights strong and vibrant again in the wake of the forgiveness they had offered each other. It never ceased to amaze him how freeing the choice to forgive could be.

"I asked . . . ," Ryan and Beth said at the same time over the kitchen table, their dinner of chicken nuggets and tater tots barely touched on their plates. The girls contentedly chowed down next to each other in their high chairs, swapping small chunks of food back and forth as if one had something different from the other.

"You first," Ryan said.

"I asked Maria. She said of course she would watch the girls," Beth said. "It's only for a few hours. She was sorta mad that I would even think to not ask her."

"Well, I asked Melanie if it would be okay if we took the girls with us," Ryan said.

"Are you kidding? These two at Windows on the World. Do they even allow that?"

"I know," Ryan said. "It wouldn't be the most leisurely meal, but I had to ask." He reached over and grabbed Beth's hand. "I need you there. Whatever it takes."

He raised her hand to his lips and kissed her knuckles one at a time.

"Me, me," said Julia, raising a hand toward her daddy.

Her parents laughed. Ryan took her hand and kissed her little knuckles too.

"Mmm, so yummy," he said, wiping crumbs from his mouth.

"Nel, Nel," Julia interceded for her twin who had extended her hand, too, but whose mouth was too full to make the request herself.

Ryan stood up and walked behind Julia to reach Nellie. He kissed her knuckles clean, too, and returned to his chair.

"So?" Beth asked.

"So, what?"

"What did Melanie find out?"

"She said we can take them if we want. No rule against it, but it was up to us."

"What do you want to do?"

"Whatever you want to do. As long as you're with me, I'm okay with either solution."

Carlyle sighed with satisfaction.

The Jolicoeur ship had been righted.

He stood up and stretched from side to side in an attempt to rid his body of the tension that had accumulated in a tight knot in the small of his back. But try as he might, the discomfort would not leave him.

Chapter 8 – The Drop-Off

Still dressed in her chenille night-robe and slippers, Mrs. Flanagan held an uncharacteristically still Nellie and swayed back and forth.

"I'm so sorry about this," Beth said.

"Not to worry, love," Fiona said. "My morning is free. Jimmy is in meetings 'til noon." She placed her hand on Nellie's sweaty brow. "Poor thing. Just woke up with this, did she?"

"Out of the blue. No warning. She was fine last night and then this morning her temp was 102. I gave her Tylenol an hour ago. There's more in the bag if she needs it. I put juice and snacks in there too. Not sure if she'll even be hungry. And if you need anything else, well, you have a key."

"We'll be fine," Mrs. Flanagan said. "Now go, catch up to that handsome husband of yours. It's not every morning ya get to eat so high in the sky. And Julia?"

"She's with Ryan downstairs. She seems to be fine," Beth said halfway out the door. "Thanks again. I owe you."

"Not a dime," Mrs. Flanagan said, closing the door behind her. "We'll just sit right here and watch the morning shows," she whispered to Nellie as she settled into her gliding chair and flipped on the TV with the remote control. She muted the volume on *Good Morning America* and began to sing.

Rest tired eyes a while, sweet is thy baby's smile,
Angels are guarding and they watch o'er thee

Sleep, sleep, *grah mo chree*
Here on your nana's knee
Angels are guarding
And they watch o'er thee

"Just a temp," Beth said to Maria. "Probably more teeth coming in, but I didn't want to risk bringing a bug into your house."

Rosie was crying in Maria's arms. Beto and Freddy were hollering as they ran up and down the hallway, still in their pajamas. Lupe had just left for her volunteer work at the soup kitchen.

"Are you sure about this?" Beth asked over the tumult. "We can take her with us."

"No, absolutely not," Maria said, patting Rosie's back. "You get out the door and enjoy your morning. It's a gorgeous day and I can only imagine the spectacular view you're going to have. Go. We'll be fine."

Julia sat in a high chair with the tortilla strips Lupe had cut up for her before she left. Beth kissed her on the forehead.

"Be good. Mommy loves you." She turned to her friend, who was slightly disheveled in her sweatpants and tank top. "Maybe it was a blessing in disguise that Nellie's not feeling well." She kissed Maria on the cheek. "We'll come back as soon as we're done."

"Take your time. I've survived a lot worse than this," she said with a smile.

It was the first time in Carlyle's role as observer of the twins that he had to travel between two locations. The girls had never been any farther apart than the length of their apartment. He had a hard time choosing where to be and when. From what Ardith had told him, it was not a common conundrum for observers, since most had only one human to watch. But as he sat on the back of Mrs. Flanagan's couch listening to her soothing lullaby, he heard a voice in his head that sounded distinctly like Madeline's say, "You have a key."

He reached into his inner jacket pocket where he had stashed the key months before and pulled it out. He had never driven the light machine because he had not needed to. Truth was, he had no idea where to even locate it.

"Okay. Great. I have a key but no motorcycle," he said to himself. He was in no mood to unravel a mystery. He was agitated by the day and he could not put a finger on exactly why.

But as he rolled the key over in his hand, it began to heat up. It became so hot, he flung it toward the lace doily on the couch. But instead of dropping, it took flight. And as Carlyle watched, the lighted outline of the awesome machine appeared between the couch and the television.

"Now is the time," the voice of his trainer again pierced his thoughts.

It was good to hear from her on this day of all days. It was a reminder that he was not alone, that he had all that he needed for his mission.

He flew to the motorcycle and seated himself on the familiar fine leather. The key had inserted itself and the engine revved, waiting for his cue to take off. He gazed at Nellie, fast asleep in her Nana's arms. She was safe.

The digital clock on the DVD player beneath the television read 8:40 a.m. as Carlyle hit the throttle and jetted from the room.

In the Gomez apartment, the chaos of the morning had settled. Julia and the twins sat on the rug in the living room playing with the boys' wooden train set. *Good Day New York* played behind them on the TV. Maria had just taken Rosie to the back bedroom for a complete change of clothes after a particularly explosive poop when Freddy began to yell.

"Bam, bam!"

She tried to censor the boys' television viewing. Freddy in particular seemed to enjoy violent scenes a bit too much for his mother's liking. *Good Day New York* was usually a safe bet. Must've been a commercial or something.

"Bam, bam, bam!" Freddy yelled again.

"Freddy, play with your trains," Maria yelled.

"Oh, oh," Beto chimed in. "Big boo-boo."

"Bam, bam."

"Mommy will be there in a minute. Pick a book and we'll read," she hollered.

Then Julia began to cry.

"Boys, leave Julia alone!"

Carlyle's eyes were glued to the scene unfolding on the television from his place on the coffee table. The commercial for some upcoming movie had given way to a breaking news story—a story that would supersede all programming for days to come. There was an explosion at the North Tower of the World Trade Center. Flames and black smoke poured from the building.

Maria marched into the living room with Rosie in her arms, prepared to bring order out of disorder. But her hand flew to her mouth as her mind tried to register what her eyes were seeing on the TV screen.

"An explosion of some sort has occurred at the World Trade Center," the voice of the reporter said.

"Ay, Dios mío," Maria whispered.

Freddy had picked up a piece of his train and was smashing it onto the top of the coffee table. Beto had one hand on the TV screen, and with the other he pointed to the enormous gash that had opened up on the face of the building.

"Big boo-boo," he said.

Julia sat transfixed by the images with tears streaming down her face as if she understood exactly what was going on.

Maria moved to the couch in a daze and sat with Rosie draped over her shoulder.

"Julia, come here, mija," she wooed the upset child.

The Agreements

Julia scrambled to her feet and flung her arms around Maria's legs. Maria boosted her up onto the couch and wrapped her close, pulling her head down onto her shoulder, averting her gaze from the unfolding news.

"Beto, move please," she said.

"Boo-boo," he said one more time before turning to crawl under the table as if in need of a safe haven. Freddy continued to slam his toy against the coffee table.

"Freddy, stop it. Stop it now!" she ordered. He looked at her with a hint of defiance before dropping the train and heading to the bookshelf. He gathered two books and offered one to Beto as he joined him under the table.

Carlyle seated himself on the armrest of the couch next to Ardith the Ardent.

"Ryan and Beth, they're up there, aren't they?" she asked.

"Yeah," he replied.

She scooted next to him until their shoulders touched. They stared intently at the TV.

Julia slid out of Maria's grasp down onto the cushions and laid her head on a velour pillow, her face away from the TV. Soon she was asleep despite the drama unfolding around her.

Shortly after a second plane crashed into the South Tower, the television hosts concluded, as so many others that day, that what was occurring was not an accident. It was an intentional attack. Maria picked up the remote and flipped from channel to channel. Each one was focused on the same bizarre scene, each one reaching the same terrifying conclusion.

Maria placed her hand on the sleeping toddler at her side and quietly began to pray.

"Father, I don't know what's happening, but you do. Please guard my friends Ryan and Beth. And Nellie . . . oh, sweet Jesus," she said with a gasp. "I don't even know if she's with them or Mrs. Flanagan. Wherever she is, keep her safe from all harm as well. And help . . . please send help. We need you, we need you, we need you," she said before lapsing into silence and staring at the scenes playing out before her on the news.

Carlyle and Ardith were also mesmerized by the television.

"Do you see that?" Ardith said.

"What?" Carlyle replied.

"The lights," she said, pointing to the towers. "Inside the buildings."

Carlyle focused.

She was right.

Up and down the height of the towers, little lights like beacons had begun to shine. Bursts of brilliant colors shot out in pairs and groups and streams.

"Heart lights?" Carlyle whispered.

"What else could they be?"

"But something . . . ," Carlyle said, ". . . something's different."

Ardith nodded.

Never before had the two observers seen the vividness of color, the strength of beaming, or the clarity of purpose of heart lights like this.

As groups of firefighters entered the buildings and began to climb, their inner lights glowed with an otherworldly vibrancy. They were charging into danger. They were risking it all for the sake of others. And it was not just these brave souls. All over the doomed structures and in the surrounding area, people seemed to be finding the courage, the strength, the love to help their fellow man.

Some would survive the day.

Many would not.

"They look like . . . ," Ardith started.

"I know," Carlyle agreed.

"Like they're remembering who they are," she whispered.

At 10:28 a.m., as the North Tower collapsed, Maria screamed and slid onto the floor beside the couch, with Rosie still in her arms, and began to sob. Beto emerged from his hiding place and stood beside his mommy, patting her gently on the back. Freddy stared at her in frozen confusion. Julia stirred and rolled over but did not, or maybe would not, open her eyes.

As devastated as Carlyle was by the events, he wished the humans could see what he and Ardith were seeing. For in that moment of destruction, a brilliant burst of light shot from the dusty haze of the failing building. And in that burst, clear and strong, a stream of seafoam green and bronze surged out over the skyline until it merged with perfect unity into all the other surging heart lights in a blazing ball of light so dazzling and intense, the observers had to shield their eyes.

    Carlyle stared into Ardith's stunned face, wondering if his own countenance was equally as ashen.

    "Are you okay?" Carlyle whispered.

    She shook her head. He pulled her into his arms as an overwhelming sorrow surged up within in him.

    They both began to weep.

    And they wept for what seemed like an eternity, long and hard and deep.

Chapter 9 – The Fallout

By the time Jimmy Flanagan had walked across the Brooklyn Bridge and all the way back to his mother's apartment, it was after 5 p.m. His feet were sore and blistered in his black oxfords, and his dress shirt was soaked through with sweat. He hung his navy-blue suit coat on the coat rack beside the front door. Bits and pieces of ash ornamented the fine woolen fabric. As Jimmy went to brush it off, he caught a glimpse of himself in the mirrored prayer of St. Patrick hanging on the wall behind the door. His wavy red hair was also bedecked with a fine layer of gray detritus. He shook his head and ran his hands through his hair, hoping to bring some semblance of normalcy to his appearance. He didn't want to frighten his mum any more than the events of the day had no doubt already done.

Stepping through the kitchen, he found his mother in the living room kneeling beside her glider. Her eyes were tightly shut, and she swayed slightly back and forth as her hands moved with practiced efficiency over her rosary beads. A small child lay bundled under an afghan on the sofa beside her. The child was not asleep but lay listless with watery eyes that registered his entrance but showed no concern. His mother was so wrapped up in her intercessions, she did not move until he spoke.

"Ma," he said quietly.

The Agreements

She looked up. Her face seemed to have aged many years since he had seen her only hours before.

"Saints be praised," she cried.

Jimmy reached down and helped her to her feet. They embraced. She wept. He held her close.

"I'm okay, Ma. I'm okay," he crooned.

After long minutes of mutual comfort, Fiona pulled back. She yanked a well-used hankie from her pocket and used it once again.

"Which one of the twins is that?" he asked.

Fiona turned to Nellie, who stared at the two adults unswervingly. She tried to tell her son, but the words would not come out. The hours of strain seemed to have robbed her of all strength. Jimmy gently set her in her glider and pulled up the ottoman to sit on himself.

"Tell me about your day," he said. "And I'll tell you about mine."

She had kept the phone close by her.

All day she had watched the ongoing horror on her television. Heard sirens rushing through the streets. Saw black smoke rising out her window over the Manhattan skyline.

Nellie had slept. She woke only occasionally, asking for water. Asking for Mommy and Daddy.

Asking for Julia.

Fiona had waited and prayed and hoped. Hoped to hear from Jimmy. Hoped beyond hope to hear from Beth.

When the phone finally rang late in the afternoon, she snatched it off the end table.

"Hullo?"

"Is this Mrs. Flanagan? Mrs. Fiona Flanagan?"

Her heart sank to her knees.

"Yes," she said.

"Mrs. Flanagan, my name is Melanie Polanski. I am . . . I was . . ."

A strangled sob.

"Take a breath, lass. I'll wait," Fiona said.

Finally, Melanie regained her composure and continued.

"Mr. Jolicoeur has you down as an emergency contact. And I'm calling to let you know . . . that . . . well, that . . ."

"That they were in the tower?"

"Yes," came the weepy reply.

The two sat in silence, strangers bound by grief, suddenly needing each other.

"I had hoped . . . ," Fiona said at last. "Do ya know for sure?"

"I'm afraid so," Melanie said. "Larry, Mr. Feldstein, called me from his Blackberry. After the plane hit. He said they were all okay. No one was hurt. But that the smoke was getting really bad. They were waiting for instructions. Looking for a way out."

"I see. Looking for a way out," Fiona repeated. "But there was no way. Those poor souls. Those poor, poor souls."

More silence.

"Uh, I hate to ask, but . . . do you happen to know . . . did they take the girls?" Melanie asked.

"No, lass, no."

"Oh, thank God," Melanie said. "Ryan had asked me if they could take them along. If the restaurant allowed it and I had told him . . . I had told him . . . God forgive me . . . I had told him they could. But they didn't. Oh, you have no idea how relieved I am."

Fiona swallowed. She waited, her grip tightening on the phone.

"Are you still there?" Melanie asked.

"Aye."

"Are you okay? I'm sorry to be the bearer of such horrible news, but at least the girls are okay. One bright moment in this terrible day."

"Well, love, it's just that . . ." Fiona hesitated.

"Was there something else?"

"I don't know how to tell ya this."

Fiona glanced over at the sick little girl on her couch.

"What is it?" Melanie urged. "You can tell me."

"It's just so . . ."

The Agreements

"Mrs. Flanagan," Melanie said softly, "it can't possibly be any worse than what I had to tell you."

Fiona closed her eyes and thought back over the rush of the early-morning drop-off with Beth and Nellie. What had she actually said?

"It's just that . . . ," she said. "Beth only dropped off Nellie this morning."

"So, where's Julia?"

"I think I remember her saying that . . . she told me that Julia . . . that Julia was . . ."

"Was where?"

"That she was with them."

Chapter 10 – The Orphans

Hector Gomez showed up at the Flanagan apartment an hour or so after Jimmy's arrival. He was still dressed in his UPS delivery uniform, and at first when Fiona opened the door, she didn't recognize him.

"Today? You are delivering packages today? Can we not stop the world for just a moment or two?" Fiona said.

"Mrs. Flanagan," Hector said. "It's me. Hector Gomez. Beth and Ryan's friend?"

Fiona's hand flew to her face.

"Of course, of course," she said, taking him by the hand and pulling him into the apartment. "I'm so sorry. My mind just isn't working quite right. Please, come in."

Hector stepped over the threshold, and Fiona reached up and hugged him. At first he stood stiffly in her embrace, but then he lifted his arms and hugged her back.

"Thanks," he said into her gray curls.

Fiona stepped back and looked into his eyes.

"It just looked as though ya might need a good hug."

Hector nodded.

"I did."

Jimmy Flanagan entered the kitchen from the hallway, having changed out of his sweaty dress shirt into a T-shirt.

The Agreements

"Can't believe they've got you out working on a day like this," he said to Hector.

"He's not working, Jimmy. He's visiting," Fiona said. "This is the Jolicoeurs' friend, Hector Gomez."

"Nice to meet you," said Jimmy with a nod. "Hell of a day out there."

"For sure," replied Hector.

The television was still on, the volume down low. Images of the day scrolled constantly across the screen.

"Not just here either. The Pentagon too," he said.

"And a plane went down in Pennsylvania," Jimmy said. "They think it might've been headed to D.C."

"So crazy." Hector shook his head. "Do they think it's over yet?"

Jimmy shrugged.

"What can I do for ya?" asked Fiona. "You've not come all this way just for a chat and a hug. Although today, I'd not blame ya."

"No." Hector replied. "Maria sent me."

"How's she holding up?"

"Not so good," he replied. "Better now that her mom is home. But it was a rough day for her . . . well, for everyone. She had all the kids. And she was by herself. I left work as soon as I could, but getting home . . . had to walk. And then all the panic and confusion. Well, you know . . . Everyone has a story today."

"Come. Sit." Mrs. Flanagan led him to the table. "I'll put some tea on."

Hector and Jimmy sat opposite each other at the round, wooden table.

"I can't stay long," Hector said. "But Maria had to know. She tried calling Ryan's office, but no one would answer her questions. She couldn't find your number, and she's been calling every Flanagan in the book, but . . ."

"Ah, yes. I'm not listed," Fiona said, pulling three cups from the cupboard.

"Yeah, I figured," Hector said. "So, have you heard anything? From . . . anyone?"

As the water warmed, Fiona came and sat at the table. She reached for Hector's hand and repeated the conversation she had had with Melanie regarding Ryan and Beth. Hector hung his head.

"Oh man . . . I was afraid of that," he said.

The three sat in stunned silence.

"Can't even let myself imagine what they went through," said Jimmy at last, voicing what each of them had been pondering privately.

Suddenly a cry went up from down the hallway. A crabby, feverish cry.

Hector sat up.

"Is that . . . ? Is she here?"

"Aye, it's Nellie," Fiona said, moving toward the bedroom. "Jimmy, will ya take care of the tea, love? She's not feeling so well, but she's safe."

"Thank you, Jesus!" Hector stood up and followed her. "Maria didn't know where she was for sure. She couldn't remember if Beth said she was with them or with you."

"She's been here all day."

Nellie lay in the middle of the bed with her arms raised.

"Hold you?" she asked.

Mrs. Flanagan picked her up, sweeping her hair off her sweaty forehead.

"It's okay love. Nana's here."

"Well, at least one piece of good news to report back to my wife," Hector said. He reached out and touched Nellie's hand. "Julia might stop crying too."

"Julia!" Fiona gasped.

"Jewels," whispered Nellie.

"Yeah, she's at my place. Been there since Beth dropped her off this morning."

"Saints be praised. Melanie said . . . well, I just assumed . . . Beth told me she was with them. I didn't know. Oh, bless the Lord."

Jimmy called from the kitchen, "Tea is ready."

Hector wrapped an arm around Mrs. Flanagan and Nellie and turned them back toward the kitchen.

The Agreements

"I think I'll take that cup of tea before I head home," he said. "And perhaps a shot of whiskey as well," Fiona offered.

"Now who can that be?" Fiona asked as someone knocked on her apartment door not five minutes later.

Jimmy got up from the table and peered through the peephole.

"Some guy," he said over his shoulder. "Older. Maybe your super?"

"Oh, I suppose. Probably checking on everyone," she said, giving Nellie a sip of water from a sippy cup. "Let him in."

The man who filled her doorway held a dirty mesh baseball cap in his hands, twisting it back and forth. He stared at Nellie and tears brimmed over his eyes.

"Nellie?" he whispered.

Fiona couldn't believe it. She wrapped her arm around Nellie and pulled her back against her.

"What do you want?" she said.

"Ma, what's going on?" Jimmy asked. "Who is this guy?"

"Ask him," she said.

"Claude," the man offered. "Claude Jolicoeur."

Hector stood up, placed both hands on the table, and leaned forward.

"Ryan's dad?" he asked.

"I am," Claude replied. Then his chin dropped. "I was."

His shoulders began to shake as he fought to maintain his composure.

Hector turned to Fiona.

"How'd he get up here anyway? You want me to kick him out?"

She took a deep breath and pondered her options. She could have him hauled out onto the street. But he would be back. His history with Ryan and Beth proved that. He was clearly distraught over the events of the day and seemed to know about his son's death. Perhaps it was not a day for more ripping and tearing.

Perhaps it was a day for listening. Perhaps he just needed to share his grief with someone. But was that all he wanted?

For years to come, she would wonder what might have happened if she had kicked him out. But not knowing what lay ahead and against her better judgment, she chose what she thought was best for that day.

"Let him stay," she said. "The man has just lost his son."

Jimmy nodded his head toward the interior of the apartment and Claude stepped inside. Hector pulled his chair to one side of Fiona and Jimmy did the same on the other side until they were positioned like guarding sentinels around Nellie.

"Take a seat," Jimmy offered, pointing to the one remaining chair opposite them.

Claude shuffled the few feet to the table and sat.

Nellie curled up into her nana's lap and hid her face from the stranger.

Long, heavy moments passed.

"I'm sorry for your loss," Fiona said.

Claude nodded and wiped his face with a soiled handkerchief he pulled from his back pocket.

"I should say the same to you," he said. "You knew Ryan better than I did these past years. And Beth . . ." He paused to clear a lump from his throat. "Her too. I, uh, never even got a chance . . ."

"Well, from what I've heard," Hector jumped in, "you made some choices long ago about being a part of Ryan's life . . . or not."

"True enough," he admitted.

"And now you want us to sit here and feel sorry for you?" Hector said. "I'm not buying it. You've got something else up your sleeve, you lousy son of a . . ."

"Okay, okay," Jimmy interrupted. "Let's keep this civil. It's been a terrible day for everyone. Let's take a breath and hear the man out." He folded his arms on the table. "Why exactly are you here, Mr. Jolicoeur?"

"Well, I'll get to the point," Claude said, still gripping his cap. "I, uh, spoke to Ryan's office, and so I know . . . I know what happened to them."

The Agreements

"How'd you get them to give you that information? They wouldn't speak to my wife," Hector said, his arms crossed, his leg jiggling under the table.

Claude hesitated.

"I guess . . . I guess I lied about who I was," he said. "Used the name of an attorney I know . . . not my finest hour . . ."

"But how'd you even know they were in the tower?" Hector asked.

Claude shook his head and took a ragged breath before he replied.

"I didn't. I was just trying one more time to talk with Ryan. I told myself, 'One more try and then I give up.' Thought maybe today in all the confusion, someone might just put me through."

"Oh, sweet Jesus," Fiona said, her chin resting on Nellie's head.

"I had no idea they were there . . . all three of them. Everyone but her," Claude said, gazing at his granddaughter.

Jimmy and Hector stole glances at Fiona.

She remained silent.

"I guess it was a blessing in disguise for Nellie to be sick today," Claude continued.

Fiona nodded.

"So, I've come to tell you," Claude, said, looking directly at Fiona, "I've come to let you know, I'll be seeking custody of Nellie. I'm the only family she's got. And I intend to take her back to North Dakota with me."

Chapter 11 – The Agreement

The discussion that followed Claude's departure that night was one Carlyle would never forget. Jimmy, Hector, and Fiona remained at the table for a long time, looking at the situation from every angle they could imagine. Could Claude really get custody? What about Child Protective Services? All agreed they didn't want the girls going into the system. But was going with their grandfather any better? What Claude did not know, because they had not told him, was that Nellie was not his only remaining granddaughter.

Could they keep that from him?

Should they keep that from him?

"I promised Ryan and Beth I would not let that man harm my angels," Fiona said. "I swore."

"But there's no way you could have known what was going to happen, Ma," Jimmy said, stroking her hand. "And he didn't seem like a total monster to me. He seemed like a brokenhearted man. A man looking to connect with his family. Maybe he's changed."

"No. Look, you heard him say it. He lied his way into that information," Hector objected. "He's the same guy Ryan warned us about."

Carlyle listened and hoped and prayed. What would be decided that night in that room would alter the course of the Jolicoeur twins'

The Agreements

entire lives. It was an anguishing decision made with the very best of intentions. As the three adults huddled and discussed, Nellie slept on the couch. Carlyle sat beside her and mulled over his training, searching for some snippet of wisdom to help him understand all that was happening.

He knew there was a master scroll written. It contained the sovereign will of the Designer for mankind from beginning to end. It would be fulfilled. It could not fail. He also knew there were individual scrolls written for each person. They each contained the dreams of the Designer for that soul and how they could participate in his master plan for the planet. But there was another set of scrolls—the shadow scrolls.

These were counterfeit copies taken by the leader of the rebels when they were cast out of the heavenlies. He used them to tempt and manipulate humanity away from their role as overcomers of the dark forces. The shadow scrolls looked like real scrolls. They read like real scrolls. In fact, it took great discernment to see where the tiny twists and turns had been added, differentiating them from the original tomes—twists that appealed to ego and desire, to revenge and vindication, to greed and self-preservation, to knowledge and reputation. Turns that seemed right but led in the very least to dead ends and at the very worst to death itself.

The tricky part was that humans were free to choose which scroll they wanted to follow. If they chose the shadows, adjustments were made, others chosen, destinies rearranged, paths altered—all based on their choice.

As Carlyle stared at the confabulation happening at Fiona's kitchen table, he wondered about choices made by somebody else on another person's behalf. It didn't seem quite fair to him that the two people with the most on the line weren't old enough to even give their input.

Nellie and Julia probably would not have chosen what was chosen for them that night.

But the deciding parties made a pact.

An agreement.

Jimmy was hesitant.

Hector torn.
Fiona anguished.
But they all agreed.
This was the best option they could see.
Julia's existence would be kept from Claude.

Fiona insisted. She had made a promise. She would protect at least one of her angels. Though it was small comfort, Hector and Fiona agreed that if it had to be one of the girls that had to go live with a difficult man, it was better Nellie than Julia. And Fiona would assert with every ounce of influence she could muster, whether legal, moral, or emotional, that Claude keep in contact with her. For if even a hint of abuse or neglect was detected, she would be on the first plane or train or whatever one took to get to North Dakota to snatch Nellie back into her care.

The even more anguishing aspect of their agreement was the intrinsic need to keep the girls' existence from each other. How could they, after all, trust a toddler or a child to keep that kind of secret from the adults in their lives? But could they tell them when they turned eighteen or twenty-one or some such adultish age? Just as they were agonizing over these details, they were jolted by more pounding at the door.

"Hector, are you in there?" Maria yelled through the door.

"Oh my, ya forgot to call your wife," Fiona said.

"I'm in so much trouble," Hector murmured on the way to the door. "Hello, corazón," he said to his wife, who stood with eyes blazing in the doorway.

"I have been waiting and waiting to hear from you and you're . . . you're sitting here . . . sitting here drinking," Maria said.

Hector tried to speak.

"No, there is no excuse." Maria raised a finger to his face and her volume rose along with it. "You have left me to worry and stew and imagine . . . and, and think every horrible thought known to mankind on this day of hell on earth. And you . . . you have been . . ."

The Agreements

Fists formed at her side. Then, like a mousetrap, they sprang up and unleashed on his chest. Hector made no move to defend himself.

"You have been drinking! What about me? What about us? ¿Cuál es tú problema? ¿Qué estás pensando?"

Fiona scurried over and judiciously but firmly seized Maria's flying fists.

"Maria, Maria," she crooned, diffusing the fury until at last Maria tore her gaze away from her husband's shame-hung head.

"'Tis not his fault, love," Fiona said. "We all . . . we just got lost in the day."

Maria sucked in a ragged breath. She blinked and shook her head as if trying to focus on Fiona's face.

"Come in. Come sit," Fiona said. "Let me get you some tea."

Like a wary child, Maria let herself be led to the table, to the chair Claude had so recently occupied. Hector shuffled behind them and then knelt beside her.

"Forgive me, corazón," he whispered.

Maria's eyes followed Fiona's movements of tea preparation before at last allowing them to connect with her husband's imploring gaze. Hector took her hands, turned them over, and kissed each palm.

"But did they . . . are Ryan and Beth . . . do you know what happened to them?" Maria whispered.

Hector took a deep breath.

"They're gone, mi amor. They didn't get out," he whispered.

Maria collapsed onto his shoulder and sobbed.

Fiona set the filled teacup on the table and lowered herself into a chair. Jimmy wrapped an arm around his mother and pulled her close. She sank into his comfort and allowed herself to join the mourning.

Carlyle watched with dripping eyes of his own. His back turned to Nellie, he was unaware that she was awake until he felt her body weight leave the couch beside him. She slipped across the room silently in her footie pajamas until she stood beside the kneeling Hector. She reached up to Maria and patted her arm. Maria sat up, her face a mess of tears and mucus, and stared at the apparition by her knee. Nellie lifted her arms.

"Hold you?" she implored.

Maria swept her up and clung to her.

"Nellie! Oh, mija." Maria gulped for air. "I thought you were . . . I thought . . ."

"Oh my gosh. I should've told you that right away. I'm so sorry. She's been here all along," Hector explained. "They didn't take her. She's safe. Both girls are safe."

Maria's tears of sorrow were suddenly mixed with tears of joy.

When the elation abated somewhat, Maria insisted on being filled in on the happenings of the day. When Claude's visit was disclosed, she gasped at his audacity and jumped quickly to the conclusion that had taken the trio much discussion to reach; Julia's existence must be kept secret. Despite the many difficulties inherent in the agreement made, she was in complete accord that it was the best possible solution to an impossible situation.

"But how do we keep her hidden?" Maria asked.

"Well, we were thinking that maybe you and I . . . the Gomez family should keep her," Hector replied.

"Of course, we will," Maria said, tucking a sleeping Nellie even closer to her bosom. "But how? Claude knows where we live. He might try to contact us about . . . about Ryan or Beth. Or what Nellie needs or likes . . . or . . . it could be anything."

"Not to mention trying to keep the whole Hernandez clan from spilling the beans . . . not that they'd mean to," Hector added as he took his wife's hand. "It's just a lot of people to ask to keep a secret."

"But we'd have to tell my mom," Maria said.

Hector agreed.

"And maybe Carmen," Maria added.

"I don't know," Hector said. "The fewer the better."

"But we're gonna need someone to cover our tracks with the rest of the family," Maria insisted. "You know how they are. They seem to know everything about everything before it even happens."

Hector sighed.

The Agreements

"This is not gonna be easy," Jimmy said.

Quiet settled among the benevolent conspirators.

"Maybe we need to make ourselves harder to find," Hector said at last.

"What do you mean?" Jimmy asked.

"Well, we've been looking for a bigger place . . . ," Hector said.

"But even if you moved, your family would still know where you were," Fiona said.

"Yes, but if we moved far enough away, they wouldn't have to see what we were doing," Hector said.

"Where would we go?" Maria asked.

Hector took a sip from his tepid cup of tea.

"I know this is a lot to ask, but . . . we could maybe go back to Washington."

"To D.C.?" Fiona asked. "What's in D.C.?"

"No," Maria said. "He means the state . . . where he grew up."

"Oh, jeez, you mean out by me? To Seattle?" Jimmy said.

"No, I've got a brother in Eastern Washington. A small town over by Yakima. I think he could probably help us out with finding a job and housing and maybe some paperwork kind of issues, like a birth certificate and stuff for Julia."

"You mean counterfeiting legal documents?" Jimmy asked, leaning back in his chair as if suddenly hit by the immensity of where their conversation had landed.

"You'd trust Raúl with all this?" Maria said.

"Look, I know it's not perfect, but none of this is perfect. Raúl has . . . he has connections that will be necessary if we have any intention of pulling this off for the long haul," Hector said.

Carlyle began to wonder if the good intentions of the choices being made had begun to give room for shadowy twists and turns. Only time would tell. He retrieved the cloth he now kept in his pocket to tend to the residual tears on his cheeks. His hand brushed over the key for the motorcycle. To think he had once been so thrilled about the machine. As he mopped his face and watched the circle of loving brokenness before him, he realized he had started to think of the marvelous apparatus as a necessity brought on by evil.

But that wasn't right. It had been prepared in advance for just such a time as this. Madeline had known he would need it.

This night, this day, had not been a surprise to her.

He pulled the key from its place and held it out in front of him.

The small token glowed in his palm. It was a reminder that though chaos and darkness appeared to have the upper hand, the Designer was prepared for all eventualities.

Carlyle sighed and looked over at Nellie. She was sound asleep in Maria's arms, completely oblivious to the massive shift that was about to happen in her life.

Was this what she had agreed to?

He wished he could remember all that was on her scroll.

He wished he could see further into the future to know what good could possibly come from any of this tragedy.

Chapter 12 – The Mountain

Before he knew what was happening, Carlyle felt himself being sucked up out of the apartment through a tube of light once again. He traveled along a bright blue portal at the speed of thought, his hand still clutching the key. In a twinkling, he found himself expelled on the shore of an enormous body of water. Small waves rippled across its surface in varying shades of orange, pink, and blue, reflecting the painted sky above them. Standing on a long, narrow raft with two long paddles leaning up against her was Madeline of the High Plains.

"Hello, my friend," she said.

"Uh, hi," Carlyle replied. "What's going on?"

He ran his hands down his uniform and arms, surprised to find himself at his original eight-foot height once again.

"Hop aboard," she instructed.

Carlyle stuffed the key back into his pocket and waded into the water. Refreshing tingles shot into his body as the water seeped through his uniform onto his skin. If Madeline hadn't been waiting, he might have simply kept walking and dove into the depths for a long soak. But instead, he climbed up onto the wooden raft and accepted the paddle Madeline extended to him. The craft was wide enough for two. Though there were slight recesses carved in the surface for sitting, they stood behind them.

"We've some ways to go. Two paddlers are better than one," she said.

"Okay," he said, shaking water from his limbs. "Where are we headed?"

Madeline pointed her oar toward a snowcapped mountain at the other end of the lake.

"To the Mount of Treasures Stored in Darkness," she said, dipping her paddle in the water and beginning to row.

Carlyle matched her stroke and the raft skimmed easily over the surface of the water. They rowed silently for some moments and Carlyle breathed deeply of the cool, heady air that blew into his face. As he did, strength flowed into his lungs and out into his arms and legs like streams into a desert. He had not realized how weary he had become.

Madeline hummed a tune in rhythm with their strokes, her face set like flint toward the mountain.

"Why am I here? Did I do something wrong?" he asked.

Madeline turned slightly and smiled.

"Just keep rowing," she said.

Beneath the perplexity he felt at his sudden relocation, he felt another emotion growing, one he was almost ashamed to admit was there. It was something he imagined a soldier on the front lines must feel when he has survived a battle and is called to the rear.

He felt relieved.

Scenes from the lives of the Jolicoeur family flashed through his mind as he and Madeline traversed the watery highway. A complex tapestry of joy and pain, laughter and tears, wins and losses wove through his memories of the time spent in their midst. And though he was happy to be where he was, going wherever he was going, his heart was still connected to those humans and he found himself interceding in his spirit for the well-being of those still residing on the planet.

With one stroke he prayed for Nellie.

With the next he prayed for Julia.

And back and forth he went, fully engaged in one realm from the reaches of another.

The Agreements

So intent was he on his supplications, he was surprised when Madeline slowed her stroke and began to direct their trajectory toward an opening in the base of the massive Mount of Treasures. A river flowed from the lake into a fissure. It was not a large crack. In fact, as they got closer and closer, Carlyle began to wonder if they and their craft would fit.

"Easy now," Madeline said. "A bit to your right. That's it."

They eased their way into the gap in the rock, their shoulders brushing either side of the opening.

"Excellent. Now take a seat and grab the handles," Madeline said as she sat and placed the paddle straight out in front of her on the length of the raft and locked it into place with a latch. She made a show of gripping the handles that stuck up from the raft's surface on either side of her hips.

Carlyle did as she said. And just in time.

The raft plummeted over a cliff in a spectacular waterfall.

"Here we go!" Madeline yelled.

They fell and fell through the deluge of spray.

Carlyle was tempted to be terrified, but Madeline's whoops of excitement reassured him that all was well.

Alarming.

Shocking.

But well.

At last, they and the raft plunged into the depths of a fathomless pool. The soaking Carlyle had considered by the edge of the lake became a reality.

He held his breath, wondering how long they would go down before they would shoot back up. Panic threatened around the edges until he remembered where he was.

He took in a deep breath of the invigorating liquid. It coursed through his body like the air, revitalizing his entire being. He gulped again and again, not caring if they ever surfaced. But at length, they did.

"Just what you needed," Madeline said, noting the smile plastered across Carlyle's face.

"I guess so," he agreed. "Now what?"

"Now we let the river take us."

"Where?"

"You will see."

The river meandered through the recesses of the mountain. Though they were deep below the surface, it was not dark. Luminous gems of every variety clung to the walls of the cavernous interior. They radiated light and color into the darkness, bouncing off stalactites and stalagmites with astonishing splendor.

Carlyle had seen riches before in various forms and in various places in the universes, but he had never seen any quite like these. They were mesmerizing in their hues, exquisite in their shapes, and breathtaking in their sheer beauty. But beyond all that, there was something else. Something Carlyle couldn't quite name.

"What are these gems?" he asked.

"They are the treasures in darkness. The riches stored in secret places," Madeline replied.

"Who are they for? The Designer?"

"Well, they are from the Designer, but they are for humanity."

"Really? I don't recall seeing anything like this in my time on the planet," Carlyle commented.

"Ah, perhaps you did but did not know it," Madeline replied. "They take a different form in that realm."

"Like what?"

Just then the raft drifted up onto a gravelly shore.

"Character, for one," she replied. "Authority, for another."

Carlyle swallowed that information down and allowed it to settle.

"Here's our stop," Madeline said, stepping off onto the pebbles.

Carlyle stood and fell into step behind his trainer, who strode in front of him.

The path they took wandered through a forest of stalagmites that reached upward to the cavernous ceiling, where stalactites reached back toward them. Water droplets gleamed on the tips of the hanging structures. Carlyle watched as a drip fell from the heights directly toward his head. It dazzled and gleamed from the

The Agreements

reflection of the radiant gems as it fell. As it was about to plop onto his face, he was bumped aside.

"Excuse me," a small being, who came only up to his waist, said as she caught the droplet in a bottle. "Can't let it hit the floor."

She smiled up at Carlyle as she recapped the glass tube and placed it carefully in a belt around her waist that held about a dozen other such tubes.

"Oh, yes, of course," Carlyle said. "We wouldn't want that."

The little one only nodded, her eyes turned up to the ceiling again and her hand already uncapping a different tube.

"Sorry. Don't mean to be rude, but we're very busy just now. Seems a wave of sadness has hit."

She caught another drop, recapped, replaced, and readied another container. Suddenly Carlyle became aware of the many others just like this small one who were scampering about the floor of the cave, collecting the drops. They were clothed from head to toe in what appeared to be silvery bodysuits that reflected the light from the glowing gems on the walls, transforming their uniforms from pink to purple to green to orange and back again as they moved. Some stopped briefly in their scurrying to hug Madeline's legs or blow her a kiss. She acknowledged their affections but urged them back to their task with a flick of her fingers.

"Carlyle, come. Let's let the tear collectors do their job," Madeline said, turning to continue along the well-worn cobbled path.

Carlyle followed her lead but kept an eye on the collectors as they dashed and leapt and reached for each dripping drop. They were very skilled at their job. Not one drop that he could see hit the floor—not even close. Though they worked with intensity, a general sense of peace flowed through their activities, as though they were not only content but also privileged to carry out their assignment.

Occasionally, a worker would run ahead of Madeline down the path and disappear through an archway at the far end of the cavern.

"Well done, Lampay. Excellent job, Alte. Way to go, Vel," she said as they passed.

Not for the first time in his acquaintance with Madeline, Carlyle wondered about her true identity. The more he knew of her, the more there was to know of her. His pondering, however, was interrupted by their arrival at an archway. Encrusted with jewels of every color along its outline, it opened up into a tunnel lined with the same dazzling mosaic. The pathway changed at the threshold from simple stone pavers to a solid trail of glistening marble wide enough for two to walk side by side. Carlyle joined his trainer and they entered the tunnel together.

"What is this place?" he asked.

"It has different names. Some call it the Tunnel of Tears. Others the Via Dolorosa."

"What do you call it?"

"The Way of Redemption."

Carlyle nodded and stared at the wondrous beauty surrounding them.

"Well, whatever you call it, it is truly spectacular," he remarked. "This is holy ground, isn't it?"

"More than you will ever know," she replied.

"Pardon me. Coming through," a small voice sounded behind them.

Madeline and Carlyle turned sideways and stepped back against the walls in order to let the tear collector pass.

"Hello, Gimmet," Madeline greeted the worker. "Full bottles?"

"Oh, it's you!" the wee fellow exclaimed as he saw her face. "I'm so glad you're here. We've been so busy in our sector."

"Ah, you're working North America, are you?" she asked, kneeling down to speak to him face-to-face.

"Got called up to help with New York City," Gimmet said.

"Yes, indeed. Much to redeem there just now," she said. "Do you happen to know whose catching for the Jolicoeur twins? Nellie and Julia?"

Carlyle bent down, too—partly because he wanted to hear the answer clearly and partly because his knees went weak at the mention of their names.

The Agreements

"Uh, let me check." Gimmet pulled a small scroll from a pouch on his belt and unrolled it. "Let's see . . . Here they are. Julia and Nellie Jolicoeur. That would be Kashi."

"Thanks so much."

Madeline kissed the small one on the cheek and rose.

"Nice to have you around," Gimmet said, rerolling the scroll and replacing it back in its spot.

"I'm always around," she said with a smile. "Now off you go."

Carlyle stood and watched him leave.

"Do we get to meet Kashi?" he asked.

"That is the plan," she said, resuming their walk. "Among other things."

In a hundred yards or so, the marble path took a sharp turn to the left. When the two of them turned the corner, a massive cavern stretched out before them. Tall winged creatures stood like sentinels around the entire circumference of the space, facing outward. Carlyle watched as Gimmet, who had just reached their boundary, spoke to a particularly large guard and handed him something. The guard perused whatever it was, nodded, and turned sideways to allow Gimmet to pass. But no sooner had the small one gone by than the enormous creature stepped back and closed ranks. Whatever was inside that circle of defense was guarded with great care.

As Madeline and Carlyle approached the ring of sentinels, they all suddenly and in perfect unison fell to their knees and bowed their heads. Madeline walked to the head guard and placed her hand on his shoulder.

"Arise," she said.

As a unit, they rose.

"Is he in?" she asked.

The guard nodded and turned aside to let them pass.

"Why does everyone seem to know you?" Carlyle whispered.

"You're not the only one I've trained," she said, marching past him into the vast space.

They walked beside a line of tear collectors who were advancing single file toward something in the center of the enormous room. Again, many greeted Madeline, but much more quietly than they had in the collecting cave, each remaining in his or her place in the line. Like the air in the tunnel, a sense of momentous solemnity filled this place, and everyone acted accordingly.

Carlyle let his gaze wander up and around. Neither the walls nor the floor held any gems but were smooth and black like polished obsidian. Beyond the circle of guards, entryways were spaced evenly around the sides of the cave. The towering sentries turned at regular intervals to allow the diminutive collectors to enter and join the line from all points around the circle. A light source of some sort at the center of the room illuminated everything with a golden glow so that the sentinels appeared to be statues formed of gold. The tear collectors' uniforms, so full of reflected color before, were now pure gold as well.

The only sounds besides the soft greetings of the workers came from the center of the room. If Carlyle didn't know better, he'd say it sounded like someone was crying or weeping or maybe even sobbing. It was not a sound he had ever heard beyond the confines of the earthly realm. He believed, in fact, that such an activity wasn't even allowed here. But the closer they came to the source of the noise, the more certain he was of his initial assessment.

And then, as if his eyes had suddenly adjusted to the light in the room, he saw what he had not seen before: a raised platform of obsidian with stairs leading up one side and down the other. Atop the platform sat a clear glass bottle that rose to about twenty feet in height. Its base was broad and sturdy, but the sides tapered upward into a narrow neck. It appeared to be about halfway filled with water. Two guards stood beside it, their heads even with the brim. Next to the bottle was a desk, simple, clean-lined, black. On its surface a huge book lay open, its pages rising so high that Carlyle couldn't see who, if anyone, sat behind it.

But as he and Madeline climbed the stairs, a hand with a golden pen became visible, writing swiftly over the pages. Then a mass of stunningly white hair appeared over the book.

The Agreements

"Peace," Madeline said by way of greeting to the being whose head was bent over the pages.

The head lifted and it became apparent where the light that lit the entire cavern came from. Carlyle felt the urge to kneel.

"Ah, Madeline," the figure behind the book said, rising to greet her with a kiss on each cheek. He was clad in a crisp, white, three-piece suit and was nearly as tall as the sentinels. His hair was gleaming white, but his face was smooth and unlined. "I see you've brought Carlyle," he added, extending his large hand down to him. The handshake was firm and efficient. "You are welcome in this place, but you must pardon me if I continue to work. As you can see, there is much to do."

"Oh, yes, certainly," Carlyle said. "We don't mean to interfere."

Madeline grabbed Carlyle's hand and pulled him to one side.

"We'll just stand here and observe, Grammateus," she said.

"Grammateus?"

The word shot from Carlyle's mouth louder than he had anticipated, and it echoed across the space and bounced from the walls. Every head swiveled to stare at him, and the guards by the bottles lifted fingers to their lips.

"Were you expecting someone else?" Grammateus asked as he resumed his place behind the open book.

"Uh, no sir," Carlyle said. "I just didn't, um, expect . . . that is, you aren't exactly like you were . . . I didn't . . ."

"Didn't recognize me?"

"Yes, sir. That's it. I'm sorry, sir."

Grammateus put the pen down and rubbed his hand over his face. The light in the room flickered.

"Expectations are a funny thing, aren't they?" he asked, looking directly into Carlyle's eyes.

Carlyle recognized those eyes. The whole world seemed to be held in them. Every person. Every circumstance. Every hope. And as Carlyle returned his gaze, he recognized something else in those eyes, something he'd not seen before in their previous encounters:

pain. The pain of the entire human race was found in his eyes. It was all he could do to keep from melting into sorrow at the sight.

Grammateus picked up his pen and said to the tear collector waiting at the bottom of the stairs, "Mele, come."

Mele climbed the stairs and stood next to Grammateus. With infinite care, the small one pulled the first tube of tears from its sheath on his belt. He read from the label wrapped around the top of the glass.

"Mario Andresu," he said.

Grammateus nodded. Mele uncorked the bottle and a sound like a man crying was released into the air. Grammateus took his pen and dipped it into the bottle of tears. He returned to the book and began to write with a sure, steady hand. In the meantime, Mele walked behind the solid, black rock the Scrollmaster occupied to the bottle on the other side of the desk. He stepped up to one of the golden guards, the open crying vial reverently raised high overhead. The guard nodded, and Mele flew up to the brim of the large bottle and poured the contents of his small tube into the liquid already contained therein. It was only then, when the tears of Mario Andresu merged with the tears of his fellow man, that the cries died down and finally ceased.

Mele descended and returned to Grammateus's side. One by one, he declared the names of the tubes of tears on his belt. One by one, the Scrollmaster dipped his pen and wrote. One by one, the tears were emptied and the cries silenced.

It was almost more than Carlyle could bear.

He glanced at Madeline. She was calm but obviously moved by the ceremony being played out before them. Carlyle followed her gaze, which was fixed on Grammateus. As Carlyle watched the pen cross the page and fill the emptiness with words, a tear fell from the writer's face. The ink smeared. It ran down the page, and words from one line mixed with words from another line. As Carlyle looked more carefully at the soft linen pages, he could see that this was not the first tear that had fallen. There were many blots and streaks all over the pages. But to Carlyle's surprise, far from making the written words messy or ugly, they somehow only added to the

The Agreements

beauty of what was written. They became more than just words. They were more like lives.

Carlyle became absorbed in the wonder of this excruciating but exquisite activity. He lost track of how many tear collectors and how many bottles of tears and how many lives passed before them. He began to understand the holy weight of this place. And he knew it was a privilege to simply be there.

"Come, Kashi," Grammateus said to the next small one in line.

Carlyle snapped to attention. Madeline placed a hand on his arm.

"Just observe," she whispered.

Kashi did as all those before her had done. Carlyle waited with growing anxiety to hear the names he longed to hear. Finally, with only two vials left on her belt, Kashi pulled one up and read, "Julia Jolicoeur."

Grammateus nodded. The tube was opened, and familiar cries wafted up into the atmosphere. The pen was dipped and words written. Carlyle's heart pounded in his chest. He moved his head around, trying to get a better view so as to read Grammateus's writing, but even when he caught a glimpse of the words, he could not decipher the language.

Julia's tears were poured into the large central bottle, and Kashi returned to the side of the Scrollmaster.

The last vial was opened.

"Nellie Jolicoeur," she said.

Again, the familiar cries, the dipped pen, the written word.

A tear fell on the page. The ink ran.

The lines written for Julia merged with the lines written for Nellie. And from their shared pain, a picture formed: a solitary heart, full of every color in the rainbow, vibrant and strong.

Grammateus turned and looked at Carlyle.

"It's for the joy," he said, a tear still coursing down his cheek.

"Joy?" Carlyle whispered. "I'm afraid I don't understand, sir."

Grammateus looked intently into Carlyle's eyes, as though measuring what lay behind them. Then he bent down and spoke into Kashi's ear. She nodded and smiled.

"Yes, sir. Of course, sir. My privilege," she said.

"Please follow Kashi," Grammateus said to Carlyle. "There are things you need to see before you return to your assignment."

Kashi reached up and took Carlyle's hand. She gave a small squeeze as if to reassure him.

"Madeline, would you stay for a while?" Grammateus asked the trainer. "Your presence brings such comfort."

"As always, I am here for you," she replied before turning to Carlyle. "Go with Kashi. Learn, observe, and be refreshed."

Chapter 13 – The Seeds

As Carlyle allowed Kashi to lead him down the stairs and toward the circle of sentries, he snuck one look back at the raised platform. Madeline stood close behind Grammateus, her hand on one of his shoulders as he continued to work. The glow on her face now was just as golden as the glow on his.

Carlyle turned his gaze forward. The path to the lone exit from the cave was the only place in the circumference of the space that was unobstructed by the giant guardians. He and Kashi walked hand in hand straight toward the opening. The doorway was not large or decorated by gems but small and plain, and Carlyle had to duck to enter. Inside, all was darkness, but Kashi seemed unconcerned. Carlyle reached out to touch the sides of the tunnel with his free hand. It was smooth as glass and a bit moist.

Kashi hummed softly as they went. Her steps sure, her song confident.

Eventually, a speck of light appeared at the far end of their path. It grew brighter and brighter, changing color with a rhythmic steadiness. Music seeped like a fog in their direction. Quietly at first, it gained volume as they advanced. It was the same song Kashi had been humming all along. Far from the somberness of the atmosphere they had just left, this song was lively and loud, filling every molecule of space with joy.

At last, Carlyle and his diminutive guide came to the end of the tunnel that opened up into a massive cave. At least a hundred times as big as the cave of tears, this space reached all the way from the base of the mountain to its peak. They stood about halfway up along a ledge that ran all along the walls of the interior, spiraling up to the top and down to the floor.

Kashi dropped Carlyle's hand and pointed to the room before them.

"Welcome to the growing room. Isn't it something?" she said. "This view never gets old."

Carlyle could understand her feelings, for what lay before them was indeed awesome. From floor to ceiling, a structure rose with layer upon layer upon layer of what looked like planting shelves. Open walls in the shelving allowed the observer to see freely into the interior of the edifice. It hummed with activity. Small ones like Kashi scurried up and down between the floors and between the rows on each floor with almost uncontainable excitement. Bending over to inspect here or point there, they chattered among themselves like tourists at the most amazing spectacle of all time.

"What are they doing?" Carlyle asked.

"Oh, they're inspecting the harvest," Kashi replied.

"The harvest? Of what?"

Kashi quirked her head upward and stared at him quizzically.

"Of the seeds of tears, of course," she said.

"Oh, uh, okay," he said.

"I forgot," she said with a small giggle. "It's your first time here. Let me show you around."

They climbed up the spiraling path until they stood opposite of where they had entered the room.

"Watch over there."

Kashi pointed to an opening next to the tunnel they had just exited. The music began to swell even louder. Then with a mighty crescendo, out from the opening shot a glorious spray of water. It not only fell down to water the floors beneath it but also shot upward to water those above as well. It flowed with great velocity and volume for quite some time. And then, like a spigot turned off, it ceased. But in its wake, crystal-like droplets clung to every surface of the tower.

Jumping up and down with excitement, Kashi said, "Come on. Let's help," right before leaping from the ledge. She laughed as she flew through the air and landed with a brilliant somersault right between a row of raised beds on the structure.

Carlyle didn't know if he could replicate her maneuver or if, indeed, he should try. But as he watched and listened to the infectious laughter and dancing coming from the many tear collectors all up and down the structure, he decided he would give it a go.

With as much strength as he could muster, he leapt across the space and tumbled onto the floor beside Kashi with a loud thump. This seemed to ignite further laughter from his tour guide. She bundled over like a ball on her knees and slapped the floor.

"That was tremendous," she said between gasps. "Just tremendous."

Soon Carlyle was laughing right along with her.

"I don't know about tremendous, but I gave it all I had," he said.

Kashi wiped the tears from her face as she stood.

"You were great. Now come on, there's work to do," she said, grabbing his hand and taking him to the outer edge of the floor they stood on. There, along the beams and supports, droplets of the water spray still clung. Kashi reached up and gently pulled one down with each hand. Carlyle reached higher and did the same.

"What next?" Carlyle asked.

"We plant," she said, walking back to a raised bed and placing each water drop down onto a layer of the richest and blackest of soils. She scooped out a hole for each tear seed, placed the seed inside its depths, and replaced the soil over the top. Carlyle followed her every step. It was surprisingly satisfying work. Again and again they returned to the edge of the room, picked up tear seeds, and returned to plant them. Above them and beside them, other workers did the same with a spring in their step and a song in their mouth.

When no more droplets remained, Kashi instructed her tall pupil to come and stand next to her beside their little plot of planted soil. All around, others did the same. And then, in perfect harmony, a chorus broke out and reverberated into the acoustically perfect cave. The tear collectors sang with total abandon in a strange but beautiful language unbeknownst to Carlyle. He closed his eyes and allowed himself to simply listen and be wrapped in its glory.

As suddenly as it had begun, the song ended. A holy hush ensued that was just as glorious as the song. Carlyle breathed deeply and felt the wonder of this place course through his body.

Gently, Kashi tugged on his sleeve.

"Carlyle," she said. "Look."

He opened his eyes and there before him, where only black soil had stood, a crop of green, lush plants had pushed through the surface and stood two feet tall. Along their branches, dangling in dazzling beauty, were gems. In the plot they had planted, the gems were a deep purple with golden centers. But other plots around them held plants of varying heights and gems of varying colors.

"Amazing," Carlyle breathed.

"Every time," Kashi agreed.

"What happens to all of this bounty?"

"The harvesters come and distribute to those who sowed in tears."

"And when is that?"

"When the time is full."

Carlyle nodded and pondered that answer.

"But we have done our part. It is time for me to return to collecting," Kashi said.

"Do you have to? Can't you just stay here? It seems so much more joyful and, well . . . fun here."

Kashi again quirked her head at an angle and stared up at her tall friend.

"If the tears aren't shed, we don't collect. If we don't collect, we don't contribute. If we don't contribute, we won't have seed. If we don't have seed, we have no harvest. Here," she said, spreading her hands to include the expansive growing room, "here is the

The Agreements

reward for going through there." She pointed to the tunnel that led back to the cavern of tears. "Here only exists because of there."

Carlyle nodded again, trying to absorb her words.

The sprightly tear collector steered him through the rows of plants back toward the edge of the structure where small ones were leaping aboard the backs of broad-winged creatures who carried them all the way to the floor.

"Why didn't we use one of these carriers on the way in instead of leaping from the ledge?" Carlyle asked, watching them fly with great ease all around him.

"Because leaping is fun," Kashi replied. "Come on."

Carlyle tried to linger and inspect the wondrous plants and produce they passed along the way. Then, just before they reached the outer rim of the structure, Carlyle noticed someone kneeling beside one of the planter boxes. She was not a tear collector but a human. It looked as though she was praying, though no sound came across her lips. She held a gem in her hands that was a soft green color edged in bronze. He watched as she lifted the gem to her bosom and held it close. It glowed brightly and seemed to burn right through her as it disappeared into her being. He was about to walk by when the woman raised her head and he saw her face.

"Lupe?" he gasped.

The woman smiled and then disappeared from sight.

Carlyle turned to Kashi, who was climbing onto the wing of a carrier next to several other collectors.

"Can humans come here?" he asked, pointing to where Lupe had been.

"If they know the way."

She smiled and waved as she and her cohorts were carried away.

"Hey, wait," Carlyle said, running to the edge. "What about me?"

A tap on his shoulder startled him.

"Come," Madeline said. "Time to return."

Chapter 14 – The Correspondence

Fiona Flanagan pulled the paper from the copy machine tucked into the back corner of the Brooklyn convenience store. She flipped it over, placed it back onto the glass surface, and pressed start. She spun the carousel of keychains and miniature license plates emblazoned with names as she waited for the second page to print. It wrenched at her heart every time. But still she looked.

Julia. There was always a plate that read Julia.

But never a Nellie.

The second page spit out onto the tray. She collected it along with the originals and headed to the cashier, a young woman with headphones plugged into her ears who stood staring at her phone. Fiona missed the elderly gentleman who had worked there for years and used to ring up her small purchase every month. He had always asked how her granddaughters were doing as she showed him the pages she had just copied. She had never corrected him about the legalities of that moniker, not wanting to confuse the issue, expose the truth, or negate the connection in her heart. She had been happy to share little snippets of life with him. But he had disappeared months ago, and though she had asked the variety of cashiers she had seen since, no one seemed to know what had happened to him.

The Agreements

As she stood at the counter, she decided not to even attempt to inquire from the latest replacement who rang up the sale, pushed her change across the counter, and said, "Have a nice day" without ever once making eye contact. Fiona sighed and tucked her folded papers into her purse as she headed down the aisle lined with cosmetics and lotions toward the exit.

A bell sounded when she pulled the front door open, and a wall of sultry air met her as she stepped out into the August day. Before she took two steps, she pulled her cardigan off and draped it through the handle of her purse. Inside the air-conditioned store, she was always glad she had it along. But on a day with temperatures in the low nineties and humidity to match, it was inappropriate wear for the walk home. She looked forward to the cooling temperatures in the coming weeks as autumn approached. But at the same time, she felt a familiar melancholy creeping up into her soul, one that arrived each September and sometimes lasted for weeks. It surprised her that even after twelve years, the pain could still take her so low so fast.

A blast from a taxi horn startled her. She was glad for the interruption, though, for she did not like to let her mind wander too far down the path from that time in her life. But try as she might, that's exactly where her thoughts returned as she walked.

Claude Jolicoeur had kept his word to her, the word he had given her on the October day in 2001 when he strapped Nellie into the car seat in his pickup truck before departing for North Dakota with his granddaughter.

"I will write every month. I promise," he had declared.

And he had. Every month for over a decade. She had stopped being astonished by his faithfulness after about five years. She had come to expect it. At one point, she had even considered traveling to the prairie state to visit Nellie and her grandpa. But she had nixed the idea, knowing that she would most likely be unable to keep her mouth shut about Julia once face to face with her twin. So, she relied upon the letters that arrived like clockwork between the tenth and fifteenth of every month. And every month, she had made the trek to Clark's Drugstore and made a copy for Maria, who had insisted she be kept in the loop.

"Hey, lady."

A young man stretched out a hand and grabbed her elbow. Reflexively, she lifted up her purse with her other arm and prepared to swing.

"Take it easy," the man said. "Just trying to keep you from falling over."

Fiona looked up, trying to orient herself to her surroundings. She was standing next to the curb with a few other people who were waiting for either the walk signal to change or traffic to thin.

"Thanks," she said.

But her rescuer was already halfway across the street. She took a deep breath and looked both ways before stepping into the crosswalk.

"My head's in the clouds," she murmured to herself.

As she continued home, she vowed to pay better attention, but within only a few feet her thoughts returned to those difficult days. It had been another heartache for her when the Gomez family had moved all the way across the country to Washington. She'd hated to see them go. But she had understood.

Hector had left on his trek toward his home state only days after 9/11, with Julia tucked into her car seat in the back of their minivan. The story they told family, friends, and coworkers in New York was that he was exploring a new job opportunity at a plant near Yakima where his older brother Raúl was already employed. And since air travel was suspended, he was going to have to drive.

The story told to the people in Washington was that Julia was their orphaned goddaughter who was under their guardianship and whom they were in the process of legally adopting. Maria had her hands full with the twins and a newborn, so Hector had agreed to relieve her of some of her stress and get some bonding time with Julia.

As crazy as it all seemed, in the wake of 9/11, people were willing to believe almost anything. The entire country's sense of what was reasonable or possible had been recalibrated in one tragic day.

As it turned out, Hector's brother Raúl had put in a good word at the plant and smoothed the way for a quick hiring process for Hector. He'd also done some legwork behind the scenes, acquiring the documents needed to legitimize Julia's presence in the Gomez family. Fiona never did ask exactly how all that was accomplished. She preferred not to know.

It wasn't long before the entire family joined Hector and Julia out west. Even Lupe had decided to go with them, which had surprised Fiona quite a lot, considering all the other relatives still living in Brooklyn.

"A word from the Lord," Lupe had offered by way of explanation. "He says, 'Go,' I go."

Some days she wished she could have gone too. But Maria had been very good about keeping her up-to-date on Julia's life. Although with five children, including Hector Jr., who was born eight years after they moved, she was not nearly as regular as Claude with her letters. Fiona's son, Jimmy, had tried to get his mother set up with an email account to make things easier, but that had not gone so well. *Easier*, it turned out, was a relative term.

As Fiona climbed the stairs to her apartment, she stopped halfway up to catch her breath. She wasn't in her seventies anymore. She was barely still in her eighties. She wasn't sure how much longer she would be able to stay in her apartment. But she hated to leave the place where she had lived with her husband and children, the place where her little angels had lived for a short time. Though Jimmy and Irene kept inviting her to come and live with one or the other of them, she wasn't ready.

Not yet, anyway.

She stopped again on the landing inside the doors and wiped the beads of sweat from her upper lip. The door to apartment 1A opened.

"You okay, Mrs. Flanagan? It's a hot one out there today," the young man who had taken over the role as building super said.

"That it is," she said.

"Still sure you don't want to swap apartments with me? First-floor living would make things a lot easier for you," he said.

"Pawsh. I'm fit as a fiddle," she said, resuming her ascent.

"Take care now. Let me know if you need anything."

She nodded, unable to say anything more while she climbed. He was certainly an improvement over the fellow he'd replaced. She thought she remembered him telling her he was from Iowa.

Once inside her home, she placed her purse on the table, pulled out the papers, and moved to the couch, where she pried her swollen, sweaty feet from her shoes and leaned back into the cushions. She fanned herself with the letter for a moment. Her eyelids drooped.

The pages slipped from her hand and drifted onto the rug beside her shoes.

The pain in her chest was sudden and thorough.

But then came peace.

Complete and perfect peace.

"Jimmy, what do you want to do with this file cabinet?" his sister, Irene, yelled down the hallway of their mother's apartment.

"What file cabinet?" he yelled back from the kitchen, where he was filling yet another box with dishes and utensils and pots and pans and all manner of kitchen trappings.

"The one in your old bedroom."

"What's in it?"

He wrapped two more salad plates with newspaper and stuffed them into the box. All the good things—the things that were too precious in either monetary or sentimental value—were set aside in boxes in the living room. Soon they would begin to haul them downstairs to the waiting U-Haul truck. He was hoping to be on the road by the next morning.

"Uh, Jimmy, I think you should come look at this," Irene said, poking her head into the hallway.

The Agreements

He dropped two more potato peelers into the box. How many could one woman possibly need?

"That important?" he asked as he came into the bedroom.

"Decide for yourself," she replied.

"Wow," he said, taking a quick rifle through the contents of the top drawer.

"Nellie Jolicoeur?"

"Yeah, looks like all the stuff from her grandpa. I mean, I knew he was keeping in touch, but this," he said, digging deeper into the drawer, "this is ridiculous."

"The bottom one is just as full."

Jimmy closed the top drawer and pulled out the bottom.

"More letters?" he asked.

"Yup. But these are from a woman named Maria Gomez."

Jimmy's head popped up.

He shut the drawer. The headache he'd been warding off all day arrived in full force. He rubbed his eyes and pressed at his temples. It had been a very long couple of weeks. He had been shocked when he had received the call. Who wants to hear that one's mother has died alone in her apartment? It was horrible having to call Irene and tell her what had happened.

And now this? How would he explain this?

"You okay? Need some ibuprofen?" Irene asked.

He nodded. She left and returned with three red tablets and a chipped juice glass with water.

"Sorry, this is the only glass I could find," she said.

He plopped the pills in his mouth and gulped down the water.

"Listen, Sis. The whole situation . . . ," he said. "It's really complicated. And Ma was . . . she was determined to keep the girls safe. I mean, we all were. We were . . . we had to . . ."

"I know. I know about both Nellie and Julia. She told me all about it—upon penalty of death if I told a living soul," Irene interrupted his confession.

"She did?"

"Oh, come on, Jimmy. Who was I going to tell? And Ma needed someone to confide in. I get it. The whole thing was an awful mess and somebody had to protect those little girls."

Jimmy sat on top of the cabinet and sighed.

"Well, I'm actually glad to hear it. Ma never told me she told you."

Irene laughed.

"She could be a wily one." She leaned forward and grabbed her big brother's hands in hers. "You did what you felt you had to do. I don't blame you. And from what I can see in those files, those two girls are healthy and happy. You did good."

Jimmy shook his head.

"Some days I wonder."

Irene stood and began to tape the bottoms of two cardboard boxes. She plopped them down on the wood floor.

"I'll fill up a box apiece of each girl's stuff. You can take them home with you and keep them. Or you can ship them back to Claude and Maria. Might be fun for the girls to see all that Ma saved and cherished. But you can decide that later. When you're more rested. Okay?"

Jimmy stood and allowed Irene to begin to empty the drawers of their contents and place them in two separate boxes.

"Okay," he said, leaving her to it and returning to the kitchen.

Just as he was emptying the last of the mismatched silverware into a ziplock bag, a cell phone went off. The familiar ring made him grab for his pocket, but upon retrieving his phone, he found it wasn't his device that was going off. He swiveled around to see Irene's phone lighting up on the counter. She had the exact same ringtone as he did.

He shook his head and smiled.

He picked up the phone.

"Hullo, Redge. It's Jimmy."

"Hullo. How's it going there?"

"Oh, we're almost at the finish line."

"Good for you. Never an easy task," Irene's husband said. "Sorry I couldn't stick around to help."

The Agreements

"Not to worry. It was good of you to make it to the service," Jimmy said. "Ma would've been so pleased to see us all together. Just wish we could've . . ."

"I know. Wish we could've done it when she was still with us?"

"Yeah," Jimmy replied.

"Me too. Me too. Say, listen, is your sister nearby? I have a supplier here who says she gave him some sort of discount last time and was wondering if it still applied. And I can't make heads nor tails of her bookkeeping."

"Sure, yeah. I'll get her. Hold on."

Jimmy strode down the hallway and whisked the moistness from him eyes before reaching the spare bedroom.

"It's Redge," he said. "Some sort of accounting dilemma."

"Great . . . Just got everything out of those two drawers. The boxes are taped up. Here. Stick these on and they'll be good to go," she said, swapping the two labels in her hand for the phone in his and walking out the door. "Redge, what's going on, love?"

Jimmy stared at the two boxes. They were stacked one atop the other with enough tape to keep them securely sealed until the next millennium. Irene was nothing if not thorough. He sighed and looked at the two labels in his hands.

On one was written:
Nellie Jolicoeur
c/o Claude Jolicoeur
PO Box 499
Grace, ND 58579

On the other was written:
Julia Gomez
c/o Maria Gomez
PO Box 382
La Verdad, WA 98901

Were they both truly happy? And healthy? And well cared for? Was that enough?

Maybe now that Ma was gone . . . maybe it was time to bring everything out into the light.

Jimmy pulled his hand over his forehead and down his face to his chin. He was too tired to think about it. At least right then. Maybe after he got back to Seattle. He knelt down by the boxes and tried to remember which twin was in the top drawer and which was on the bottom.

"Nellie. She was on the top drawer," he said to himself, unpeeling the back of the label addressed to North Dakota and sticking it on the top box. "And Julia on the bottom." He moved Nellie's box off and adhered the label addressed to Washington on the bottom box.

Irene wandered by the door, still engaged in discussion with her husband. She peeked at Jimmy.

He mouthed, "All good," and gave her a thumbs-up.

And so, the two boxes traveled across the entire United States from New York to Seattle in the back of Jimmy Flanagan's rented U-Haul. Upon arrival at his home, Jimmy and his sons unloaded the truck into the space cleared out for the incoming belongings in the basement. The boxes stuffed with documentation of the Jolicoeur twins' separate lives took up residence in a far corner behind stacks of other boxes atop Fiona's kitchen table.

Chapter 15 – The Dress

It was not what Nellie usually wore to school. But it was a special occasion. Carlyle smiled as he watched her admire herself in the full-length mirror hung on the back of her bedroom door. She was not much of a "primper," but something about putting on a pretty dress had softened her edges and brought out a feminine side she usually kept well hidden. She turned one way and then the other, tugging at the cap sleeves to get them just right. Her cropped black hair was shiny and fluffy. She patted it down, unused to it being uncovered by a baseball cap or a motorcycle helmet.

It had been quite the outing when Papa Claude had driven Nellie to Bismarck for a day of dress shopping. She had protested vehemently.

"Not gonna wear any dumb ole dress," she had declared. "Even if you buy me one, I'm never, ever, ever gonna wear it."

But Papa Claude had learned a trick or two over the years of raising his headstrong granddaughter. Negotiations. It was all about negotiations. If she would wear a dress to the all-school assembly, he would let her ride her dirt bike to school the rest of the week. And maybe more if she kept the dress on for the entire day and did not slip into the bathroom to change into her usual jeans and T-shirt.

She had not agreed right away to the terms laid out. The ride to school from their house through the Carlsons' pasture was half a mile, and she had to be really careful not to rile up the cows or drive through cow pies. But it would be great to see the look on everyone's faces when she parked next to the other dirt bikes the junior high schoolers and high schoolers kept in the covered lot next to the cafeteria. Only a handful of her fellow eighth graders were allowed to drive their motorbikes to school. She longed to be part of the select few.

"No bows, polka dots, or ruffles," she had demanded.

"Agreed," Papa had said.

Carlyle admired the dress she had settled on with the help of the saleslady at JCPenney. It was stretchy and soft, with small blue and white triangles on a black background. The colors made her eyes pop. A thin black belt cinched in the waist over the A-line skirt. He had to chuckle about the shoes. No way was she buying fancy shoes. Claude had compromised on that one item, and they had purchased a pair of crisp white Converse. She had not been allowed to wear them until the day of the assembly, though, so they actually looked quite presentable.

"Nellie, let's go," Claude yelled up the stairs.

"Coming," she yelled back with a final spin.

Carlyle followed her out into the hallway of the two-story farmhouse.

"Wow," her grandpa said when she made her appearance at the top of the stairs. "Pretty as a picture."

Nellie scrunched her nose as if annoyed, but the blush on her cheeks belied the pleasure she took in his words.

"Now let's get a move on," he said.

"Are you gonna stay for the assembly?" she asked.

"Planning on it."

She nodded and headed out the back door. Carlyle knew she was nervous about the part she'd been asked to play. He knew that she needed all the support she could get. But the rich color exuding from her amber heart light told him she was determined to do a good job.

Carlyle wished, and not for the first time, that he could remind her of the treasure she carried. The one from the depths of the

The Agreements

Mount of Treasures Stored in Darkness. He had been surprised upon returning from that journey with Madeline to find tucked inside his inner vest pocket two gemstones. Each was brilliantly cut with exquisite luster, one a soft green and the other a shimmering bronze. At first, he had wondered if he should be alarmed. He didn't want to be accused of stealing. But as he held the stones in his hands, a still, small voice whispered, "Do not fear. Give them to the orphans."

It was odd. He knew the twins had lost both their parents, but for some reason he had almost forgotten they were orphans. They had been cared for and fought for and loved from the moment Ryan and Beth had departed the planet, but they were indeed orphans.

So, one night, as each girl slept in their separate beds, in their separate towns, in their separate lives, Carlyle had placed the gems gently on their bellies, both gems on both girls. He had watched as the gems had become part of their inner beings, so deep within them that once absorbed, even Carlyle could no longer see them. But they were there, and he knew it. He wondered though—did they?

"Next on our agenda this morning, we are going to hear from one of our own whose life was deeply impacted by the events of 9/11," Mr. Holmes, the principal of Roosevelt Junior and Senior High School, said into the microphone. He and the school board had decided that as part of the opening week assembly, they would mark the anniversary of 9/11 with a special presentation. "Nellie Jolicoeur, as you all know, lives with her grandfather here in Grace, and the reason for this is, of course, because Nellie's family died in the attack on that terrible September morning twelve years ago. So, while we are very happy she is part of our community, we also want to acknowledge the great loss she suffered that brought her to us. And we want you to see the human side of what most of you students may think of as only a historical event from long ago."

Carlyle watched as Mr. Jones, the music teacher, sidled up next to Nellie behind the midnight-blue curtains on the side of the stage.

"Are you ready?" he whispered into her ear.

Nellie stepped back and away as she nodded.

"I'm sure you'll do great," he added. "You look terrific in that dress."

Carlyle didn't like the way the older man was looking at Nellie.

"Please give a round of applause for our own Nellie Jolicoeur," the principal said, and the gymnasium filled with clapping.

"Oh, there's your cue," Mr. Jones said, putting his hand on Nellie's back.

Nellie brushed his hand away and stepped out onto the stage. Mr. Jones slid back into the wings where the pep band waited for their turn on the morning's agenda.

Carlyle viewed Nellie's progress as she walked past the big white screen hanging down from the proscenium ceiling to the microphone set up on the far side of the stage. The junior high students sat on the floor of the gym in fairly straight lines, grouped according to their first-period classes with their teachers sitting on chairs on the outside edge of the lines. The high school students sat behind them in folding chairs similarly divided. A smattering of parents and grandparents stood leaning against the brick walls beneath the basketball hoops and beside the exit doors, chatting quietly among themselves. In the middle of the gym, the librarian sat on a chair next to a rolling cart. On top of it was a laptop. She gave Nellie a quick nod to let her know she was ready. Nellie nodded back.

A picture of Ryan, Beth, Julia, and Nellie appeared on the large screen at the center of the stage. Carlyle fought back the tears that threatened to spill from his eyes at the sight of the family all together.

"This is my dad, Ryan; my mom, Beth; my sister, Julia; and me," Nellie said. "We lived in an apartment in Brooklyn, which is part of New York City. Julia and I were born in Brooklyn. My dad was a lawyer in Manhattan and my mom stayed home with me and my sister."

The picture changed to the skyline of Manhattan prior to 9/11, with the Twin Towers standing tall and proud above everything else.

The Agreements

"This is what Manhattan looked like from where we lived. Those big, tall buildings are the World Trade Center."

The students quietly oohed at the impressive cityscape. Most of them had never seen a city bigger than Bismarck, although a few had been as far as Minneapolis. But the IDS tower there was no match for the skyscrapers of New York.

"I don't really remember what it looked like. I was only a year and a half when—" Nellie's head dropped.

Mr. Holmes stepped over and asked, "You okay? Need a break?"

Nellie shook her head. He backed away and she resumed.

"There was a restaurant on the top of one of the towers called Windows on the World. That's where my family went that morning. I didn't go 'cause I was sick. They left me with our neighbor, Mrs. Flanagan. They never came back."

Nellie nodded at the librarian over the faces of all her schoolmates. The picture changed to a night view of the city from the same perspective. But instead of the towers, only two beams of light shot up from the ground and into the heavens.

"This is called the Tribute in Light," she said, turning to take in the picture herself. "The Twin Towers are gone, but every year on 9/11 they shine these super bright lights up into the sky all night long. Just so people don't forget. There's a park where the towers used to be. And a memorial with the names of everybody who died carved in bronze. They invited Papa and I to come and see it when it was dedicated. But I didn't want to go. I don't even really remember all that stuff. Grace is my home."

Nellie turned to Mr. Holmes, who came from his spot by the curtains and stood next to her.

"Let's thank Nellie for sharing this very personal story," the principal said, leading the crowd in a round of applause.

Nellie gave a small wave to her grandpa as she left the stage. He was leaning up against the gymnasium wall under one of the district championship banners. Claude waved back as Elsie Shatzenpfeffer, the school nurse who stood next to him, handed him a tissue.

"Beautiful," she said. "Just beautiful."
Carlyle agreed.

Nellie was the last student in the history classroom at 3:35 p.m. Carlyle watched as her teacher exited to take up his position as hall monitor.

"Great job today, Nellie. Real proud of you," he said before he left.

It felt good to hear his praise for Nellie. It felt good to have other kids see her and acknowledge her as more than just the girl who won nearly every dirt bike race in the county. She picked up her history text and notebooks and stuffed them next to several other books in her backpack. She didn't seem to hear Mr. Jones enter the room until he cleared his throat. She jumped and her backpack dropped to the floor with a clunk. He was only a few feet from her.

"Sorry. Didn't mean to startle you," Mr. Jones said. He lifted up the clarinet case in his hands. "Wanted to make sure you took this home with you so you can start practicing."

"Thanks."

Nellie reached out and snatched it from his hands. The music teacher didn't move.

"You did a beautiful job up on stage today," he said.

Nellie acknowledged his compliment with a small nod.

Carlyle stood up on the edge of the desk.

"And you looked so pretty. I don't believe I've ever seen you in a dress before," the music teacher said, moving closer.

Nellie blushed. Whether from pleasure at his words or anger, Carlyle couldn't quite tell. She turned around to pick up her backpack.

And that's when Mr. Jones made his move.

He pressed up against her back as if trying to see something over her shoulder.

The Agreements

"Is that yours too?" he said, pointing to a pen atop the desk. As he did, his arm brushed up against Nellie's breast and lingered there.

Nellie froze.

Mr. Jones made no move to back away.

Carlyle could see the vein in Nellie's neck pulsing wildly.

Then, without warning, Nellie grabbed the handle of her clarinet case, swung around, and nailed the man in his private parts.

The music teacher groaned and doubled over.

Carlyle cheered and flew after her as she fled from the room as fast as her new shoes would take her. She didn't stop running until she had made it all the way home, raced up the stairs, slammed the door to her bedroom, dropped her backpack and clarinet case, and flung herself onto her bed.

Carlyle had heard the rumors whispered among Nellie's friends about Mr. Jones. Everyone said he was odd. Everyone knew to steer clear of his wandering hands.

"Never alone with Jones."

Everyone knew that. Everyone, it seemed, but the grown-ups. They all talked about him like he was some sort of musical genius. And he really could play the piano like nobody's business. But if he was a genius, what was he doing teaching music to kids in Grace, North Dakota?

Nellie stood up and stared at the reflection of herself in the mirror, the same reflection she had so admired only hours before. She ripped the dress off over her head and threw it across the room.

"I'll never wear another dress again as long as I live," she vowed, pulling jeans and a T-shirt from her dresser drawers. Once re-dressed, she climbed back into bed, pulled the quilt up to her chin, and clutched her teddy bear to her chest. She cried into her pillow until exhaustion pulled her into sleep.

Carlyle stared at the discarded dress, his hands clenching and unclenching. He was surprised at the depth of emotion he felt.

Mr. Jones had not only trespassed upon Nellie's physical safety; he had ripped into her psyche and stolen a piece of her soul.

And Carlyle was more than angry. He was enraged.

Chapter 16 – The Talk

When Claude rang up the final bill for the day, it was already ten to six. He didn't like to stay so late at the shop, but the hours he had spent at the school that morning had cut into his productive work time. A smile tugged at the corners of his mouth as he recalled Nellie's courage. Talking in front of the entire school was something he would never have done, not as a kid and not as a full-grown adult.

"Shouldn't be surprised," he muttered to himself.

It was Nellie after all. And Nellie did whatever Nellie made up her mind to do.

He flipped the sign hanging in the front door to Closed and twisted the deadbolt to the locked position. Yanking his jacket off the hook by the back door, he turned off the lights and exited into the alley. He climbed up into the cab of his 2001 Silverado. It had a bunch of miles on it—292,674, to be exact. It still ran great, but he knew the time was approaching when he really should think about getting something newer. Problem was, unlike any other vehicle he'd ever owned, the truck held too many good memories. It was the truck he had driven to and from New York. The rig that had carried Nellie home to Grace for the first time. The vehicle they had taken together to races the past few years. Sometimes they'd fill the back bed with dirt bikes and go out to the flats north of town. Nellie

The Agreements

and her friends Eric and Jason loved to run the course out there. And Claude loved to take them. Just like he'd loved to take his son all those years ago.

Ryan.

How he wished he had it all to do over again.

Claude sighed and eased the truck out onto Main Street and turned south toward home. It was hard for him to remember that part of his life. Before Grace. Before sobriety. Before Nellie.

When he'd moved to North Dakota, he'd been a lonely, depressed divorcé. The only reason he'd stopped and stayed in Grace was because as he'd been driving through on his way to God only knew where, he'd spotted a For Sale sign on the town's only auto repair shop. After making a few inquiries, he'd decided, what the heck, might as well give it a go here as anywhere. Might as well do the one thing he knew he was quite capable of doing. The deal had all gone down so smoothly, he'd almost felt like it was meant to be. Like maybe he'd stumbled onto some sort of destiny.

For several years, he had been content to work twelve- or fourteen-hour days at his garage. There hadn't been any reason to rush home to the farmhouse on the edge of town that was much too big for a single guy like himself, the only thing available to purchase when he'd arrived. So, many nights he'd just sleep on the couch in the office. He would microwave another chicken pot pie, drink another six-pack of Miller or two, and maybe watch an old movie on the little black-and-white TV that sat atop the mini fridge. He had had no friendships to speak of, except maybe the bartender at the Elks lodge. And even that guy would only be nice until Claude had had one too many drinks. Then he'd kick him out the door. Which really hadn't bothered Claude all that much. But when his business had started to take a hit because people didn't trust him or his work anymore, he'd hit rock bottom.

Life in Grace had only turned around once he had looked squarely in the mirror and realized the main source of his failure to thrive was staring right back at him. He'd finally owned the fact he was an alcoholic and needed help.

As Claude drove past the First Lutheran Church, he tipped his hat to Pastor John, who was just locking up for the day himself. The pastor raised a hand in return and smiled. Claude wondered where he might be if it weren't for that faithful man of God and the band of brothers and sisters he still met with once a week in the fellowship hall of that building. It was this very group that had first suggested he make amends with his family. And his ex-wife Julia, God rest her soul, had made a way for him to do that.

Lord knew she had every right to be angry with him until the day she died, but she had forgiven him—even blessed him in his new life. She'd prayed he would do well. If he'd had more courage, he might have tried to reconcile with her. But it would never have worked without Ryan's willingness, if not forgiveness. And his son . . . well, he had been a different story.

Some nights he still laid awake and stared at the water stain on his bedroom ceiling and wondered. Wondered what might have been had he been a better father. What might have been if he could have proven to Ryan that he had changed. What might have been if he'd just had the chance. And then, inevitably, he wondered about that day. Had there been a moment of grace? An eleventh-hour cry when his son had realized there was no way out, that no one was coming to rescue them, that he was breathing his last breaths—had he softened even then? And then, inevitably, tears streaked down the valley of crow's-feet onto Claude's pillow. He would never know. Could never know.

But he prayed and he hoped. Because he had to.

The house was dark when Claude pulled into the driveway of the farmhouse. Odd. Nellie usually started some sort of dinner if he was late. Macaroni and cheese and waffles were her specialties.

"Hello," he yelled, dropping his jacket on the chair by the woodstove and hanging his keys in the small key box by the back door. "I'm home. Sorry I'm late."

No answer. No backpack. No schoolwork on the table.

"Nellie," he called into the living room, though they seldom used that room.

The Agreements

He flipped on lights, checked the bathroom and the back bedroom they used as a TV room.

Not there.

The stairs creaked as he ascended to the top floor.

"Hey, you up here?"

The door to her room was shut tight.

He knocked.

No answer.

He pushed it open just enough to peek in. Nellie lay on her bed underneath her quilt. She was fast asleep with her teddy bear tucked under her chin, the one he had claimed off the shelf in her Brooklyn bedroom, the bear that had belonged to her mother. She looked so young and vulnerable—like she was still his little girl.

Claude eased the door open and stepped into the darkened room. Before he could reach out and touch the base of the lamp on her nightstand, he stubbed his toe on something in the middle of the rug. The light revealed the culprit: her backpack. He picked it up and set it on the end of the bed along with the clarinet case that also sat abandoned on the floor. As he did, he noticed the dress wadded up and lying by the closet.

It wasn't like Nellie. She was neat as a pin—almost too neat. Sometimes he worried about her need to have everything put away, cleaned up, and in its place.

He stepped over to the closet and bent down to pick up the dress.

"You can give it away," came the voice of his granddaughter.

He turned the dress right side out and draped it over the end of her bed.

"Why would I want to do that?"

"'Cause I'm never wearing that stupid thing again."

"But you looked so nice in it," he said, sitting on the edge of the bed. "Did someone tease you or something?"

Silence.

"Well, I suppose that's up to you," Claude said.

More silence.

And then he remembered—she was not a little girl anymore. It wasn't the first time he'd felt completely out of his element with this maturation process. He'd had "the talk" with her a while back, and if awkwardness could kill, they'd have both been dead. After he'd said all he knew to say, she'd said, "I already know all that stuff," and left the room.

And now this.

What was he up against now?

He reached out to the lump of covers over her feet. As soon as contact was made, she withdrew them like a turtle into its shell.

Claude sighed and pulled his hands back into his lap.

"I'll make us some omelets. Ham and cheese?" he offered.

She nodded.

He stood and walked toward the door.

"Green peppers," Nellie said.

"Green peppers," Claude repeated. "Can't forget those. Anything else?"

"We got any onions?"

"Come look for yourself," he said over his shoulder, relieved to be talking about something as uncomplicated as food.

Chapter 17 - The Race

The hum of a lone dirt bike zipping around the earthen track played in the background as Nellie and her buddies Eric and Jason relaxed on the berm overlooking the track while sipping their sports drinks. The September sun was warm but tempered by an encroaching autumn breeze. The boys' riding boots and gloves lay haphazardly beside them where they had pulled them off, while Nellie's boots sat perfectly upright by her feet, each one with a glove sticking out like a rooster's comb from the top. There were no official races at the track that Saturday because harvest was in full swing. Only those who lived in town and whose parents hadn't hired them out to a local farmer to earn some harvest cash were available to ride. And that was practically no one.

Nellie was thankful that her best buddies were "townies." Eric's parents ran the local post office where Eric worked every Saturday morning. He wasn't allowed to handle the mail and stuff it into the PO boxes that lined the length of one wall in the old brick building. He was not, after all, a certified federal employee. But his father had decided that the only "certification" required for sweeping and cleaning was being able-bodied and desperate for cash—which Eric generally was, especially since anything extra he wanted to do, such as dirt biking or hockey, came out of his own bank account.

Jason's dad was the county sheriff and his mom a teacher. Nellie wasn't sure what Jason did to earn money, but he always seemed to have some. She guessed it had something to do with the fact that he was the baby of the family and the only boy. While Jason's mom doted on his three older sisters, his dad spared no expense to give his only boy everything a boy could want—including the brand-new dual sport Honda standing below them. It rode like a dream both on and off the road. Nellie knew because Jason had let her take it out for spin or two. Not that she would ever let her grandpa know that, since he didn't allow her to drive anywhere but on the dirt tracks and trails.

They had argued about it just last week.

"You just aren't old enough or big enough yet," Claude had said to her.

"Papa, I'm five foot seven and growing every day, according to you," she had retorted. "Besides, Jason can handle it, and he's shorter than me."

"Well, I don't care. Can't imagine how the sheriff can turn a blind eye to his own son driving on the road without the proper license."

"It's just so he can get to the track by himself. Less than half a mile from their house. Wouldn't you be relieved to not always have to haul me and my bike around?"

"No, I would not," Claude had replied. "Don't push me, young lady, or you won't be riding anywhere."

And that was the end of that.

Looking down at her used Kawasaki next to the brand-new Honda sent a small shot of envy through her heart. But she quickly shook it off. Papa Claude had worked hard to get her the bike she had and thanks to him, it was in tip-top shape at all times. Besides that, she loved her bike—the way it handled, the green paint job, the size and weight and power. She'd ridden it so much that everything about it was second nature to her. It was her baby. And etched into the handlebar, where she could glance down at it before every race, was the name she had given to her: Jewels.

The Agreements

"Hey, you looked great up there on stage the other day," Eric said with a final gulp of his orange drink.

"Ooh, got a little crush on our Nel-girl, do ya?" Jason teased.

Nellie punched him in the arm. "Shut up, Probst."

"No, I didn't mean you looked great—" Eric stammered. "I mean—yes, you did look nice, but what I meant to say was you did a great job."

Nellie gave a nod of acknowledgement, her eyes carefully avoiding Eric's.

"I meant to tell ya right after school, but you went running off."

"Yeah, what the heck happened?" Jason said. "We saw you take off down the hall, and then Jonesy came out of the classroom hunched over like an old man."

Nellie pulled at a clump of grass by her leg and shrugged.

"Nothin' happened. Just needed to get home," she said.

"Ah, come on. You were flying down that hall like a bat out of H-E-double hockey sticks," Eric said.

A fly buzzed past Nellie's nose and she swatted at it.

The lone rider on the track sped past them, kicking up a cloud of dust. Nellie waited for it to settle.

"He was bugging me," she said at last.

"About what?" Jason asked.

"Clarinet."

"So, you punched him in the gut for bugging you about practicing?" Eric asked.

"I didn't punch him in the gut," Nellie said. "And it wasn't about practicing."

"Then what?" Jason prompted.

Nellie pulled her knees up to her chest.

"He tried to touch me," she admitted softly.

"Ugh. He's such a creep!" Jason said.

"So, what'd ya do?" Eric said.

A small smile tugged at the edge of Nellie's mouth.

"I hit him in the nuts with my clarinet case," she said.

Jason and Eric gaped at her before bursting into laughter and falling to their sides.

"Oh, my gosh." Jason gasped for breath. "You are the best!"

"My h-h-h—" Eric, too, tried to talk over the spasms. "Hero."

Nellie smiled and rolled her eyes.

"He had it coming," she said.

Eric sat up, brushing a clump of dirt off his cheek.

"He's had it coming for a long time, Nellie. But nobody ever does anything."

"I've even told my dad what everyone says about him," Jason added. "But he said no one's ever filed a formal complaint, so there's nothing he can do."

"You should file a complaint," Eric said.

"Nah. It wasn't anything much," Nellie said. "But if he ever tries anything like that again . . ."

Just then a red pickup pulled off the highway and onto the gravel road leading to the track.

"Great," Eric said. "Looks like Shrek has arrived."

It was the name they'd given to Karl Franks for his hulking frame and ogre-like personality. But they would never say that to his face. He was a junior, and no eighth grader in their right mind would risk that. Most of the time Karl was just full of bluster, but sometimes he could be a real jerk. One never quite knew what to expect.

As the older boy parked and lowered his dirt bike out of the back of the truck, Nellie and her buddies pulled their boots and gloves back on and clambered down to their bikes.

"Let's go wait for your grandpa down by the highway," Eric said, taking his helmet off his handlebars.

Nellie and Jason nodded their agreement over the roar of Karl Franks' bike coming to life. But just as they were about to make their exit, Karl drew up next to them and flipped up his visor.

"Nobody gonna stick around for a little race?" he sneered as he gunned his engine.

Jason and Eric shook their heads in unison and rolled their bikes toward the exit road.

"Looks like your knights in shining armor are just a couple of wimps," Karl said to Nellie, who stood by her bike glaring at him.

The Agreements

"They'd never beat me anyways," he said with a final smirk before snapping his visor back into place and driving toward the track's starting line.

Wordlessly, Nellie slipped on her helmet, mounted her bike, started her Kawasaki, and pulled onto the starting line next to Shrek.

"What's she doing?" Eric said, hitting Jason on the shoulder.

"Holy buckets," Jason said. "I think she's gonna race him."

He kicked down the stand for his bike and ran back to where the two dirt bikes sat waiting to tear down the track. Eric did the same. Before Karl could take advantage of an unfair start, Jason sprinted in front of the racers, tore his bandana from his back pocket, and waved it to get their attention. Karl and Nellie acknowledged their starter with a nod. Jason raised his hand with the bandana high in the air for a second, held it, and then jerked it down in a flash of red.

Off the racers sped in a flurry of dust down the first straightaway. Karl, who had a bigger bike, easily took the lead. Eric and Jason climbed up the berm to get a better view of the whole track. Karl took the first jump with ease, but Nellie was close on his heels. Her bike may not have been as powerful, but her riding skills were just a notch above her competitor's.

Eric and Jason jumped up and down, screaming.

"Go, Nellie, go!"

"Get 'em, girl!"

At the first hairpin turn, Karl stuck out his inside leg and easily maneuvered around the bend. Nellie swung a bit wider, attempting to avoid his back tire and the dirt it kicked up toward her face.

Over another set of jumps, around another turn, Karl maintained his lead, but Nellie was never far behind him. Then suddenly they came upon the kid who had been riding at a leisurely pace around the track by his lonesome. Karl swerved around him on one side and Nellie swerved on the other, clipping the edge of the track and spraying loose dirt out behind her.

"Hang on!" Jason yelled.

"Jeez louise," Eric added, hiding his face in his hands.

Karl's lead increased around the last turn, but as he zoomed toward the last set of two jumps, Nellie came around the turn and gunned it.

"She's gonna jump both at once!" Eric said, gripping Jason's arm.

And sure enough, that is just what she did. As Karl roared up and over the last obstacles, Nellie flew like a ball shot from a cannon over both at once. She landed right next to Karl, whose head jerked twice to the side as if unable to believe what he was seeing.

Jason and Eric scrambled down the hill to the finish line, whooping and hollering.

It was going to be close.

With her head pressed forward over her handlebars, Nellie gave it all she had. All she and Jewels had. By the barest of margins, Nellie's front tire crossed the line ahead of Karl's.

And her fans went wild. They leapt and skipped and jumped down the track to where Nellie had stopped and was tugging off her helmet.

"You did it!"

"You beat him!"

Nellie wiped the sweat from her forehead and smiled. Karl Franks drove right on past, his eyes fixed straight ahead.

"Remember what I said about her earlier?" Eric asked Jason, staring at Nellie with open admiration.

"Oh, I'm with you now buddy," Jason said, holding a hand up for Nellie to slap him a high five. "She's definitely my hero too."

Chapter 18 – The News

"Rosie, please get your siblings," Maria Gomez said as she sprinkled grated cheese over the corn, zucchini, and ground beef in the frying pan. "Food is ready. We need to eat and get going."

Rosie nodded but did not budge from in front of the computer where she was engrossed in her role as mayor of a Sim City.

"Now, mija," her mother prodded.

"I know, I know. I just gotta put these fires out."

"The fires can wait."

"But I can't let it get near my power plant. I may have a meltdown."

"Rosalinda Maria Josefa. If we are late, your father may have a meltdown. Now turn that off and do what I asked."

Rosie paused her game and sulked across the kitchen toward the top of the stairway.

"Jewels, Beto, Freddy, Junior, food's ready," she yelled.

Maria glared.

"I could have done that. Go downstairs to the TV room and get them. And knock on Lita's door."

With a final roll of the eyes, Rosie acquiesced.

Maria lifted the frying pan off the stove and set it on the trivet in the middle of the long oak table. Three place settings lined each side, with one at the end closest to the stove for herself. Hector's place at the head of the table sat vacant. He was already at city hall, probably pacing the floor, Maria guessed, and sweating through the freshly pressed shirt and sport coat they had just purchased in Yakima the week before. She smiled and shook her head.

A seat on the city council hadn't exactly been his idea, but after much urging of his fellow employees and friends, he had agreed to give it a go. He had never believed he'd actually win. And now that he'd been elected, he was a bundle of nerves. She hoped that after the swearing-in ceremony he might calm down and begin to enjoy his new position in the community. It had been a bit of a risk, they knew, to enter into the world of politics, where candidates' personal lives were often placed under a microscope. But it was La Verdad, not Washington, D.C. And besides, everyone in town already knew them and how they lived. No one had ever once, in the decade plus that they'd lived there, questioned Julia's presence as their adopted goddaughter. No one had any reason to do so.

She checked to make sure all the burners were off on the stove before stepping over to the computer and pulling up her email. Hector's friends and cousins had all accepted her invitation to join them for the ceremony, but not his brother Raúl. Which didn't surprise her, but she had hoped that maybe he might lay aside his most recent issue with Hector, at least for one night. She knew it would mean a lot to Hector, and the kids always loved seeing him.

Despite Raúl's issues with his brother, he seemed to genuinely care for his nieces and nephews. He'd take them snowmobiling or dirt biking or to the monster truck rallies—without ever inviting Hector, of course. The kids all enjoyed the outings, except maybe Julia, who, more often than not, opted to stay home.

Maria had assumed it was just because she wasn't really interested in the activities. But recently she had begun to wonder if there was something more behind her choices, like maybe Julia wanted to show some kind of solidarity with her dad. She couldn't quite put a finger on it. She made a mental note to just flat out ask her what the issue was, just like she'd asked her husband the night before what the latest dispute was between him and his brother.

The Agreements

Hector had vaguely alluded to Raúl doing something stupid at work.

Raúl was always doing something stupid at work, something to make Hector's life more difficult. Raúl hated the fact that his baby brother, who had worked at Eastside Cold Storage fewer years than he had, was now his manager. In fact, when Hector had first gotten the promotion, which Raúl believed wholeheartedly should have been his, Raúl had mounted a slur campaign with some of his buddies in an attempt to get Hector demoted or even fired. But it had come to nothing. The higher-ups knew which brother they wanted in management—and it wasn't Raúl.

Maria checked the list of responses to her invitation one more time. Nothing from Raúl or his wife, Cynthia. She sighed and wondered again what a sweet woman like her saw in a guy like him. Quickly she scrolled through her other messages. Suddenly she pulled back from the screen and then leaned back in to make sure she was seeing what she was seeing.

An email from Jimmy Flanagan.

It was over a month old. Admittedly, she wasn't the greatest at checking her emails, but how could she have missed this? The subject line caused her heart to constrict. With a small tremble in her hand, she clicked the mouse and opened the message.

"What happen, mija?" Lupe asked, coming up behind her daughter and laying a hand on her shoulder.

The troops had all barreled into the kitchen and were already sitting at their places, waiting for their mother. They knew better than to start dishing up without saying grace, and they knew better than to start saying grace without an adult presiding.

"Yeah, come on. We're hungry," Freddy said.

"Thought we were in a hurry," Rosie mumbled.

Maria patted her mom's hand.

"Would you pray with the kids? I'll be right there," she said without turning from the computer.

"Not good news?" Lupe said.

"Uh, no. I'll tell you later."

Lupe squeezed Maria's hand and went to man her position.

Maria reread the email.

Fiona Flanagan was dead.

The news settled like a lead weight in her gut.

The sounds of Beto and Freddy disputing portion sizes, Julia encouraging Junior to try a few more bites, and Lupe cleaning up Rosie's spilled glass of milk played in the background, unattended by their mother. Her mind had been transported back to a different time and place. To a dear, dear woman. To an agreement made. To secrets kept.

Her elbows on the desk, she leaned her head into her hands and allowed the tears to trickle down her face. The war of conflicting emotions that she usually kept closely guarded concerning this era threatened to pull her under. She reached up and grabbed a paper towel from the roll that hung under the cabinet next to the computer and wiped her face. With a deep breath and a straightening of her shoulders, she closed the email and turned around.

Julia's eyes locked onto hers—her beautiful, sapphire eyes that never seemed to miss a thing.

And suddenly in Maria's mind it wasn't Julia's face she saw but Beth's.

Tears sprung fresh to her eyes.

"Mami? What's wrong?" Julia asked.

Maria shook her head and wiped her cheeks.

"I . . . ," she started. "I just got some sad news about an old friend in Brooklyn."

"Señora Flanagan?" Lupe said. "She has died, no?"

Maria stared at Lupe while the rest of the table quieted.

"Where did you hear that?" Maria asked.

"I just feel it. In here," Lupe said, touching her heart.

"How long have you 'felt it'?" Maria said.

"Two, maybe three weeks."

"Two or three weeks! And you didn't think to maybe clue me in?"

Lupe shrugged and said, "Is not for me to tell."

Maria took another deep breath in an attempt to keep her exasperation with her mother to a minimum.

The Agreements

"Wasn't she . . . didn't I know her?" Julia asked. "Is she the one who sends you letters all the time?"

Maria got up, walked over to Julia, and placed a hand on her cheek.

"Yes, she writes me, and yes, you knew her. She was your neighbor before . . . well, before you came to live with us. Do you remember her?"

Julia's eyes misted over and her chin dropped to her chest. Maria gently put her finger under her chin and lifted it up. Every face around the oak table was turned to Julia, and a rare silence settled in the room.

"I'm sorry," Maria said. "She was a lovely lady. You girls used to even call her your nana."

"I don't remember her," Julia said.

"Then what has you so upset?"

"I had a dream," Julia began. "Last night. About . . . about them."

"About your family?" Maria asked.

Julia nodded.

"What happened?"

Maria kneeled beside Julia's chair.

"Nothing . . . I just saw a face."

Maria nodded.

"Whose face?"

Julia fumbled with her fingers in her lap.

"Mine . . . except not mine. I think it was Nellie." She stopped. The sound of the dog whining in his kennel filled the quiet.

"Did anyone feed Perro?" Maria asked quietly as she waited for Julia to continue.

A collective shake of the head.

"Beto, go do it."

He hesitated.

"Ahora, por favor," his mother urged.

"But I wanna hear," Beto said.

"Yeah, come on Jewels," Freddy said. "We ain't got all night."

"Oh my gosh. What time is it?" Maria shot up and looked at the clock above the stove. "Ay, we have got to go."

She cupped Julia's face in her hands.

"We can talk about this later. Okay?"

Julia shrugged and Maria sighed.

"Just leave everything," she commanded the rest of the children. "Rosie, take Junior to the bathroom and clean his face. Beto and Freddy, wash your hands, tuck your shirts in, and get in the car."

"I want Jewels," Junior whined, refusing to leave his seat.

Rosie planted her feet beside his chair and tugged at his hands.

"Mom, he won't come with me," Rosie said.

"I want Jewels," he repeated.

"Yeah, well so does the Queen of England," Rosie said, with a final jerk of his arm that pulled him onto his feet. "Let's go, ya baby."

"A little less attitude and a little more action, please," Maria said to the pair of them before turning to Lupe. "Mom, do you mind staying and cleaning up?"

"Okay, that's fine," Lupe said. "But her," she said, nodding toward Julia, who remained in her chair unmoving. "She stays too."

Maria gently brushed her hand over Julia's long, dark tresses and then stepped close to her mother.

"Okay. She can stay. But you know the rules," she said quietly.

Lupe waved her hand at her daughter.

"Yes, yes, I know. Go. Hector won't be happy if you are late."

"And please feed the dog," Maria said as she exited.

Lupe stood with her hands in the warm, soapy water, washing the frying pan and softly humming to herself. She glanced down at Julia, who was bent over stuffing the last of the dirty dishes into the dishwasher.

"Is full?" she asked.

Julia nodded, her ponytail bobbing as she did.

The Agreements

The table was cleared and wiped clean. The leftovers were put into Tupperware and stashed in the fridge. Perro was fed. And still Julia had not uttered a word.

From his spot on the windowsill just above the sink, Carlyle wondered what she was processing behind those beautiful blue eyes. Judging from her slouching shoulders, crinkled forehead, and intense blue aura, he guessed she was thinking about something deep. Not a surprise—she was often thinking about something deep.

Julia shut the door on the dishwasher and pushed start. As the appliance whirred into action, she stood and kissed Lupe softly on the cheek. At thirteen years old, she had to bend to do so. Carlyle smiled and wondered how long it would be before this budding beauty would be taller than everyone in the household, except maybe Freddy, who seemed destined to surpass even his dad.

Julia shuffled to the table and sat with her elbows folded on the wood surface, her eyes appearing to contemplate something outside the kitchen window beside Lupe's silver hair. If Carlyle didn't know better, he almost might have believed she was looking straight at him. Perro scampered across the floor, his toenails clicking on the tile surface, and stood at Julia's feet with his paws up on her thighs. With one hand, Julia scooped the Chihuahua-terrier mix up and set him in her lap, where he circled once and curled into a ball. She sat back and ran her hand over his short, brown hair. A sigh escaped her lips and her shoulders relaxed.

"Here it comes," thought Carlyle.

"Was she nice?" Julia asked.

Lupe set the clean pan into the dish rack and pulled the plug from the sink. As she wiped her hands on a fresh kitchen towel from the drawer, she turned and asked, "Señora Flanagan?"

Julia nodded.

"Yes, she was nice. A good woman."

Julia turned her attention back to the dog in her lap.

"Did we like her?"

"Yes, you and Nellie liked her. You liked her cookies," Lupe said with a smile. "Are you sad because she died?"

"I guess. I mean, it's sad when anyone dies . . . but I don't really remember her."

"She called you her angels."

Julia looked up.

"Her angels?"

"Sí, her angels."

Again, Perro became the focal point of Julia's attention. Long, quiet moments passed, and Carlyle wondered if that was it. Surely that couldn't be all. He flew to the center of the table and settled on the napkin holder.

"I make some tea. You want some?" Lupe asked, moving to the stove and turning on the burner beneath the teapot.

Julia shrugged.

"Cocoa?" Lupe suggested.

Julia nodded.

As the water warmed and Lupe shuffled around the kitchen finding mugs, spoons, tea, and hot chocolate, Julia remained still, save for the constant stroke along Perro's back.

"Do you believe in angels?" Julia asked.

"Of course."

The kettle whistled and Lupe poured the steaming water into two mugs. One she set on the table in front of Julia with a spoon and a packet of hot chocolate while she turned to ready her own cup of tea. The spoon clinked against the inside of Julia's mug as she stirred the mix around. Lupe hummed as she prepared her tea and sat down across from the granddaughter of her heart.

"Sometimes, when I dream," Julia began and stopped. She blew on the hot chocolate.

"What?" Lupe said. "Tell Lita. You will feel better."

"I see her. I see Nellie," she said, peering at Lupe from beneath her thick, black lashes. "And she makes me laugh."

"She did," Lupe agreed.

"Did she?"

"Oh, yes. The only one who made you laugh from your belly."

Julia smiled and raised her mug for a tentative sip. Too hot. She stirred some more.

"Sometimes . . . I think . . . ," she said. "Sometimes, deep in my heart, I think she's still alive."

Lupe froze.

Carlyle gulped and waited.

"She is alive," Lupe said quietly.

"I know," Julia said. "Mami tells me she is always alive in my heart."

Lupe drank her tea.

Some noise undetectable to humans perked up Perro's ears. He stood and leapt from his spot in Julia's lap, barking as he ran toward the back door. After what he deemed an appropriate time, the barking ceased, and he ran to his small kennel by the pantry and curled up.

"But Lita, there's something else." Julia pulled the spoon from the mug, licked it, and set it down. "Sometimes when I see Nellie, I think I see something, or more like *someone* else."

Lupe swallowed and nodded.

"It's like there's always somebody else with us. Somebody who's not really a somebody. Does that make any sense?"

Carlyle's entire body rushed with shivers and he sat to attention.

"I've wondered if it might be an angel, but he's not very big . . . at least in my dreams he's not."

"What does he look like?" Lupe prompted.

Julia shrugged.

"Does he have the wings?" Lupe asked.

Julia shook her head.

"No. He kinda looks like a security guard or someone like that, 'cause he has on a blue uniform."

Carlyle leapt to his feet and jumped up and down on the napkins, causing one to slip from its spot and flutter to the table. Julia, lost in her memories, hardly seemed to notice. But Lupe stared at the puffy green square before pulling it toward her. She scanned the space above and around the table. Carlyle sat back down slowly, surprised by the physical manifestation his dancing had produced. For the first time in a very long time, there seemed to be an overlap between his world and Julia's.

"Does he talk to you?" Lupe asked.

"Sometimes. But mostly he just watches."

"Ah, a watcher."

"Is that like an angel?"

"Sí, but only for to watch."

"But why was he watching?"

"I think God sends him here to learn."

"To learn?"

"To learn of us. Of you."

Julia sipped tentatively at her cocoa.

"Why? What's so important about me?" she asked, wiping a drip of froth from her lip.

Lupe lifted a finger and pointed it at her granddaughter.

"You are very important. What do I teach you? You are . . . ?"

Julia sighed and blew out a breath.

"A daughter of the King."

"Yes," Lupe clapped her hands. "A daughter of the King. Una princesa. Muy importante."

Julia stared into her cocoa.

"Do you think he might still be watching?" she asked.

"Quizás, mija. Maybe."

Carlyle fell back into the cushy pile of paper product and pumped his fists into the air.

She remembered.

Chapter 19 – The Payment

Lupe sat in her favorite recliner in the TV room, her book lying in her lap. When Julia realized she was sound asleep, she switched off the lamp beside her abuela's head and tucked the throw blanket around her feet. Returning to her spot on the sofa, Julia pulled her open journal onto her lap. She chewed on the end of the pen as she read over the lines she had written:

Always
Never far
Though nowhere near
Always with me
In my dreams
I hear you laugh
Always joy filled
Sometimes I laugh
Along with you
Always longing
To touch your face
To hear your voice
Always hoping
That I will wake
And you'll be there - Always

She sat back into the plaid sofa cushions and gazed up at the ceiling fan. A single tear slipped from the side of each eye and she let them fall, wondering once again if in her entire life she would ever feel whole.

Perro began to bark furiously in the kitchen. Julia got up and ran toward the stairs.

"Perro, be quiet," she half yelled, half whispered.

Perro ignored her plea. Julia took the stairs two by two.

"Hey, I said—"

She slid to a halt in the doorway to the kitchen.

"Tío?" she said to the man standing on a chair with his hands reaching into the cupboard above the sink.

Another man standing by the sliding glass door that led out to the deck snatched Perro off the tile floor and clamped a hand over his snout. The dog squirmed but couldn't get away.

"Hey, ah, Jewels, what are you doing here?" Raúl asked as he slammed the cupboard shut, stuffed an envelope into his pants pocket, and climbed down from the chair. "Thought you'd be with your very important papa tonight."

Julia shook her head.

"They didn't leave you here all by your lonesome, did they?"

She shook her head again.

"So, who's with ya?"

She pointed toward the family room.

"Lita," she said.

"Who's Lita? You said nobody would be here," the other man said as the dog continued wrestling in his tattooed arms.

Raúl turned to his cohort.

"Keep it down, would ya?" he said. "She's just an old lady. Don't worry about it. And Jewels won't tell anyone. Will ya, mija? Besides. Nothing to tell. Just getting something your dad owes me."

The other fellow chuckled and set Perro down. The dog scurried to Julia, who swept him up.

As she held the trembling dog, she flashed back to a day in August when she had held the same quivering ball of fur in her arms. She had just pulled into the driveway on her bicycle and was about to press the code to open the garage when the side door had flung open and a whimpering Perro had scampered out. He had spun around in a few frenzied circles and then sped toward her. Securing her bike on its stand, she had knelt down to comfort the obviously upset canine.

Raised voices had filtered through the paneled garage door.

"Jeez, Raúl. Leave the dog out of this. You gonna throw me out the door next?"

"Maybe. If you keep acting like a little shit too."

Julia hadn't meant to eavesdrop on her dad and uncle's heated conversation. In fact, she had carefully stepped off the concrete and over to the grass, intending to quietly go around the house to the back door. But just as she'd navigated underneath the side window of the garage and turned the corner, she'd heard something that caused her to freeze as if caught in a game of red light, green light.

"Julia is legally our child. And no one has any reason to question that."

"You wanna keep it that way?" Raúl's voice had held a menace she had never heard from him before.

"Oh, come on, man. After all this time, you're gonna throw that in my face?"

Raúl had chuckled.

"What do you expect when you become a politician?"

"You know I didn't even want to run. Everyone just kept saying I should . . ."

"And Lord knows little Kiki don't wanna let anybody down."

"Shut up. And don't call me that."

"Oh, that's right. Only Papi could call you that. His little Kiki. His little pet."

"Raúl, I am not going to stand here and have this same old crap conversation. I've got better things to do with my time."

Julia had made ready to run for the back door of the house as she'd heard footsteps crossing the garage and the side door opening. But the next sentence had stopped her in her tracks.

"Fine. I'll just take the story to the newspaper. I'm sure they'd be happy to pay me a few nickels for such a sordid tale about Mr. Keep La Verdad Clean."

The door had clicked shut. And though she'd pressed her ear to the wood siding, she could not make out all the details of the conversation that followed. All she knew for sure was that it had involved her.

And money.

The scraping sound of the chair being pushed back under the table brought her back to the present situation.

"Your papa told me to come tonight," Raúl said. "So, no need for you to go telling tales to Lita or anyone else. Got it?"

Slowly Julia nodded.

"See, nothing to worry about here, Rico," he said, turning to his stocky companion.

"Dude, you didn't tell me you had such a pretty niece," Rico said, his eyes racing up and down her lean frame. "That's one tall drink of water for a thirsty man."

Raúl hit him in the chest.

"Back up, bro. She's only thirteen," he said.

"Don't make me no never mind. I like 'em young," Rico said.

Raúl grabbed him by the shirt and spun him away.

"Get outta here before you get us into real trouble," he said.

Rico lifted his hands up in the air in surrender.

"Dude, I'm just saying," he laughed, backing away.

"Just shut your face," Raúl said as he pushed Rico toward the sliding door. Following him quickly to the exit, he turned one last time to face Julia. "Remember"—he lifted a finger to his lips—"silencio."

He slid the door shut and disappeared into the dark.

Chapter 20 – The Truck

"Maybe I should tell Rosie," Julia thought as the two of them sat on the curb in the gathering twilight, waiting for their ride on the following evening. But the memory of Raúl's last words gave her pause. Besides, he had said her dad had told him to come. Maybe it really wasn't that big of a deal.

"I thought Papi said 7:30. The corner of 13th and Vine at 7:30," Rosie said, glancing from her wristwatch back to the street. She absentmindedly rubbed the silver cross that hung perpetually around her neck, a sure sign that she was anxious about something.

"They'll be here soon," Julia replied, picking the bag of campaign signs back up from where it had toppled off the curb beside her. "What's the big hurry?"

"*Amazing Race* starts in like twenty minutes."

"Ah, yes. Very important," Julia remarked.

"It's the season premiere. So, yeah, it is very important."

The sisters had walked the grid assigned to them by their father with garbage bags and screwdrivers, removing campaign signs from all the telephone poles and yards in the southeast corner of town. Beto and Freddy had been assigned the southwest corner and Maria and Junior the area around their home. Hector had covered the rest of town by himself in the van.

In the flurry of activity that had led up to the special election for the open seat on the city council, the Gomez family had all done their part to get Hector elected. And now that he had been elected, they were all called on to pitch in again. Since Keep La Verdad Clean was Hector's campaign slogan, he'd insisted that all the election signs get cleaned up—not just his, but his opponents' too.

Of course, the physical cleanliness was secondary to the moral and fiscal integrity Hector was hoping he could help restore to city government. Julia had read all the newspaper articles about the former mayor with a sense of outrage that someone in his position could be so crooked. Misuse of funds. Sexual harassment. Racism. It seemed he had been kept in office by virtue of the amount of property he owned and the number of wealthy farmers who benefitted from his form of good-old-boys politics. But when the behind-the-scenes shenanigans had been revealed by one fed-up city employee after another, the formerly loyal backers had pretty much thrown their leader under the bus.

The head of the council, Catherine Martinez, had stepped in as temporary mayor until a special election could be held. Despite opposition from a few of the old guard cronies, Mrs. Martinez was duly elected as mayor and Hector as a city councilmember in her place.

"I can't believe how many of Papi's signs were ruined," Rosie said, continuing her scan up and down the street.

"Some people aren't very nice," Julia said.

"I know. But don't you think it's kinda weird?"

"What's weird?"

"Well, the whole power trip. I mean, it's not like La Verdad is New York City or someplace important like that. Why does anybody think it's such a big deal to be the king of the hill if the hill is only the size of an anthill?" Rosie said.

"You have a way of getting to the bottom of things."

A grimy white box truck turned off 13th Avenue onto Vine and parked in a driveway directly across from where the girls sat. The house at that address sat back from the street behind a wall of overgrown shrubs. A broken-up sidewalk led from the street to the

The Agreements

front steps, where one iron railing remained standing while the other swung crazily off into the shrubs. A short, thick man hopped down from the driver's side of the truck and walked through the dilapidated carport to the back of the house. The truck remained running and loud music poured from the cab's open window.

A cold shiver ran up Julia's spine.

"Let's go, Rose," Julia said, grabbing her garbage bag by the tied end and standing up.

"But we're supposed to wait here," Rosie protested.

"No, let's go."

"Okay. Jeepers. What's gotten into you?"

"Don't know. Something doesn't feel right over there." Julia nodded toward the truck.

As Rosie picked up her swollen garbage bag, a seam suddenly burst and campaign flyers slipped out like a mudslide.

"Rats," Rosie said. "Now what?"

"Just leave it. We'll come back for it when Papi picks us up."

"Seriously? No way would he want us to leave all this mess."

Rosie bent down and began to slide as many signs as she could back into the bag. Julia sighed in frustration but set aside her bag to help.

"Hey, you two," a voice shouted from across the street.

Julia and Rosie looked up at the same time but didn't respond to the man standing behind the running truck.

"You deaf or something?"

The man began to walk toward them. Julia's stomach flopped as he got closer.

"Did you two pretty ladies happen to see if a dark blue car left this house recently?" the man asked.

Rosie shook her head. Julia stood stock-still.

"Well, well, well," the man she recognized as Rico said as he neared them, "if it isn't the tall-drink-of-water niece. And who's this other cutie?"

Julia dropped everything in her hands and pulled Rosie behind her.

"Hey, no need to get all scared there, uh . . . Jewels, isn't it?" Rico said.

"How does he know your name?" Rosie whispered.

"Just asking for a bit of information, ya know? Nothing else," Rico said. "Wondering if you saw my friend leave his house, that's all. Did you see anything?"

Julia shook her head.

"Oh, yeah, that's right. You're not a big talker." Rico stepped closer still. "But that's cool. Just the way I like 'em. Pretty and quiet."

A honk from down the street alerted them to Hector's impending arrival. Rosie jumped from behind Julia and flailed her arms like a mad semaphore signaler.

"Papi, over here!"

Rico flashed a sneering smile at Julia and backed up a few steps before turning to flee for his truck. By the time Hector pulled up with Beto and Freddy in the van, the box truck was pulling away in a hurry.

"Boys, get out and help the girls get everything in the back," Hector ordered Beto and Freddy, who piled out the side of the van.

"What the heck, Rosie? You trying to make La Verdad dirty or something?" Freddy said as he gathered handfuls of signs from the pavement.

Rosie ran to the driver's door, where Hector's window was down.

"Papi, did you see that guy? Did you see him?"

Julia dragged her bag to the back of the van. Beto helped her stuff it in on top of the other bags already filling the space.

"Yeah, I thought I saw someone walking away. Who was it? Was it a friend of yours?" Hector replied.

"No, ew! He was creepy and weird. He kept saying we were 'pretty ladies' and 'cuties' and stuff like that. And then he said, 'Aren't you the tall-drink niece?' or something. And then he called her Jewels. He knew her name," Rosie gushed.

"What?" Hector looked in the rearview mirror to where Julia stood. "What's she talking about, Jewels? Did you know that guy?"

Julia did not respond.

"Well, he knew you," Rosie said as she collected the last of the escaped detritus and took it to the back of the van.

"Jewels? You gonna tell me what's going on?" Hector turned his head to Julia as she took the seat behind him.

"Can I tell you when we get home?" she asked.

"Ah, come on," Beto whined, climbing in next to her from the other side. "Tell us too."

"Yeah, Jewels," Freddy chimed in. "It's the only interesting thing that's happened all night."

Rosie slid the door shut behind her and sat next to Beto.

Julia remained silent with her eyes fixed on the plastic floor liners.

"Leave her alone, guys," Hector said, putting the car into drive. "We'll talk at home, mija. Okay?"

He glanced in the rearview mirror. Julia looked into his reflection. Their eyes locked. Hector's hand froze on the gear shift.

"Come on, Papi," Rosie said. "*Amazing Race* starts in like five minutes."

Julia averted her gaze and Hector shifted into drive, gradually rolling away from the scene.

Chapter 21 – The Valley

On his way back to North Dakota, back to Nellie, Carlyle tried to reset his mind. Transitioning from one twin to the other was always a bit of a challenge. Although, as far as time and space went, there was no actual travel time, he sometimes liked to take advantage of quantum physics and dip into a different dimension. It allowed him to gather his thoughts. To check his emotions. To process the latest developments.

He didn't like the things swirling around Julia and Rosie. He and Ardith the Ardent had discussed it at length. They had never really trusted Tío Raúl. His heart light was always veiled behind a dark cloud of anger. But they trusted Rico even less.

"I think he's the first man I've ever encountered whose heart light is completely undetectable," Ardith had said one night during their midnight-watch discourse.

"Yeah. It's hard to even imagine what color it might be," he had agreed.

Carlyle shook his head to scatter the memories of Julia and Rosie and Ardith. He leaned forward and focused on the path ahead of him.

Nellie. Back to Nellie.

He smiled to himself, thinking about their last moments together at the dirt bike race with Karl Franks. It was the most fun

The Agreements

he'd had in . . . well, in eons. The thought of flying next to her on his motorcycle as she flew over the last set of jumps on her Kawasaki brought a sheer shot of joy to his system. She had been brilliant.

And he had loved it.

Suddenly, Carlyle was jarred from his musings as his motorcycle took a sharp turn to the right. He yanked on the handlebars, thinking that perhaps he had lost control. But no amount of yanking could alter the machine's trajectory. It was as if an unseen driver had taken over. The bike accelerated to speeds he did not know it possessed. Carlyle gripped the handlebars tightly.

The bike began to shake, but it did not slow down. Sounds like roaring wind, fire, and water whipped past his ears. Carlyle ducked all the way down over the front tank and held on for all he was worth.

Just when he thought he and the machine might shake to pieces, they broke through a wall of sound and shot out onto a wide-open plain of absolute white silence.

The motorcycle came to a complete stop. No skidding. No jarring. It just stopped.

Carlyle sat up, shook his head, rolled his shoulders, checked his limbs. All intact.

He looked to his left. To his right. Ahead and behind. Above and below.

All was snowy white and gossamer bright. He sat for a moment, adjusting to the perfect, undistracted peace of this strange, new place. The silence was weighty and smelled of fresh rain. He closed his eyes and absorbed the tranquility. It was exhilarating and calming at the same time. The cares and concerns of the world of the Jolicoeur twins loosened and dissipated like grains of sand in the grip of a mighty wave. Every molecule of his being relented to the cleansing power of it until he felt as if he might dissolve completely under its influence.

"Relaxed?" a familiar whisper broke into the silence.

He smiled, knowing who it was before he opened his eyes.

"Hello, Madeline," he said, turning to the see his trainer seated next to him on a silvery white horse.

"Hello, my friend. Ready to go?" she said. Her hands were wrapped within the long tendrils of her mount's mane and her own long braid swathed around her neck. The animal lifted his head and pawed at the powdery white surface. "Easy, Jett," she said, leaning close to his ears. "I was asking Carlyle, not you."

"Where are we headed?" Carlyle said.

Madeline smiled and clicked her tongue. Jett shot forward with a leap.

"Follow me," Madeline called over her shoulder.

The motorcycle roared to life as if reignited by her voice. Carlyle clutched the handlebars and laughed.

"I guess I'll find out."

The horse galloped with unrestrained strength, its hooves never touching the floor of the endless white terrain. Carlyle had to use all his skill and all his daring to keep within sight of the magnificent animal and its rider. They rode and rode farther and deeper into the dazzling white. With every inch of advance, Carlyle experienced another measure of serenity—of bliss. It was so intoxicating, he began to wonder if he should even be driving. Thankfully, when he had reached the absolute limit of his capacity, Madeline pulled Jett to a halt, turned, and waited for her student.

"Here we are," she said when he pulled up next to her.

Carlyle looked around but saw nothing different from what he had been seeing since the moment he had broken into this pristine sphere.

"Uh, and where would that be, exactly?"

Madeline stroked Jett's forelock and whispered something in his ear before dismounting. The animal nickered and galloped away.

"Come," she said to Carlyle, unwinding her braid from around her neck and letting it drop like a cape down her back.

He alighted from his bike and followed Madeline's receding form.

She began to climb a set of stairs that appeared beneath her feet with each step. At the apex of the flight, she turned and waited.

The Agreements

"Ready?" she said.

"For what?" he asked, ascending to meet her.

She reached forward and pulled on a doorknob that suddenly manifested in her grasp. An invisible door swung open. Madeline stepped through. Carlyle followed. They stepped together onto a broad stone balcony.

Far below them, stretched out as far as the eye could see and beyond, was a tangle of roads, highways, byways, paths, and trails so dense the surface that held them up was completely obscured. It was the most confusing-looking place Carlyle had ever seen, especially when experienced in juxtaposition to the uncluttered clarity through which he had just journeyed.

Anxiety niggled at Carlyle's heart as he stared at the chaos. Madeline placed a hand on his shoulder.

"Don't worry," she said.

The two set off to the right along a cobbled road that ran atop a thick wall. They were the only travelers as far as Carlyle could see.

"What is this place?" he asked.

"The Valley of Decision," she replied.

Carlyle peered to his left over the unfathomable landscape of intertwining pathways.

"It looks complicated," he observed.

Madeline gave no comment but continued to walk straight ahead.

In the faraway distance, a marble tower loomed. As they approached its colossal base, the tip of the edifice simply disappeared somewhere in the blue firmament above them. Its surface was smooth, white marble with veins of silver gray sparkling in random paths throughout. A dark wooden door at the bottom was the only thing that interrupted the homogenous exterior.

Madeline approached the wooden entrance and knocked. The door opened of its own accord, and the traveling duo stepped into the tower's dark, hollow interior. The door swung shut behind them and they were engulfed in utter darkness.

"Now what?" Carlyle whispered.

Madeline reached into the blackness and grabbed his hand.

"We ascend," she said, and they shot upward through her reverberating words.

He couldn't see her face, but he knew she was probably grinning from ear to ear with the thrill of their flight. He knew that he was.

As they soared higher and higher, a speck of light appeared above them and grew larger. At last they flew through the lighted opening and arrived at the edifice's apex, at what appeared to be an enormous observation deck. A wall of golden pebbles standing at least six feet tall enclosed the area. Along the far side, overlooking the Valley of Decision, stood rank upon rank of gigantic winged creatures. Dressed from head to toe in bronze armor, they each held a spear in one hand and a shining, fiery shield in the other. Atop their heads, helmets of pure light glowed like molten lava. Those closest to the edge had one foot upon the golden wall, ready to leap over it and launch out above the valley at a moment's notice. Each faced forward, but with an ear turned back and up as if awaiting some sort of signal.

Carlyle and Madeline watched as, one by one and two by two, the winged warriors hurled themselves off the tower and took flight in quick succession. As those disappeared from view, others filled their places and followed their lead. Their ranks never thinned, for as some left, others arrived in an unending stream of departures and arrivals. The activity was constant and swift, but never frenetic or disorderly. No words were spoken among the ranks. The only sound Carlyle could hear was the unceasing beating of enormous wings.

After observing for long moments, Madeline touched Carlyle's shoulder and directed him to follow. They walked to their right, keeping close to the back wall of the observation deck and out of the warriors' flight paths. On the far side of the space, Carlyle saw what looked like the bottom of yet another white tower rising upward, but as they drew closer, he realized the structure was made not of stone but of fabric. The pure-white folds of the flowing material rose heavenward, and Carlyle strained to see what might be at the top. But try as he might, all he could see was more fabric and an almost-blinding sheen reflecting off its surface.

The Agreements

Madeline once again grabbed him by the hand. With the other, she reached out and touched the hem of the garment. In an instant, the two of them were carried skyward and deposited on a broad area covered by the same shining cloth. Beneath his feet, the surface felt strong but pliable. It molded around his feet and then sprang back into place once he stepped forward, almost as if something living resided just below the fabric.

A wall of wooly white cascaded beside them and down beyond the place where they stood. It held within itself the most inviting shades of softness and the fiercest flames of passion. Carlyle was tempted to both fall into its comfort and flee from its holiness. Madeline walked right into the tumbling tresses and vanished.

Carlyle remained frozen in his spot. When his trainer did not return, he tore his eyes away from the place where she had disappeared and looked out and about for the first time. Far below him was the platform with the army of fiery ones launching out into flight over the Valley of Decision. From this vantage point, the valley was no longer a jumbled, chaotic mess but what looked like a woven tapestry of the most extraordinary beauty. Threads of every hue and shade intertwined in an ornate landscape of patterns and shapes. Gold and silver wound through in various places, sometimes as nothing more than a shimmering thread and sometimes as broad swaths like opulent rivers. As he stared, the scene before him moved and pulsed and breathed. Colors shifted and patterns changed. Valleys lifted and mountains leveled. Crooked places became straight and rough places became smooth. The entire scene vibrated with breathtakingly beautiful vitality and life.

"Enjoying the view?" Madeline asked, suddenly by his side again.

He nodded.

"Well, if you like that, you're going to love this. Let's go," she said, and she began to walk back to the place she had entered the waterfall of white.

Carlyle trailed behind Madeline with some trepidation. She vanished once again into the wooly white wall, and Carlyle reached out a tentative hand to push aside an opening for himself.

Immediately upon contact with a single strand, a jolt of electricity shot up his arm and jerked him into the depths of the tresses, where he found himself next to Madeline beside the entrance to a golden tunnel.

She handed Carlyle a pair of heavy-duty earmuffs.

"Wear these," she said.

Obediently, he placed them over his ears.

They stepped inside the tunnel. It was warm and dimly lit. The walls vibrated constantly, and, despite the earmuffs, Carlyle was nearly overwhelmed by the volume and density of words that rushed all around them. He was relieved when they reached the end and turned to the left, away from the intense stream's direct path. They stepped out onto a luminous stage. Carlyle shielded his eyes from the almost-blinding light that streamed through an oval-shaped opening. Madeline handed him a pair of sunglasses.

"Put these on," she said.

He gladly donned the deeply darkened spectacles.

"Now take a look."

Madeline pointed him back toward the lighted hole. The living tapestry of the Valley of Decision was spread out before him in all its glory, but from this vantage point Carlyle was able to see every human being within its fabric. Millions and billions of souls—alone, in groups, in cities, in nations. It was more than his mind could comprehend. Seeming to sense his overload, Madeline pointed to one spot on the fabric and said, "Watch there."

As if given a telescopic lens of some sort, Carlyle was able to focus on just one soul: a young girl in a school lunch line. Braces engulfed her thin legs and she shuffled forward with effort. A boy behind her shoved her and she toppled forward. Another boy reached out and caught her. She looked up with tears in her eyes. Behind her, they laughed. But her rescuer smiled and helped her forward. Strokes of silver, amber, and periwinkle splashed across the lenses of Carlyle's vision.

Then he saw a woman standing in a tiny apartment in a run-down tenement building, a baby in her arms, a toddler clinging to her leg, and a pistol in her hand. In the doorway stood a man yelling

The Agreements

and swinging his arms wildly in a drunken rage. The baby screamed. The child froze in terror. The woman tried to calm them all with pleas of desperation and threats of defense. But the man paid no heed. He lunged forward and the woman raised the gun. Deep shades of purple enveloped the scene and obscured the outcome.

Yet another soul was set before Carlyle's eyes: a man in a business suit, sitting in front of a computer. His index finger trembled over the keyboard. He pulled his hand back into his lap and reached for a mug of coffee. He sipped the warm liquid, his eyes trained on the screen in front of him. He closed his eyes and took a deep breath. He set the mug down and pressed a few keys. Chartreuse filaments entangled with orange fibers fell like a curtain.

On and on in swift succession, Carlyle watched as individual after individual made decisions. Some were small, some large, some tragic, some beautiful, some selfish, some kind. All were saturated with a great diversity of hues. All were sucked down into and absorbed by the fabric of history, shaping it, morphing it, infusing it with such a heady mixture of love and loss, triumph and failure, war and peace, the simple and the profound, he could not look away.

When he absolutely could not take in anymore, he shook his head and wiped his eyes beneath the dark lenses, surprised to find tears streaming down his cheeks.

"I don't understand," Carlyle whispered.

"What?" Madeline asked.

"How? How does it all become something so beautiful?"

Madeline nodded, took his hand, and led him away from the brilliant opening. He returned the sunglasses to her as they ventured back through the dim, warm tunnel; out through the fiery, white curtain; and back to the cloth-covered platform. She reached up and took off his protective headgear.

"Hold still and look."

She pointed toward the cascade of white they had just walked through. The massive amalgamation of tresses swung toward them, and a huge profile appeared. It had a trim, white beard around a set of full lips and a strong nose beneath eyes so full of light, their color was indescribable. White lashes and thick brows framed the eyes as they scanned the valley unceasingly.

"Grammateus cannot speak to us in this place, for his vigil is constant, his focus unwavering. But he was happy to allow you a glimpse, if ever so slight, into his perspective," Madeline explained.

Carlyle opened his mouth and stared.

"Have we been . . . uh, inside . . . ?"

Madeline merely smiled.

Chapter 22 – The Hullabaloo

"Sorry the coffee isn't fresher. Wasn't expecting any takers 'cept myself today," Claude said as he poured the last cup into a mug for Elsie Shatzenpfeffer. "Milk or sugar? Got some of each."

"Black is fine," Elsie said from where she sat in the rigid plastic chair next to the candy dispenser in the lobby. Her puffy down coat was draped over her shoulders, guarding her from the chill of the window behind her that read "Jolicoeur Auto & Truck Repair—Serving Grace since 1991." A red turtleneck rose up under her chin and hugged her firm torso. Black, formfitting snow pants stretched over her legs and tucked down into her snow boots. An avid runner during the summer months, she turned her physical energies to cross-country skiing during the winter.

Claude emerged from behind the service desk.

"I'd offer to have ya sit back here on the couch, but it's awful messy," he said, handing her the warm mug.

"Oh, not a problem," Elsie said. "I won't be long. Just got done skiing and wanted to check on how Nellie was doing."

Claude leaned back against the tall counter with both elbows and sighed.

"Well, she hasn't been in this morning. Said she had 'things to do.' Wouldn't say what exactly. Never a dull moment with that girl," he said, scuffing his leather work boot along the mat that ran the length of the counter. The mat was damp from the deposits of snow left from the various customers who had come and gone during the day. "Thought she might pop over this afternoon. Got a few chores for her but haven't seen hide nor hair of her."

"Well, I guess I'll just have to check on how you're doing instead," Elsie said, taking a sip of the coffee.

Claude glanced at her soft brown eyes that seemed to be measuring him over the rim of her mug. Something like adrenaline shot through his system. The woman made him darn uncomfortable at times. If it weren't for the fact that her former husband had been his AA sponsor for years until his untimely death in a farming accident, he might have avoided her attentions more actively. But he knew she was good people, knew she meant well. If she just weren't so attractive . . . He wiped his oily hands along his equally oily jeans, suddenly self-conscious about his appearance.

A red truck pulled into the parking spot directly in front of the shop, its tires crunching over the layer of snow next to the curb. A thick mountain of a man eased his way out of the driver's door and lumbered toward the entry.

"Looks like I got a customer," Claude said, stepping back around the counter. He clicked on the mouse next to the computer, waking up the screen. A bell jangled with the opening of the door.

"Otto," Claude said with a nod to his customer.

"Claude." Otto Franks nodded back. "Elsie."

"Hello, Otto," Elsie replied.

"Got your bill right here," Claude said. "Let me just print out a copy. Everything running alright?"

The printer behind the counter buzzed to life.

"Yeah, running great. Got another truck that'll need your attention. But we'll wait 'til after the holidays," Otto said, pulling his wallet from his tan Carhartt overalls. He eased a credit card out with his thick, calloused fingers and set it on the counter. "Heard about the doings up at the school."

Claude grabbed the card. He kept his eyes averted and gave no response.

The Agreements

Otto turned to Elsie.

"Were you there for all the hullabaloo?" he asked. "I'm guessing you were in the thick of it, being the school nurse and all."

"Well, yes, I was," she said with a quick nod, her salt-and-pepper bob swinging forward along her chin line.

"Heard there were some pretty gnarly injuries." Otto ran a hand over the stubble on his chin. "That fella ever gonna play the piano again, ya think?"

Claude made eye contact with Elsie and shook his head behind Otto's back.

"Now Otto, you know I can't tell you those things. Client-patient confidentiality still applies, even for school nurses," she said.

"Here ya go." Claude handed the card and receipt back over the countertop. "Truth is, Otto, we don't know a whole lot just yet."

Otto folded the receipt over the credit card and stuck the whole bundle into his coat pocket.

"Well, if ya ask me, the guy had it coming, from what I've heard. My boy tells me Mr. Jones isn't all that he wants everyone to think he is."

Claude shrugged.

Otto turned to go.

"Heck of a way to kick off Christmas break, eh, Elsie?" he said.

"Certainly not the usual way. That's for sure," she agreed.

"Well, if I don't see ya, have a merry Christmas," Otto said, reaching for the door handle.

The bell jangled again, and Otto stepped out into the waning light of the December afternoon. Claude let out a deep sigh and leaned onto the counter.

"I suppose that's all I'm gonna hear about 'til this whole thing gets settled," he said.

Elsie stood and walked over to the counter. She set her mug down and reached over to touch Claude's hand. He sucked in a deep breath.

"It's going to be okay," she said. "Nellie only did what she saw fit to do."

He blew out the breath, pulling his hand back and running it through his thick mop of gray hair.

"Yes, but she's not the one with crushed fingers. Michael Jones is, and he's the one who's filing charges against my Nellie for assault, bodily harm, loss of livelihood, and on and on," Claude's voice rose with every word. "He even claims it's not the first time she's hurt him."

He put his elbows on the counter and dropped his head into his hands.

"I haven't wanted a drink so bad in . . . in I don't even remember when."

"I suspected as much," Elsie said, crossing her arms on the counter and leaning in toward Claude. "When my Earl, God rest his soul, was your sponsor, what would he have told you?"

Claude massaged his face with his hands and remained silent.

"He would have said, 'This too will pass, whether you lose yourself in the bottom of a bottle or not.' You've come too far to throw it all away now, Claude. And besides, which version of you do you think Nellie needs right now?" Elsie asked. "I know I've never raised a child of my own, though Lord knows I would've loved to . . . but I've been around a lot of tough situations with kids in my nursing career. And I can tell you this right now—this isn't really about you. It's about your granddaughter."

Claude let his hands drop.

"I don't even know all that happened yesterday. She won't tell me," he said.

"Well, I'll tell you what I know. Truth is, Michael Jones isn't really a client. The students are my clients," she replied. "So, from what I can tell, Nellie walked in on Mr. Jones doing something inappropriate with Kenny Larson. She grabbed the kid, yanked him away from Jones, and scrambled for the door. When Jones tried to follow, Nellie smashed the door on his hand. Broke several fingers and almost severed another. She came and found me immediately. I stashed the two of them in Principal Holmes's office and ran back to the music room. It was pretty gruesome. I did what I could and called 911 right away. The EMTs couldn't tell me if they could save

The Agreements

the one finger or not." She stared at the white-tailed deer on the calendar behind the desk. "Kenny is a second grader. Can you even imagine? What the hell was he doing to a second grader?"

"I don't want to imagine," Claude replied. "And Nellie's not saying. Only thing she said was Kenny is too embarrassed to talk and if he doesn't want to talk, then she won't force him. She's babysat that kid for a couple of years and they're pretty tight. Poor little guy. And my Nellie is the one in trouble. Who's holding Jones accountable for his actions?"

Elsie shook her head and sighed.

"Kenny's not the first," she said. "I'm sure of it."

"Then why won't anybody do something? What's wrong with us?"

"I guess it's because it's kids' words against a respected grown-up's word. And maybe because nobody wants to believe that something like this is happening in our little town. I asked Sheriff Probst about it, and he told me that he's just been waiting for somebody to file an official complaint. Without it, his hands are tied. Short of putting some sort of surveillance camera in Jones's office, he's got no evidence of wrongdoing."

A dazed silence fell between them. Elsie walked back to the chair and picked up her coat.

"You have any booze stashed around here?" she asked.

Claude shook his head.

"You sure of that?"

He nodded.

The phone's ring interrupted her inquisition.

"Jolicoeur Auto and Truck," Claude said into the receiver.

Elsie turned to go, but Claude held up a finger, which caused her to halt by the door.

"What's she doing there? Is she okay?" he asked the party on the other end. "Okay. I'll be right there."

He dropped the receiver into place but didn't move.

"Claude? Who was that?"

He glanced up.

"Sheriff Probst."

"And?"

"And he says Nellie is down at the station."

"Is she alright?" Elsie asked, walking briskly back to the counter.

Claude lifted his shoulders in a shrug.

"I guess. He says she's okay but she's not alone. Whatever that means. I need to get on down there right away."

"I'm coming with you," Elsie said.

"Okay," Claude said, flicking off the lights, grabbing his coat and keys, and locking the front door. "I'll drive."

Chapter 23 – The Exposure

Five miles out of town, down highway 271 between Grace and Maltby, sat the Wells County Sheriff's Office. Normally the parking lot held only the small fleet of cars used by Sheriff Probst and his three deputies and occasionally a pickup truck or SUV from someone needing intervention from the law or discharge by the law. But on that late Saturday afternoon, the lot was nearly full of minivans, SUVs, and a few pickups. Carlyle watched down the hallway through the double glass doors that led out into the parking lot as headlights swept past and another car pulled in. Nellie sat in the waiting room in the cracked vinyl chair near the hallway. Next to her, with his feet tucked up under him, was Kenny Larson. Together they hunched over his mom's phone playing a video game. His parents could be seen through the window of Sheriff Probst's office filling out paperwork while the sheriff made entries on his computer and answered their questions.

On the other side of Nellie sat Kaya Wannamaker and her dad, Steve. Their coats were draped over their laps and small puddles of melted snow gathered under their feet. With one hand the dad held his daughter's hand, and with the other he tapped his thigh with a rhythm of unremitting fury. He gave a terse nod to Ron and Darlene Meyers, the latest arrivals, as they passed the waiting room with their daughter Megan between them on their way to the front desk.

Across the room from Nellie were Candice Loderquist and her mom, along with Josh Reynolds, his folks, and the entire Peters family. The room was overcrowded and stuffy. The air smelled of damp boots and barely controlled anger. Besides initial greetings and small whispers between family members, no one spoke.

Standing with their backs turned beside the pop machine and coffee dispenser were Principal Holmes and Superintendent Florhaug. They conversed in hushed, clipped phrases while the coffee in their Styrofoam cups grew cold. With every arriving parent, the two took turns trying to calm the livid and assure the perplexed that they were acting. Something was being done. Their children were being heard and Mr. Jones would be held accountable.

The heart light of each person in the room pulsed with extraordinary strength. Their combined energies sent arcs of light shooting around the room from one person to the next, even without a word being shared. Carlyle sent up a silent cheer for every brave soul who made their way through the darkening twilight into the gathering light of justice.

Deputy Bollinger stepped out of her office with Karl Franks.

"Thanks for coming in," she said to the burly teenager.

"About time," he said, stuffing his ball cap on his head. As he turned to go, Carlyle saw him give Nellie a quick lift of the chin before zipping his coat and making for the exit.

The deputy walked into the waiting room with a clipboard. She ran a pen down the list and called out, "Kaya Wannamaker."

"Here." Kaya's dad's free hand shot up. He leaned over to Kaya and looked squarely in her eyes. "We can do this," he whispered.

Nine-year-old Kaya slid from her chair, her hand gripping her dad's as they stood.

"I'm going to ask you a few questions, Kaya. Is that okay?" Deputy Bollinger asked.

Kaya's lips quivered.

"Your dad will be right beside you. But you are the one who will have to answer the questions. Can you do that?"

The Agreements

Kaya looked up at her dad, then back at the deputy.

"I think so."

"Okay. Follow me then," the deputy said, leading the pair behind the reception desk into a windowed office next to the sherriff's.

A gust of cold air wafted down the hall from the front entry. Carlyle looked up from his perch on the back of Nellie's chair to see Claude and Elsie passing Karl in the double-doored entryway and striding down the hallway toward them.

"Nellie?" Claude said, entering the waiting area.

Heads swiveled and stared at the new arrivals. Claude gazed from one face to the next around the entire room and back to Nellie's.

"Mr. Jolicoeur."

Superintendent Florhaug swiftly crossed the space with his hand reached out in greeting. Claude shook the offered hand with one half-hearted pump.

"What's going on here, Andy?" he asked the administrator.

"Well, uh, it's quite the thing," Andy Florhaug said, retrieving his hand and stuffing it back into his pants pocket.

Principal Holmes joined them and shook hands.

"John," Claude acknowledged the handshake. "You wanna fill in some blanks here for me? What are all these people doing here? Is Nellie in trouble?" He kept his voice low, though it was nearly impossible for every word not to be heard by every person in the confined area.

"Claude, I just have to tell you . . . I, uh, we are . . . we are doing everything we can to address and rectify the situation," the principal said.

"I'd say that's a bit of a stretch there, John," Josh Reynolds's dad spoke up.

Every head shot up. Nellie and Kenny lost track of the game and let it roll, unattended, in their hands.

"Now, Trevor. Let's not get all worked up and cast blame. A man's reputation and career are on the line here. We need to proceed with the utmost care for his sake, as well as the sake of the students. So, we are going to do all we can to make sure you are all heard and everything that needs to come out into the light comes out," Superintendent Florhaug addressed the challenge.

"Oh, I'm not saying you won't. Although I'd say there's more than one career on the line here," Trevor said. "I'm just saying you aren't the ones who are seeing to it that this situation gets addressed and rectified. I'd say that credit needs to go where credit is due."

He turned his gaze to Nellie. She sunk back into her chair and dropped her head. Carlyle wished he could lift her chin and help her see the gratitude and admiration in the midst of the anguished countenances around her.

Elsie unwound her scarf, unzipped her coat, and made her way to Nellie. She knelt in front of her and placed a hand on her knee.

"Did you do all this?" she asked.

Nellie shrugged.

"She called my daddy," Kenny Larson volunteered. "She said she would come with me."

"Is that true?" Elsie asked.

Nellie nodded.

Claude sat in the chair Kaya Wannamaker had vacated.

"Did you talk to Mr. Larson?" Claude asked his granddaughter. "What did you say?"

"Just told him what happened to his son," she said, her eyes still down in her lap. "Didn't want Kenny to get in trouble."

"She saved me, you know," Kenny said, his eyes beaming at Nellie. "She's very brave."

A slow blush crept up his heroine's neck as she turned and smiled at her young friend.

"You are the brave one. You were the first one to tell Sheriff Probst your story," she said, and Kenny scrunched his nose to keep the tears from falling.

"So, how did all these people get here?" Elsie asked as she stood from her crouch and sat next to Claude.

"Chuck Larson called us," Trevor Reynolds said. "He got the word out about what had happened with Nellie and Kenny. And he said every parent needed to have a serious conversation with their children, without coaching or prompting, but with ears to hear what they might not want to hear."

"None of us would be here if Nellie hadn't stood up for what's right," Mrs. Loderquist said.

"You should be real proud of your girl," Mr. Peters added.

Claude stared at his granddaughter in wonder.

Carlyle crossed his arms over his chest and leaned back against the wall, mesmerized all over again by the rich gleaming of Nellie's burnished amber glow.

This girl was absolutely brilliant.

Chapter 24 – The Trap

The Christmas Eve service at Glory of the Lord Church was over, and Julia was relieved and exhilarated at the same time. The candles were extinguished and the overhead lights back on. People were milling about, exchanging hugs and best wishes before heading home for dinner and presents. Pastor Valdez still stood by the back doors of the sanctuary, greeting the regulars and those making their biannual appearance with equal measures of enthusiasm. The giant tree by the altar twinkled with a blanket of white lights. Pine boughs wrapped in red ribbon draped the communion railing in front and the balcony in back. Julia breathed in the scents of the season, quietly relishing what had just transpired.

  She had to admit that once she had begun to sing her solo, she had actually enjoyed herself immensely. Despite the nausea, she had closed her eyes and opened her mouth, and the music had lifted from somewhere deep inside her and flowed out freely. Every other sound had hushed and there had been only the music, only the beautiful words—*silent night, holy night, all is calm, all is bright*—each one stronger, surer than the last until it felt like a stream of joy was rushing from her mouth. And for the first time that she could remember, she had felt like she was doing exactly what she had been born to do.

The Agreements

"Julia, that was so wonderful," Mrs. Ramirez's voice interrupted the memory. "You sing like an angel."

"Why haven't we heard this before?" her husband asked. "You've been holding out on us, I think."

Julia shrugged and ran her hands nervously over the soft velvet of her new dress.

"It's not like we haven't tried to get her to sing before," Maria jumped into the conversation. "Just had to be her decision. Julia, can you tell the Ramirezes thank you?"

"Thanks," Julia said, letting her eyes briefly meet the elderly couple's.

"Well, I hope it won't be the last time you share your gift with us," Mr. Ramirez said. "We sure did enjoy it." He reached out and surreptitiously slipped something into Julia's hand.

She opened her hand a crack and looked down. It was a twenty-dollar bill. She gaped back at Mr. Ramirez and over to her mom. Maria was checking her phone and hadn't seemed to notice.

"A little something just for you," the old gentleman whispered to Julia with a wink.

"Where are you headed for the rest of the evening?" Mrs. Ramirez addressed Maria.

"We have tamales heating up over at Cynthia's place. She was just texting me, letting me know everything is ready."

A slight pause hung between them.

"Oh, well, isn't that good of her," Mrs. Ramirez said.

"She heard from that good-for-nothing husband of hers?" Mr. Ramirez asked.

Maria put her hand on Julia's back.

"Why don't you go find your coat and your siblings? I'll meet you out by the front door."

Julia nodded and left, happy to be dismissed. She didn't want to hear the explanation again. The fact was, it wasn't Tía Cynthia's fault that her husband had vanished.

"She is still a part of the family and we will treat her as such," Hector had told the children when all the planning for the usual Christmas activities had come into play in the midst of the mystery about Raúl's disappearance. He'd been gone for weeks. No answering his cell phone. No explanation. Just gone.

Julia was sure it had something to do with her.

She hadn't wanted to tattle on Raúl, but after the incident with Rico in September, Hector had pried out the full story about what she had seen and heard, going way back to the argument in the garage. She had expected him to be angry, but another emotion had emerged the more she'd disclosed to him, one she had never seen before in her dad: fear. She would never forget the look in his eyes, nor could she jar from her mind the snippet of conversation she'd overheard between the two brothers when Hector had called Raúl shortly after her revelations. Most of it had been indecipherable from across the hallway and through the bedroom door. But one line had been crystal clear.

"If I go down, you go down too. So not one penny more," Hector had yelled. "Not one!"

The next day, Raúl had left town. He had not been heard from since.

"Hey, Jewels. Nice gob," Beto said passing Julia in the hallway with Junior in tow.

"You're the bestest singer in the whole world," Junior said yanking his hand free from Beto's and flinging his arms around Julia.

She put her hands under Junior's chin and lifted his face.

"And you are the bestest listener," she said.

"Jeez, enough of that mush," Beto grabbed the back of Junior's coat and pulled him away. "I'm starving. Let's go get some food."

"But I want Jewels," Junior whined.

"After tamales, Santa is coming," Beto bribed. "At least for good little boys."

"Santa!" Junior's eyes lit up and he took off so quickly, Beto had to run to catch up.

"See you there," Julia laughed at her brothers as they disappeared from sight.

She continued down the hallway toward the last room, where she had left her coat and mittens before the service alongside those

The Agreements

of the other members of the youth choir. Only a few people swept by her, offering smiles and congratulations on a job well done. The lights were already off in the youth room, but enough illumination spilled in from the hall lights to assist her in finding her way to her things, which lay over a round table in the back corner. She placed the twenty-dollar bill into the inside pocket of her jacket and zipped it shut. She noticed Rosie's purple, down-filled jacket still lying next to hers and picked it up before turning to find her. Just as she was about to step out of the room, Rosie whirled around the corner.

The two girls screamed in unison as they bumped into each other.

"Oh my gosh, Jewels," Rosie laughed. "You scared me half to death."

"Yeah, well, same to you," Julia replied with a shudder.

"Is that mine?" Rosie asked, pointing to the purple coat her sister was gripping against her chest like a life preserver.

"Yeah, here. We better get moving. I think everyone's already out front."

"Okay, okay," Rosie said, digging through her coat pockets. "Hey, did you see the Christmas card Teacher Sylvia gave me? I thought I put it in my coat. There's a Target gift card inside."

"Nope. Maybe it slipped under the table."

Rosie ran across the room and Julia stepped out into the hallway to wait.

"Hey, Jewels," a male voice came from the far end of the hallway.

Julia swung around.

"Tío?" she said, squinting into the semidarkness.

Raúl stood in the open back exit, silhouetted by the lights coming in from the alley behind the church.

"Guilty as charged," Raúl said.

"Where have you been?" Julia said.

"Around."

Julia stood still.

"So, I was thinking maybe I owe you an apology," Raúl said, stuffing his hands in his fleece-lined jean jacket and leaning against the doorframe. "You know . . . it being Christmas and all."

Julia offered no response.

"I know the last time I saw ya, I might have sort of given you a scare. Didn't mean to do that . . . so, uh, sorry about that."

Julia backed up and looked into the classroom, but Rosie was nowhere in sight.

"I know the wife is serving up tamales for everyone at my house. Need a ride? My car's right out back," he said. "What do ya say?"

"No," Julia said softly. "Thanks, but Mom is waiting for us."

"Oh, I cleared it all with her. She's in on the little surprise we've got planned. Me showing up for Christmas dinner and smoothing everything over. You know how she likes all that lovely-dovey family stuff, right? So, what do ya say?"

Before Julia could think of what to say, Rosie came rushing out of the room.

"Found it," she said. "It was underneath the table. Somebody must've bumped it off . . . you okay?"

Julia nodded in the direction of Raúl. Rosie swung around.

"Tío? Is that you?" she said.

Raúl stood to attention.

"Rosie. What are you doing here?" he said.

"I think maybe I should be asking you that," she said. "My dad's been trying to get ahold of you for days and Tía Cynthia is worried sick. So, you tell me. What are you doing here?"

He pulled his hands out of his pockets and held them out like a man caught red-handed.

"Was, uh, just gonna give y'all a ride over to the Christmas doings but, uh, Jewels here seems to think she's too good for a ride from me."

"I didn't say that," Julia whispered.

"Mom and Dad are waiting for us," Rosie said.

"He says Mom said it would be okay," Julia said. "Says he wants to surprise everyone for Christmas."

"Really?"

"That's what I said," Raúl said. "Your folks are long gone. Got tired of waiting for ya. But, hey, maybe the two of you just want to walk. No skin off my nose."

Raúl turned to leave out into the darkened alley. Rosie grabbed Julia's hand.

"Come on. Let's go. It's too cold to walk."

She dragged Julia behind her out the rear exit of the church. Directly ahead of them, under a streetlight in the alleyway, was Raúl's classic muscle car.

He was already climbing into the driver's seat when Rosie yelled, "Tío, wait up! Come on, Jewels. He never lets us ride in this car. Let's go!"

Reluctantly, Julia allowed herself to be drawn along.

Raúl's head sagged and he let out a sigh before standing up and opening the back door of the car.

"Alright, I guess it will be the two of you then," he said.

"Of course. Duh," Rosie said. "Where she goes, I go."

"If you say so," he replied.

The two girls scooted across the seat of the impeccably restored vehicle. Raúl shut the door behind them and ran his hands over his wool beanie before getting back behind the wheel.

If Julia wasn't mistaken, she thought she heard him mumble to himself just before the engine rumbled to life, "Feliz Navidad, hermano."

Maria said goodbye and Merry Christmas to person after person as she stood by the front door until the entire lobby was empty. Hector, her mother, and her sons were outside in the minivan idling at the bottom of the entry steps. She flagged down Pastor Valdez, who was inside the sanctuary, picking up stray bulletins, candy wrappers, and candles from the pews and the floor. He smiled and headed toward her as she strode toward him.

"Have you seen my girls?" she asked.

"Not since the end of the service. What a beautiful job they did tonight. Especially Julia. Oh, the heavens opened up when she sang. So amazing." He seemed lost for a moment in the memory. "But you can't find them? They're not with the boys?"

"No, they both went back to get their coats. I told them to meet me by the front doors."

"Well, let's go take a look in the classrooms. Maybe they're still chatting with someone," he said, leading the way to the Sunday school room wing. "I think the choir was leaving all their things in the youth room. Let's check there first."

He flicked on the lights as they entered the darkened room. No girls. No coats. Nothing out of place.

"Maybe they left their things somewhere else," he said, ushering Maria back into the hallway and into the next rooms. As they approached the back exit, a cold draft seeped through a crack between the door and its frame. Pastor Valdez went to tug it shut. "This door doesn't like to close unless you give it a yank."

They checked all the restrooms, the choir loft, and the fellowship hall. But still, no girls.

"And you're sure they're not in the van?" Pastor Valdez asked when the two reentered the lobby.

"I'm pretty sure, but I'll go check," she said.

She ran out to the van and opened the door to the front passenger seat.

"Still can't find them?" Hector asked from his place behind the wheel. "Where the heck could they have gone?"

Maria shook her head.

"Jewels said, 'See you there,'" Junior piped up from his car seat.

"Did she, Beto?" Maria asked.

"Yeah, when she was going back to get her stuff. That's what she said," Beto confirmed.

"Well, maybe they walked to Cynthia's," Hector said. "It's only four blocks."

"I can't imagine they would've done that in this cold," Maria said. "But maybe so. They're certainly not in the church."

The Agreements

"Get in and we'll go look. We'll probably drive right by them if they're not already there," Hector urged his wife.

"There is trouble," Lupe spoke up from her place behind Hector.

"Excuse me?" Hector said, looking in the rearview mirror at his mother-in-law.

"Trouble. I feel it."

"Now Lupe, let's not blow this all out of proportion," Hector urged.

Maria froze in her place, staring into her mother's eyes.

Pastor Valdez walked up behind her.

"Find them?" he asked.

Maria turned and shook her head.

"We're thinking they probably walked. No need to be too worried." Hector peeked around Maria. "We'll call you when we get to Cynthia's to let you know they're alright."

"You do that, Hector," the pastor replied.

"My mother thinks there's trouble," Maria whispered.

Pastor Valdez's eyebrows shot up.

"Hmm, well, I'll be praying. But I'm sure they're safe and sound somewhere. Just lost in all the hubbub. Be at peace, my friend," he said. "And feliz Navidad."

"Yeah, uh, for sure. Feliz Navidad."

Chapter 25 – The Boxes

Jimmy Flanagan smiled at the small bundle in his arms and brushed a finger softly over his baby granddaughter's sleeping brow. It was the first time all evening he had gotten the chance to hold her. His sons and their families had just left the big Christmas Eve family shindig. They had in-law engagements the next day and so needed to trundle the troops home for at least a few hours of sleep in their own beds. Jimmy understood. And he didn't begrudge the other grandparents time with the grandkids—especially at this time of year.

But secretly, he was delighted that his daughter Rowen's in-laws lived too far away to split the holiday. It meant she and her husband Parker and their kids were gone entirely every other year, but when they were home, they were all in. His wife had taken their grandson, Hudson, up to bed with promises of a bedtime story from one of his new books. Rowen was busy stuffing a large garbage bag with crumpled-up wrapping paper, discarded ribbons, ripped-up boxes, and all matter of the leftovers of what had only hours ago been beautifully wrapped Christmas presents.

"This is ridiculous," Rowen said, tying up the string of a second full bag and opening another. "I told you not to go crazy with the gifts, Dad."

"Ah, come on. Don't rob a man of his joy."

The Agreements

"But Dad, Hudson is only two, and Fiona isn't even a month yet. How much do you think they could possibly need?"

Jimmy laughed.

"It's not about need, you know. It's about want. And the want isn't even theirs. It's your mum and I and what we want to do for them."

"I know that. And I don't deny you your right to spoil them a bit, but it's Parker and I who have to haul all this stuff home and live with it."

"Yup," Jimmy said. "Get used to it."

"Where is Parker, by the way?"

"I sent him on a little errand for me."

Just then his son-in-law entered the expansive open living room with two more presents, a large one that reached from just below Parker's chin nearly to the floor and a smaller box balanced on top.

"These the ones?" Parker asked.

"Dad! Now what?" Rowen protested.

"Santa gifts," her dad replied.

"But it's the size of a small house!"

"It's just a wee workbench and tools. He'll love it." Jimmy looked down to see Fiona's deep-blue eyes staring up at him. "Can't tell you what the one for Fiona is, for she's looking right at me and I'll not be giving up Santa so soon in her life."

"Well, you can keep that big ole thing here. Hudson can have all the fun he wants with it at your house."

Rowen reached down, grabbed a handful of crinkled paper, and crammed it into the bag.

"Bah humbug," Parker said, setting the gifts down by the tall stone fireplace. "Come on, Row. Your folks are just having some fun with the kids. Didn't your grandparents ever spoil you?"

Rowen stopped where she was.

"Seriously? You're gonna bring up granny right now? She was very kind and generous with what she had," she said as tears lit her eyes. "But she didn't spoil me. She didn't have the money to spoil me."

"Ah jeez, hon. I'm sorry." Parker walked over and pulled his wife into a hug. The bag in her hand dropped and she let herself melt into his arms. "I didn't mean to bring up your gran. I know it's your first Christmas without her."

Jimmy glanced up and smiled through his own tears. Parker could be dense at times, but he had a heart the size of Texas. Baby Fiona wriggled in his arms, demanding his attention.

"It's the mercy of God, I think," he whispered for her ears alone. "One leaves and one arrives."

"Hey, Pops," Parker said over Rowen's head, "I saw a couple of other boxes downstairs hidden under some things. Looked like they were maybe presents for somebody else. They're all packed up with address labels and stuff. Want me to bring 'em up?"

Jimmy dropped his head back against the couch and let out a sigh.

"Oh, man. Speaking of my mother . . . I forgot all about those," he said. "They're not Christmas presents, but they do need to be sent." He looked back at Parker. "When you're done there, would you mind bringing them up and setting them on the bench in the front entry?"

"Sure thing, Pops."

Chapter 26 – The Attempt

The back door of the dirty, white box truck opened and a flashlight illumined the two girls curled up under the blankets in the corner. Cigarette smoke blew in on the wings of a cold gust.

"Get up," Rico ordered.

Two sets of terrified eyes peeked up over the grimy covers and blinked back the bright rays. Rico climbed into the back of the truck with a brown paper bag in one hand and the flashlight in the other.

"Get up if you want to pee somewhere else besides in your own drawers," he said, the cigarette in his mouth bobbing as he talked. "There's food and drinks in the bag when you get back. Wouldn't want you to be telling your important daddy we weren't humane."

"Come on, Rose," Julia said. She began to unfold her frozen limbs and Rosie followed suit.

"Where are we?" Rosie demanded. "What are you gonna do with us?"

"Oh, now don't you worry your pretty little head about that," Rico sneered, trying to touch her cheek with the back of his hand.

Rosie jumped back.

"Don't touch her," Julia said, wrapping an arm around her sister and steering her to the door.

"Leave 'em alone," Raúl said, reaching up to help Rosie down from the truck. "Hector won't pay a dime if we hurt them."

"Like you didn't hurt us when you stuffed us in the back of this dirty heap of a truck?" Rosie snipped.

"If you'd have just done as you were told, nobody would've gotten hurt," Raúl replied.

"Seriously?" Rosie spat back. "You think we were just gonna calmly cooperate with this ridiculous . . . stupid . . . idiotic . . . kidnapping or whatever the heck it is you're doing to us? Where are you taking us, anyways?"

"As far away as I need to make your daddy know I'm serious."

"Well, if you think you're gonna get tons of dough out of him, you're nuts. You think living with five kids, a wife, and a mother-in-law is cheap?" Rosie continued.

"Jeez, Gomez," Rico said, handing Julia down. "That one sure is sassy. Why don't ya put her in her place?"

"Just shut up," Raúl snapped. "She wasn't supposed to be part of this."

"Oh, really? And Jewels was? What did Jewels ever do to you?" Rosie asked.

"That, mija, is none of your business," Raúl said.

"Um, I am standing in the freezing cold in the middle of nowhere, so I'd say it has become my business," Rosie snapped back.

"Holy shit. Are you gonna stand out here discussing details, or are you gonna take advantage of our offer of a potty break?" Rico interjected from the back of the truck.

"Let's go." Julia grabbed Rosie by the hand.

"Well, this is the stupidest thing ever," Rosie spouted at her uncle as Julia led her away. "What is the matter with you? Have you gone insane?"

Raúl grabbed her other hand and yanked her back toward himself.

"You better zip it, sister. Just 'cause you got mixed up in this thing by mistake doesn't mean you can go disrespecting me. Now get out there and do your business or I'll put you both back into the truck and you can figure it out in there." He pushed Rosie toward the side of the two-lane highway.

The Agreements

"Yeah, just shut up and go," Rico added.

"Where are we supposed to go?" Rosie yelled into the wide-open darkness.

The night was pitch black. There were no buildings anywhere, and the closest lights were only tiny twinkles on the far horizon. Even the moon and stars were covered by a thick layer of clouds.

"Out there somewhere," Raúl said. "And don't bother screaming for help. There's nobody around for miles."

Julia grabbed Rosie's hand once again and the girls stepped gingerly over a ridge of hard-packed snow onto the icy shoulder of the road. Rico flashed the light on them.

"Don't try anything, either. There ain't nowhere to go."

"I can't pee if you shine that thing on me," Rosie grumbled.

"Let 'em alone," Raúl said.

Rico flicked off the light and jumped down to the road. He leaned against the truck and took a long drag on his cigarette, blowing the smoke out in perfect circles.

"Can't believe we actually pulled it off," he said as the last smoke ring disappeared into the night.

"Yeah, well, not exactly as planned but . . . Rosie's the one who insisted on coming along," Raúl said. "Hector has no one to blame but himself for raising such a hardheaded kid."

"Maybe ole Hector will cough up twice as much. Double for our trouble," Rico chortled.

The sound of feet clambering over a snowdrift disrupted them.

"Crap," Raúl said, leaping toward the ditch. "Give me some light."

Rico turned the flashlight on and scanned the snow-covered field beyond the ditch until the beam caught two scurrying shadows in its glow.

"They're running," Rico yelled, throwing his cigarette on the ground as he leapt into action with Raúl out in front of him.

"Hurry, Jewels," Rosie said, slipping and scrambling over the snow in her good church shoes.

"Go, just go," Julia urged her on. "They're coming."

"Get that one," Rico hollered. "I've got this one," he said as he gained ground on Julia with every stride. Within seconds he had the back of her coat in his grip and threw her to the ground.

Raúl pursued Rosie. His heavy boots broke through the icy snow, where she skimmed over the top. He cussed, wrenched himself free, and hurled himself after her frantic footsteps.

"There's nowhere to go, Rose," he yelled.

But she ran on. He redoubled his efforts. When he got within a few feet, he flung himself at her and tackled her to the ground. They lay panting on the hard, cold ground.

"Get her?" Rico's voice echoed through the dark.

Raúl lifted his head and readjusted his beanie that had nearly fallen off.

"Yeah, I got her," he yelled back, pulling himself and his captive to their feet. "I never meant for you to get caught in all this. Why couldn't you leave her alone?"

Rosie glared at her uncle as she wiped snow from her face and hair.

"She's my sister."

He shook his head.

"Nah, she ain't your sister. She's some orphan that your dad and mom felt sorry for. She don't even belong in this family."

"She's more family than you are!"

Raúl shoved her toward the truck.

"Just get moving. And don't do anything stupid. It'll only make matters worse."

"Worse? I'm in the middle of nowhere with two wackos. How could it get any worse?"

He shook his head and pushed her forward.

"Oh, trust me," he said. "It can get worse."

Back inside the truck, the girls grabbed the brown paper bag and tucked themselves tightly under the covers. Their frozen fingers fumbled with the plastic bottles and chip bags they found inside. In the pitch black, they couldn't tell what they were about to eat or drink until it was in their mouths.

"Doritos," Rosie said.

"Mountain Dew," Julia added.

They tried to savor the snack, eating one chip at a time completely before moving on to the next.

"Not exactly tamales," Julia shivered.

Rosie dropped her head onto her sister's shoulder. Her brave exterior cracked, and she began to sob. Julia carefully secured the lids on both their drinks and then wrapped her arms around her.

"I'm sorry. That was stupid to bring up," she whispered.

"I-I can't . . . even . . . believe . . . this is . . . happening."

Julia nodded into the darkness.

Rosie continued to weep, and uncontrollable shivers wracked her body. Julia shut her eyes and pulled her little sister closer. It wasn't often that Rosie was the one in need of strength. Silently, she prayed for wisdom. Suddenly a song filled her heart. And though at first she thought she could not possibly sing, she opened her mouth, and the words spilled out and filled their tiny comforter sanctuary:

Silent night, holy night
All is calm, all is bright
Round yon virgin, mother and child
Holy infant, so tender and mild
Sleep in heavenly peace
Sleep in heavenly peace

Slowly, Rosie's sobs subsided. Her trembling calmed. Julia continued to sing every verse until at last her sister slept in her arms and her own eyelids drooped heavily onto her cheeks.

Chapter 27 – The Promise

Morning sun peeked under the truck bed's door in a harsh slash of gold. Julia and Rosie still slept in a tangled heap in the corner as the temperature outside slowly climbed and warmed the truck's interior. Smells muted by the cold began to emit memories of cargoes past. Minutes turned to hours, and still the truck rumbled on. Unconsciously, the girls tugged the covers off their faces, seeking fresher air. Sweat dripped down their faces and into their tangled hair. But still, they slept.

Finally, the vehicle slowed, veered off at an exit, and came to a halt. Sounds of other people and vehicles sifted in muffled waves into the back bed of the truck.

"Fill 'er up. I'm gonna get some coffee and grub," Rico said as his footsteps passed the cargo door.

The trickling of gas flowing into the tank followed.

Suddenly, the back door opened and brilliant sunshine broke in. Raúl climbed in quickly and closed the door behind him, leaving a small crack for light. He walked to the corner and bent down.

"Hey, wake up."

He rustled the blankets. Julia's eyes slowly blinked open. She stared at her uncle in a daze.

"Don't make a sound," he warned, tapping on Rosie's arm. "You too."

The Agreements

Rosie rolled over and sat up, struggling to open her eyes. Julia sat up beside her.

"If you promise to be good, I will take you to the bathroom. But if you think you're gonna pull some kind of stunt like last night, I swear, I'll leave you in this truck all day. Got it?" he said, kneeling and speaking directly into their stupefied faces. The girls both nodded mutely. "Wait here. I'm gonna move the truck right next to the restrooms in the back. I'll be back."

He jumped off the back bed and secured the door. Julia unzipped her coat and flung the blankets to the side. Rosie wiped the sleep from her eyes and shook her head as if trying to rid her mind of cobwebs.

"You okay?" Julia reached over and took Rosie's hand.

"I don't know. I feel like I've been asleep for about a week," Rosie mumbled.

"Yeah, me too."

The sound of flowing gasoline stopped and the engine of the truck rumbled back to life. As the wheels rolled forward, Julia struggled to her knees.

"Let's get ready," she said.

Slowly they got to their feet, their hands pressed against the walls for balance.

"Listen to me," Julia said. "If we see any way to escape, we are going to take it."

"What? You heard Tío."

"I know, but we have to keep trying. And if only one of us can get away, I want it to be you."

"No way. I will not leave without you."

"Listen to me," Julia said. "He only wants me. It's my fault you're even in this mess."

"It is not your fault, Jewels."

"It is. I'm the reason Tío has been able to blackmail Papi for money."

"What? That's crazy. Why?"

"I don't know for sure. But I think it's something about my adoption not being legal or something."

The truck lurched to a stop and the girls fought to remain upright.

"That is crazy talk," Rosie said. "And it doesn't make any difference. I am not leaving here without you."

"Yes, you are." Julia grabbed both of Rosie's hands. "Promise me. If we can, you will try. Promise."

Tears filled Rosie's eyes.

"Don't make me," she cried.

"Rose, this is just what big sisters do. Besides," she said, reaching up to brush away the tears, "you'll be able to get help, and then Papi can come rescue me. Right?"

Rosie nodded slowly.

"Okay . . . but only if you can't make it too. I promise, cross my heart and hope to die, that I'll come back with help."

The girls hugged each other.

The back door opened just enough for Raúl's head to peek in.

"Ready?" he whispered.

"Yes," Julia whispered back.

"You come only when I say so," he ordered, swinging his head around to make sure the coast was clear. "Okay. Now!" He reached in, pulled them out one after the other, and hustled them to the small, single-stall women's restroom. "Get in and don't lock the door. I'm gonna stand right here 'til you're done. Hurry up."

As soon as the girls entered the grubby room, they saw the window on the wall inside the stall. The big lower pane was locked shut with a padlock, but the smaller upper pane was swung open for ventilation.

"Can you fit through there?" Julia whispered.

"Yeah . . . maybe. But where am I gonna go?"

"I saw a farmhouse not too far across the field. You get out and run toward that house. I'll stall as long as I can. Come on. Climb up on the windowsill," Julia urged.

"It's too high up," she said, climbing up onto the sill and reaching for the opening.

Julia stood on the toilet rim and leaned onto the windowsill.

The Agreements

"Step on my shoulders," she said. "It will give you a few more inches."

Raúl pounded on the door.

"Get done in there," he hissed.

Rosie paused, leaned against the window, and reached behind her neck.

"What are you doing? You've gotta go," Julia urged.

"Take this," Rosie dangled her baptism necklace down to her sister. "I want you to have it."

"But . . ."

"I won't go if you don't. It'll remind you that I promise to come back for you."

"Okay, okay." Julia grabbed it from her hand and stuffed it into her coat pocket. "Now go."

Rosie hoisted herself up and Julia boosted her feet as she went. With every ounce of strength they possessed, the sisters worked their precarious plan.

"There's a bar out here," Rosie called back over her shoulder. "I got it."

With one last boost from Julia, Rosie's body slid out.

Julia quickly jumped down, used the facilities, flushed the toilet, waited a few seconds, and flushed it again. She rushed to the sink and splashed cold water on her hands and face before running her fingers through her hair. Her cheeks were flushed a deep pink in the reflection in the cracked mirror. Slowly she shuffled to the door, making whispering noises as if she were still talking to Rosie. She cracked the door and Raúl grabbed her by the wrist.

"Where's Rosie?" he whispered with a fake smile on his face as a gray sedan rolled by within ten feet of them.

Julia was tempted to holler and wave her arm to the people in the car but she resisted, knowing that every second was precious for Rosie.

"She isn't feeling too good. What did you put in that pop, anyways?" she whispered back.

"Just a little something to help you sleep," he said, the smile vanishing from his face as his gaze followed the taillights of the sedan out of the parking lot and passed over the field just beyond where they stood.

"What the . . . where is she going?" he muttered as his hand left her wrist and he ran toward the edge of the pavement.

Julia ran behind, tugging at his coat.

"Let her go."

Raúl suddenly halted with one foot on the outer curb of the parking lot. Julia nearly toppled over into him.

"You said you only wanted me," she said, righting herself beside him.

The two of them stood and watched Rosie bob up and down through the dried cornstalks of the field. She was already halfway to the farmhouse.

"You're doing the right thing," Julia said.

Raúl stared off at the receding figure of his fleeing niece.

"Well, there's always a first time," he mumbled.

Suddenly Rico had Julia in his grasp, escorting her firmly back to the truck with one hand while gripping a bag of snacks with the other.

"What the hell is going on here?" he said over his shoulder to Raúl. "Where's the other one?"

Raúl shrugged.

"I let her go."

"You let her go? What the freakin' heck is wrong with you? She's gonna squeal like a stuck pig," Rico hissed as he steered Julia back to the truck.

An old Ford pickup pulled into the parking spot next to them.

"We better put Jewels up front with us," Raúl whispered.

A gray-haired man in a straw cowboy hat stepped out of the truck. He bobbed his chin upward in greeting to the two men with the tall, pretty girl between them. Raúl nodded back as he made his way to the driver's door.

"Gonna be a warm one," the man said, his eyes squinting at the trio.

"That's what they say," Rico replied, opening the cab door and assisting Julia up inside. "Here, hon, here's your treats," he said, pulling a bag of trail mix out of the sack in his hands and dropping it onto her lap.

Rico climbed in behind her, slammed the door shut, and locked it.

"You shouldn't have let her go," he said to Raúl. "She's gonna get us caught."

"Maybe we should just drop this one off somewhere, too, and be done with this whole stupid thing," Raúl said. "I've gotten my pound of flesh out of ole Hector by now."

"Oh, no you don't," Rico said, popping the tab on his energy drink. "You told me we could get some easy money out of this pretty little miss. And I aim to do that. One way or another."

Julia scooted closer to her uncle and peered up into the rearview mirror. Rosie was nowhere in sight.

She took a deep breath and prayed the people in the farmhouse would be home.

Would be nice.

Would be helpful.

Because if they weren't . . . she couldn't allow herself to think about that.

Casting a sidelong glance to the men she was sandwiched between, she realized she had plenty to worry about all by herself.

Chapter 28 – The Search

For the Gomez family, a most hellacious Christmas Eve rolled over into an equally hellacious Christmas morning. Every present still lay unwrapped in a mound under the tree at Tía Cynthia's house. Tamales and beans and rice still sat in pans on the stove and in the oven, warming and waiting for someone to have an appetite. Beto, Freddy, and Junior lay passed out in the living room on couches and recliners. Hector, Maria, Pastor Valdez, and Detective Mason sat around the kitchen table, drinking yet more coffee. Cynthia shuffled around the room with bleary eyes. Hector's cousin and her kids, along with Cynthia's folks who had gathered for the hoped-for festivities, had all gone home.

When Hector and Maria had not found the girls at Cynthia's, every family member with a vehicle hit the streets of La Verdad and searched for hours. Lupe immediately closeted herself in a back bedroom and began to pray. Maria phoned Pastor Valdez, who arrived within minutes. And when the search parties turned up nothing, they called the police. Cynthia and the other family members worked their phones, calling everyone they could think of who had been at church that evening and might have seen anything. Pastor Valdez sent out messages to every pastor and priest in town, asking for their help and their prayers.

The Agreements

When the hours piled up without any leads or sightings, Hector began to press the police to issue an Amber Alert. The problem was they didn't have much information to give out that might possibly help in tracking the girls down, a requirement for the alert to be sent out. Everyone in the family agreed Raúl was probably part of whatever was happening, but no one had proof. His muscle car had been found under a tarp in the alley behind a house on Vine Street—not a place he would ever have left his precious vehicle if he wasn't in a hurry to get out of town.

"They could be halfway to Mexico by now," Hector argued.

"I know, and I have given the state patrol their descriptions and all the information we have—which isn't a lot," Detective Mason said. "If we just had some sort of lead about a possible vehicle . . ."

"You know, I just remembered something," Pastor Valdez said. "When Maria and I were looking for the girls in the church, I noticed that the back exit door was slightly cracked open. No one hardly ever uses that door, so I thought it was a bit odd. It's always locked from the outside, so it can only be used as an exit. We don't have any cameras back there, but maybe one of the houses behind us along the alley has a security camera or something? I don't know. I'm just throwing out an idea."

"Good, that's good. Let me call down to the station and get someone on that," Detective Mason said. He picked up his phone and headed to the back deck, where he could make his call in relative privacy.

Maria followed him with her eyes, straining to read his lips through the sliding glass door. Hector rubbed her back gently.

"He'll tell us everything we need to know, mi amor," he said. "We have to trust him."

"Trust? How can I trust anybody right now?" Maria said.

Just then, Lupe appeared in the entrance to the kitchen. They had not seen her all night.

"Did you get some sleep, Mom?" Cynthia said, greeting her with a hug.

Lupe shrugged her off and marched directly over to where Maria and Hector sat. She set a small slip of paper on the table in front of them.

"I did not sleep," she said. "I pray."

Maria grabbed her hand and kissed it.

"Gracias, Mamá. We need every prayer we can get."

"What is this?" Hector said, picking up the piece of paper.

"I see it," Lupe said. "I see the truck and those numbers."

Pastor Valdez peeked over at the note in Hector's hand and then back up at Lupe.

"Are you saying this is the vehicle that the girls are in?"

"Sí," Lupe said.

"Did you see it at the church?" he asked.

"No. I see in here," she said, pointing to her forehead.

"Did the Lord show you this?" Maria said.

"Yes, he show me," Lupe replied.

"Is this the license plate numbers?" Hector asked.

"Yes, but is only some," Lupe said.

The sliding door opened and Detective Mason stepped back into the room.

"Brisk out there," he said with a shiver. "The guys are on the way to check with homeowners along the alley."

Maria leapt from the table with the slip of paper in her hand.

"This is it. This is the vehicle that took the girls away," she said, sticking it in front of the detective's face.

He leaned back to avoid a finger in the eye and reached up to take it carefully from her.

"Hmm . . . large white truck with box on back. You mean a box truck?"

He looked around the table and room, seeking the source of the note. Lupe stepped forward.

"Yes, a box truck."

"Did you see the truck?" he asked her.

"Detective, my mother-in-law sees things in the spirit when she prays," Hector explained. "So no, she didn't actually see the truck."

"No," Lupe fired back. "I see it."

The Agreements

"We know, Mamá, but not like in person. Only in your spirit," Maria said, patting her arm.

"Same thing," she said, brushing Maria's hand away.

"I'm not an expert or anything," Cynthia said from behind them. "But in my experience, Lupe has been pretty darn accurate when it comes to stuff like this. A few years ago, I lost my wallet for like a week. And finally, one day Lupe was over here and she prayed about it for a few minutes and then told me where she thought it was—wedged between the back seat and the trunk of my car, under a blue blanket."

"And was it there?" the detective asked.

"Yup. Exactly like she said it was, down to the color of the blanket," Cynthia replied.

Beto stumbled into the kitchen, wiping sleep from his eyes. "Can I get a tamal?" he asked.

"I'll get it for him, Maria," Cynthia said. "Come here, mijo, I'll get you a plate."

Beto shuffled toward his mother first.

"Any news?" he asked.

She wrapped her arms around him and shook her head.

"No, not yet."

He pulled back from her, his shoulders sagging.

"Thought I heard someone say something about a vehicle," he said.

"Well, not exactly," Maria said, caressing his cheek. "Just one of Lita's words from the Lord."

"What'd she see?" he asked. "Most of the time she's right, ya know."

"I see big white truck with big box," Lupe said, demonstrating the size and shape with her hands. "It is white, but not white. Sucio. Dirty."

Suddenly Beto's eyes lit up and he turned to Hector.

"Hey, Dad, remember that truck we saw that day when we were picking up campaign signs? The one where Jewels and Rosie were? The one where that guy came out and talked to them and knew Jewels's name?"

"Hey, yeah, you're right, mijo," Hector said, standing to his feet. "It was a big white box truck that was really dirty. And it was that guy . . . uh, Raúl's buddy . . . Rico. That's his name. Rico. He was the one who was with Raúl when we were all gone and Jewels saw them."

"You know what?" Cynthia chimed in. "I've seen that truck around whenever Rico has shown up. I've totally seen it!"

"Well, looks like I'd better run these numbers and see if there's a truck matching your description, Lupe," the detective said. "I'm gonna head down to the station and do this myself. I'll let you know if I find anything. And if this pans out, I'll get that Amber Alert issued right away." He paused in front of Lupe. "Ya know, I've heard of police departments hiring psychics, but I never believed in any of that stuff. Looks like you may just prove me wrong."

"Is not psycho. Is God," Lupe corrected.

"I believe her," Pastor Valdez added. "He's the God who knows all things. Guess we just don't ask very often about this sort of thing. Did you see anything else, Lupe?"

"No. But I feel. I feel heat. Warm. Like a desert."

"Hmm, well, could be they headed south," Detective Mason said. "Good job, buddy," he said as he passed Beto. "Every little bit helps. Every little bit."

Beto beamed and a ray of hope entered the house.

An hour later, Freddy sat with his disheveled head next to Beto's at the kitchen table, attacking his second plate of tamales. Beto was on his third. After a night with no appetite, the brothers had awoken with growling stomachs. Cynthia and Lupe had happily dished up plates for them and any who were ready to eat. Pastor Valdez had shoveled down a quick plate before heading back to church for the Christmas Day service. He was fortified both in body and spirit after the interesting developments of the early morning, spurred on by Lupe's word of knowledge.

The Agreements

An Amber Alert was issued, and with the distinct possibility that the girls had been taken across state lines, the FBI was notified.

Maria and Hector sat side by side on the couch in the living room with Junior laid out across their laps. He still was not ready to eat or to be far from his dad and mom. His little, warm body gave his parents a certain measure of comfort. The TV was on, but they watched without really seeing a thing. Their eyes drooped with weariness, but sleep only came in short increments of ten or fifteen minutes before rushes of adrenaline shook them back to consciousness.

Maria's phone rang and vibrated on the couch beside her. She glanced down, hoping to see Detective Mason's number, but the number was one she had never seen from somewhere in Nevada. She flipped the phone over and let it ring until it quit, not wanting to have her phone tied up with some telemarketing call, should an important call come in.

Suddenly Hector's phone went off. Without even looking at the number, he picked it up and answered.

"Yeah, this is Hector," he said.

"Papi? Papi, it's me," a sobbing voice filled his ear.

He sat straight up and Junior nearly rolled off onto the floor.

"Rosie! Is that you?"

Maria bolted upright and snatched the phone from his hand.

"Mija, is that you? Are you okay? Where's Jewels? Where are you? Are you hurt?" the questions shot from her belly like a burst dam.

The sobbing on the other end continued without words.

"Oh, hello," a deep male voice came on the line. "Uh, is this Hector or Maria Gomez?"

"Do you have my daughters?" Maria yelled. "If you hurt them, I will track you down and—"

Hector grabbed the phone back from his hysterical wife.

"This is Hector Gomez. Who is this?"

"Uh, this is Frank Longfellow. Say, listen, I'm not gonna hurt your girl here. Uh, Rosie, is okay. She's okay," Frank assured him. "And we're here to help however we can."

Maria jumped from the couch with a befuddled Junior in her arms to meet Lupe, Beto, and Freddy, who were standing in shocked attention all in a row.

"It's Rosie. She's okay," Maria cried, tears flooding her eyes.

The twins enveloped her and Junior in a group hug. Lupe sat next to Hector, who continued his conversation with Frank.

"Julia?" Lupe whispered.

"Say, Frank, can you let me talk to Julia?" Hector asked.

"Well, now, I, uh don't know about her. We just have Rosie here with us. She flagged us down, coming running through our cornfield. Got a couple acres for the cows and such. We was just about to head out for Christmas dinner at my son's, and then there she was in our driveway. Good thing we hadn't left yet."

"But isn't her sister with her?"

"She's been real emotional. My wife has been trying to get the story straight. But from what I can tell, I think the other girl . . . uh, Julia did you say?"

"Yes, yes, Julia."

"She, ah, is still in the truck. Seems she helped Rosie get free but couldn't get out herself."

Hector and Lupe stared into each other's eyes and then back at Maria.

"I'm real sorry to have to tell you that," Frank added.

Hector shook himself back into action.

"Okay, listen, Frank, where are you exactly?"

"We're outside of Sparks, Nevada. 'Bout twenty miles east of there, towards Clark."

Hector flagged down Cynthia, who stood in the hallway wringing a dish towel.

"Cynthia, get Detective Mason on the line. I'm gonna try to talk to Rosie, but I want to get this information to him right away."

Cynthia nodded and hustled to her phone.

Maria turned back to her husband and mother, her sons still by her side.

"What's wrong?" she asked. "Are they hurt?"

Lupe walked over to her daughter.

"It's Julia. She is not with Rosie. He says she is still in the truck."

Maria dropped to her knees with Junior still clinging to her neck.

"No, no, no," she groaned.

Lupe knelt beside them.

"Not just one, Mami," Maria cried into her mother's shoulder. "Not again."

Chapter 29 – The Flyer

New Year's Eve of 2013 was relatively balmy in Grace, ND. A few snowflakes fell in the early morning hours, but by 9:00 a.m., they were well on their way to melted mush.

"Ah jeez," Eric said, leaning against the broom handle and staring out the plate glass window of the post office. "The rink's gonna get sloppy."

"Well, quit standing around then," Nellie said from the other end of the lobby, dumping her dustpan into the large rolling wastebasket beside her. "That's why I came. So you could get out of here early."

Eric resumed his sweeping chore.

"Nobody else has to work on New Year's Eve," he grumbled.

Nellie shook her head and laughed.

"Oh yeah, right. Mucking out stalls and feeding pigs and milking cows—none of that is work."

Eric glared at her.

"Get moving, Gretzky, or they'll start the game without us," she said, slapping her broom like a hockey stick across the linoleum tiles.

A lean, balding man stepped into the lobby from behind the wall of post office boxes and headed toward the front entry.

"You keeping him in line, Nellie?" Mr. Nelson said.

The Agreements

"Yes, sir. We're almost done," she replied.

"You sure you don't want to come and help more often?" he asked, pulling a ring of keys from his pocket. "The place always looks a lot nicer when you've done the cleaning."

"Gee, thanks dad," Eric huffed.

"Well, it's the truth. The girl pays attention to details. You'd do well to follow her example." He stepped through the first set of glass doors and unlocked the second set. "Time to open up shop," he said, reentering the lobby. "Why don't you kids move your operations to the back? I've got a few things for you to do there that won't get in the way of folks coming to check their mail."

"Dad, the guys are waiting for us," Eric moaned.

"And they'll be waiting even longer if you want to stand around and complain," Mr. Nelson said, disappearing through the door that led to the back operations of the mail business.

Nellie and Eric gathered up their cleaning products, brooms, and garbage bins as the front doors opened and in walked Sheriff Probst. Jason shuffled in behind him with his head down and only a quick glance up toward his friends.

"Mornin'," the sheriff said with a tip of his broad-brimmed hat. "Surprised to see you here, Nellie. Thought you might be at the rink by now."

"Just about," Nellie said.

"Well, say, I'm actually glad that I caught the both of you at once," the sheriff said. "I've got something here I'd like you to take a look at. Already showed it to my son, and he says he doesn't know anything about it."

He pulled a letter-sized piece of paper from a manila folder he had tucked under his arm.

"You know how I come down here and post notices for missing kids?" he said.

"Sure. Like those?" Eric said, pointing to the corkboard hanging on a side wall.

"Yup, just like that. Except this one is sort of curious," he replied, staring at the new notice and then up at Nellie. "Now you guys know this is very serious stuff here. Right?"

Eric and Nellie nodded solemnly.

"And if anyone were to, say, think it were funny to make up a missing-persons poster as some sort of prank, they could be in serious trouble? Right?"

"Dad, of course they know that," Jason said. "We're not stupid."

Sheriff Probst gave his son a weighty glare.

"Why don't you just hold your tongue, mister, while we sort this all out?"

Jason let his eyes drop again and stuffed his hands into his parka.

Mr. Nelson's face appeared in the window of the door to the back. He opened the door a crack and stuck his head out.

"Everything okay out here, Lyle?" he asked the Wells County sheriff.

"Well, now, I'm not quite sure, Jack. You wanna come out and take a look at this?"

Mr. Nelson stepped into the lobby, wiping his hands on his pants.

"Mornin', Jason. Come to give your buddies a helping hand?"

Jason did not reply.

"Say good morning, Son," Sheriff Probst said.

"Mornin'," Jason mumbled.

"Look the man in the eye and speak up," his dad said.

"Good morning, sir," Jason enunciated clearly, with his eyes lifted to meet Mr. Nelson's. "Not here to clean the place. But I am here to help my friends . . . and I'm hoping they can help me."

"Well, that's rather cryptic," Mr. Nelson said. "What did you want me to look at, Sheriff?"

He stepped over to the law enforcement officer. The two men stood shoulder to shoulder and stared at the paper, then up at Nellie, and then back at the paper.

"You kids know anything about this?" the postmaster asked, taking the piece of paper and holding it out to them.

Their eyes popped open and they both leaned closer to stare at the picture on the top of the flyer.

The Agreements

"It looks like Nellie . . . 'cept with long hair," Eric said.

"That's what I said," Jason added.

"That about sums it up, alright," said Sheriff Probst. "Got any ideas about where it came from?"

Nellie was still staring at the flyer. Her face had gone completely white.

"Now Eric, if you or your buddies had something to do with this, we can get it taken care of right now," he said. "As long as it never happens again."

"We didn't do this," Eric said. "I swear. Wouldn't even know how."

"Told ya," Jason mumbled.

"Well, somebody did," Mr. Nelson said, putting a hand on his son's shoulder. "You think it might be some of the older kids, like Karl Franks, maybe? Maybe he hasn't gotten over that race you told me about with Nellie."

"I'll look into that," Sheriff Probst said. "That's a good idea. Anybody else you can think of, Nellie?"

"Maybe it's Mr. Jones," Eric said. "He's about as pissed off as anybody could be at Nellie."

"Watch your language there, son," Mr. Nelson said. "But you have a good point."

"Yeah, I wondered about that too," Sheriff Nelson said, typing notes into his phone.

"You okay?" Eric said to Nellie. "You look like you've seen a ghost."

Slowly she lifted her eyes to meet Eric's.

"I think she's my . . . my sister," she whispered.

"Huh?" he replied. "I thought she was dead."

"Yeah, me too," Jason said.

Nellie's head dropped to her chest.

"Guys, be nice. Can't you see she's scared?" the postmaster chided.

"Sorry. But it's the truth. Isn't it, Nel?" Eric said.

She nodded.

203

"Oh, I'm sure there's some explanation other than a ghost," Sheriff Probst said, pushing his phone into his pocket. "I'll just take that for safekeeping." He tugged the paper gently from Nellie's clenched hand.

"But it says Julia," she said.

"Yes, it does. But other folks know you had a sister named Julia," he added. "We're gonna find out who's behind this. I promise."

"Where does it say she went missing from?" Jack Nelson asked.

"Someplace out in Eastern Washington. Town called La Verdad. Family name of Gomez. That's about all I know. But that may be just a bunch of hooey too. I'm gonna go do some more checking." The sheriff placed the notice back into the folder and tipped his hat before placing a firm hand on Jason's shoulder. "Let's go. Time to lace up those skates."

"Believe me now?" Jason said as the two headed out the door.

"Never said I didn't believe you," his dad said. "Just said I needed more information."

The trio left standing in the Grace post office were somber and silent.

"How about we get through these last few chores and then you two can grab your skates and go join Jason?" Mr. Nelson said.

"Come on, Nel."

Eric put his hand in Nellie's and gently tugged. For once, she didn't resist his leading.

It was only much later in the afternoon that Mr. Nelson saw the name on the large box at the bottom of the sorting bin. The packages had arrived from Bismarck on the noon truck, and he was just getting around to getting through all of them. It was addressed to Nellie Jolicoeur, care of Claude Jolicoeur. The postmark was from Seattle, but the return address said Brooklyn, New York.

The box was too big to fit into the Jolicoeur PO box.

He slapped himself on the forehead.

"It's her birthday tomorrow," he said.

He decided then and there that he would make a special delivery to the Jolicoeur place right after work. It was the least he could do for his best junior janitor, especially considering the strange doings of the morning.

As Claude drove around the house and up the driveway, he noticed all the lights were out, save for a small flicker behind the shades in the family room.

"Nellie, I'm home," he announced as he entered through the back door, kicked off his boots, and hung his coat behind the door.

"Hello? Anybody here?" he hollered, flicking on the kitchen lights and then the one in the hall as he shuffled down the hallway in his stocking feet, coming to a halt behind the couch in the family room. Nellie lay cocooned in her purple-and-yellow fleece blanket along the couch's length, her eyes glued to some sort of snowboarding competition playing on the big-screen TV.

"Sorry I'm so late," he said. "Had quite the lineup of rigs today. Wasn't expecting it to be so busy on New Year's Eve. You eat yet?"

Nellie shook her head.

"How was the hockey game?" he asked.

"Okay."

"Score any goals?"

"Nope. Cami."

"Hey, that's great. She's getting to be quite the skater. You ever hang out with her?"

"Sometimes."

"Just think it might be nice for you to have some girlfriends, ya know."

"Whatever."

Seeing that his granddaughter was not exactly in a talkative mood, he opted to retreat to the kitchen.

"I'll whip up some French toast and bacon. Sound good?" he asked.

"Whatever."

He sighed and headed to the fridge, where a bright pink note hung, stuck under a magnet of Mount Rushmore.

"Fresh eggs. Top shelf. Elsie," it said. He smiled, wondering how she always seemed to know just when they needed to restock.

"Did Elsie—uh, Mrs. Shatzenpfeffer stop by?" he yelled down the hall.

"Yeah," came the response.

"Did you thank her for the eggs?"

"No."

"Why not?"

"Forgot."

It was a roller coaster, this parenting thing. About the time he was patting himself on the back about what a wonderful girl he was raising, he got reminders that there was still a long way to go. He pulled the fresh eggs from the fridge, along with bacon and milk, and set them on the counter. He was retrieving a pan from the bottom drawer of the stove when someone knocked on the back door.

"You expecting anyone?" he hollered, making his way to the door.

No response.

He set the pan on the stove and moved to get the door.

"Well, Jack," he said, seeing the postmaster on his back stoop. "What can I do for ya? Come on in. Did ya eat yet? I'm just about to make us some dinner. You're welcome to join us."

"Thanks, but no. I'm on my way home. I got this in today and thought I would get it to you right away, seeing as we're closed tomorrow," Jack Nelson said, holding the box out to Claude. "I know it's Nellie's birthday tomorrow and didn't want her to miss out on any presents."

"That's mighty thoughtful of you," Claude said, taking the box. "Golly, this thing is heavy."

"Yeah, makes you wonder what might be in there," Jack said.

Claude turned the box around to read the return address label.

"Flanagan, Brooklyn, New York," he read aloud. "Hmm, that's weird."

"I sort of thought so, too, since the postmark isn't New York, but Seattle."

"That is a bit odd, but the really weird thing is this looks like it must be from Nellie's friend, Mrs. Flanagan. She passed away several months ago. Her son sent me the obituary."

"Where does he live?"

"Ah, yup. That's probably it. I think he's out in Seattle. Must be from him."

"Well, hope it's something good," Jack said, beginning to back down the stairs. "Have a good New Year's, and tell Nellie happy birthday."

"Will do. And thanks for getting this to us," Claude said as he slowly shut the door and stared at the box in his arms.

"What's that?" Nellie said from her spot in the middle of the kitchen doorway. She was still draped in her fleece blanket.

"Well, I'm, uh, not totally sure," Claude said. He set the box on the table. "It's for you. Seems like it might be something from Mrs. Flanagan."

"Didn't she die?"

Claude nodded and tucked his hands into the depths of his Wranglers.

"Then what do ya mean it's from her?" Nellie said.

"Got her address on the return label. But I think her son sent it. Might be something she had set aside for you."

"Can I open it?"

Nellie walked to the table and ran a hand tentatively over the box. The two stared at the package. Claude turned and grabbed a pair of scissors from the hook beside the refrigerator.

"The suspense is killing me," he said. "Let's get her opened up."

Nellie's face lit up as she put the scissors to work on the plentiful layers of tape that secured the box. At last, the top flaps sprung free and Nellie gave the scissors back to her grandpa before pushing the flaps open. A picture of a girl of seven or eight in a pink, sparkly tutu standing with her arms in soft, open curves lay on top of a pile of papers. The girl's dark hair was pulled back from her face in a bun, and a cautious smile underlined her deep-blue eyes.

The blanket dropped to the floor as Nellie's hands flew to her mouth.

"What is it?" Claude said, coming back to the table from having returned the scissors to their rightful spot. He peered into the box, reached in, and lifted out the five-by-seven picture of the young ballerina.

"Holy cow. Never seen you in a tutu before," he said. "How the heck could somebody do this? Some sort of computer thing or something?"

Nellie slowly retrieved the next piece of paper from under the cardboard flaps. It was a crayon drawing of the Twin Towers. Fire spurted out from the sides of the buildings and angels filled the sky. On the bottom of the page was written "We will not forget." And it was signed.

Julia Gomez.

Nellie let out a cry and dropped the drawing like a hot potato.

"Did you know?"

Nellie glared at her grandfather with such severity that he put his hands up in self-defense.

"Hey, hey, what's going on?" Claude asked. "Did I know what?"

He picked up the discarded drawing. His eyebrows furrowed and his pulse quickened.

The back door reverberated again with three loud knocks. Claude backed up to the door and pulled it open, still peering at the childish sketch and then back at his seething granddaughter.

"Evenin'," Sheriff Probst said. "Mind if I come in?"

Claude motioned him in.

"Got something on your mind, Sheriff? We're sort of in the middle of something here," Claude said.

"Sorry to interrupt. But, uh, you're gonna want to hear this. Nellie," the sheriff said, removing his hat and holding it in two hands in front of his belt, "I, uh . . . well, I did some checking . . . and, well, I don't know how to tell you this, but—"

"She's alive, isn't she?"

The sheriff nodded.

"What is going on here?" Claude looked back and forth between the law enforcement officer and his granddaughter.

"Well, Claude, it would appear that Nellie's twin sister, Julia, is alive."

Claude put both hands onto the back of a chair to steady himself.

"Say what?"

The sheriff reached into his pocket and drew out the missing-persons flyer. He unfolded it and handed it to Claude.

"She's alive, but . . ."

Sheriff Probst lowered his head and twirled his hat.

Nellie suddenly turned and ran for the stairs, taking them two at a time. Her bedroom door slammed so hard, the mugs hanging from pegs on the kitchen wall rattled. Claude stared up the path Nellie had beaten as the sound of objects hitting walls resounded from her room.

"Need me to go check on her?" the sheriff offered.

"Uh, no. Best to leave her alone for a bit, I think," he said, peering back at the missing-persons flyer in his hand. "You mean to tell me Julia is alive?"

"Yes, sir. That would appear to be the case."

"But how?"

"Don't rightly know just yet."

"And she's missing?"

"That appears to be the case, as well."

Crashing glass coupled with an agonized cry from upstairs filled the house. Sheriff Probst dropped his hat on the table as he raced across the kitchen and up the stairs with Claude close behind him.

Wendy Jo Cerna

Chapter 30 – The Captor

It was her fourteenth birthday, but Carlyle was pretty sure Julia was unaware of that fact. She lay curled up under her coat on a filthy mattress that neither cushioned nor shielded her from the cold cement floor. Three other girls on three other mattresses lay crammed next to her in the cold, windowless room. The metal door was locked and bolted shut. A plastic bucket sat in the corner for use as a toilet, its reeking aroma only partially stymied by a plastic bag they used as a lid. A lone light bulb shone from the ceiling with a frayed string for a cord. Without its frail light, the darkness would have been absolute.

They were all asleep due to the latest round of whatever drug it was their captors used to subdue them. Carlyle knew the drug was in itself an evil thing, but he couldn't help but feel a sense of relief for Julia whenever she could experience a few hours of oblivion from her situation. It was the third such horrid prison that she had been in over the past three days. It was nearly inconceivable to him that she had wound up in such circumstances.

After Rosie's escape, Raúl and Rico had argued all the way to Southern California about what to do with Julia—right in front of her, as if she weren't even human but some sort of

The Agreements

merchandise. Raúl wanted to just dump her at a rest stop somewhere and head for the border. He was done with the whole escapade and wanted nothing further from it except to save his own skin. Besides, he reasoned, he had accomplished his main goal, which was to cause his brother pain.

Rico, on the other hand, was not content with that minor achievement. He wanted money. And he convinced Raúl that he knew a way to get some.

They ditched the box truck in the Wholesale District of Los Angeles. A peroxide blonde dressed in leopard-print leggings and a barely there tank top came and picked them up in a shiny red convertible. Her unabashed public display of affection with Rico left no doubt in Carlyle's mind that the two were intimately acquainted. He hoped that maybe, just maybe, the woman, who was in reality only a girl herself, might be sympathetic to Julia's predicament. And at first, she seemed as if she might be.

They drove together to a ramshackle little house not far from LAX. While Rico and Raúl plotted in the kitchen, the woman, named Cassandra, took Julia to the bathroom and helped her find everything she might need for a shower.

"It'll make everything seem better," Cassandra told Julia as she hung out in the bathroom with her, humming along to Beyoncé tunes that blared from her phone and reapplying her makeup while Julia showered, allowing the steaming water to pour over her and slip down the rusty-rimmed bath drain. Cassandra even offered Julia a change of clothes, which she politely declined, preferring her disheveled Christmas dress over the skimpy jean skirt and halter top offered to her.

"Mmkay," Cassandra said. "But you gonna stick out like a sore thumb."

"To who?" Julia asked.

"Whoever see ya."

"But who's gonna see me?"

"Shit, girl, you ask too many questions," Cassandra replied with a raised eyebrow. "But you stick with me, and maybe we can get you outta this mess you all in."

"Would you help me?" Julia asked. "Would you call my dad and mom? Please. They've gotta be so worried. Please."

Cassandra appeared to be contemplating doing just that when Rico barged into the room and hauled Julia out by her wrist.

"Don't get all chummy, you two," Rico warned sternly.

It wasn't until later, much later, that the wink that passed between Rico and Cassandra behind Julia's back registered with Carlyle.

They locked Julia in the bathroom overnight. She tried everything she knew to escape—from attempting to pick the lock to removing the hinges on the door—but her attempts were quickly squelched and her imprisonment further fortified with a chair stuck under the doorknob in the hallway. She cried herself to sleep on the grungy linoleum floor with the damp, threadbare towel Cassandra had scrounged up for her as a pillow.

After only a few hours of sleep, Carlyle jumped to his feet as he heard the chair being removed from the hall and the door lock popping open. Julia was so tired, Cassandra had to shake her by the shoulders to get her to wake up.

"Shh," she said with a finger over her lips. "You want outta here?"

Suddenly awake, Julia sat bolt upright and nodded vigorously.

"Then follow me," Cassandra said.

She led her past Rico's snoring form sprawled on the bed in the room near the bathroom, past Raúl's equally dormant body curled up on the couch in the living room under a tattered windbreaker, through the odor of stale beer and cold pizza drifting from the kitchen, and out the front door. They ran down the broken-up sidewalk beside the already-busy four-lane street in the early morning hour.

"Where are we going?" Julia whispered as they ran.

Cassandra laughed.

"You don't gotta whisper no more. We shook those losers. They gonna sleep 'til noon, and we'll be long gone. Come on."

She grabbed Julia's hand as they continued to run away from the house and toward a busy commercial intersection. Carlyle

The Agreements

remembered the furtive glance he took back at the house, making sure they weren't being followed. He had shaken off the notion that he had seen Rico peering through the iron bars of the bedroom window. He remembered thinking that surely that had just been his paranoia. If Rico had seen them escaping, surely he would have busted down the door and raced after them.

It was several more intersections later, at a McDonald's where people headed to work were ordering Egg McMuffins and McCafés, that they stopped.

"Can I use your phone to call my dad?" Julia asked right away.

Cassandra pulled her phone out of an interior pocket of her jean jacket. She pressed some buttons and hmphed.

"Crap, I forgot to charge it," she said. "Gonna have to find someone with a cord or something." She replaced the phone into its secure spot in her jacket and then searched through several other pockets. "Hey, I got a few bucks. You hungry?"

Julia's crestfallen face brightened slightly, and they went to the counter and ordered breakfast. As they were just about finished with their meal, two teenage girls walked through the front doors. They were dressed in matching black uniforms, with snug wraparound tops that dipped precariously low in front and skintight black leggings. A red logo was embroidered along the rim of each left breast pocket.

Cassandra jumped up.

"OMG," she yelled as the two girls rushed over to her and they all hugged like long-lost friends. "I can't even believe it. What are you guys doing here?"

Julia listened quietly as the three chatted it up. Finally, Cassandra turned back to her and stared at her and then back at her friends, as if a scathingly brilliant idea was being hatched under her bleached roots.

"Julia, these are my friends, Tina and Char." As she introduced them, the girls sat down one on either side of Julia. "They work, like, just down the street at a totally rad spa. Hey, you guys got a phone on ya?"

Both girls shook their heads.

"Nah, we left 'em at work."

"Dang. Julia really needs to make a call," Cassandra said, stuffing the last of her muffin into her mouth. "But you think it might be okay to take her to the spa and get her some help?"

"You in trouble?" the one called Char said.

Julia looked at Cassandra, who said, "Go 'head. Tell 'em. I ain't even heard your whole story yet."

And so, Julia told them the whole sordid tale. The girls seemed interested, appalled, and compassionate at all the appropriate moments. And Carlyle again hoped that rescue was just around the corner.

"I was so scared. Rico and Tío were talking about some guy that might want to buy me like a prostitute or something," Julia quietly admitted.

Tina choked on the sip she was taking from Cassandra's Diet Coke.

Char reached out and touched Julia's arm.

"That is so crazy," she whispered.

"Good thing you ran into us," Tina managed to say between attempts to clear her vocal cords of soda.

Carlyle was so excited.

They took Julia to the spa and situated her in a well-outfitted room with a glass of sparkling water and the promise of a cell phone. He watched her relax against the plush upholstery of an overstuffed chair and sigh. And he joined her with a sigh of great relief.

Until he heard the deadbolt slide into place on the door.

Then the real nightmare had begun.

Carlyle was brought back into the present situation at that same sound. But this time the deadbolt was sliding back and the door being unlocked. A big, burly guy dressed in a skintight black T-shirt, designed no doubt to accentuate the rippling muscles beneath it, stepped in and kicked at the feet of the girl lying next to Julia.

"Get up," he demanded. "And clean up."

He threw a damp towel into the girl's face. She slowly pulled the towel off and sat up, her head bobbing and her eyes still closed.

"Jeez, Manny, give me a sec," the girl grumbled.

"Five minutes. Put this on," Manny said, dropping a slinky, pink dress next to her and exiting.

The dead bolt slid back into place.

Cassandra, Tina, and Char had disappeared after their successful mission of luring Julia into the trap. What they got out of the deal, Carlyle could only imagine. Over the course of the last three days, they had been replaced by a series of nameless, faceless girls of varying ages, shapes, and ethnicities, all evidently equally as ensnared as Julia.

Julia's eyes opened and she watched the girl strip off her black spa uniform like an automaton. She wiped the towel over her face, neck, arms, and body. The dark bruises that marked her torso and thighs caused Julia to cringe.

"Where are you going?" Julia whispered.

The girl turned to her with blank eyes.

"To work."

"But . . . I thought you had to wear your uniform . . ."

The girl, who must've been only slightly older than Julia, let out a brittle laugh.

"Different uniform for different work," she said as she slipped the pink dress over her body. As if by magic, every sign of abuse disappeared under its skimpy covering.

"Why don't you have a uniform?" the girl said, eyeing Julia's coat and bedraggled dress.

Julia shrugged.

"I don't think I'm qualified to work in a spa."

The girl stared for a second and then asked, "You a girl?"

Julia nodded.

"Then you're qualified," the older girl said, tugging the plunging neckline even lower.

Manny reentered the room and ran his eyes over the girl.

"Get your hair up," he ordered, and the girl pulled her straight black hair into a bun. "Better," he said. "I'll be right back."

He threw a dress at the next girl's feet as he grabbed the one in the pink dress by the wrist. She offered no resistance as they left the cramped quarters.

Carlyle watched as one by one the cell emptied until only Julia was left. She sat with her back against the wall and her knees drawn up to her chin. Her fingers rubbed the cross that hung around her neck. Her Christmas dress that stuck out from under her coat was dirty and torn.

Once again, the door swung open. A pit of anxiety and anger grew in Carlyle's insides. How could the Designer not intervene? Carlyle knew that if he had it within his power, he himself would find a way to rescue these girls and punish their captors. But his hands were tied. He wished he could simply turn away and not see what he was seeing.

In walked Manny. Next to him was another man Carlyle had never seen before—a young, athletic-looking man dressed in an expensive suit, with gold jewelry sparkling on his neck, wrist, and fingers. His dark blond hair was slicked back from his face and a musky cologne wafted all around him.

"This the new girl?" the guy in the suit asked Manny.

"Yup, just got her in last night, Boss."

"Stand up," the boss ordered Julia.

Julia pressed back against the wall and used it to help her stand.

"Pretty, maybe, if you got her cleaned up," the boss said.

"Yeah, fresh too. Don't think Rico had a chance to ruin her, from what I can tell. Had to shuttle her around pretty good though," Manny said.

"Oh, yeah? She got people looking? Thought Rico told you she was an orphan."

"As far as I know, just got an uncle who was more than happy to get rid of her."

They spoke quietly to each other as if Julia couldn't understand a word they said. Or as if it didn't matter if she did.

"Yeah. It's been kinda weird. We get her settled in and all of a sudden the cops show up. Twice now, like she's got some kinda GPS on her or something," Manny said.

"Well, does she?" the boss asked.

"If she does, we can't find it."

The man raked his eyes over Julia from head to toe.

"Get her outta that coat and party dress and into something nicer. Then bring her up to my office. I think I'll see to this one myself," the boss said. "But run her through the shower first. And empty that thing, will ya?" he said, pointing to the bucket. "Customers are starting to complain."

"Yes, sir," Manny said as his boss exited. Turning to Julia, he said, "Time to grow up, little miss. Let's go."

He held the door open for Julia. Carlyle watched her face as what little color she had in her cheeks drained away completely.

The plate of fruit slices, cheese, and crackers reflected in the deep blue of Julia's eyes as she stared at it. She almost looked like herself again, Carlyle noted, after the shower and fresh change of clothes. But not quite. Her face was sallow, and the enormity of the white leather couch she sat on made her appear younger than she was. The new dress she'd been given was silky blue and sleeveless. She had begged Manny to let her keep her coat on, and for unknown reasons, he had acquiesced.

"Go ahead. It's for you," the boss said from his leather chair on the other side of the glass coffee table. One leg lay crossed at the knee over the other, and his foot bobbed slowly up and down inside its fine Italian boot. "What would you like to drink?"

"Um, just water, please," she replied before reaching out to the food with shaking fingers. She piled two slices of cheese and some apple slices between two crackers and stuffed it into her mouth. Crumbs sprinkled down onto her lap. She brushed them into her hand and licked them off.

"Take it easy," the man laughed. "You can have as much as you want."

He poured water from a beautiful silver pitcher into a tall glass.

"Ice?" he asked.

Julia shook her head.

"Ah, yes, silly of me to ask. I can see you're a bit chilly as it is. Perhaps a bit of food will warm you up and we can get rid of that old coat."

Julia tugged the open flaps of her coat tighter.

"So, Julia . . . that's your name, right?"

She nodded again while making another cracker sandwich.

"My name is Winston, but the girls just call me Win."

Julia peered at him and popped the food into her mouth.

"How old are you?" he continued.

She took a gulp from the water and wiped her lips with the back of her hand.

"What day is it?" she asked.

Winston laughed.

"Do you keep track of your age by the day?"

She stared at him without so much as a smile.

"Well, it's actually New Year's Eve. At least for a few more minutes," he said after consulting his thick gold watch.

"Then I'm fourteen."

"You weren't fourteen yesterday?"

She shook her head again as she chewed another generous mouthful.

"Is today your birthday?"

He leaned forward, onto his knees.

Julia nodded.

He slapped his pleated wool pants and stood up.

"Then we must have a special celebration," he announced.

Carlyle stayed close by Julia's side as the boss man went behind a bar at the side of the room and bent down to retrieve something. He reemerged with a dark green glass bottle in his hand.

"Since it's both New Year's and your birthday, we must have champagne," he said.

The Agreements

What adult thought giving a fourteen-year-old champagne for her birthday was appropriate? Carlyle steamed the thought over in his mind.

Winston set two champagne flutes on the counter from off a hanging rack. He carefully worked the cork until it popped and shot up into the air. Julia recoiled at the unexpected noise, making him laugh again.

"It's wonderful stuff," he said as he captured the overflowing bubbly in the two glasses. "I think you're going to like it. It's sure to warm you up."

He glided back to the couch and handed a glass to Julia before sitting right next to her.

"To your fourteenth birthday," he said, raising his glass in the air.

Julia held the glass near her lap.

"Well, come on. Raise a glass," Winston urged.

Julia shook her head.

"I'm not supposed to drink alcohol."

Winston took a swig from his glass and set it on the table. He took Julia's glass and set it next to his.

"Who are you, Miss Julia, that you are so prim and proper?"

"Lita says I'm a daughter of the King," Julia said quietly.

Winston sat back and perused her face carefully.

"A princess, is it? And here I'd heard you were an orphan."

Julia stared into her lap.

"I am an orphan," she whispered.

Winston reached out and pulled one of her hands into his.

"Well, then, we have something in common," he said.

She looked up into his eyes.

"What happened to your parents?" she asked softly.

"My mother died when I was very young in a boating accident. I don't even remember her," he said, stroking a finger over her palm. "And my father, well, he died trying to be a hero."

"I'm sorry."

"No need for that," he said with a sharp laugh. "He wasn't much of a father, really. More devoted to his business than his family. What about you? How did you wind up all alone in the world?"

"I'm not all alone," she said, retrieving her hand. "I have a family. They adopted me after my parents died in the Twin Towers."

Winston Chambers's spine stiffened and his head cocked.

"On 9/11?" he said.

She nodded.

He reached for his glass of champagne and took a long draw. For the first time since he'd entered into the presence of the man, Carlyle detected a slight glow from his heart light. It was a deep, deep blue with hints of gold. But then, as quickly as it appeared, it was snuffed out, as if drowned by the alcohol.

"Well, my little orphan," he said, setting the glass back down and leaning forward to cup her face in his outstretched hand. "We are more alike than you know."

Julia tried to pull back, but Winston clamped his fingers around her chin.

"Relax," he said. "Things will go better if you'll just relax."

"What things?"

Winston stood and pulled her upright.

"Things only a man like me can show a princess like you." He tugged a side of her jacket off one shoulder and bent down to kiss her revealed skin. Julia tried to jump away, but he had her hands firmly in his grip. "Don't make me hurt you."

Julia froze.

"Come with me, little princess."

He yanked her forward, toward a door on the other side of the office. His charming politeness had been replaced with a harsh edge.

Just then the lights in the entire room began to blink off and on. Winston's phone went off. He reached into his pocket with one hand while keeping Julia close with the other.

"I told you, I don't want to be disturbed," he hissed into the phone.

The voice on the other end sounded urgent. Carlyle watched as the arrogant confidence that had been on Winston's face morphed into rage.

"Get my car. Meet me at the back. Now!"

He dragged Julia to a bookshelf and pressed a button under the third shelf. The bookshelf slid to one side and an opening at the top of a stairway appeared. He pushed her through the opening and hit another button that caused the shelf to begin to close.

"What the hell is so important about you?" he said over his shoulder as he dragged her down the stairs.

Carlyle followed close behind them as they reached a heavy metal door at the bottom of the stairs. Winston cracked it open. The sound of sirens split the air. A deep-gray BMW zipped up to the door with Manny behind the wheel. Winston ran toward it, opened the back door, and pushed Julia into the back seat. He jumped in behind her.

"Go, get out of here," Winston ordered, hitting the back of the leather driver's seat.

Carlyle watched out the back window as they peeled down the alley. Girls in various degrees of dress dashed out of back exits and fled in the opposite direction. He cheered their escape, but the cheers stuck in his throat at Winston's next words.

"You, little orphan-princess," he said, sticking a finger under Julia's chin, "you may be more trouble than you're worth."

Julia slid as far away from Win as possible and gripped the armrest on the door as the car zipped and skidded around corners.

"Take us to the plane," Winston ordered Manny. "Feels like SoCal has gotten a little too hot. Let's see what Seattle is like this time of year."

Chapter 31 – The Intervention

It wasn't hard to locate Elsie Shatzenpfeffer on New Year's Day. The First Lutheran Church was having a special service to call in the new year with prayer and song. She was in her usual Sunday-morning spot in the fifth pew back from the right when Deputy Bollinger tapped her on the shoulder and motioned for Elsie to come with her. The thirty or so other gathered believers watched the two women hustle down the side aisle into the foyer as the pastor led the crowd in singing, "O God, our help in ages past / Our hope for years to come."

"I'm really sorry to interrupt you. But we've got a situation out at the Jolicoeur place. We're hoping you can help," the deputy said.

"Of course. I'll do whatever I can. Has someone been hurt?" Elsie asked.

"Well, no, not yet at least."

"What do you mean? What's going on?"

"Grab your coat and I'll explain everything on the way."

Elsie hustled across the foyer to the coat closet. She thrust her hands through the camel wool sleeves, pushing out her gloves and scarf as she did. With practiced motions, she wrapped, buttoned, and gloved herself on her way out the front doors. Deputy Bollinger was waiting for her in her black-and-gold sheriff's department rig.

The Agreements

Elsie climbed in and the SUV took off with lights flashing. Elsie buckled her seat belt.

"What's this all about, Karen?" she asked.

"Seems Claude fell off the wagon last night," Karen Bollinger replied.

"Oh, no."

"Nellie called us about thirty minutes ago. He had gotten a bit aggressive with her."

"Did he hit her?"

"Don't think so, but scared her pretty good," the deputy said, whipping the steering wheel around as they cornered onto county road 191. "Scared himself, too, from the looks of things."

"What has he done?"

"Got himself barricaded into a bedroom on the top floor. Nellie thinks he's got a gun with him."

"Oh, dear God."

Elsie prayed quietly under her breath as the SUV rumbled onto the gravel drive leading to the Jolicoeur house. Sheriff Probst's rig was there, along with two other Wells County vehicles.

"Got the whole cavalry here," Karen said, pulling to a halt beside her boss's truck.

"What do you need me to do?" Elsie asked.

"Come in and talk with the Sheriff. He's got a plan."

"Is Claude . . . do you think he might be dangerous?"

"We think the danger is mainly to himself."

Elsie took a deep breath and squared her shoulders before opening her door. She picked her way across the frozen ruts of the driveway behind the deputy and entered the house through the back door. Inside the kitchen, Sheriff Probst and his two other deputies stood in a close huddle. Nellie rushed from the stool where she was sitting into Elsie's arms even before the older woman was all the way through the door.

"I didn't mean to make him so mad," Nellie cried. "Please help him."

Elsie wrapped the pajama-clad girl in a hug as best she could, being a few inches shorter than the growing teen.

"I'm gonna try, sweetheart. I'm sure gonna try," she said.

The law enforcement officers opened rank and the sheriff stepped over to the new arrival.

"Thanks for coming," Sheriff Probst said. "Quite the deal here. Never seen him like this before."

"No, it's been a very long time since anyone's seen him like this," Elsie said.

Nellie stuck close to Elsie's side, their hands intertwined between them.

"Any idea what set him off?" Elsie asked.

"Now that's a long story," Deputy Bollinger said. "But here it is in a nutshell."

The deputy commenced to give a brief synopsis of the recent developments in and around the flyer, the mysterious box, and the realities about Julia. He also summarized Nellie's shocked reaction he had helped mediate the night before. Elsie listened in stunned attention.

"My goodness," she said when the briefing was over. "That is . . . uh . . . that is very unexpected."

"He kept saying, 'I shoulda known. I shoulda checked. This never would have happened,' stuff like that," Nellie added to the story. "I was so mad I just didn't think about . . . about him."

Elsie slipped her arm around Nellie's waist.

"Blaming himself for pretty much everything, it seems," the sheriff surmised.

"How much has he had to drink?" Elsie asked.

A deputy held up two empty bottles of Jack Daniels.

Elsie's eyebrows shot up, but she gave no comment.

"That's all we know of. Might have more with him. Haven't been able to get him to open the door. That's where you come in, Elsie. Nellie says Claude listens to you better than anyone," Sheriff Probst said.

"Well, I'm not sure that's true," Elsie shrugged.

"Is so," Nellie said.

"Whether it is or isn't, you're the best bet we've got right now. Ready to give it a go?" the sheriff asked. "I'll be right there in the

The Agreements

hallway with you. Karen will stay down here with Nellie, and I'm gonna post these two outside in case . . . well, in case he tries some sort of crazy escape. Okay?"

Elsie blew out a quick breath and her wispy salt-and-pepper bangs lifted briefly off her forehead.

"Okay. I'll try."

Deputy Bollinger extracted Nellie's hand from Elsie's and led her to the cushioned seat under the window. The other two deputies headed outside while Elsie and the sheriff mounted the creaking stairs to the second floor. As they approached the closed bedroom door at the end of the hallway, the sounds of whispered and slurred self-reprisals slipped under the door.

"Stupid, stupid, stupid," Claude said over and over. A loud bang like a fist hitting a desk caused Elsie to jump backward into the sheriff.

"It's okay," he said, steadying his negotiator and easing her toward the door. He set her slightly to the right of the doorframe for safety's sake.

She tapped quietly on the door. Claude's moaning ceased.

"Claude, it's Elsie," she said.

"Go 'way."

"Well now, I don't think that's such a good idea. Seems to me like you could use a friend right now," she said, checking back with the sheriff.

He nodded his encouragement.

Quiet filled the narrow hallway.

"Claude? Are you listening to me?" Elsie prompted.

"Don' wanna listen," came the reply. "Heard too much."

"Yes, I know all about that. About Julia. That's quite a surprise."

"I shoulda known!" he yelled.

Elsie flinched back against the wall.

"Wait," Sheriff Probst mouthed to her. "Breathe."

She closed her eyes and did as instructed.

"Okay," the sheriff whispered. "Try again."

She leaned back toward the door.

"Claude, we can work this through together. But you've got to calm down," she said. "You hear me?"

A moment passed.

"Yeah, I hear."

"Okay, well, I'm not sure how all this happened with Julia, but I'm sure the sheriff is going to help you figure that all out. But you know what my Earl would have said, don't ya?"

The cuckoo clock in the living room sounded the half hour. More seconds ticked by.

"Can't change the pass at the bot'em of a bot'el," Claude's answer was spoken so quietly Elsie almost missed it.

"That's right, that's right."

She turned to the sheriff. He gave her a thumbs-up.

"Do you think maybe you could open the door, Claude, and let me in?" she asked.

"Jus' you?"

"Yes, just me. Just you and me. We can talk this through, and nobody has to get hurt. Okay?"

The scraping of a chair along the wooden floor inside the bedroom caused Sheriff Probst to back up into an alcove.

"I'll be right here," he whispered to Elsie. "Keep the door open."

She nodded.

Whatever was propped under the door handle was removed and the lock popped up before the bedroom door squeaked open. Claude stood unsteadily in his undershirt and jeans. His eyes were bleary, his silver hair a tousled mess, and his cheeks covered in white stubble. In his hand, lying alongside his leg, was a shotgun.

"Now, Claude," Elsie said. "I'm not gonna talk to you with a gun in your hand. Can we set that outside the door while we talk?"

He stared at his friend and then down at the gun and then back at her.

Slowly he lifted it to her. She grabbed it with both hands and gingerly set it in the corner of the hall.

"Thank you," she said. "Mind if I come in?"

The Agreements

Claude swung his arm wide and staggered to a chair by the window. Elsie took up a spot on the end of the bed and began to talk. Claude's head hung on his chest and tears dripped onto his lap as she spoke quietly and gently of all the good in his life: of Nellie and his friends in Grace and of his many years of business and service to his community. She praised his faithfulness and work ethic, his sincerity and skill, his wisdom and patience. And she spoke of a new day. A fresh chapter. That tomorrow could be day one—again.

Claude's breathing deepened and his chin dropped farther. Elsie leaned closer. He was asleep. She tiptoed out into the hallway and summoned the sheriff. He slid out of his hiding place and into the room. He pulled the handcuffs from his pocket.

"Do you have to do that?" Elsie whispered.

"Afraid so. Gonna take him to the station for the night," Sheriff Probst said, slipping the cuffs over the sleeping man's wrists before waking him.

Claude's eyes opened and blinked several times.

"Come on, buddy," the sheriff said. "Time to go dry out."

Claude stood to his feet with the sheriff's help and staggered across the braided rug. He stopped in front of Elsie.

"Sorry," he said to her. "Shoulda checked. Shoulda known," he murmured on his way down the stairs.

Elsie stopped at the top of the stairs and tried to gather herself. She had begun to shake as soon as the sheriff placed Claude in the handcuffs. Several deep breaths and a quick prayer of thanksgiving slowed her racing heart. Even so, she gripped the handrail and took the steps slowly on her way into the kitchen. Nellie sat huddled staring out the window, watching her grandpa being tucked into the back of one of the deputy's sedans.

Deputy Bollinger met Elsie beside the table.

"You able to take Nellie for the night?" she asked.

Nellie's head swung around at the mention of her name.

"Yes, of course," Elsie said. "I could use some girl time. How about you?" She reached out a hand to Nellie and the girl untangled her legs and stood to accept it. "Why don't you go upstairs and change? Grab a few things for overnight?"

Nellie nodded and turned to go to her room.

"Oh, and Nellie," Elsie said. Nellie stopped halfway up the stairs with her back still turned. "Don't think I've forgotten."

Nellie turned slightly.

"There's a cake and ice cream waiting for you at my house. Your grandpa asked me a few days ago to have it ready for you after church today before . . . well, before all this happened."

Nellie acknowledged the news with a small tip of her head before continuing on her way.

"It's her birthday today?" Deputy Bollinger asked when she was out of sight.

Elsie nodded.

"Fourteen. Today."

"Heck of a way to celebrate," the deputy remarked.

Friday morning found Claude Jolicoeur sitting up on the bottom bunk in his cell at the Wells County Jail. He was dressed the same as he had been the night before, save for the fleece pullover stamped with the sheriff's department logo over the right chest. Sheriff Probst stood beside the open cell door with a sheet of paper in his hands.

"Been chatting with the law enforcement folks out in Washington State," he said, perusing the report he held. "They were happy to hear from me. Seems they were attempting to contact you yesterday afternoon but couldn't reach you."

Claude ran a hand over his stubbled face and nodded.

"Did you tell 'em where to find me?" Claude asked.

"Well, now, you know I had to, Claude."

Claude slumped back against the wall.

"Suppose that won't work in my favor far as Julia goes?"

"Don't suppose it will."

The Agreements

"Have they found her yet?"

The sheriff shook his head.

"Don't know all the details, but it seems she and another younger girl were snatched on Christmas Eve by a disgruntled uncle and some other shady fellow. FBI is in on the investigation. Said they had a couple of leads in a couple of states. Even found the vehicle they were snatched in abandoned in LA somewhere. Thought they were close, but no luck yet."

"Still can't believe she's been alive this whole time," Claude said.

"How you feelin' about all that? Had you pretty shook up yesterday."

Claude leaned forward onto his knees.

"Sorry about all that, Lyle. Didn't mean to make such a scene. Just kept thinkin' about everything and kept getting madder and madder. Mostly at myself. How could I have been so stupid? I shoulda known she was still alive."

"Now come on buddy, 9/11 was a crazy time. Especially in New York, from what I remember. Too much going on for anybody to know everything. I'm sure the, uh"—he looked down at the report—"the Gomez family was counting on all the chaos to keep you in the dark."

"And the Flanagans too. If Nellie hadn't have been sick that day when I came to Mrs. Flanagan's apartment, they'd probably have told me she was dead too."

The two pondered that possibility in silence.

"'Course after my performance yesterday, nobody is gonna believe I should even have Nellie, let alone Julia."

"Get yourself cleaned up. Down the hall to the left," Sheriff Probst said. "Elsie's coming to pick you up in a about fifteen minutes."

"She's a better friend than I deserve."

"Think she'd like to be more than a friend, if you'd let her."

The sheriff tossed the remark out under his breath. He didn't see the look on Claude's face turn from utter surprise to pleased perplexity because his attention was diverted by the sound of shouting and scuffling from down the hall and the sudden appearance of Deputy Bollinger.

"Sir, we've got a situation next door," she said.

"Jones?" Probst asked.

The deputy nodded.

"You got Michael Jones in here too?" Claude said, rising to his feet.

"Now, Claude, you just mind to getting yourself ready to go and leave Michael Jones to us," the sheriff replied, pointing a warning finger at him as he backed out of the door behind his deputy.

Chapter 32 – The Apprehension

Raúl Gomez threw his head back and tipped the beer can all the way up over his mouth. A few drops dribbled their way onto his tongue. He crushed the can and tossed it toward the overflowing trash bin beside the couch. The can hit the stack of other crushed cans and ricocheted off onto the dingy shag carpet. He stared at it and let it lay there. On the muted television, scenes from a holiday movie showed a family gathered around a table laughing and eating. He ran his hand half-heartedly under the pillows beside him, searching for the remote, but to no avail. His eyelids closed and he toppled over onto the couch, his feet still on the ground.

For nearly an hour he slept, unaware of his surroundings. The little brick house with no air-conditioning, the barred windows and tiny fenced yard, the constant buzz of traffic on the four-lane street, the intermittent roar of jet engines rattling the windows, the smell of day-old pizza and beer—none of it reached his consciousness.

But slowly, images drifted into his mind, disturbing his alcohol-induced stupor: a gas station; a cornfield; a girl running; deep-blue eyes filled with fear and something else, something he couldn't quite understand—something like victory. He swatted at the vision. His hand crashed against his own cheek, ending his temporary oblivion.

The sound of a car pulling into the driveway gave him just enough motivation to sit up and stumble to the window. He pushed open the metal blinds to see Rico getting out of his red convertible. Cassandra got out of the passenger seat, and the two of them met at the hood of the car. The security light from the carport illumed them locked in a passionate embrace.

Raúl let the blinds snap shut and wandered toward the back bedroom. He didn't want to interact with Rico and his lover. It was amazing to him that women found the guy remotely attractive. Cynthia always called Rico "a deluded Don Juan with testosterone poisoning." She was right about that. She was probably right about a lot of other stuff too. He dipped into the bathroom and locked the door as he heard Rico and Cassandra come crashing and laughing through the front door. If he didn't need the money, he would've left as soon as Julia had been set up and sent off.

"As soon as we get her settled, you'll get the rest," the guy named Manny had told them. "Gotta make sure she works out. You know the drill, Rico."

"What drill?" Raúl asked the bleary-eyed man looking back at him from the mirror. He was beginning to wonder if there even was more money. He'd never been a part of anything like this before. Some gambling. A little drug running. Even a bit of forgery. But trafficking? "How the hell did you wind up here?"

The cold water he splashed over his face brought a measure of clarity to his thinking. Maybe he should just forget about it and head for the border. Maybe find a job down there. His Spanish was good. Maybe get on a fishing boat. Take tourists out. Be in the sun all day.

"Gomez, get done in there. Cassie has gotta pee," Rico said, pounding on the bathroom door. "Dontcha, little Cassie Boo Boo?"

Cassandra giggled.

"Oh, baby," she said. "Don't make me laugh or I'm gonna wet my pants."

The door handle rattled and Rico banged against it again.

"Open up, man," he yelled.

Raúl's head dropped back and he stared at the molded ceiling.

"Jesus, get me outta here," he sighed.

The Agreements

***

Lupe Hernandez sat up in her bed in the quiet of the night in La Verdad, Washington, and switched on her bedside lamp. She fitted her reading glasses onto her nose before grabbing the small spiral notebook she kept on the nightstand and pulling the pen from its place in the wired binding. Quickly she scribbled the fragments from the dream before they flitted away: a small house with barred windows; a busy, four-laned street; a red convertible; airplanes flying overhead; and a name—La Brea. She peered up at the ceiling fan. Not just La Brea. She stopped and prayed. And then she wrote, "South La Brea."

She ripped the page from the notebook, removed her glasses, and dropped her legs over the side of the bed. Her terry cloth robe lay on the stuffed chair by her door. She slipped it on and scurried into the darkened hallway in her bare feet. At Hector and Maria's bedroom door she stopped and knocked. A light came on inside the room.

"Who is it?" Hector's sleepy voice reached through the door.

"Lupe."

Some ruffling and shuffling ensued. The door opened to show Hector in his checkered boxers and Maria struggling to right a pillow behind her back where she sat under a puffy comforter in their queen-sized bed.

"What is it, Mami?" Maria asked.

Lupe's eyes showed no signs of the deep slumber she had so recently arisen from. She raised the notebook page in her hands as she rushed to the side of the bed. Hector shuffled after her.

"Raúl. Is here," she said, pointing to the details on the paper.

"What? Can I see that?" Hector asked, and Lupe handed the paper to her son-in-law.

"I see him in my dream," Lupe said.

"You had a dream about Raúl?"

"Sí, with an address. South La Brea."

"Was there a city or a state?" Maria said.

"No, but it is warm like California. And many airplanes."

"Planes? Maybe it's near an airport?" Hector handed the paper to Maria. "Think we should call Mason?"

Maria perused the words Lupe had scribbled.

"What have we got to lose?" she said.

"I will make coffee," Lupe said, heading to the kitchen.

"But Lupe, he might not come over or even answer his phone. It is the middle of the night," Hector said.

Lupe's thick white hair shook over the back of her neck.

"He will come," she said on her way out the door.

When the front door came crashing in on the little brick house on South La Brea, the sun was just beginning to brighten the skies over Inglewood, California. Rico scrambled for the back door in nothing but his briefs. He was met by the forearm of a police officer across his trachea as soon as he stepped over the threshold. Cassandra screamed and hid under the threadbare sheets on Rico's bed. A female officer allowed her to get dressed before cuffing her.

Raúl, however, sat up in his bed and calmly buttoned the plaid shirt he had removed only hours before. He offered no resistance to the two burly law enforcement officers who busted open his flimsy bedroom door with guns drawn. The taller, thicker one brusquely flipped Raúl onto the bed and secured his hands behind his back in handcuffs.

"Raúl Gomez, you are under arrest for the kidnapping of a minor and intent to traffic said individual," the other officer said. "You have the right to remain silent. Anything you say can and will be used against you in a court of law. You have the right to an attorney. If you cannot afford an attorney, one will be provided for you. Do you understand the rights I have just read to you? With these rights in mind, do you wish to speak to me?"

Once upright and face to face with his arresting officer, Raúl said, "Nope."

The Agreements

Only after he was situated in the back of a squad car did he allow himself to wonder, "How the heck did they find us?"

Chapter 33 – The Investigation

"Hector, I have to be frank with you," Detective Mason's voice drifted down the hallway of the Gomez home. "This new information complicates our investigation significantly."

Rosie strained to hear the discussion playing out at the kitchen table while staring at the pictures on the coffee table in the family room. It was some of the contents of the mysterious box that Hector had picked up the day before. The package had been sitting at the post office for days, but in all the chaos of the girls' abduction, picking up the mail had not exactly been high on the list of priorities. Maria had opened the box as soon as he'd brought it home and then had stuffed it under her bed without letting anyone see what was in it. But Rosie, recently returned safely to the nest in La Verdad, had seen the look on her mother's face, and she had known whatever was in that box was super important. So, she had made sure to watch from a distance where it was stashed.

She had waited until her parents were deeply engrossed in a conversation with Detective Mason in the kitchen to sneak into her parents' room and pull the hidden package from its place under the bed. Thinking back on the moment she'd first realized the box's contents were all about Nellie, she wished that perhaps she wouldn't have screamed quite so loudly. Perhaps then her parents and the police detective wouldn't have come running. And she might've been able to simply push the evidence of the duplicitous life they'd all been leading back under the bed—back into the darkness. But much to her chagrin, she had been found out in the midst of her snooping, and her family's deepest secret had been laid bare on the bedroom floor right in front of Detective Mason.

"Kids," the detective said, marching down the stairs to address the Gomez children, who sat side by side on the couch, "I know I said you could have a look at a few of these photographs, but now I'm going to have to ask you to leave them alone."

Rosie, Beto, and Freddy set whatever they were holding down and leaned back into the couch silently.

"Jewels looks funny," Junior said, waving a photograph of Nellie in her dirt bike outfit in front of Rosie.

Freddy grabbed his wrist and wrestled it from Junior's hands. "It's not Jewels, dummy," he said.

"Is so," Junior insisted.

Rosie pulled her little brother up onto her lap. She brushed the hair back from his forehead.

"No, buddy. It's not her. It's her twin sister. Her name is Nellie," she explained.

"No. You're her sister," Junior said, struggling to free himself.

Lupe sat forward in the recliner.

"I will take him," she said to Rosie, her arms extended to Junior. "Ven aquí, mijo."

Junior slid out from under Rosie's arms and ran to his abuela. She enveloped him in the blanket on her lap and began to hum into his ear.

Peace descended on the room. Or at least on Junior. The other siblings just stared at the detective. It had been one thing for them to discover that Nellie was alive and well and living with her grandfather in North Dakota. It had been quite another thing to realize that their parents and even their grandmother were not shocked by this information but, in fact, seemed to have known it all along and had kept it from them.

All of them.

Even Julia.

"Someone is coming soon to box everything up," the detective said. "So, if you could maybe find somewhere else to play or whatever, that would be a big help." He turned to head back to the kitchen.

"Do you know who sent the box?" Rosie asked.

The detective stopped and turned back to the three somber Gomez kids.

"Yes, we just chatted with Mr. Flanagan," he said. "Seems he thought he was sending a box of Julia's pictures and drawings and such that his mother had accumulated over the years back to your folks and another box of Nellie's stuff back to her grandpa."

"But he mixed them up?" Rosie asked.

"Appears to be the case."

"Has he known about Julia and Nellie all along?" Rosie continued her line of inquiry.

"Can't go into those details with you," the detective said.

"Because he might be guilty too?" she said.

The detective shifted uncomfortably in his department-issued boots.

"Guilty of what?" Beto whispered.

Rosie stared at the law enforcement officer, who appeared to have lost his tongue.

"Of kidnapping," she said. "Julia has a real family and it's not us. Mom and Dad took her and kept her from them."

Junior suddenly popped up from Lupe's lap and leaned toward his siblings.

"Did we stole Jewels?" he asked.

"Okay now, I think we need to just stop right here." Detective Mason put his hands in a time-out signal. "This is not a conversation I am going to have right now. So, why don't you all find something else to keep you occupied. Got it?"

The detective turned and climbed the stairs without waiting for an answer.

"You hear him," Lupe said as she pulled Junior back into her arms.

The Agreements

Beto and Freddy stood up quietly and shuffled off to their room on the far side of the family room while Rosie wandered upstairs toward hers. She stopped in the hallway and stared at the lineup of family pictures on the wall. Each child had a frame assigned for his or her school pictures. She let her eyes shift from Julia's frame to her own, where her new sixth-grade photo smiled back at her. A photo that showed a girl who saw the world as an adventure waiting to happen. A girl who was confident that life held nothing but promise. A girl who felt safe and secure. Her chin dropped. She wasn't so sure she was that girl anymore.

"Our intentions were only for Julia's good," Hector's voice drifted out from the kitchen.

"I understand that, but the fact remains that you are not her next of kin. Mr. Jolicoeur is, and he legally has every right to accuse you of kidnapping," Detective Mason explained. "The contents of the box appear to show that your fears over his competency were not justified."

"But we couldn't have known that. Ryan and Beth were terrified of letting that man get anywhere near the twins. Jimmy Flanagan will verify that fact if you ask him," Maria protested. "Fiona, Hector, and I promised them we would do everything within our power to protect them."

"And we will sort that all out," the detective said. "The fact remains: you lied about Julia's death. You took a child without permission from the court-appointed legal guardian. You broke the law."

Rosie winced. Nellie's sudden reemergence shed her family in a new light. They weren't just victims—they were suspects.

"Look, we don't care what happens to us. We will tell you everything you want to know about the twins and Ryan and Beth and all of that, but right now we need you to give all your time and energy and resources to finding Julia," Hector pleaded.

"Please," Maria added. "Please just find her. It's been a week. How could you not know anything? She can't just have vanished into thin air."

Detective Mason sighed and set his crossed hands up on the table.

"We have strong reason to believe she's still alive. We've gotten some leads."

"What is it?" Maria leaned over and touched his hands. "Please."

"Can't tell ya, I'm afraid," the detective said. "Especially now, since . . . well, since this new information has come out."

Maria retracted her hand and huffed in frustration. The detective leaned back against the wooden dowels of his chair and gave Hector a penetrating stare.

"Listen, if I were you, Hector, I'd give Mayor Martinez a heads up about the box and everything."

"Yeah, I've thought about that," Hector said, shaking his head slowly. "Last thing I wanted to do was to put this town through more scandal."

The detective pushed his chair back and stood.

"Wait. One more thing," Hector said. "Any word on my brother?"

"Can't tell you that either," he said, punching a number into his phone.

The sound of the phone dialing filled the tense quiet.

"Agent Reese here," came the voice on the other end.

"Yeah this is Mason," the detective said, moving to the back door. "We've got an unforeseen situation over here at the Gomezes' . . ."

His voice trailed away and out the back door, where Perro barked ferociously from his kennel at the sheriff's passing form.

Rosie stepped into the kitchen. Her parents sat with their backs to her, their hands united on the table, their heads bowed together with foreheads touching.

"Papi," she whispered. "Can I come in?"

Hector and Maria's heads parted.

"Of course," Hector said, scooting back his chair and reaching out an arm.

The Agreements

She rushed forward and climbed onto his lap. Maria rubbed her daughter's back.

"I'm sorry," she said. "I shouldn't have gone snooping . . . I shouldn't have . . ."

"No," Hector said. "You shouldn't have . . . but I think . . . I think maybe it's better that it's all out in the open. And really, mija, it's us who shouldn't have put you in that position. We're the ones in trouble here, not you."

"Are you . . . ?" Rosie asked, her head still bent into Hector's neck.

"What, mija?" Maria prompted.

"Are you going to jail?"

Maria and Hector's eyes locked.

"We don't know what's going to happen," Hector said.

Rosie's body began to shake with pent-up sobs.

"But we love Jewels . . ." she quaked.

"Of course we do," Maria soothed her. "Of course we do. That's why we made her part of the family to begin with. Because we loved her and we wanted to keep her safe."

Rosie sat upright.

"But you didn't," she said as tears and anger lit her eyes. "You didn't keep her safe!"

She untangled herself from Hector's embrace and stood on her own two feet.

"You should have left her with her grandpa!" she yelled. "And . . . and . . . her real sister."

She spun around and fled the room.

Chapter 34 – The Quest

"Papa, can we go to Washington?" Nellie said to her grandfather at the conclusion of her bedtime prayers.

Carlyle sat on the top rail of the brass bed frame, enjoying the familiar bedtime ritual, one he wasn't sure Nellie would indulge much longer.

Claude sat on the edge of her bed and tucked the quilt up under her chin.

"You don't have to do that anymore, ya know," she said, pushing the quilt back down.

"Do what?"

"I'm fourteen. You don't tuck fourteen-year-olds into bed."

"Sorry. Old habits," he said, retracting his hands.

"Well, can we?"

Her grandfather rubbed a hand over his chin.

"Why? You thinking of leaving me, now that you've seen my ugly side?"

Nellie grabbed his hand.

"Never," she said. "I just want to see where she lives . . . lived . . . lives. And meet her, uh, her family. Didn't I used to know them too?"

The Agreements

"Yup, long time ago. They got a couple of boys about your age you used to play with," Claude nodded. "But what about school? It's starting up again real soon."

Nellie's gaze dropped and she tucked the teddy bear hidden under the quilt closer.

"I don't think I'm gonna be much good in school . . ."

The wind whipping down from Canada rattled her bedroom window.

"Honey, you know we're hoping and praying Julia's gonna be found real soon, but there aren't any guarantees. You've got to go back to school sometime."

Tears erupted in the corners of Nellie's eyes. Claude heaved a deep sigh and Carlyle leaned forward. She wasn't the crying sort.

"I suppose I owe ya after my little . . . uh, breakdown or whatever that was," he said, hanging his head.

The clock downstairs cuckooed ten times.

"It's okay," Nellie said. "Between the whole Mr. Jones thing and then finding out about Julia . . . it's been a little overwhelming around here. I sorta broke down myself, if you'll recall."

Claude let out a long breath, as if he'd been holding it for days.

"Is Mr. Jones gonna be okay?" Nellie asked. "I didn't mean to ruin his life. I just wanted him to stop doing all that . . . you know . . . all that stuff."

"Now, you listen real close," Claude replied, and Carlyle leaned in even closer at the intensity in his voice. "Michael Jones trying to take his own life is not your fault. He has been making choices for a long time. I don't know why . . . maybe he doesn't know why. Probably got his own set of demons he battles every day. I'm not his judge. But him sitting in that jail cell and having to face up to all the harm he's caused . . . well, I think it was just more than he could bear."

"Yeah, I guess . . . but is he gonna live?"

"Don't know," Claude said. "Heard they transferred him to a hospital in Bismarck. He's still alive, but that's about all I know."

Another gust of frigid wind howled around the farmhouse's exterior, and a low moan whistled down the chimney.

"It's gettin' late. How about I talk to Sheriff Probst in the morning? I can see if he has any more details he can give us about Mr. Jones. And I'll ask if he thinks it's a good idea or not for us to travel out to Washington. Seems the Gomezes are cooperating fully. Says everything he's heard from out their way is that they're real nice folks. Upstanding citizens."

"Then why did they take her? Isn't that like kidnapping or something?"

"Yeah, legally that is what ya call it, but . . ." Claude's eyes wandered to the blackness of the winter night outside the window.

"But what, Papa?"

"But maybe it's not that simple. The more I think on it, the more I'm wondering if maybe it isn't more a matter of me reaping what I sowed. I mean, I wasn't a very good papa to your papa. In fact, I was downright lousy." He continued to stare into the faraway past and the darkness it contained. "Maybe what the Gomezes did wasn't right in the eyes of the law, but maybe it was right in the eyes of a higher law," he said, returning his gaze to the deep blue of his granddaughter's eyes.

"Then why didn't they take me too?" she whispered.

Now the tears that threatened sprang up in Claude's eyes.

"That, baby girl, would be because God knew I couldn't live without ya," he said, his hands automatically moving to tuck the edge of the quilt up higher. At the last second, his eyes popped open, realizing what he was doing, and he let the blanket go.

They both laughed, bringing a smile to Carlyle's face.

"I know, I know. You're a young woman—not a girl," he said. "Alright if I still kiss ya goodnight?"

Nellie nodded.

Maybe there were some things that couldn't be outgrown, Carlyle mused to himself.

It was the same spot Carlyle always took on their road trips in the pickup: on the top of the back seat, leaning up against

The Agreements

the window, where he had a clear view of Nellie and the road ahead. Most of the time the back bed of the truck was filled with dirt bikes and the back seat with some of Nellie's buddies. But this time when Carlyle looked back, the truck bed was enveloped by a fiberglass canopy and its cargo consisted of two suitcases, a shovel, a couple of heavy blankets, an emergency roadside kit, and five heavy bags of sand. Winter driving across North Dakota, Montana, Idaho, and half of Washington was no joke. One had to be prepared.

They'd taken the interstate all the way to Butte, Montana, on the first day under startling-blue January skies. The mood in the cab was a forced lightheartedness, with country music playing on the radio and the driver and passenger engaging in road games. Nellie already had sixteen different state license plates and twenty-four letters recorded in her notebook, the one Eric had given her the night before—the one that said "Good Luck Nellie & Julia" in bold black Sharpie on the front cover and "Come back soon" on the inside.

The following morning, as they pulled out of the parking lot of the Super 8 in Butte, light snow flurries began to fall from a leaden gray sky. Claude had spoken to Hector on the phone the previous night to give him an update on their progress. The Gomezes were expecting them for dinner that night, but the road report said to anticipate some delays at higher elevations due to heavy snowfall, so they had agreed to keep the schedule flexible. Carlyle wondered if maybe Claude would like to delay the upcoming meeting as long as possible. The conversations between the two "fathers" of the two girls had been a bit tense thus far.

The evening after Claude and Nellie's bedtime chat, Sheriff Probst had connected the two parties via Skype on the computer at the sheriff's office. Claude had left Nellie and Elsie in the waiting room, so the two females and Carlyle were not privy to much of the details of the conversation. But they had heard a few of the more heated moments, when voices had been raised and the sheriff had had to step in to cool things off. The sanitized and brief report from Claude when things were all said and done had been, "It went well."

Nellie and Elsie had been a bit skeptical about that until he had said to his granddaughter, "If you really want to go, we'll go."

If school hadn't been starting up, Elsie might have joined the journey, just to make sure her friend Claude remained on the wagon. She'd left him with a stern warning to call her immediately if he even thought about taking a drink. Carlyle had to smile when he thought about the exchange between the two adults beside the truck in the frigid dawn air right before their departure—the Tupperware container of fresh baked cookies and pumpkin bread she had tucked into his hands after her little lecture, the short words of thanks from Claude, the awkward silence like two teenagers on a first date, the tender kiss on Elsie's cheek, and the glow in her eyes. Nellie had covered her face with both hands and looked away. But Carlyle had soaked in every moment. Romantic love was a tricky thing between humans, but it sure was something when they got it right.

On the way to Missoula, the snow flurries picked up and the wind began to blow. Soon the white stuff was flying over I-90 in horizontal sheets. Claude shifted the Chevy into four-wheel drive and slowed his speed. The traffic around them thinned while the frozen precipitation thickened. The AM station was tuned to the Montana Department of Transportation station. Nellie's notebook lay unopened in her lap, where her fingers absentmindedly picked at the corners while she stared straight out the windshield.

"Heavier-than-expected snowfall in Western Montana between now and 3 p.m. mountain standard time," came the recorded message from the radio. "Chains required over Lookout Pass. Accident eastbound on I-90 at milepost 28. Left lane closed to traffic. Please drive with extreme caution. This message will be updated and repeated every fifteen minutes."

Claude flipped off the radio.

"Looks like maybe we should hunker down in Missoula for a few hours until this weather lightens up," he said. "It'll almost be lunchtime by the time we get there at the rate we're going anyways."

The Agreements

Nellie nodded, her eyes still fixed straight ahead as if her concentration could help her papa's. They pulled into the Cracker Barrel in Missoula just after noon along with what looked like a fleet of semis and cars.

"Appears we aren't the only ones looking for refuge," Claude said as they parked.

The place was packed. They waited forty-five minutes for a table. All around them folks chatted about the weather.

"I heard another foot by nightfall."

"Skiers will be happy."

"How's it lookin' between here and Coeur d'Alene?"

"Not sure if I'm gonna risk it," one trucker said to another. "Lots of chatter on my radio sayin' it's real tough up on the pass."

"Weather guy said it's supposed to calm down. But they didn't forecast this, so who knows."

Carlyle flew next to Nellie as she wandered through the old-fashioned general store attached to the restaurant. She picked out a couple of different candies with the money Claude gave her: gummy bears for her and Red Vines for her papa. She plodded back to the stuffy waiting area in her snow boots and handed the licorice to Claude.

"My favorite," he said, ripping open the cellophane and tearing off a long, red rope.

"Yeah, I know," Nellie said. She tore her bag of colorful goodies open carefully, allowing just enough of an opening to extract one bear at a time. A green one appeared at the breach first and she plopped it into her mouth. "I wonder what her favorite is."

Claude looked down at Nellie, but didn't ask who "her" was. She'd been asking similar questions ever since they'd discovered Julia was alive.

"Do you think she likes to ride bikes?"

"Wonder if she knows how to skate."

"Will she sound like me too?"

"Think she's as tall as me?"

None of the questions Claude or Elsie had been able to answer. Carlyle speculated that it was part of what drove their current expedition—this incredible hunger to find someone who could answer her questions, someone who knew her other half.

When at last they were seated, it took another inordinately long amount of time for a waitress to appear. Thankfully, when she did, she was a matronly woman who was managing to keep her good humor in the midst of the sudden rush of business.

"Sorry, folks, about the long wait. Weren't expectin' such a full house today," she said, sweeping a stray hair back behind her ear. "I'm Julia. I'll be your server today."

Nellie's jaw dropped along with the menu she had just received. The edge of the multipage bill of fare caught the edge of her water glass and tipped the whole thing over.

"Good golly, miss molly," the waitress laughed. "I sometimes have that effect on folks. Hank," she yelled at a passing busboy, "get a towel over here, please." She turned back to Nellie. "You alright, hon?"

"She's fine," Claude said, although Carlyle could see from the way Nellie's chin quivered that wasn't quite true. "Why don't you give us a minute?"

"Sure thing," the woman named Julia said. "Oh, and by the by, I'm not sure where you're headed, but I just heard the pass is closed westbound now too. Some sort of multivehicle accident. Not expectin' it to open for a while."

"Thanks. We were hoping to get to Washington tonight, but maybe not. Any inexpensive hotels nearby?" Claude said.

"Motel 6 just down the road, but ya better get over there pretty soon. You won't be the only ones looking for a place to bed down."

Carlyle suddenly felt the tug, the one that said, "Time to swap spots."

He pulled the golden key from his pouch and his motorcycle appeared out of thin air. As he mounted the light-filled vehicle, he took one last look at Nellie and Claude. They'd come so far. He prayed a way would be made where there seemed to be no way. A way that somehow led them back to Julia.

Chapter 35 – The Suffering

The scene that he encountered when he reached Julia brought Carlyle and his machine to a screeching halt. He couldn't move, just sat on the bike in midair and stared. The thing he had dreaded had come to pass.

Winston Chambers lay on top of his silent victim, doing the thing he had intended to do since the moment he'd met Julia. Her eyes were filled with terror as she gazed past her rapist's bare shoulder at the elaborate ceiling tiles in the dimmed lights of the massage room. She didn't struggle or scream or even move. It was as though she was simply hoping to vanish until the vile deed was done.

Carlyle bent over, his hands still gripping the handlebars. A surge of anger swept through every fiber of his being until he could contain it no longer. He lifted his face to the heavens and screamed, "No!" His exposed rage resounded in waves past the confines of the small room and posh spa beyond the boundaries of city, state, and nation, through the ozone and layers of earthly atmosphere, and into the realms of heaven and the heart of the Designer himself.

A hand gently touched his shoulder.

"Carlyle," Madeline said.

He sat up with a start and turned toward her voice. She sat beside him in a small chair just like the one he found himself sitting in. Her ebony eyes shone with compassion.

"I'm here," she said.

Her voice sent a balm of peace into his churning heart, a peace he both welcomed and resisted. How could he accept it when one of his charges was in such a place of turmoil and destruction?

He shot to his feet and in that instant, he realized where he was. He was back.

They were back.

In the place where it had all begun. In the office of the Scrollmaster. The same messy, cluttered, unorganized space from which he had departed. And there, seated behind the paper-strewn desk, sat Grammateus.

Carlyle slammed his hands onto the desk and leaned toward the small man in the white suit.

"You need to do something and you need to do it now!" he yelled.

Grammateus did not move or utter a word.

Carlyle turned back to Madeline.

"What is wrong with you two? Don't you see what's happening down there?"

Madeline, too, remained mute to his cries.

In his fury, Carlyle spun around and swept his arm across the desk. Papers flew everywhere.

"Maybe if you cleaned this place up and put things in order, you would know," he said, falling back onto his chair, his anger spent for the moment.

Grammateus and Madeline glanced at each other and then back at their friend—for he was indeed their friend.

"Perhaps it's time," Madeline said.

"Perhaps," Grammateus agreed.

"Finally," Carlyle said. "I'll do whatever you need me to do. Just show me how to stop this insanity."

Grammateus slipped his glasses off and pinched the bridge of his nose.

The Agreements

The quiet that followed nearly drove Carlyle mad.

"What are we going to do?" he demanded.

The Scrollmaster placed his folded hands onto the desk and gazed intently into his agreement agent's eyes.

"We are going to do what they decide to do," he said.

"Are you kidding me?"

"He doesn't kid," Madeline interjected.

Carlyle swung on his trainer.

"But what they are deciding to do is—what *he* is deciding to do—leaves her without any choice! How can you allow him to decide anything?"

"We know. But you seem to have forgotten," she said.

"Forgotten what?"

"Love always requires choice," Grammateus said. "If I remove the ability of one person to choose between the light and the dark, the true and the counterfeit, the right and the wrong, then I must remove the ability of all. And as you yourself have witnessed, before they step into time, they all agree to take the risks involved with life on planet earth."

"But this! Why would anyone in their right mind agree to this?"

"You are absolutely correct. No one in their right mind agrees to suffer simply for the sake of suffering. That would be not only absurd, but insane. But in a world that has been invaded by rebellion, suffering comes to all, and they can choose what to do with it just as I chose when I suffered," the diminutive man behind the desk said.

"Excuse me?" Carlyle sat back. "You suffered, sir?"

Again, the trainer and Scrollmaster exchanged glances. He tipped his head as if to defer to her.

"Carlyle, I have taken you to other places and shown you many things. True?" Madeline said.

"True," he said, folding his arms across his chest.

"And you have seen Grammateus in other surroundings, in other roles."

Carlyle nodded casting a quick glance at the Scrollmaster.

251

"You have seen him in the cave of tears and the Valley of Decision. You have felt his compassion and marveled at his perspectives."

"I suppose so."

"But I have not yet shown the most pivotal place—his most vital role."

"Okay. Then show me."

A slow, sad smile spread over Madeline's face. She reached out and grabbed his hand.

"Follow me."

It was pitch black.

Carlyle blinked and squinted into the obscurity.

Weeping was the only sound that pierced the darkness.

Slowly his eyes began to adjust.

People stood on all sides of Carlyle, old and young, rich and poor, male and female. All were eerily quiet, save one woman who knelt on the ground before them—the source of the weeping.

He wanted to go. To comfort her. But he was reluctant to interrupt.

"Don't worry. They can't see us," his trainer said. "Let's go to her."

They walked to the side of the kneeling woman, who continued to sob. Her tear-ravaged face was turned upward. Carlyle followed her gaze.

He rocked back onto his heels in horror.

The body that hung suspended in midair with arms spread wide was nearly unrecognizable as a man. Almost every inch of his naked form was covered by bruises and open gashes. Blood ran in rivulets from the top of his head all the way to his nail-pierced feet. His face was a mass of wounds. His lips were split open. His eyes were swollen shut. A crown of long, angry thorns protruded from his blood-matted hair. His lungs expanded and heaved with every anguished breath.

The Agreements

It was the most horrific thing Carlyle had ever seen. And though he wanted to look away, he could not tear his eyes from the man's face.

"My son, my son," the woman beside him moaned and rocked back and forth, completely unaware of Carlyle and Madeline's presence.

Carlyle's heart wrenched for her.

"What has this man done?" he whispered to his trainer.

"Nothing deserving of this," Madeline replied.

Carlyle stared at the brutalized man.

"Then why is he there?"

"Because he agreed," she whispered as a tear breeched the rim of her eye and slid down her cheek.

Carlyle's face whipped back to stare at the man.

Could it be?

Was it him?

With great difficulty, the man with his arms spread wide lifted one swollen eyelid. And through that tiny crack flowed so much love, Carlyle was nearly knocked backward. It was love enough to envelop the entire world and every soul that ever was and was to be. He had seen that look only one other place.

"Grammateus," he murmured. "But why? If he has done no wrong, then why?"

Madeline took in a deep, ragged breath.

"For the joy," she said. "For the joy set before him."

With one convulsive breath, Carlyle was gone. Whisked away from the woman and the darkness and the broken, innocent man, from the suffering Grammateus. He and Madeline stood side by side in a vast, expansive space. Carlyle shook his head, closed his eyes, and breathed deeply. His knees felt like liquid, and his hands quivered by his side. Madeline patiently allowed him all the time he needed.

Eventually, he opened his eyes and wiped the dampness from his face. A stone wall stretched upward and outward before him.

"Where are we now?" he asked, almost too weary to speak.

"Let your spirit adjust, my friend," Madeline said.

Carlyle focused on breathing deeply. He could not close his eyes, for when he did, the scene they had just left blazed in full color in his mind.

"Ready?" she asked.

He nodded.

Madeline stretched out a hand and something like a massive stone rolled to one side, revealing an opening. She stepped through and he followed.

It must've been a room they had entered, for there was a ceiling above them, but as far as he could see from their position atop a massive stairway, there were no walls.

"Come, follow me," she said as she began to descend.

Down they stepped until slowly they passed through a thick, filmy layer of cloud and Carlyle could see what appeared to be rows and rows of bookshelves. But these were not your average library shelves. They were as tall as the tallest tree and as wide as the widest river. Their length? That he could not discern, for the rows simply went on and on, disappearing from sight. And their number? He scanned from side to side. They were innumerable. And every square inch was stuffed with books of every size, thickness, and color.

"I thought the scroll room was big, but this . . . this is awesome," Carlyle said.

"Indeed. It is awesome."

"What's in all the books?"

"Ah." Madeline smiled, letting her gaze scan the length and depth and breadth and width of what lay before them. "Every pain. Every sorrow. Every wound, sickness, disease, and wrongdoing. Every crime committed and harsh word spoken. Every arrogant thought. Error in judgment. Accident. War. Pestilence and plague. Every broken relationship, argument, and fight. Everything that has ever gone wrong in every life that was ever lived on planet earth. It's all here."

"Wow, that's, uh, that's not what I expected . . . but what does this have to do with . . . with, well, where we just were?"

"It's the joy set before him. It's what his suffering paid for. He owns all of this." She spread her arms out wide. "Every book, every page, every word, every jot, and every tittle."

A long, low whistle escaped from Carlyle's lips. "That is truly something," he said, allowing himself to try to absorb the enormity of the prize that was won. "But . . ." He paused and stroked his beard while gazing out over the incalculable collection of tomes.

"What are you wondering?"

"Well, if he already purchased, so to speak, all of this," he said slowly and carefully, "then why is it . . . why do they still suffer?"

"Come, let's go back to the top," Madeline said. They climbed steadily upward until they reached the place they had entered and turned back to view the expansive vista. "The lingering existence of suffering has to do with the fact that man has forgotten."

Carlyle waited for her to continue, but she turned and was about to open the door through which they had entered. He reached out and grabbed her shoulder.

"Wait," he said. "What exactly have they forgotten?"

Madeline peered into his eyes.

"They've forgotten who they are."

Carlyle took a step backward.

"You mean if they reclaimed their identity . . ." he began to process aloud what he thought she was saying.

"And their position," she added.

"If they reclaimed their identity and their position, they could eradicate all suffering?"

Madeline nodded and smiled.

"A way has been made by the sacrifice given," she said. "They need only receive it and walk in all the fullness of who they truly are."

Chapter 36 – The Song

"Get in there and shut her up, will ya?" Manny said, dragging a young woman by the elbow.

They were in the basement of the Sheer Pleasure Spa in Seattle—the latest stop in Winston Chambers' quest to continue his business while still evading the law.

"Why? Beats the whimpering she was doing before," the woman said, yanking her arm free and tugging the neck of the oversized sweatshirt back up over her shoulder. She was in her late teens or early twenties, attractively built, with thick, brown hair. She might have been a model under different circumstances. But her worldly eyes, cigarette-stained teeth, and dull skin testified to the youth and innocence that had been stolen from her, leaving her a weary shadow of who she might have been.

"Chrissy, just do as I ask, will ya? Her little songs are making me crazy," he said, inserting a key into a locked door. "I'll make sure you're compensated."

"I need some new bras," she said. "And not cheap ones. Victoria's Secret."

Manny rolled his eyes.

Chrissy began to walk away.

A quiet melody slipped out from the room.

The Agreements

"Alright, alright," Manny replied. "I'll take ya myself. Just get in there and shut her up."

Chrissy turned around slowly with a smug smile on her face. Manny pushed the door open and she walked past him in silence.

She stopped in the middle of the doorframe and peered into the dimly lit room. A lone night-light of some sort flickered from a socket near the floor. It wasn't much of a room, more like a closet that had been emptied out and fitted with a solitary mattress. Julia lay curled up on her side, facing the wall, under a thin blanket.

"Thought you said she was with Win last night?" Chrissy whispered to Manny, who hovered behind her.

"She was. All night."

"Then why's she singing?"

They stood in silence and listened to the clear, reedlike notes of Julia's voice as it bounced off the concrete wall.

"This little light of mine, I'm gonna let it shine," Julia continued to sing, seemingly unmoved by or unaware of their presence.

"Who knows," Manny snarled. "Maybe she's outta her mind. Just get her to shut up."

He shoved Chrissy across the threshold and shut the door behind her. She stepped onto the end of the mattress and slid down the wall until she was seated with her knees drawn up under her sweatshirt, facing Julia. Unlike Manny, she found the music flowing in the room to be soothing. So for several long minutes she sat and soaked in the melody. A sharp rapping at the door jarred her into activity. She reached out and placed a hand on Julia's feet. Only then did the younger girl open her eyes and turn to look at Chrissy. But her song did not cease.

"I'm gonna let it shine, let it shine, let it shine, let it shine . . ."

Chrissy stared into Julia's eyes. She had expected to see terror or hopelessness or even madness. It wouldn't be the first time that a girl simply lost touch with reality after experiencing what Julia had just experienced, especially with the younger girls. And especially for a girl like Julia, who Chrissy suspected was not familiar with sex, let alone the business of sex. But that is not what she found in

Julia's eyes. Instead, a sense of intense strength shone from their violet depths.

"Hide it under a bushel, no, I'm gonna let it shine . . ."

Tears lit the older girl's eyes. She knew this song. Long ago and far away, her grandma had sung it to her like a lullaby. But that was before. Before her grandmother had died and left Chrissy alone to drift across a quagmire of unwelcoming relatives and a minefield of foster homes.

She didn't remember all the words, but she began to hum along, eliciting a faint smile from her fellow captive.

"Hey!" A loud bang on the door caused both girls to jump. "Shut the hell up! Now!"

Quiet settled into the small space. Chrissy breathed deeply. It was almost as if she could smell the lotion on her grandma's skin.

"How do you do that?" she whispered to Julia.

"What? Sing?"

Chrissy nodded.

"Don't know," she replied. "When I couldn't cry anymore, I decided to try singing."

One of Chrissy's eyebrows rose high and to the left.

Julia sat up.

"Can I sit by you?" she asked.

"Sure," Chrissy said with a shrug, and Julia quickly snuggled in next to the older girl, throwing the flimsy blanket over both of them.

"Singing makes me feel better," she said. "Reminds me of my abuela."

"Your grandma?"

"Yeah."

"Mine too."

The girls turned to each other, and their eyes locked for a brief moment.

Chrissy turned away and added, "But I haven't thought about that in, like, forever. For sure, not since I've been with Win. Never felt like there was anything to sing about."

The Agreements

Julia nodded and the girls both stared straight ahead at the concrete wall that was so close, if they stretched out their legs, their toes would have touched it.

"Where's your grandma now?" Julia asked.

"In heaven, I guess. If anyone deserved to go, she did."

"Sorry. Not about the heaven part . . ."

Chrissy nodded and dampness appeared at the edges of her heavily lined eyes. She quickly wiped it away.

"Where's the rest of your family?" Julia asked.

"Don't have any," Chrissy said with a shrug. "At least any who want me or me them."

"Sorry about that too."

"Well, don't go feeling too bad. Win takes care of me."

A hardness crept into Chrissy's voice so different from how she had just been speaking that Julia peered sideways to see what had come over her.

"Like he 'took care' of me?"

A harsh snicker left Chrissy's mouth.

"Yeah, like that, and lots of other ways too. You're not his first, ya know, and you won't be his last. So don't go thinking like he's always gonna be stuck on you. You're just the latest addition. Pretty soon he'll get over you and move on to the next . . . or he'll come back to me." Her little speech wound down to self-talk. "He always does. Eventually . . ."

Julia wrapped her arms around her knees and hugged them tighter.

"Do you want him to?" she asked.

Chrissy shrugged.

"Sure. He loves me, ya know?"

Julia's eyebrows furrowed as she set her chin on her knees.

"It doesn't feel like love to me."

The door swung open.

"Let's go, Chrissy," Manny said. "You did your job."

Chrissy didn't budge.

"Come on. Get back to your room. Get rested for tonight."

"She says she's gonna keep singing unless I stay," Chrissy said.

Julia kept her face down to keep her surprised look at Chrissy's assertion hidden from his view.

Manny sighed deeply.

Chrissy made like she was going to stand up.

"Okay, fine. It's your ears."

"Nah," he growled. "Sit down. Keep her quiet. But you better be ready to go tonight."

She slid back down next to Julia as if resigning herself to an assigned task. Manny slammed the door. The deadbolt slipped into its spot.

Julia turned a cheek to rest on her knees.

"Thanks."

"Nobody likes to be alone," Chrissy said, tossing her long, brown hair behind her back.

Julia smiled.

"Oh, I'm not alone. I'm never alone."

Chrissy sat back and stared. Maybe she had guessed right the first time. Maybe this girl was a bit mad. But the more she looked into her shining eyes, the more she knew that was not true. This girl was saner than anyone she'd talked to in a very long time.

"What do you mean . . . not alone?"

Claude switched on the light that sat on the nightstand between his bed and Nellie's in their room at Motel 6. She was moaning and thrashing from side to side and tugging at the sheet, as if to escape its confines. The comforter lay in a heap on the floor. He slipped from under his covers and sat up.

"Nellie," he said. "Wake up."

Neither the light nor his voice seemed to penetrate her consciousness.

He slid his feet into the slippers that lay waiting to be filled beside the bed. Not that he really needed them to shuffle the few feet over the carpeted floor to his granddaughter's bed; it was just a habit developed over years of living through harsh winters and cold

The Agreements

hardwood floors. Many was the night that he had donned these same slippers to make the trek from his bedroom and down the hall to Nellie's to calm her after another of her vivid, disturbing dreams. He had learned after receiving a stunning left hook to the cheek that it was best to try to wake her without touching her, if at all possible. He stood beside the bed and gently shook the mattress.

"Wake up, honey. It's just a dream."

Still she flailed from side to side.

Keeping his head back at a safe distance, he reached out and shook her shoulder.

"Nellie, come on. Wake up."

Suddenly, she threw the sheets off her body and bolted upright into a sitting position, her breathing quick and ragged, her eyes fixed straight ahead. Claude sat on the edge of the bed, facing her.

"You're okay. I'm right here," he said.

Slowly she blinked and pulled her eyes away from whatever distant shore she had been seeing to turn and look at her grandpa.

"That's it now. Take a deep breath," he continued.

She did as he instructed.

"Where are we?" she asked.

"Motel 6. Missoula, Montana. Remember?"

Nellie scooched back against the padded headboard and looked around.

"We couldn't get over the mountains . . . too much snow . . ." he added.

Slowly she nodded.

Claude reached for the plastic water bottle on the nightstand.

"Take a sip," he said.

Again she obeyed, then handed it back to him.

He screwed the lid back on and replaced the bottle to the stand.

"Okay now, you wanna tell me what you were dreaming?"

He had also learned over the course of the years that Nellie needed to process whatever she had been dreaming out loud. Whenever he had attempted to skip that part and just tuck her back into bed, he would inevitably have to return to her bedside sometime shortly thereafter within the same night and go through the ordeal all over again. Better to stay awake and get it over with. Besides, he had found that her dreams where really quite remarkable. Not like his own that he could seldom remember or connect to much of anything in his day to day life. No, her dreams were intensely real and strongly linked to her world—past, present, and future.

"They were singing," she began, her eyes returning to the place far away.

"Who was?"

"The kids. Girls and boys. Lots of them."

The digital clock by the lamp clicked to 3:33 a.m.

"Do you remember what they were singing?" Claude prompted.

"A song from Sunday school. 'This little light of mine, I'm gonna let it shine,'" she said, singing the melody as she spoke. "And they were. They were shining. All kinds of colors. It was pretty."

"Hmm, I can imagine it sure would be."

They sat in silence as Nellie's eyes flickered back and forth across the replay screen in her mind.

"And there was a conductor. A man," she continued.

"Did you know him?"

"Not at first. He had his back to me. And his arms could only go so high. There were chains on his wrist."

Nellie grabbed a pillow from beside her and hugged it close to her chest.

"And there were men. Lots of men. Sitting in rows. Listening to the kids sing."

Claude nodded and waited for her to go on.

"The men had signs hanging around their necks with one word each."

"What were the words? Do you remember?"

She nodded and looked to her left as if to read each word one at a time.

"Rejected. Abandoned. Abused. Beaten. Scarred. Orphaned. Homeless."

Her head moved to the right with each word and then stopped at the spot straight ahead of her.

The Agreements

"Honey, you okay? Was there another word?" Claude said, gently reaching out to make contact with her ankle.

"It's not a nice word," she whispered.

"That's okay. It's just you and me. I'm not gonna get mad at you for saying a bad word if it's what you saw. Just tell me."

"It said, 'bastard,'" she said and then turned to look at Claude. "I don't even know what that means. Just that it's not nice."

Claude stroked his stubbly chin before answering.

"Well, it can mean a couple of things. First, it can mean someone who was born to a mom who wasn't married. Or to a mom who was married but the baby wasn't her husband's baby. Another word for that would be *illegitimate*."

"Oh," Nellie replied.

"It can also just mean someone who's mean or bad. Some people say it about people they really hate or who've done them wrong."

Nellie nodded and slid the pillow onto her lap, plumping its sides up absentmindedly.

"Well, I don't know which one this guy was. But he looked really sad. And he was bald with a big black moustache. And he had chains on his feet. All the men did."

Claude watched as goose pimples appeared on Nellie's legs and arms where they stuck out from her flannel shorts and T-shirt. He reached down and pulled the comforter off the floor.

"Here. Let's get you warmed up again," he said, tossing the cover over her extended legs. She pulled it up over the pillow to her chin.

"Was there more?" Claude asked.

"Yeah," she said, clutching the plaid comforter. "Somebody started to sing a solo. And I walked up past the conductor to see who it was. And, I think . . ."

"What? What do you think?"

"I think it was me . . . or maybe it was her . . . I couldn't tell. She looked just like me, but she sang . . . she sang like an angel. And when the words came out of her mouth, they looked like lights.

Like laser beams. And the beams hit the chains around the men's feet and the chains came off. They just fell off."

"Hmm, were you scared when the men were free? Did they come after you or something?"

"No. They just stood up and took off the signs and set them on their chairs, and then they disappeared. Why?"

"Well, you were thrashing around pretty good. Thought maybe someone was chasing you or something like that."

"Oh, that," she said. "That was because of him."

"Okay, wait. I thought you said all the men disappeared. Who are you talking about?"

"The conductor," her voice trailed off. "I saw his face. He still had on his chains. And he asked me. He said, 'Will you free me?'"

"Who was it, honey?"

"It was . . . uh . . . it was Mr. Jones."

Claude nearly slid off the edge of the bed.

"Jones? That bast—" Claude caught himself in mid oath. "What did you say? Did you let him off the hook?"

Nellie dropped her chin.

"I didn't. I couldn't."

"Well, I can understand that . . ."

"But she just kept singing . . ."

She looked up into her grandpa's eyes. Tears trickled down her cheeks.

"I tried to stop her. But she wouldn't. She wouldn't stop singing."

Chapter 37 – The Reunion

The winter dusk was about to settle in when Claude and Nellie drove past the city limits. A yellow ribbon tied in a big bow embellished the sign that read, "La Verdad, WA—Population 3,427." As they passed the Chevron station at the edge of town and drove all the way into the center of town, they noticed more yellow ribbons on streetlamps and stop signs and shop doors.

"What are those for?" Nellie asked, whipping her head around to catch each passing flash of yellow.

Claude let up on the gas pedal so he could take it all in himself. As they eased to a halt at the red light in front of the Downtown Diner he said, "Look over here." He rolled down his window so she could see more clearly what he saw on his side of the street.

"Bring Julia home," Nellie read the words painted in yellow and surrounded by hearts on the diner's windows. A lump formed in her throat. "Is that . . . do they mean our Julia?"

"Can't imagine there's too many Julias in a town this size. Especially Julias who need to be brought home."

The light turned green and a quick beep from the car behind them urged them to pull forward. They continued their slow journey through town despite the pressure from the tailgater, who thankfully turned off to the right a few blocks later. Several people scurried along the sidewalks near the drugstore, movie theater, and dry cleaners, their heads bowed against the blustery north wind. A woman walking her dog nearly ran into a parking meter when she looked up and made eye contact with Nellie as they drove past. Nellie turned back in time to see her stopped in her tracks, her hand over her mouth, her terrier straining at the leash.

As they passed city hall, the reader board above the door flashed "Bring Julia Home." On the next block, the message board at Glory of the Lord Church added the words "We Believe" underneath the plea for Julia.

Nellie's heart was gripped with a mixture of awe and sorrow and excitement. Here was an entire town that cared about the very thing she cared about—her sister.

Claude flicked on the left turn blinker.

"Here we go," he said. "A left on Sierra, go five blocks, and a right on 10th Street. We're almost there. You ready?" He cast a glance her way in time to see her give a quick nod.

They drove in silence through the last stretch until they pulled up in front of the Gomezes' tan, split-level house. Yellow ribbons wrapped around the mailbox, the light fixtures on either side of the garage, and the base of the tree in the middle of the yard. They stood out like brilliant sunflowers against the snow, even in the deepening January twilight.

Claude parked the truck beside the curb where a shoveled sidewalk cut across the yard to the house. Before either of them could even unhook their seatbelts, the front door flung open and a young boy leapt out onto the cement stoop. He peered out at the truck intently and then ran back through the door and slammed it shut.

"Well, hope the rest of them are friendlier," Claude mumbled. He reached over and grabbed Nellie's hand. She had gone deeply still. "You sure about this? We can turn around right now and drive home if you've changed your mind. No skin off my nose."

But Nellie shook her head as she tugged her stocking cap down over her hair and zipped her down jacket up under her chin.

"Okay then, let's go do what we came to do," he said.

The Agreements

As they approached the front door, once again it opened and light from inside the house spilled out onto the path. A little dog shot through the opening, yapping and spinning at their feet. Claude stepped back as it nipped at his ankles.

"Perro," the man standing in the doorway yelled at the dog. "Stop that. Come here!"

The dog ignored his commands and turned his attention to Nellie. She reached down and put her hand in front of his snout. Perro leaned in warily and sniffed. Then both of his front paws came off the ground and he spun around like a ballerina in a jewelry box, causing Nellie to smile.

"Can I pick him up?" she asked.

"Sure. He seems to know you," the man said.

Perro settled right into Nellie's arms, tucking his nose into the crook of her elbow. The man who stood in the doorway smiled at Nellie, but his face sobered as he turned his gaze to Claude and extended his hand.

"Hector," Claude said, giving the hand a quick shake.

"Claude," Hector said.

For a moment, the two men glared at each other like the banty roosters in Elsie's chicken coop. Nellie looked from one to the other, wondering who would back down first.

"Hector," a woman's voice from the top of the stairs inside reached them. "Invite them in."

Hector stepped back and swept his arm over the threshold and into the house. "Pasa te. Come in," he said, his eyes locking on Nellie as if he couldn't quite believe what he was seeing.

"Maria," Claude said with a nod to the woman descending the stairs toward them.

She returned his nod, but her gaze was glued on Nellie.

"Nellie," she said, as bright tears lit her eyes. "I'm Maria. I don't suppose you remember me . . ."

Nellie ran a hand down Perro's back before replying, "No, ma'am, sorry, I don't."

"No, well, that doesn't matter. I'm . . . we're just so happy that you're here."

"Yes, ma'am. Me too," Nellie said, venturing a glance upward at Maria and Hector.

Suddenly, the little boy who had first opened the door slid down the stairs on his rump and landed at Nellie's feet.

"Junior," Maria scolded. "That's not how we greet guests. Now stand up and give a proper welcome."

Junior stood up, tugging his best button-down shirt over his slightly paunchy belly. He stepped close to Nellie and peered upward.

"I thought you said she was a girl," he said.

"Junior." Hector grabbed his son by the shoulder and yanked him backward. "You apologize to Nellie. Right now."

"But she doesn't—" Junior protested.

"Now, Son."

The grip on Junior's shoulders tightened. He looked up at Nellie through thick, black eyelashes.

"Sorry."

"Maybe you should take your cap off," Claude said quietly to his granddaughter.

She reached up and pulled the stocking cap off with one hand and adjusted her thick, short tresses.

Junior's eyes lit up and he launched himself with open arms to Nellie.

"Jewels," he yelled, wrapping her up in a tight hug around her waist. "You got a haircut!"

Nellie stood stock-still and Perro let out a low growl. Maria sucked in a deep breath and the tears that had threatened before burst forth in a flood. Hector froze.

A girl about Nellie's age came down the stairs into the crowded entryway.

"Good grief, Junior, why do you have to be such a doofus? This isn't Jewels. It's her twin. This is Nellie," she said, prying Junior away from Nellie. "Obviously. You look a lot like Jewels, but I can totally tell the difference. I'm Rosie. Those are my brothers Beto and Freddy," she pointed to the two boys staring over the wooden railing from the living room. "And that's Lita, our grandma." She indicated the short woman in the apron at the top of the stairs. "Kick off your boots and I'll show you around," she said, lifting Perro from his perch.

Nellie shed her boots and handed her coat and cap to Maria's extended hands before following Rosie up into the house.

"We eat now," Lita announced from the kitchen doorway to the three adults gathered in the living room. "Ahorita, por favor. It's hot." She wiped her hands across her gingham green apron and turned back to her culinary duties without another word.

The minutes Hector, Maria, and Claude had spent awkwardly chatting about the road conditions, the weather, the stop in Missoula, and other inconsequential minutiae upon first arriving had slowly evolved into more substantive conversation. And when it had, the children, who had stood in uncomfortable silence, had been encouraged to find other things to keep themselves occupied while the adults talked. Rosie had grabbed Nellie's hand and led her to the bedroom she shared with Julia. Junior had attempted to follow but was left standing in the hallway.

"I wanna stay with Jewels," he yelled while pounding on the closed door.

"Not now," came the yelled reply from his older sister. "And it's not Jewels! It's Nellie!"

He crumpled to the floor in a heap and began to cry.

"Beto and Freddy, please retrieve your brother and take him downstairs. Bribe him with first dibs on the Wii or something," Maria instructed her older sons from her place at the far end of the couch next to the recliner where Hector sat.

After some fairly serious negotiations, Junior agreed to the terms laid out and allowed himself to be carried on Freddy's back to the basement.

Left to themselves, the adults sat quietly with their own thoughts, wondering where to begin, what to say, how to start.

"Uh, Mr. Jolicoeur," Hector ventured at last.

"Just Claude, please," Claude said from his spot at the opposite end of the couch from Maria.

"Okay, Claude," Hector resumed. "I want to reiterate what I said on the phone last week."

"No need to go through all that again," Claude said.

"Well, now, I disagree," Hector said. "I, uh, we need to say some things face to face. If we're gonna figure this whole thing out in a way that's best for Nellie . . . and for Julia . . . we're gonna have to be totally square with one another."

Claude gave a small nod.

Apologies were given.

Responsibility was taken.

Forgiveness was asked.

"Alright, now it's my turn," Claude said. "A week ago, I would have said you were completely in the wrong to do what you did. I would have gladly had you arrested, prosecuted, and thrown in jail. I was hopping mad."

The rattling in the kitchen where Lita was busily preparing dinner quieted considerably.

"But I had what you might call a come-to-Jesus moment last week," Claude said, wiping his palms over the stiff denim of his best Wranglers.

He proceeded to come clean to them about how he'd gone on a bender, had the cops called on him, and wound up in jail. As he finished his confession he added, "Scared the bejeebers outta Nellie . . . and me. Thought I was long past all of that, but guess not."

Hector and Maria didn't respond.

"Ryan had a point, ya know," Claude said. "I wasn't a good dad, and maybe I'm still not . . ."

"I don't think that's true," Maria said. "I read all the letters you sent to Fiona. She sent me a copy of every one of them."

"She did?" Claude said.

"She did. I insisted because I wanted to know . . . I needed to know if Nellie was okay. We had agreed that if any hint of abuse or neglect showed up, we were going to show up on your doorstep and do whatever needed to be done to make things safe for that girl.

The Agreements

Because we promised . . . we promised Ryan and Beth . . ." Maria's words choked to a halt and the room fell silent.

And that was when Lita appeared with her announcement, "We eat now."

Hector extracted himself from his leather recliner and stood.

"I'll get the boys," he said, heading toward the family room in the basement.

"And I'll get the girls," Maria said. "Claude, if you want to wash up before we eat, follow me. There's a bathroom just down the hall."

As they stepped into the hallway, the sound of soft crying filtered out from under the door that led to the girls' bedroom. Maria and Claude stopped in their tracks and listened.

"Maybe they're not ready to eat yet," Claude offered in hushed tones.

"Guess I'll find out," Maria said.

Claude waited and watched as she tapped gently on the door below the pink and purple wooden letters that spelled out "Julia and Rosie."

"Girls, can I come in?" she asked into the small crack between the door and the frame.

The sound of crying drew to a halt.

"Okay," Rosie replied.

Claude gave Maria a nod before he retreated to the bathroom and shut the door behind himself.

"Everything okay in here?" Maria asked the two girls huddled side by side on the bottom bunk—Julia's bunk.

Nellie wiped both hands across her tearstained face. Maria pulled a tissue from the box on the desk that sat beside the bunk beds.

"Here, mija," she said, offering it to Nellie.

Nellie received it wordlessly and continued the mop up she had begun with her hands.

Rosie scooched to the edge of the bed.

"She wanted to know what happened on Christmas Eve," she said to her mom. "So, I told her."

Maria knelt beside the bed. She set one hand on Rosie's and reached the other out to touch Nellie's crisscrossed legs, but Nellie pulled away.

"I wish I could make this all go away. That we could all just go back to living our normal lives," Maria said.

"With my sister here with you," Nellie snipped.

Maria hung her head and took a deep breath before replying, "No, my wish goes farther back than that. I wish I could make 9/11 disappear and bring your mom and dad back to life and have you grow up with your sister and all of us be really great friends back in Brooklyn. But . . ." her voice caught in her throat, "but that is not within my power to make happen."

Silence settled in the bedroom. The toilet flushed in the bathroom next door and the sound of water running in the sink seemed inordinately loud.

"We're sorry, Nellie," Rosie whispered at last.

"Truly. We are," Maria echoed. "We didn't mean to hurt you. Only protect you and Julia. If we could have hidden you, too, we would have . . . but it just didn't . . . the way things went . . ."

"I wouldn't have gone with you anyways," Nellie said. "I like living with my grandpa. And Julia would too. What you did was wrong. You took away from me the only family I had left. You had no right to do that."

A knock on the door interrupted her rebuke. Claude poked his head in the door.

"Sorry. Am I interrupting something?" he said.

None of the three women in the room replied.

"I, uh, think dinner is waiting. Nellie, why don't you come and get washed up?" he asked.

Nellie slid from her place on the bunk bed, carefully stepping around Maria and averting her gaze from Rosie.

Claude lingered in the bedroom.

"She can be pretty tough," he said to Maria, who was busily wiping her face and blowing her nose into a tissue.

"She has every right to be upset with us," Maria replied.

The Agreements

"Well, now, I think I probably have my fair share of blame to take for this whole situation," Claude said, extending a hand to help her up from her place beside the bed. "Nellie will come around. We just need to let her process all this . . . this new stuff."

Maria nodded and tried to offer up a smile.

Rosie stood and wrapped an arm around her mother's waist.

"I think Nellie just might be the one to help us find Jewels," she said.

"Oh really?" Maria said. "Why is that?"

"'Cause she's her twin and 'cause I think she's willing to do whatever it takes to get her back."

"If you just wanna follow me, I can lead you over to Raúl's . . . uh . . . Cynthia's place and get you settled in for the night," Hector said after dinner.

It had been decided that scrunching Claude and Nellie into the Gomezes' already-crowded abode maybe wasn't the best idea, given the nature of the visit. And since the closest hotel was twenty-five miles away, an alternative had been found. Raúl was in federal custody in California and Cynthia had left the day before to drive down to see him. She was more than happy to offer their place to the Jolicoeurs.

"It's the very least I can do," she had said to Maria when asked about the arrangement. "I wish to God there was more."

Junior had put up a fuss, having grown attached to Nellie very quickly. Twice over dinner he had again called her Jewels. Nellie had said, "I don't mind" when Lita had scolded him for his bad manners. Which, of course, had only endeared Nellie more fully to his four-year-old heart.

"Well, those were some good enchiladas and frijoles," Claude said when he and Nellie were by themselves in the pickup cab. "Way better than Taco John's."

"Uh, yeah," Nellie said with a small grin. "Way, way, better."

"It's been real good of them to let us come, you know."

"I guess."

Claude turned the key in the ignition and pulled out behind Hector's van.

"From what I can tell, these folks truly love Julia and have given her everything she's needed," Claude said as they turned onto Main Street.

"Everything except us," Nellie replied.

"Well, now, I suppose that's true enough."

They drove past Glory of the Lord Church to the other side of town, where they pulled up in front of a brick rambler. Hector parked in the driveway and stepped carefully over the icy surface to the attached garage. He punched a code into the pad by the door and it began to glide upward.

"I'm only gonna say this once," Claude said as he turned off the truck. "Don't let unforgiveness settle in your heart. Trust me. I've done it, and it'll eat ya alive."

Claude undid his seat belt and was about to open his door when Nellie reached over and put her hand on his.

"I'm trying, Papa," she said.

"I know," he said, patting her hand. "Me too."

They exited the truck and retrieved their suitcases from the back.

"Watch your step over here," Hector said as they approached the garage. "Shoulda had the boys come and shovel this."

The trio made their way into the garage and past a jacked-up Toyota Tacoma that gleamed as if freshly polished under the fluorescent garage lights.

"That an '07 or an '08?" Claude asked, running a hand admiringly over the metallic blue paint.

"It's an '07. Raúl's pride and joy. Can't believe he left it here," Hector replied.

"It's a beauty," Claude said. "Looks like he took good care of her."

"Yeah, takes better care of his rigs and his bikes than his wife."

"Does he have dirt bikes?" Nellie piped up.

"Dirt bikes. Street bikes. Dual sports. Trikes. Got a shop full out back. Perfect condition, every one of 'em. Used to take the kids out all the time . . . well, before he decided I was his enemy. It's a real shame. He was good with them and they loved riding. Got to be pretty good at it too. Especially Freddy. And Rosie, for that matter. Beto's a bit more cautious," he replied.

"What about Jewels?" Nellie asked.

"Ah, not so much. She tried it, but not really her cup of tea. What about you? You like to ride?"

She nodded.

"Oh, she likes it alright," Claude said. "She can ride the hair off a dog. Just like her dad."

"Really? Cool. You should let the kids know," Hector said over his shoulder as he opened the door to the house. Turning back to Claude, he added, "Never knew that about Ryan. He always seemed like the academic, urban kind of guy."

"Guess he sorta became that alright, but there was a time he loved getting grimy riding on dirt tracks and working on bikes. Just wish he could see her now . . . see us now," Claude said.

"Yeah, me too," Hector said before heading down the hallway. "I'll get some lights on in here and turn up the heat a bit."

Nellie and Claude trailed behind him. They stepped onto the tiled surface of the dining area with the kitchen in front of them and the living room to their right. Hector was in front of them, adjusting the thermostat.

"Should warm up pretty quick," he said. "You can take your pick of bedrooms. The bathroom is right here," he said, turning on the light. "You saw where the kitchen was. Cynthia said anything you can find to eat is yours. She's really a great gal and she feels just terrible about what Raúl did. We all do."

He had turned to stare at a photograph displayed prominently on the wall between the bedroom and bathroom.

"That him?" Claude said.

"Yup, that's Raúl and Cynthia. No kids. Never wanted any. Too much of a hassle, he always said," Hector said.

Nellie stopped beside them and she looked up to follow their gaze. Her hand flew to her mouth and her suitcase tipped onto its side.

"You okay?" Claude said, leaning over to right the fallen luggage.

Nellie mutely shook her head. Her face had gone ashen. Hector and Claude exchanged concerned looks.

"It's been a long couple of days. Maybe she just needs to lie down and get some rest," Claude said.

Nellie grabbed her papa's hand and pointed to the photograph. "That's him," she whispered.

"Yes, honey, that's Raúl," Claude said. "But he's in jail. In California. He can't come here. He can't hurt you."

"No, I know that," she said. "But he's the guy . . . the guy from my dream."

Claude stared back at the picture of Raúl and Cynthia that showed a heavyset blonde woman standing behind a man with her arms wrapped lovingly around his shoulders. He was thinner than she, with a shiny, bald head and thick, black moustache over his posed studio smile.

"The one with the sign that said—" Nellie stopped and glanced at Hector and then back at her grandpa. "You know, with that word."

Claude nodded knowingly.

"Uh, I'm not sure what's going on here, but if it's something I should know or shouldn't know, I'm totally cool either way," Hector said.

Nellie's grip on Claude's hand increased.

"That's up to her," Claude said.

Nellie continued to stare at Raúl's picture, her eyes flickering back and forth as if the dream was superimposed over his image. Quietly, she began to retell the story that had played out in her sleep the night before. Her words poured out steadily and surely until it came to the word emblazoned on the sign that hung around Raúl's neck.

"I'm sorry, Mr. Gomez," she said.

The Agreements

"Hector. Please call me Hector."

"I'm sorry, Mr. Hector, but the word was 'bastard,'" Nellie said.

Hector stepped backward as if to avoid a slap.

"Listen, uh, Hector, she has these dreams from time to time," Claude said. "And they're pretty vivid and stuff. But, you know, it's hard to say how much really means anything or not. So, let's not take this too personal or . . ."

"No, uh, it's not that," Hector said, smoothing his fingers over his own deep-black moustache. "It's just . . . uh, Lupe asked me about that very thing just a few days ago."

"What did you tell her?" Nellie asked.

"Told her I didn't really know, but that there were rumors. Rumors my mother refused to even respond to, and my father . . . well, he let us know quite firmly that such talk was forbidden. But he never treated Raúl the same as me. Always stricter. Tougher. Even downright abusive at times. I always thought it was just 'cause he was the oldest. Higher expectations and such . . . but maybe not. Maybe there was something to those rumors."

Claude nodded. Nellie leaned back against the wall across from the picture and continued her assessment of Raúl. An awkward silence settled in their midst as each one considered the ramifications of this word for Hector's older brother.

"Well, I will let you two get some rest," Hector said with a roll of his shoulders as if to release a pile of tension. "Think I could use some myself. Lupe will have something whipped up for breakfast. If you've never had homemade breakfast burritos, you'll not want to miss that."

"That sounds good. What time?" Claude said.

"Well, she's up by five, but you don't need to be there until eight or nine," he said as he began to make his way back to the garage. "The house keys are in the bowl on the kitchen table. I'll close the garage door on the way out. Oh, and Detective Mason will be over at our house about ten, along with an FBI agent from Seattle. We're anxious to hear about the latest developments."

"Us too," Claude replied.

"And we can discuss, uh, in further detail the . . . you know, the legal issues and such," Hector said, with one hand gripping the doorknob. "And we'll go from there."

"Yes, we'll go from there." Claude said.

"It's sort of strange to have you here with Nellie and not Julia," Ardith said to Carlyle as the two of them sat watching Nellie play video games with the Gomez kids. It was Saturday and they had all finished up their breakfast burritos and been ushered to the basement so that Detective Mason could converse with the adults along with FBI Special Agent Brenda Reese.

Junior sat in Nellie's lap, which didn't seem to interfere with her ability to manipulate the controls or to soundly beat first Freddy and then Beto in the latest Sonic video game, much to the delight of her rabid four-year-old fan.

"Yeah, it's sort of strange, all right," Carlyle replied, leaning back against the window frame where the two watchers had taken up their posts.

"Nellie seems to be softening up a bit," Ardith said.

"Well, she's a good kid, ya know," Carlyle said, adjusting his uniform over his chest where the buttons seemed suddenly to want to burst. "She's tough, but she's got a good heart."

The two watchers sat in companionable silence, enjoying the sight before them.

"How's Julia doing?" Ardith asked.

Carlyle didn't reply right away. Every time he let his mind wander back to Julia's plight, he was flooded with emotions, not the least of which was anger. But since his latest expedition with Madeline and Grammateus, he was beginning to see things from a different perspective.

"Julia is doing amazingly well, all things considered," he said. "I don't know how, but she seems to be finding herself . . . her true self, if ya know what I mean."

Ardith nodded. "I'm aware of that possibility," she said.

The Agreements

"What do you mean?"

"I've just heard from some of the senior agreement facilitation officers that humans seem to return to their primordial essence under the most difficult of circumstances. They just cut through all the trivial and get down to the original."

"If only it didn't take such . . . I don't know . . . such pressure."

Maria slipped into the room and silently stood for a few moments observing the scene playing out in her family room before she spoke up. "Sorry to interrupt guys, but Agent Reese needs to talk to the girls."

Not a single head even turned to acknowledge her.

"Go, Nellie, go!" yelled Junior.

"Come on, Beto," urged Freddy.

"I'm trying," Beto replied.

"She's got you again," Rosie said, jumping up and down beside the big-screen TV.

"Ah, man!" Freddy said, throwing a pillow across the room as the game finished with Nellie as the victor once again.

"Hey, no throwing stuff," Maria lifted her motherly voice over the tumult.

This time every head swiveled and stared at her as if stunned by her presence.

"Good for you, Nellie. Always nice to see these boys put in their place," she said. "Now come on, girls. Let's go upstairs."

"But it's my turn to play," Rosie whined. "Why do we have to go upstairs now?"

"Because the FBI agent in our dining room who has traveled all the way from Seattle needs to ask you girls some questions," Maria said.

Nellie eased Junior off her lap. He turned around and gripped one of her hands before announcing to his mother, "I'm with her."

Beto and Freddy stood up and switched off the Wii and the TV.

"Us too," they said in unison.

Carlyle and Ardith smiled at the unified front the young people presented.

"Not every day you see those two voluntarily shut down their gaming," Ardith commented.

Maria crossed her arms over her chest and assessed the solemn lineup before her with a spark of appreciation in her eyes.

"Okay," she answered. "But only if you agree to sit quietly and not cause a ruckus."

"Okay," the boys chimed all at once.

"And," she added, "you must not discuss anything you hear with anyone outside of the people in this house right now. Can you do that? Even you, Junior. Not one word."

The boys looked from one to the other as if suddenly realizing the gravity of what was transpiring upstairs. Nellie squeezed Junior's hand for reassurance.

"We can," Beto said, acting as the group's spokesman.

Carlyle and Ardith followed the crew as they exited the room.

"Wow, will you look at that," Carlyle said, pointing to the atmosphere surrounding the five children, which had begun to vibrate and glow with an intertwining of all their heart lights.

"Sure enough. Beautiful. 'The whole is greater . . .'" Ardith began.

"'. . . than the sum of its parts,'" Carlyle finished with a smile.

Chapter 38 – The Friends

"If you don't want everybody else getting sick, you'd better get her some help," Chrissy said to Win.

"Oh, she's just got a cold or something," he replied, buttoning up his freshly pressed dress shirt as he stood in front of the full-length mirror at the foot of the bed.

Chrissy tugged the silk sheets up over her naked frame.

"I'm just sayin' . . . she was burning up with fever last night," she said.

"Tell Manny to give her some Tylenol or something," Win said as he tucked his shirt into his designer slacks and buckled his crocodile belt around his tightly muscled waist. "That girl . . . the little princess," he muttered. "She's strange. Been trouble since the day I met her."

"She's just a kid, ya know," Chrissy said quietly, knowing she was pushing her luck but also knowing if anyone could get Julia some help, it was her. Chrissy had been with Win longer than any of the other girls, at least the ones in Seattle—since she was thirteen. And though he went through stints of forsaking her for the newest addition to his business, he tended to return to her whenever he needed someone to not just service his desires but actually talk to him. Yes, there were occasional violent reminders of her position in his life, but he usually followed up the abuse with something really nice, like a new pair of shoes or a necklace or a nice dress. Something to show her what she had believed until very recently—that he loved her.

"Her crazy singing has got all the other girls stirred up and restless," he said.

"I don't know," Chrissy said. "I think it's sorta soothing. Seems to help her cope. Everybody needs something to get them through."

Win swung around and stared at her.

"Since when are you Mother Teresa?"

Chrissy drew back into the pillows at the harshness of his retort. But then a little smile played at the corners of her mouth, though any sense of happiness failed to reach her eyes.

"I care about you," she said, crawling out of her cozy spot across the bed to run her hands over his chest. "And she's a part of what you do. I'm just looking out for you, babe."

Win let her hands caress him, soaking in her adoration. Then he grabbed her fingers and flung them down.

"Well, don't go thinking you know what's best for me," he said, turning back to assess his reflected image. "And don't go getting too attached to that kid. I'm shipping her off to the East Coast in a day or two. As soon as Manny can arrange it."

"To Carver? Really?" she said, dropping back onto her heels. "That guys a freakin' psychopath."

"Yeah, so what? Why do you care?"

Chrissy leaned over the edge of the bed and grabbed her underclothes and velour sweat suit off the floor. "Don't get me wrong," she said, pulling the newly acquired outfit onto her thin frame. "I'd be happy to see her go. She's takin' up too much of your attention already, as far as I'm concerned. But it probably won't help your reputation any to be passing along dirty packages."

Win let out a sigh.

"Fine. Tell Manny to get her whatever you think she needs," he said, slipping his Rolex onto his wrist and then checking the perfection of his hair one last time in the mirror. "But no doctors. You got that?"

"Sure. Whatever you say, babe."

Win slipped on his leather loafers, grabbed his sport coat, and headed toward the door.

"Clean this place up," he said as he exited.

"As always," she whispered to the door that slammed behind him.

Chrissy tucked the extra blanket around Julia, who lay curled up in a ball on the mattress in her tiny room. Even though her head was covered by the hood of her down jacket, which was zipped up all the way past her chin, she was trembling from head to toe. Despite the racking chills, she managed a weak smile for her visitor.

"Th-th-th-thanks," she whispered. "I h-h-hurt. All . . . all . . . over."

"Shh, now. That Tylenol is gonna kick in soon and we'll get that fever down. Okay?" Chrissy said, snapping shut the lid of the water bottle and placing it snugly between the wall and the mattress. She reached over and pushed some loose black strands of hair back under Julia's hood and rested her hand on the younger girl's forehead.

Julia's skin was hot and even in the room's dim light, it had taken on a distinctly yellow hue. Chrissy was no nurse, but she knew this wasn't good. A small grip of anxiety settled in Chrissy's chest. She didn't want to see Julia go anywhere and certainly not in the state she was in. Win was no angel, for sure, but she'd heard even worse things about Carver and his gang on the East Coast. But besides that, she didn't want to see her go, for her own sake.

Without even thinking about what she was doing, Chrissy began to hum one of the melodies Julia had been teaching her over the past few nights. The sick girl sucked in a deep, ragged breath and seemed to relax under the song's influence. The trembling eased and Julia's eyes flickered shut. After ten minutes or so, Chrissy gingerly stood up off the mattress, trying to avoid any movement that might disturb her now-sleeping friend. As she backed toward the door, she kept her eyes on Julia and offered up a prayer for her healing. Once again, she wasn't quite sure how she even knew to do that. Praying wasn't something she'd done for a very long time, until just a few nights prior.

She leaned against the door and remembered the strange but wonderful presence she had encountered that night with Julia. Manny had sent her once again into Julia's room to get her to stop singing, because she was the only one who seemed able to get the job done. What he didn't know was that Julia only agreed to stop singing if Chrissy would agree to stay and talk. At first it had seemed odd to the older girl. After all, she was seventeen, almost eighteen, and Julia was barely fourteen. But that wasn't the biggest issue. The years were only a small gap between them. It was their life experiences that were like the Grand Canyon.

It was only after Julia told her about the early tragedy in her life—of losing her dad and mom and twin sister on 9/11—that Chrissy slowly began to tell her own tragic tale. Of a teenage mother addicted to drugs. Of a father she had never met. Of sexual abuse and violence in places that were meant to be safe. And of the death of her beloved grandmother from a random bullet in a drive-by shooting. Julia listened with rapt attention and empathetic tears—and, much to Chrissy's surprise, not an ounce of judgment. It wasn't what she expected from what she would've labeled a "church girl." But there was something different about Julia. Win was right about that. Something that did stir up the hearts of the other girls. Something that smelled of hope and glowed like light. Something Chrissy longed for more than any drug or attention she had ever known. Something that made the love she thought she felt from Win feel like a twisted counterfeit of a pure reality.

"Chrissy," Julia's whisper pulled Chrissy back from where her mind had wandered.

She knelt back down onto the mattress and crawled up beside her young friend.

"What do you need?"

"Take this," Julia said, pulling her clenched fist up and out of the cocoon of blankets around her.

The Agreements

"What is it?" Chrissy said, opening her hand to receive a small wad of paper.

"Some money and a phone number."

Chrissy stared at the twenty-dollar bill.

"Where did you get this? If Manny finds out you've been taking money, there'll be hell to pay."

"It's mine," Julia reassured. "I've had it in my coat pocket since I got here."

Chrissy opened up the crumpled piece of paper and pulled it closer to her face. In the dim light she could barely make out the penciled numbers.

"Whose number is it?" she asked.

"My dad's," Julia whispered. "He's your way out."

An otherworldly gleam filled Julia's eyes, and Chrissy wondered if perhaps her friend had begun to hallucinate. She folded the money and paper back into a small parcel and tried to put it back into Julia's hand.

"You should keep this. You might just need it," she said.

Julia refused to accept the returned items.

"No," she replied. "I've seen it. You are getting out—and soon."

Chrissy reached out and ran her hand over Julia's forehead. It was warm, but not nearly as feverish as before.

"But I've got nowhere to go," Chrissy protested. "And there's no way I'm going anywhere without you."

"No. I'm not strong enough just yet. But it's okay. I need you to go first."

A strange burning sensation filled Chrissy's heart and her cheeks flushed deep pink.

"But . . . nobody goes anywhere around here without Manny knowing. How do you suppose I could possibly get out?"

The gleam in Julia's eyes intensified and a little giggle erupted from her lips. Her eyes scanned the room above and around Chrissy.

"Can't you see them?"

Chrissy whipped her head around in the small, shadowy space. Two nights before, when they had been talking, she could have sworn there was someone else in the room with them, but she hadn't said anything and she certainly hadn't seen anyone. But she had felt a presence. A beautiful, soothing presence. It was there again, even thicker than before. Goose bumps rippled over her skin from the top of her head to the tips of her toes. But try as she might to see what was causing this reaction, she couldn't see anything except the concrete walls.

"No . . . I don't . . . are you . . . what are you talking about?" she said.

"The fiery ones. They're here."

Tears unexpectedly rushed to Chrissy's eyes.

"No, now listen, hon," she said. "You've been really sick, and I think you're seeing things. So, you just try to sleep. I'll sit here for a minute with you. Okay?"

"Okay. But promise me you'll keep what I gave you."

"Alright. I'll keep it."

"And when the doors open, promise me"—Julia reached out and gripped the older girl's hand—"promise me you'll walk through."

Something in the way she spoke half scared and half inspired Chrissy.

"Sure. Sure. If the doors open up all by themselves, I promise. I'll go," she said, squeezing Julia's hand.

"And call Dad. He'll help you," Julia said as her eyes began to droop and her grip eased.

"Okay, okay," Chrissy said, setting Julia's hand back by her side. She peered at the money and the slip of paper one more time before sliding them inside her bra. She leaned back against the cold concrete walls and peered into the air. "God, if you're really here and you've really got a way out, then show me," she whispered. "And one more thing," she said after a momentary pause. "If I do get out, you'd better have somewhere in mind for me to go . . . somewhere better than this."

Chapter 39 – The Fear

"Am I nuts to even think about letting her do this?" Claude's voice sounded as tense as Elsie had ever heard it.

She held the phone close to her ear, settled her forearm onto her kitchen table, and let her eyes rest on the words of the Good Book open before her. She'd been reading when he called. Reading and meditating and praying—something she'd done a lot of since Claude and Nellie had left for Washington.

"Els, you still there?"

"Yes, I'm here. I'm just thinking. It's a lot to take in," Elsie replied.

"I know. Boy howdy, do I know," Claude said. "Sorry if it's too much."

"No, don't be sorry. I told you to call whenever you needed to talk. Just didn't expect it might be something like this," she said.

"Me either."

The two old friends sat in silence, he in his truck outside Cynthia and Raúl's house in La Verdad and she in the kitchen of her two-bedroom house in Grace.

"Are you smoking that old pipe of yours?" Elsie asked.

A moment of smoke-filled quiet preceded Claude's response.

"Guilty as charged. Thought it was a better choice of vice than a drink."

"Well, I'll give you that, alright," Elsie said. "So, this FBI agent. What's her name?"

"Reese. Brenda Reese."

"Agent Reese honestly thinks Nellie would be safe?"

"Well, she can't say that with 100 percent certainty, but she said they'd take every precaution available to them."

"It just seems like such a risk," Elsie said. "Isn't there someone else better qualified for the job?"

"Sure. That's what the FBI originally wanted to do. They've been working on finding a double who looks like Julia for days. That's why they wanted to meet Nellie. Better than looking at pictures, Agent Reese said."

"I suppose she doesn't get an identical twin option every day," Elsie admitted.

"She was in the middle of totally assessing Nellie when Nellie piped up and said, 'Why not just use me?'"

"Oh, I can just hear her now. And see the look on her face of complete and utter determination."

"You know it," Claude nodded. "Agent Reese just sat in her chair and stared into those deep-blue eyes, and Nellie stared right on back. Could've heard a pin drop in that room. Then Agent Reese turned to me and said 'What do you think, Grandpa? Think she could do it?'"

"Of course, she could do it," Elsie said. "That girl can do anything she sets her mind to. That's not the question. The question is *should* she do it."

"Took the words right out of my mouth."

"And I suppose you can't really find a better double than a true double. Hard to beat that."

"True. Plus, the agent grilled Rosie pretty thoroughly about what Julia was wearing when she last saw her and any other details she could think of that might convince the bad guys that they're looking at Julia and not someone else. Do you know what Rosie said?"

"What?"

The Agreements

"Well, I don't suppose I should really be telling you any of this, but since we've gone this far," he said, lowering his voice, "Rosie said she gave Julia a necklace the day they were separated. A necklace Beth had given to her on the day she was dedicated to the Lord as a baby. She described it perfectly, right on down to the inscription on the back and the scratch on the left side. Agent Reese was so excited. She said it was things like this that can make or break an operation."

"Don't that beat all," Elsie commented. "A necklace from Beth ... it's almost like ..."

"Like what?" Claude prompted.

"Like their mom is playing a part ... with a little act of kindness done years ago, she's reaching into today. Making a difference for her girls."

Quiet settled once more over the airwaves.

"Do you know the one thing Nellie told me that scares her?" Claude asked, letting out a slow stream of smoke that drifted up and out of the cab through a small opening in the window.

"No, can't imagine."

"She said she's scared of having to act girlie, 'cause acting girlie is what makes things unsafe."

"Hmm, well now. I suppose having experienced what she experienced with Michael Jones and now seeing this whole thing with Julia ... I suppose a person could reach that conclusion, alright."

"Then she told me she's not sure she even knows how to act like a 'real girl' would act."

"What? She's as real a girl as any."

"I know that and you know that, but apparently she doesn't know that. We had quite the talk about it on the way back over here from the Gomezes'. She even told me she thought God might have made a mistake. That she was really supposed to be a boy."

"Oh, for darn sake," Elsie blurted. "You don't have to be all caught up in makeup and clothes and dance recitals to be a girl! The good Lord makes us females in a wide variety. I used to ride bucking broncos in the rodeo when I was her age."

"You did?"

Elsie laughed. "I sure did. Better than most every boy in the county too. And that's because Mama sat me down one day after one of those boys, who I'd just showed up quite badly, shoved me to the ground and told me to get back into the kitchen where girls belonged. Mama told me that day that just 'cause God might've wrapped me up in female packaging didn't mean that he didn't fill my soul with strength and courage and a sense of adventure. And who was to say that riding a bucking bronco wasn't just as much where a girl belonged as cooking in the kitchen, if that's what was put in her heart to do?"

"Sounds like your mama was a spunky gal."

"Oh, you have no idea," Elsie replied. "I took her advice to heart, and I've got the trophies to prove it."

"Well, I'll be. You might have to show those to Nellie."

"I'll have to dig through a few boxes in the attic, but I would be delighted to do that for her when you get back."

"Yup, when we get back," Claude's voice trailed off. "If we get back . . ."

"Now, you listen to me, Claude Jolicoeur. Don't you let your mind wander off to the worst-case scenario. We've got to hope for the best and believe. I was just sitting here reading before you called, from the book of Esther. You know that story, don't ya?"

"Sure," Claude said with a sigh. "The orphan girl that wound up being the queen and saving her people, or something like that."

"In a very small nutshell, yes. She had a relative who was her guardian, just like Nellie does. Except hers was a cousin instead of a grandpa. Cousin Mordecai. And do you remember what Mordecai said when that young woman was placed in a position to be the heroine—a very dangerous position that could have cost her very life?"

"Remind me."

"Let me read it." She picked up her reading glasses. Placing the tortoiseshell spectacles on the end of her nose, she slid the Bible out a few inches into the best light. "It says here in chapter four and verse fourteen—and this is Mordecai talking to Esther—'For if you remain completely silent at this time, relief and deliverance will arise for the Jews from another place, but you and your father's house will perish. Yet who knows whether you have come to the kingdom for such a time as this?'"

Quietly, she slipped the glasses off and set them on top of the written pages.

"Maybe Nellie was born for such a time as this," she said. "Maybe this is part of the plan for her life. And maybe her being the kind of girl that isn't afraid of much of anything is an integral part of that plan."

Claude let out a deep sigh.

"That's what I'm afraid of," he muttered.

Lupe nestled the dried nine-by-thirteen pan back into its spot in the drawer beside the stove and turned back to the sink just in time to grab another wet dish from Claude's hand before he could set it in the drainer. They were the last ones in the kitchen after the post-Sunday-service dinner. The kids had cleared the table and loaded the dishwasher before disappearing into Julia and Rosie's bedroom. Hector and Maria had returned to church to fill Pastor Valdez in on the latest developments.

"Quite the shift in weather," Claude remarked to Lupe, his arms elbow deep in the soapy water in the sink.

"Yes, it's how it is sometimes here. Cold then no so cold then cold," she replied.

"Not complaining. Was glad to see the sun shining and the ice melting when we got up this morning. Will make the driving a lot easier tomorrow."

"It is much better."

They continued to work in quiet tandem, Claude scrubbing and rinsing, Lupe drying and putting away.

"Might not have been the best idea to go with you all to church this morning," Claude said. "Think Nellie felt like Princess Di in the middle of the paparazzi."

Nellie had caused quite a stir among the congregation when she and Claude had entered the sanctuary with the rest of the Gomez clan. Pastor Valdez himself had had to get behind the pulpit before the service even began to offer a brief clarification that this was indeed not Julia but her twin sister Nellie. Whispers and skeptical glances had continued throughout the hour of worship such that Pastor had been prompted to instruct the many well-wishers and gawkers to let the entire Gomez contingency exit before anyone else left their pews.

"Yes," Lupe agreed. "It was a little difficult. But she is what she is."

Claude stopped his scrubbing to look at her.

"What do ya mean by that?" he said.

"She is a princess," she stated. "A daughter of the King, no?"

"I suppose that's true," Claude said with a chuckle. "You're not the first one to remind me of her being royalty lately. It's a good thing, I guess, but sure comes with a lot of responsibility."

"You are scared," Lupe said.

Claude nodded.

"Don't be."

She turned to the pantry with her latest dried dish. Claude watched her march with certainty to her task and march back just as briskly.

"How can you say that?" he asked as he pulled the plug from the drain and swished water around the sides of the sink to clear it of soap and food scum.

Lupe stretched her damp towel over the handle of the oven door.

"You sit. I get coffee," she said.

Claude sat down and waited. He pulled his cell phone from his pocket and checked it for messages. A text from Elsie. "Praying," was all it said. He would've acknowledged it with a thanks of some sort, but he had yet to figure out the darn texting thing. Nellie usually handled that for him. There was a voice mail from Agent Reese. He swiped across it and pressed the start arrow.

The Agreements

"Will meet you at the Gomezes' at 0700. Ready to roll by 0730. Tell Nellie to get a good night's rest."

Lupe set a cup of steaming coffee on the table before him.

"Milk?" she asked, holding up a small carton.

"No," Claude said, covering his mug with one hand. "Black is good for me."

She poured some into her own mug and sat across the table from her guest.

"You will not be alone," she said.

"I know. We've got the FBI, and Jimmy Flanagan will do his part. And even Raúl has agreed to help in exchange for some leniency and such, but . . ." Claude said.

"Not just those. There are more. Many more," she said, waving off his words like a bee from a picnic lunch. "I have seen them. Los ángeles del fuego. The fiery angels. They will help."

Nellie's grandpa sat back in his chair and stared across the table at Julia's grandma. She sipped her coffee and peered back at him over the brim. She set the mug down and reached a hand across the checkered plastic tablecloth. Claude slowly reached out and placed his own much-larger hand in hers.

"You are not alone. She is not alone," she assured him with a squeeze of his well-calloused hand. "Never alone."

Chapter 40 – The Plot

The four Gomez children, plus Nellie, knelt in a huddled circle on the carpet in the girls' bedroom. Their heads nearly touched in the middle as Beto counted.

"One hundred eighty-six, 187, 188, 189. That's it. One hundred eighty-nine dollars and a few odd cents. That should be plenty to get you there and back."

"And you've got the keys to the shop and the three-wheeler?" Nellie asked, turning her head to Freddy.

"And the phone and charger?" Rosie added.

"Check and check," he replied.

"And Snoqualmie Pass is going to be clear tomorrow?" Beto asked.

"The DOT website says the road should be bare and dry. Might be a little chilly, but we can bundle up," Freddy said.

"And you're sure we can ride that thing that far?" Rosie asked.

Freddy's eyes narrowed at the challenge in her voice.

"Rode it all the way to the Tri-Cities and back last summer with Beto behind me," he replied.

"You did?" Rosie said. "Did Tío Raúl know?"

"He's the one who rode right beside us the whole way," Freddy replied.

"Does Daddy know?" Junior asked.

The Agreements

"No," Beto said, leaning his face closer to his little brother's. "And he better not ever find out. Right?"

Junior's lower lip began to quiver.

Rosie patted her baby brother on the back and glared at Beto. "Getting him all upset is not gonna help our cause here."

Beto backed up onto his haunches.

"And your friends are in? They're not gonna rat on us, right?" Nellie asked.

"No way. They love Jewels and they'd do whatever we asked if they thought it might be part of getting her back," Beto assured her.

"And you know how important your part is, right?" Nellie said to Junior, who was tucked right by her side.

He flashed her two thumbs-up. She gave him a quick side hug.

"I really appreciate this, guys," Nellie said.

Beto and Freddy shrugged like it was no big deal. Junior reached up and wrapped his arms around Nellie's neck.

"Well, I think it's the least we can do for you, seeing as we've been the ones to have Jewels all these years. I think we owe ya," Rosie said. "And besides, I promised her I'd come back for her, no matter what."

"To Nellie and Jewels—reunited," Beto said, reaching his hand into the center of the circle over the stack of bills.

"To Nellie and Jewels—reunited," the other Gomez siblings said, mimicking his actions.

Nellie smiled at them and placed her hand atop the pile of hands. "To us . . . all of us . . . reunited," she added.

They pumped their hands down once and then threw them up into the air.

Rosie began to gather the money into a pouch.

"Hey, Freddy, what did you do with the twenty dollars Lita gave you at Christmas? Everybody else's is in the pot," she said, sitting back on her heels.

The circle opened up like a flower in bloom as each one followed her lead.

"Spent it, I guess," Freddy said.

"On what?" Beto said.

"Stuff," his twin replied with a shrug.

"Great. We coulda used that right now," Beto said as he pushed Freddy backward.

Freddy's arms sprawled out and his back slammed into the bottom rail of the bunk beds. In a flash, he was back on his knees and shoving Beto the other direction. Beto fell flat on his back and Freddy pounced on top of him with fists flying. Rosie sprang to her feet, stuck her slipper-clad foot into Freddy's side, and gave a swift push. He toppled to his side into the lowest dresser drawer, causing the entire chest to tip precariously forward. Nellie leapt up just in time to keep it from falling squarely on top of Freddy. Rosie shot her hands out just in time to catch the jewelry box that was headed for the floor while Beto rescued one flying American Girl doll and Freddy half caught, half collided with the other when it landed headfirst on his stomach.

Junior burst into applause. "Yeah, you saved 'em! You saved 'em both!"

The older kids all turned to stare at the now-giggling youngest child. Then they looked back and forth to one another and erupted in laughter.

The door opened and Lupe stepped in.

"Everything is okay?" she asked.

"It was awesome, Lita!" Junior said. "Freddy was hitting, then Rosie was kicking, then he fell and stuff went all over and they caught it!" He got so excited by his own animated review of the melee, he jumped to his feet and ran and gave Lupe a hug around the waist before running back to the middle of the room and plopping down crisscross applesauce.

Lupe stared at the rest of the crew, who all scrambled to look cool and collected.

"That's all?" she asked.

"Yes, Lita," Rosie, Beto, and Freddy said in unison.

"Yes, Lita," Nellie added.

Their grandmother was about to shut the door when her eyes landed on the pile of money lying on the floor.

"What is that for?" she said.

The Agreements

"Oh, uh, this?" Beto said. "We were just . . ."

"They were showing me all their Christmas and birthday money," Nellie said.

"Oh, sí? Why?" Lupe said.

"'Cause," Rosie added, "we're gonna send some with Nellie and her grandpa to, uh, to you know, help with the cause and stuff."

"Yeah, just in case they need something along the way or something," Freddy said, shedding the doll from his lap.

Lupe assessed their faces one by one.

"Ten cuidado, niños," she said. "Be careful."

Then she left.

Everyone slumped to the floor.

"Yeesh, that was close," Beto said.

"Well, if you two could behave for like more than two minutes," Rosie glared from one older brother to the next.

"He shoved me," Freddy said, pointing at Beto.

"You were being a selfish ding-dong," Beto replied. "Want me to do it again?"

"See what I mean?" Rosie said, putting her hands on both of their chests. "I rest my case."

The twins glared at each other but backed down.

"What did Lita mean?" Nellie asked as peace was restored once again.

"About what?" Freddy asked.

"That thing she said before she left," Nellie said.

"Oh, that. She was just telling us to be careful," Beto replied.

"Do you think she knows what we're planning?" Nellie whispered.

The five sat in silence, pondering that possibility.

"Nah," Freddy said, "she was just talking about us fighting and stuff . . . I think . . . maybe . . . pretty sure."

Chapter 41 – The Opening

The miniature digital clock glued to the headboard read 6:43 a.m. when the knocking started.

"Go away, Manny," Chrissy grumbled loud enough to penetrate the locked door. "I just barely got to sleep."

But the banging on the door only increased.

"Un-flipping-believable," she said, rolling onto her back and rubbing both hands over her weary eyes.

Bam, bam, bam.

"Quit knocking and just open the damn thing," she yelled as she threw off her blanket, flung her feet over the side of the bed, and sat up. She flicked on the lamp that sat on the short chest of drawers that contained all her worldly possessions. Everything in the tiny space was a perk from Win's on-again, off-again favor. She yanked up her underwear and pulled the straps of her lacy camisole back up onto her shoulders.

A key turned in the lock and the door swung open. Chrissy quickly reached for her velour jacket on the floor and tugged it on when she saw that the man standing on the threshold was not Manny or any of the guys who worked for him.

"Dude, you can't be back here," she said.

The man was dressed in crisp, gray coveralls with the emblem of a crown stitched on his chest pocket. His jet-black hair and prominent ebony forehead nearly touched the top of the doorframe, and his shoulders tested the seams of his uniform until it seemed a wonder that they didn't burst.

"Are you with the laundry guys?" Chrissy asked. "I thought you only picked up on Thursdays."

"There's been a change of plans," the man said, pulling a small notebook from the pocket of his coveralls. He looked at her with his deep-chocolate eyes, flipped open the notebook's cover, and ran his fingers down the top sheet of paper.

"Lombardi, Christina Benedetta," he read. "Is that you?"

Chrissy zipped up her jacket, crossed her arms, and stuck out her chin.

"So, what if it is?" she said. "My uniforms are cleaner than pretty much everyone's. What's your problem?"

He looked up and smiled, and his previously serious countenance softened into a genuine warmth.

"Just making sure I have the correct room," he replied, closing the notebook and sliding it back into his pocket.

"Well, if you're not here for the laundry, then you're gonna have to make an appointment like everybody else in this joint. And I am off duty, mister."

The man did not reply.

"I will scream, ya know, and when I do, Manny's gonna come, and you do not want to mess with him. So I suggest you get on outta here," she said, leaning back into the padded headboard and pulling her legs onto the bed.

"Fear not. I mean you no harm," he said. "I am here for your welfare."

Chrissy rolled her eyes and let out a brittle laugh.

"Well, I ain't heard it said quite like that before," she said.

The man stepped into the room.

Chrissy reached for the lamp, readying it as a weapon.

"Come, the time is now," he said. "The door is open."

Chrissy froze in her spot with the lamp raised above her head. The hair on her arms stood to attention and her heart fluttered rapidly.

"What did you say?" she whispered.

"The door is open."

Slowly, she lowered the lamp and set it back in its place. The man waited.

The door is open.

Julia's face flashed across her mind and her own words echoed in her ears.

She had made a promise.

She pulled open the top drawer and took out the bottoms to her Juicy Couture tracksuit and a pair of flip-flops. The stranger turned his back and stood like a sentinel in the doorway as she dressed.

"Who are you, anyways? A new janitor or something?" she said.

"Not exactly."

"How do I know I can trust you?"

"The phone number and the money," he said over his shoulder. "You'll want to bring those with you."

Chrissy's eyes popped wide open. She spun around and dropped to her knees. Her head disappeared under the bed as one arm reached into her hiding place beneath the mattress. She gripped the note and the money from Julia in her hand and stuffed them both into her jacket pocket as she stood.

"I'm ready now," she said.

"Good. Follow me."

Chrissy stepped into his shadow and out into the empty hallway. The familiar smell of lavender, mango, and mint massage oils mingled with her suddenly activated deodorant. She quickly checked both ways, expecting Manny or one of his cronies to appear at any moment. But no one did. The two walked swiftly, almost as if flying, to the end of the darkened hallway past all the other locked doors. Chrissy tapped the stranger on the back as they passed Julia's room.

"Can we bring my friend?" she whispered.

"Now is not her time," he replied over his shoulder. "Come."

They turned left down another hall. Chrissy moved even closer to her rescuer and grabbed a handful of his gray coveralls. To the

The Agreements

right was Manny's office. She could see him through the half-opened blinds of the window sitting behind his desk, sipping coffee and staring at his luminous computer screen. Just as they were square in the middle of his window, he looked up and straight at them. Chrissy stopped dead in her tracks.

"Be not afraid," the stranger said. "Don't stop."

Manny lifted his mug, took a drink, and returned his eyes to the screen as if he hadn't seen a thing. Chrissy exhaled. The escaping pair continued on their way.

"What about the guard? And the lock?" she whispered, poking her head around his shoulder.

The stranger turned his head sideways with a finger to his lips to silence her. They walked past more locked doors toward the final turn that would lead them to the rear exit to the alley. Chrissy gasped as she saw the hulking form of the guard sitting on a barstool beside the door. His chin lay on his chest, which rose slowly up and down in a somnolent rhythm, his back leaning against the wall. Suddenly the sound of chains rattling and falling to the floor filled the hallway as the back exit door swung open and brilliant sunlight flooded in. Chrissy blinked rapidly at the brightness and shrank back. A hand reached for hers and drew her out of the darkness and into the light. Instinctively, she lifted a forearm up to shield her face, certain that the guard was awake and about to accost her. But nothing happened.

When she dropped her arm, Chrissy found herself at the far end of the alley, beside a busy street. She spun around, frantically trying to figure out where she was. Way down the alley, a full block away, she spotted the deep red of Sheer Pleasure Spa. She swung back around. The stranger in the coveralls was standing beside the street, almost out in the traffic, with one arm waving up and down. A bright-green car with yellow stripes and a taxi light on its roof pulled over.

"Tell him to take you to 13 Coins on International Boulevard," the man said, opening the back door of the taxi for her to get in.

Chrissy stepped into the car and sat. She looked up to say goodbye and thanks, but the man was gone.

"Miss," the taxi driver said, looking at her in his rearview mirror. "Where to?"

"To 13 Coins on International Boulevard," she said while she peered up and down the sidewalk for any sign of the man in the gray coveralls.

"Uh, miss," the driver said.

Chrissy tore her eyes away from her search and looked at him.

"You're gonna have to close that door before we can go anywhere," he said.

Chapter 42 – The Call

Hector tried to keep the anxiety he felt in his heart from showing on his face as he joined Maria, Lupe, and the kids on the front lawn. His family didn't need to know how concerned he truly was about the unfolding events in their lives. It was 7:15 a.m., and Agent Reese stood with her hands stuffed into the pockets of her khaki trench coat beside the sedan that was parked alongside the curb in front of Claude's truck. Both of the vehicles had their engines running.

"So, we are headed to Jimmy Flanagan's house in Bellevue. You've got the address and the directions, yes?" the FBI agent in charge addressed her remarks to Claude.

"Yes, ma'am," Claude replied.

"Should get there well before noon if we can get out of here soon."

"Sounds about right," Claude replied.

"Just stick right behind me and call if you need to stop," she said. "And don't putter. I'll be cruising right along."

"He doesn't putter," Nellie said.

"I suspected as much," the agent said. Turning back to Claude, she said, "It would be a whole lot quicker if we just flew, you know."

"I know," Claude replied. "But I think Nellie and I could use some time to sort of decompress and process this whole thing before we get into the, uh, mission, or whatever you call it."

"The sting operation," Agent Reese said.

"Yeah, that."

"Fair enough. My team has a few things to get into place before we arrive, anyway," she said, running a hand through her short, auburn hair and tamping it into place. "Well, best say your goodbyes. Soon as you get in your rig, I'll be ready to roll." She walked around the hood of her vehicle and sat down behind the driver's seat.

Maria was the first to encircle Nellie in a fierce hug while everyone else watched. After several long moments, Maria pulled back and looked directly into Nellie's eyes.

"You can do this," she said, zipping Nellie's down-filled jacket a few inches higher, though it wasn't really necessary in the morning's mild temperatures. "I have no doubt in my mind you can. Since the day you were born, you have been fearless and strong. Do you hear me?"

Nellie nodded as Maria released her and Hector moved in for a farewell embrace.

"You know we'll be praying," he said, patting her back and stepping away without making full eye contact. "Kids, come on, give Nellie and Claude some love." It took extreme effort to keep his voice from shaking.

One by one, the Gomezes hugged first Nellie and then Claude.

Maria stepped alongside her husband and entwined her arm through his crooked elbow, above where his hands were deeply entrenched in his hoodie pockets. Her touch released the waterworks he had been trying to control, and tears spilled down his face. She reached up and gently wiped them away.

"Way to go, guys," Maria said to her kids as she wiped her own eyes. "You're doing a better job than your dad and I at not blubbering like babies."

"That's 'cause crying won't help nothin'," Junior piped up.

The Agreements

Rosie quickly got a hold of Junior's jacket hood and yanked him back up against her legs.

"Ouch. Why'd ya do that?" Junior said, swatting her hand away.

"Just keeping you out of the way," Rosie said.

"I don't wanna be out of the way," he protested. "I've got an important job. Nellie said so."

"A job?" Lupe interjected over the lip of her steaming coffee mug.

"To be brave," Nellie said quickly. "To be brave for me and for Jewels. Right, buddy?"

Junior looked up at her and gave her a big wink.

Hector had to chuckle at his antics, but he noticed his mother-in-law was not amused. She was looking slowly from one grandchild to the next as she sipped from her morning drink. Not one of them seemed to be able to meet her gaze.

"Well, sure wish I could go with you," Hector said, reaching out to shake Claude's hand. "But leaving town is out of the question for us . . . as you know."

"For now," Claude said, returning the handshake and placing his other hand on Hector's shoulder.

A short honk from the sedan split the air at the same time as Hector's phone rang in his pocket.

"Guess that means it's time to go," Claude said.

The two Jolicoeurs settled themselves into their rig. Nellie rolled down her window right away and reached out a hand to Rosie, who came running to grasp it.

"Hello," Hector said into his phone while keeping his eye on the farewells and backing up under the maple tree still wrapped in yellow ribbon.

Rosie stepped up onto the truck's sideboard and whispered something into Nellie's ear. Maria walked over and put a hand on her daughter's arm.

"Come on, mija. We need to let them go," she said. "And you guys need to get ready for school. It's a big week. You've got a lot to get done before the science fair on Wednesday."

In the midst of all the noise, Hector couldn't quite make out who the person on the other end of the line was, let alone what she was saying.

"Excuse me . . . thirteen what? Where?" he said, putting a finger into the ear away from the phone.

Rosie stepped back onto the lawn as the FBI agent pulled out into the street with the Jolicoeur pickup close behind. Nellie hung her head out the window and waved to the family tableau on the yard.

"Wait. Slow down, slow down," Hector said, hunching into the phone as he tried to concentrate on the caller's voice over the wave of adrenaline coursing through his body. "Um . . . um . . . yeah . . . Where? Okay . . . What did you say your name was?"

Rosie turned to stare at the sound of the rising agitation in her father's voice.

"Wait!" Hector yelled, running toward the street.

The two vehicles were already at the stop sign at the corner.

"Boys, run after them!" Hector ordered.

Freddy and Beto stared at him.

"Go! Now! Just do it," Hector urged them into action.

The two boys took off into the street, their arms flailing like windmills on hyperdrive, trying to catch Claude's attention. They cut through the neighbor's yard at the corner of the block and sprinted onto the next street where the two vehicles had turned, yelling as they went. Suddenly the brake lights lit up on Claude's truck. Freddy raced to the driver's side, where Claude already had his head out the window.

Hector kept talking to the woman on the phone, hoping he could keep her engaged in conversation.

Claude laid on the truck horn and flashed his lights before backing up around the corner. The black sedan followed suit in a hurry.

When the two rigs stood once again in front of the Gomez house, Agent Reese jumped from her vehicle and yelled over the roof of the car, "What the hell is going on, Hector?"

"It's a girl, or a woman. I don't really know," he yelled as he sped toward her with the phone. "Her name is Chrissy. Says she's friends with Julia."

"Where are they?"

"Not together. She's at 13 Coins in SeaTac. She says Jewels is being held at some spa."

Agent Reese snatched the phone from Hector and held it to her ear.

"This is Agent Reese of the FBI. Who am I speaking with?" she said as she slid back into her car with the phone.

Hector stepped away and back to Claude's truck, where he explained what was going on. Maria slipped between the parked cars and stood beside him as he recounted the conversation with Chrissy.

"Holy mackerel," Claude muttered.

Nellie leaned around her grandpa.

"Is Jewels okay?"

"Uh, well," Hector said. "She's alive. But the girl said Jewels has been sick."

"Sick!" Maria said. "What kind of sick?"

"Didn't say. Just sick."

Beto and Freddy rejoined the group, breathing heavily.

"What the heck is going on?" Freddy huffed.

"Yeah, tell us what's happening," Rosie demanded from her spot on the curb where she stood next to Lupe, who had restrained both her and Junior from entering the fray.

Before Hector could reply, Agent Reese got out of her car and marched back to where they stood. She held the phone back and away from them.

"She's still on the line. I need to make some calls and get someone to her ASAP. Can you keep her talking while I do that?" Agent Reese said to Hector.

"Sure, sure. Whatever you need," he said. "But what should I say?"

"Doesn't matter, as long as you keep her calm and keep her where she is," she said, handing the phone back to its rightful owner. "Claude, change of plans. You're gonna have to drive by yourself. I need to get to Seattle ASAP, and you won't be legally able to follow at the speed I will be going. You okay with that?"

"I can handle it," Claude replied.

She put both hands on the ledge of the driver's side window of the pickup and leaned in close.

"But don't even think of not being in Bellevue before noon. Got it?" she said.

"Ten-four," Claude replied.

"Alright then," she said with a pat on the metal frame. "I'm off," she said, jogging back to her sedan. As soon as she pulled away from the curb, bars of red and blue lights flashed to life from the front and rear of her vehicle, splashing across the bodies still arranged by Claude's pickup and on the Gomez lawn.

"Uh, hello, Chrissy? You still there?" Hector said as Maria tucked her head right next to his phone. They both plugged their free ears as Agent Reese's tires screeched around the corner by the stop sign.

Chapter 43 – The Love

Although Claude had told Agent Reese that he and Nellie needed the drive time to process, there wasn't much talking going on between the two of them as the miles sped by. Carlyle sat in his usual spot on the top of the back seat as they travelled I-82 through the hills past Yakima.

Claude's cell phone pinged where it rested in Nellie's lap.

"Who is it?" Claude said.

"Elsie," she replied. "Again."

"Tell her we're just about to I-90 outside of Ellensburg and I'll give her a call when we get to the Flanagans'."

Carlyle noted how much deeper the blue of Claude's heart light became at just the mention of Elsie's name.

"Can I text Eric too?" Nellie asked.

"Yes, but remember, no details. We're still in La Verdad, as far as he's concerned."

"I know," she replied. "It's not like he's gonna track our GPS or something."

Her fingers flew over the phone's small keyboard for several minutes.

"Uh, that sounds like details," Claude remarked.

"Well, it's not," she said, flipping the phone back over in her lap. "Just thought I'd send one to Rosie too."

"Okay, but nobody else back home. You know how fast news can get around Grace."

"Faster than me and my Kawasaki on a straightaway?"

"Not quite that fast."

Silence once again settled into the Silverado's crew cab. Carlyle peered into the large rearview mirror on Nellie's side of the truck. Then he checked the one outside Claude's window. No sign of them. Nellie must've warned them to stay back a bit farther. Their sudden appearance in the rearview mirrors as they were passing Selah had caused Nellie's face to blanch.

After Agent Reese had sped away, Claude and Nellie had stayed and listened to the remainder of Hector's conversation with the mysterious Chrissy. Lupe had gathered the Gomez kids and hustled them back to the house to get ready for school, seeming only slightly suspicious at their instant cooperation. The extra minutes Claude had spent debriefing with Hector and Maria once they were off the phone must've given Freddy and Rosie time to get to Raúl's place. They had certainly not wasted any time getting on the three-wheeler and getting out of town. Carlyle had to admit he was both surprised and impressed by their efficiency in implementing their wild hair of a plan.

Fortunately, Claude hadn't seen them—or at least seen them for who they were. Beneath their helmets they were hard to recognize, but it had caused Nellie's heart light to flash an astonishing shade of intense yellow.

Even after the scare of being busted had passed, the amber glow within the younger Jolicoeur twin had continued to intensify. Carlyle sensed the growing urgency within Nellie with every passing mile. They were getting closer and closer to Julia.

In the instant he thought her name, the light machine appeared and he was whisked up onto its seat and off like a rocket ahead of the Silverado, headed straight for Seattle.

***

The Agreements

When Carlyle arrived in Julia's tiny concrete cell, there was a woman sitting on the mattress beside the teenage girl. She held Julia's head in her lap and hummed softly as she gently ran a hand over the sick girl's forehead and down her tangled hair. Something about her was very familiar. Carlyle left his light machine near the ceiling and situated himself between Julia's curled-up knees and the wall. He peeked under the cascade of blond tresses that fell from the woman's head like a curtain.

What he saw caused him to fall abruptly back against the wall.

"Hello, Carlyle," the woman said, looking up at him. "I've been wondering when you would show up."

Carlyle stared at her visage. He almost didn't recognize her. She was herself and yet beyond herself. But as she returned to her ministrations, an extraordinary seafoam green light emerged from her being and filled the space.

"Mom?" he said. "I, uh, I mean, Beth?"

"One and the same," she replied.

"But how? That is . . . are you . . . can you?"

Beth smiled at him.

"It's a thin place."

He had, of course, been taught about thin places in his training with Madeline—the places where the distance between heaven and earth becomes so small that you can see into one from the other.

"Can Julia . . . does she know you're here?" he whispered.

"I believe so," Beth said. "She told me she loved me and then fell fast asleep."

Carlyle leaned back against the cold stone wall.

"But how did you . . . I mean, we've never met before," he said. "How do you know me?"

"Just because your vision has been limited doesn't mean mine has," she replied.

He crossed his arms over his chest and his brows furrowed. Beth let out a chuckle.

"Now don't pout," she said. "Everything has its order. One day you'll know fully. But your current parameters, or what you think of as restrictions, are serving their purpose."

Carlyle's facial features relaxed and the room fell quiet, save for Julia's soft, steady breathing. Seconds and minutes and hours ticked by.

The sound of a key being inserted into the door split the stillness. The deadbolt slid back and the door opened. Manny's face appeared first and then Win's.

Carlyle wondered if they might be able to see a glimpse of Julia's mom, given the thinness of the room's atmosphere, but it soon became evident that their vision was only and completely earthbound.

"Like I told ya," Manny said, "she's here. They're all here. It's only Chrissy that's gone."

Manny's face disappeared, but Win remained staring at Julia.

"She doesn't look so great," he said.

"Well, she's got water in there and a whole bottle of Tylenol. What else do ya expect me to do?" Manny's muffled voice filtered around the door.

Win swung around to face his head of security and grabbed him by the front of his leather jacket.

"I expect you to keep them from disappearing," he snarled.

"Hey, hey, hey now, Boss," Manny said. "It's just Chrissy. She'll be back. She always comes back."

Win slowly released his grip.

"How many guys you got looking for her?" he asked.

"As many as we can spare and still keep this place secure," Manny said.

"Find her."

"You got it, Boss."

"Twenty-four hours, Manny. That's it."

"Sure thing, Boss."

"And if she's not back by then, we pack this place up."

"Where are we going?"

The Agreements

"Just do your job and we won't have to go anywhere," Win said.

"What about her?" Manny said.

"Who? The princess?"

"Yeah, you know. What if she keeps getting sicker?"

A moment of silence passed and then another.

"Just do what you do, Manny. And leave me out of it," Win said as his steps began to recede down the hallway.

Manny poked his head into the room one last time and stared at Julia, his eyes shifting back and forth as if calculating his next move.

"Twenty-four hours," he said quietly to himself before shutting the door and sliding the deadbolt back into place.

Carlyle stood up and glared at the door.

"This is crazy," he said to Beth. "We've got to get her out of here."

"We?"

"I mean, you know, somebody. Somebody has got to get her out of here."

Beth did not reply.

"Did you know Chrissy escaped?" Carlyle said as he began to pace back and forth along the space over the edge of the mattress.

"Yes," she replied.

"Do you know how?"

"With some assistance from the fiery ones, I believe."

"The ones from the high tower?"

"Yes, the very same."

"But . . . why would they . . . what about . . . ," he said, coming to a halt. "If they could help Chrissy, why wouldn't they help Julia?"

Beth sighed deeply, leaned down, and kissed her daughter's cheek. Then she lifted her eyes and gazed at Carlyle.

"Everything has its order," she said.

And then, she was gone.

Carlyle sank down beside Julia and stared at the place her mother had just occupied. There was a shining, grand goodness that hung like a residue in the air. Possibilities flowed from it like a life-giving stream into his heart and filled his imagination. He let his mind wander beyond the confines of the room to the many places Madeline had shown him during this assignment. There was so much he didn't understand about the Designer's plans for the human race. Yet Beth's appearance in the thin place had reminded him once again that at the core of it all remained this one thing: love.

"And love," he reminded himself, "love never fails."

Chapter 44 – The Quarry

It wasn't as if he had fallen asleep, for watchers never sleep. But the tapping on his shoulder pulled Carlyle up and out of what he imagined sleep must be like. A little giggle behind him caused him to spin around. And there, standing in glorious purple light, smiling broadly, was Julia. Carlyle was dazed. He gaped at her sudden change in appearance and at his own. They were equal size. Then he surveyed the space around them. The concrete walls were gone. The grubby mattress and airless space had been replaced by a broad, open plain of waving grass and endless azure sky. Down the middle of the plain stretched a narrow gravel path, just wide enough for the two to walk side by side.

"Let's go," Julia urged.

He hesitated, still scanning their surroundings.

"What are you waiting for?" she asked.

"It's just that usually when I'm here . . ." he replied.

"You've been here before?"

"Well, not exactly here in this spot, but, yes, here."

"Okay. So, what usually happens here?" she asked.

"Usually, someone meets me. I guess you'd call her a friend."

"Ooh, I'd like to meet a friend of yours," Julia said, joining his search. "What's her name?"

"Madeline," he said. "Madeline of the High Plains."

"Well, this sure looks like a high plain."

"Yeah, this is definitely her kind of place," Carlyle said as the two of them turned in a slow complete circle. "But I don't see her."

"Maybe we're supposed to find her," Julia suggested.

"Could be."

Julia reached out her hand and Carlyle slipped his into hers. It was odd to communicate so freely with her—at least to him, although she seemed totally unfazed by the turn of events.

"Let's go," she said.

And off they went.

Julia swung their joined hands back and forth in rhythm to their steps. Absolute silence reigned, save for a faint pulsing frequency that exuded upward from the ground through their feet and into their bodies. It was constant, steady, and full of a life force that seemed to shake away the weightiness of earthly cares like heavy snow being shaken off drooping branches. The farther they journeyed, the faster they moved without any effort to increase their pace. Soon the grass was speeding by them on either side in a verdant blur, as if the path itself were propelling them faster and faster.

The two of them came to a sudden halt at the edge of an enormous canyon. As far as their eyes could see and beyond, layers of precious stones ran in sparkling strata along every wall. A sound like tinkling bells and cymbals reverberated all around them. Julia let her toes dangle over the edge and looked straight down.

"Look, Car," she said. "Look at the miners."

He stared at the scene spread out below them.

The broad opening of the canyon grew ever smaller in tidy increments all the way to the bottom, where a glittering river flowed, reflecting the many colors of the surrounding rocks. Along the ledges that jutted out like layers on a massive wedding cake, an army of beings were busily at work excavating precious gems from the rock. Clothed in immaculate blue coveralls, their tools glimmered in silvery arcs as they swung them. Every contact with the rock sparked pure percussive notes. Rhythms and melodies emerged and echoed and mingled.

The Agreements

Carlyle and Julia watched closely as a group of four workers directly below them dug out an opal so large it took all of them to remove it and set it gently on the stone at their feet. With great care they chipped away small areas of sediment that clung to the opal's surface. Then they all replaced their mining tools into their tool belts and pulled silky kerchiefs from their pockets. With vigorous circular motions, they buffed the opal until it shone so brightly Carlyle and Julia had to squint to keep watching. The workers then stepped back from their task and admired the exquisite gem. With great joy, they slapped one another on the back and shook one another's hands in congratulations on a job well done.

Without any signal or call that the two observers could perceive, a winged angel landed on the ledge next to the opal. He was four times the size of the miners, yet as he towered over them, he bowed slightly in their direction and they bowed back. The angel, garbed from neck to toe in luminescent light, turned his back to the stone and knelt down. He opened his wings wide to reveal a golden carrier strapped to his back. Prongs stuck out from a flat, golden surface like an empty setting of a ring awaiting a stone. The miners situated themselves at each corner of the opal and lifted it onto the carrier. It fit perfectly and securely into its place. One of the miners tapped the angel's wing and the angel propelled himself off the ledge and soared out over the canyon.

"Can we follow him?" Julia said.

"I suppose we can," Carlyle said.

Without so much as a moment's hesitation, Julia launched herself off the ledge of the canyon and glided with ease in the path of the angel, as if flying were her natural mode of transportation. Carlyle followed suit. On every side of them angels similar to the one they followed joined their ranks and flew in formation, like highly trained jet pilots, with wingtips breathtakingly close but never touching.

The ever-increasing entourage flew down the length of the canyon, past hosts of miners along countless ledges. At the very far end of the canyon floor, a lake appeared. Its surface was glossy and flat, without so much as a ripple. They seemed to be headed directly for its shores.

Suddenly, the angels broke rank and whole banks of them veered off in one direction, while others went another. The angel Carlyle and Julia had been following jetted steeply to the left and disappeared in a host of other delivery angels. In the blink of an eye, the sky around them was clear of the entire flying contingent.

"Now what?" Julia asked.

And then, as if in response to her question, a magnificent airplane materialized next to them. The plane was shaped like a cone with an active lightning bolt jutting from the front tip and a brilliant aurora of fire emanating from the spherical rear end. As they watched, three hatches opened along the length of the plane. In the front cockpit sat Madeline.

"Climb aboard," she said.

Julia clapped her hands.

"You're Madeline of the High Plains, aren't you?"

"Indeed, I am," Madeline replied.

"I knew we'd find you! I just knew it," Julia said, climbing onto the wing of the aircraft and up into the seat behind Madeline. "Although maybe it was you who found us."

"Maybe a little bit of both," Madeline said. "Come on, Carlyle. Hop in."

When both passengers were in their compartments and the hatches lowered, the aircraft shot straight upward at a tremendous speed. They looped-de-looped back over themselves before barrel-rolling forward. A broad grin lit Carlyle's face. Madeline was at it again. Even over the roar of the engines he could hear her laugh. And, much to his surprise, he could hear Julia laughing as well. In fact, she was whooping and hollering as if she were on the most fantastic of roller coasters. In all the time he'd known her, he had never heard her be so freely expressive.

At some length, Madeline eased up on the throttle as the plane approached what looked like one of the walls of the canyon. Beneath them was the mirrorlike lake, with the river flowing out behind them. Carlyle shook his head and chuckled. They had flown in a complete circle, back to where they had begun. As they eased forward, the canyon wall evaporated and an opening into a large cave appeared. Madeline drove straight into the space and settled the aircraft gently on a floor of polished granite. Their individual hatches opened and the three emerged from their compartments onto the wing.

"Can we do that again?" Julia asked immediately.

"How about if I teach you to fly yourself?" the pilot answered while unwrapping her lush braid from its swirl around her neck.

"Seriously?" Julia said.

"Completely seriously," Madeline replied. "But not right now. Now we have places to go. Follow me."

A silver staircase emerged from the plane's wing and they descended onto the cavern floor. Carlyle and Julia fell in behind Madeline as she led the way across the enormous empty space at a brisk pace.

At the far end of the cavern were bronze double doors fitted snugly into a wall of gold. As they approached, the doors swung open of their own accord and Madeline stepped across the threshold, with Julia and Carlyle close behind. Before them stretched a tremendous, long cavern with a soaring ceiling and golden walls lined with blueprints. From three feet above the floor to fifty feet, the blueprints covered every square inch of the walls for as far as the eye could see. Hovering all along the way at various heights and distances were pairs of miners carefully studying the drafted design. One busily scribbled in a small notebook while the other scanned along the parchment with a finger and read something aloud to his partner. After they had acquired whatever it was they were looking for, the pair flew off and out the front of the cavern, which opened out into the canyon and the lake. The space hummed with activity like the inside of a beehive.

As Madeline, Carlyle, and Julia walked past the workers, some turned to wave and greet Madeline, who returned their greetings, calling each by name but stopping to chat with none.

"Does she know everybody?" Julia whispered to Carlyle.

"Everywhere I've been she does," he replied.

"Do you know where we're going?" she asked.

"Not really," he said. "But usually, about now is when he shows up."

"Who?"

"The guy we've come to see," he whispered back.

"And who is that?"

Carlyle pointed to a pair of men walking toward them from a long distance away.

"The guy in all white on the left is named Grammateus."

"Who's the other one?"

"Not sure," Carlyle said. "But I'm sure we're about to find out."

Suddenly, Julia took off sprinting straight toward the two men. Carlyle was about to join her, but Madeline put a hand on his chest and stopped him.

"Let them be," she said.

The man next to Grammateus took off running toward Julia with his arms open wide.

"Daddy," Julia cried. "Daddy, it's me!"

Ryan swept Julia up in his arms and spun her around. With her head buried in his chest and her feet flying out behind her, the pair looked like a merry-go-round bathed in an aura of plum and bronze light.

"My girl. My Julia!" Ryan sang out as they spun.

Grammateus stood motionless beside the father and daughter, with his hands clasped behind his back. From the place where Carlyle and Madeline remained at a respectful distance, the light that glowed from the Scrollmaster's face made it plain to see that he was immensely satisfied with the reunion.

"Come," Madeline said to Carlyle once the spinning had stopped and the two Jolicoeurs had settled into a quiet forehead-to-forehead conversation.

At their approach, Julia looked up and smiled.

"Car," she said. "This is my dad!"

Ryan reached out a hand in greeting and Carlyle shook it.

"Sir," Carlyle said. "It's wonderful to see you again. I'm so you glad you . . . you made it."

Ryan laughed.

"It only takes a moment," he said.

"Yes, sir. I believe that is true," Carlyle replied.

"Oh, I know it's true," Ryan said, placing a hand atop Carlyle's shoulder. "And, hey, thanks for watching over my girl and bringing her here."

"Well, I'm not sure I, uh, brought her exactly," Carlyle replied. "More like she brought me, I think."

Grammateus cleared his throat and the watcher, the father, and the daughter turned to him.

"If you three will follow me," he said. "I have things to show you."

Turning to Madeline, he said, "I believe you have another appointment."

"Yes, indeed," she said and then vanished.

"Where did she go?" Julia asked.

"To meet with the Designer," Grammateus replied.

"Do we get to meet him too?" she inquired.

Grammateus smiled and peered deeply into her eyes.

"If you have seen me," he said. "You have seen him."

"Oh," Julia said, meeting his stare with equal intensity. "Then I think . . . I think I like him very much."

Grammateus broke out into laughter. Every being in the entire space paused to listen to the wondrous sound of it.

"But will Madeline be back?" Julia asked when the laughter finally faded. "I didn't get to say goodbye."

"Not to worry, dear one," Grammateus replied. "She has simply gone ahead of you. Now come, let's see what you have come to see."

With that, he raised up off the floor and glided to a spot halfway up the blueprint-papered wall. The miners who were busy about their business in that area bowed at his presence and then returned quietly to their work. Grammateus motioned for Ryan, Julia, and Carlyle to join him, and they did.

"Right here," Grammateus said, pointing to a place on the schema. "This is the exact spot from which the Jolicoeur line was hewn. Do you see?"

Ryan and Julia leaned in together, their hands clasped between them.

"Ah, that looks like my mother," Ryan said, excitedly indicating a rich amethyst stone embedded in the plans.

"Is that your dad?" Julia asked, pointing to a deep sapphire stone next to it.

Ryan gazed at the stone quietly for a moment.

"Yes, I suppose it is," he replied.

"Ooh, here's Mommy," Julia said, with her finger on an exquisite green tourmaline.

"That's her, alright," Ryan agreed. "And look right beneath her. That's you, and that's Nellie."

Julia and Carlyle pressed even closer to the plans.

"Place your hands on your gemstones," Grammateus directed.

Julia and Ryan reached out a hand each and laid it over their own stone.

"Tell me what you feel," Grammateus instructed.

Carlyle watched in fascination as the light from the stones shone so brightly, they penetrated both of their hands and lit up their faces.

"It's pulsing," Ryan said.

"Like a heartbeat," Julia added.

"Exactly," Grammateus said. "The heart of the Designer lives in every stone hewn from this quarry. Each one a piece of him. Each piece a part of his plan."

Ryan pointed with his free hand to his father's stone.

"Even this one?" he said.

"Touch it and see," Grammateus replied.

Ryan hesitated and then set his hand over the place where Claude's stone resided.

Silent moments passed.

The Agreements

Then, through the hand of the son, a blue light began to glow. Faint at first, it grew in intensity until Ryan pulled his hand away, as if to save it from fire. He gazed back at Grammateus.

"I never knew," he said.

"I know you didn't," Grammateus said. "But it's true. After years of following the counterfeit, he has returned to fulfilling his authentic scroll."

"Well, I'm glad to hear it," Ryan said. "Thanks for showing me."

"My pleasure," Grammateus replied. "But know that it is for more than just your benefit I have revealed these things."

Ryan nodded and smiled at his daughter. He sighed with satisfaction and looked back to Grammateus. Their eyes locked. Carlyle sensed the two of them were having a conversation, but what it was he could not guess, for not a word was spoken. Then Ryan turned around to face Carlyle squarely.

"Keep them close," he said with a fatherly intensity that sent a rush of adrenaline through the watcher's being.

"I will, sir," he replied.

Then Ryan placed both hands on Julia's cheeks and kissed her forehead.

"We must part for now," he said. "But I will see you soon."

"Don't go," Julia pleaded.

"If I don't go, you can't go," Ryan said.

"But I don't want to go!"

"I know, but Nellie needs you."

"Why would Nellie need me? Isn't she with you?" she protested even as Ryan disappeared from sight. She spun around and faced Grammateus and Carlyle. "Please don't make me go. I want to stay with Daddy!"

The Scrollmaster gently put a finger under her chin and turned her face back to the blueprint.

"Tell me what you see," he said.

Julia looked up and around and away in search of her dad, but Grammateus turned her attention back to what was directly in front of her. Julia took a deep sigh and surrendered to his direction.

"Nothing," she said. "Nothing but what I've already seen."

Then Grammateus passed a hand in front of her face and something like scales fell from her eyes. She sucked in a small gasp.

"Oh my. Now I see them," she said, leaning closer. "But just barely. They're so dim."

Carlyle strained to see the hundreds and even thousands of tiny gems that had suddenly appeared all around the girls' stones. They were like grains of sand, they were so small, and some blinked off and on as if the sparkle within them was about to die.

"Who are they?" she asked.

Grammateus swept his hand across the area and gathered up the miniscule grains. Then, with his palm open, he blew on the collection and it flew in a glittering arc toward Julia's heart.

"They are the forgotten and forsaken ones," he said.

Carlyle watched as something like lightning penetrated Julia's chest and arced through her entire body in fiery flashes.

She cried out.

The cavern disappeared.

In less than a breath, they were back in the darkened cement cell.

Julia slept curled up in the fetal position on the dingy mattress with Carlyle seated near her head. She quivered slightly and awoke.

Her eyes were not feverish.

They were fiery and focused.

Chapter 45 – The Double

"This must be the place," Claude said to Nellie as he eased the Silverado around another bend on the winding, tree-lined street and into a gravel parking spot across from a two-story contemporary house. The yard was equal parts organic and architecturally designed plantings, still green and glossy in the misty January sunlight. A paved walkway led up to the mahogany, double-doored entry. The driveway in front of the three-car garage was full of black SUVs displaying government license plates. Two gray sedans filled the spots next to the curb.

"Looks like we're the last ones to the party," he said.

Nellie nodded silently, assessing the Flanagan home.

Just then, the front doors of the house opened and a short, middle-aged man with thinning red hair appeared in the opening, dressed in a black vest over a long-sleeved shirt. The man zipped up the vest as he a left the doorway and approached them. Claude rolled down his window.

"Morning, Claude," the man said with a small tip of his chin as he planted his feet a yard short of the pickup.

"Morning, Jimmy," Claude said.

"Been a few years," Jimmy said, stuffing his hands into his vest pockets.

"Yup, a few years," Claude agreed.

Nellie watched the two older men let their eyes settle anywhere but on each other.

"Okay if we park here?" Claude asked.

"That'll be fine for now," Jimmy said peeking around Claude. "Hello, Nellie. I'm Fiona's son, Jimmy."

Nellie didn't reply.

"Don't expect you'd remember me. We only met a handful of times when you were a wee child."

Nellie remained silent.

"Well," Jimmy said, clearing his throat. "Let me help you with your bags. We've got a place all set up for you in the apartment over the garage."

"Surprised you let them invade your place like this," Claude said as they unloaded the suitcases from the truck bed.

"Well, the powers that be were pretty persuasive," Jimmy replied.

"Oh yeah? How's that?" Claude asked.

"They gave me the option to cooperate or pay up," Jimmy said.

"Now, I thought I made it clear to Agent Reese that we don't want to press any charges," Claude said.

"Guess the feds aren't quite as forgiving as you," Jimmy said.

"Well, I'll be . . ." Claude said as the trio made their way up the path to the front door. "What about Hector and Maria?"

Jimmy stopped with his hand on the front-door handle and shrugged.

"I am not privy to that information," he said. "But I'm guessing they'll be facing some sort of judgment."

"I don't think that's right," Nellie piped up, and the two older men swiveled around to look at her. "We're the ones who were wronged. And if we say we don't want to press charges, then how can they press charges?"

The Agreements

Claude looked to Jimmy. Jimmy looked to Claude, then back to Nellie.

"I'm not sure," Claude said. "But you can be sure I'll be having further conversation with Agent Reese about all this."

"Come on in," Jimmy said, swinging the tall wooden doors open.

The scene that greeted the two Jolicoeurs as they entered the open space of the Flanagan home was like something straight out of the movies. The long dining room table at the far end of the living area was littered with computers and electronic equipment. Men in button-down shirts with sleeves rolled up sat at chairs or stood leaning over shoulders viewing whatever was on the computer screens as they engaged in intense conversations. None of them so much as turned to acknowledge the newcomers.

"Good thing my wife isn't here to see this mess," Jimmy muttered.

"Where is she?" Claude asked, perusing the technical hubbub.

"Went to ride out the storm at my daughter's place," Jimmy replied. "Follow me. This way," he said, moving past another group of people huddled around what looked like a map spread out over a long coffee table in the living room.

As they passed, one of the heads bent over the map popped up and Nellie recognized Agent Reese, who quickly left her spot in the encircled group and made her way over to them.

"You made good time," she said to Claude.

"I was instructed not to putter," he replied.

"Jimmy will get you settled, and then we need to get to work. We've got a lot to go over before tomorrow. You ready for this, Nellie?"

Nellie nodded.

"We've got the best in the business right in this room. You'll be in good hands all the way," Agent Reese said before returning to her team grouped around the map.

Jimmy led them into the kitchen with its sleek white cabinets and marble-covered island. Seated on the barstools beside a woman in holey jeans and sweatshirt was a younger blonde woman in pink velour loungewear. The two were so deeply entrenched in a quiet conversation that they didn't seem to notice the latest arrivals. Jimmy and Claude were already halfway up the staircase on the other side of the kitchen leading to the apartment when the younger woman jumped from her seat and screamed.

"Oh my God! You're out! You made it!" she yelled, launching herself toward Nellie, who spun around just in time to be enveloped in a flying hug from the blonde girl.

Every head across the entire space shot up. Hands reflexively reached for holsters on hips and chests. Suddenly Nellie, locked in the girl's fierce grip, could see at least five weapons pointed in her direction.

The other woman who had been sitting at the island jumped up and threw herself between the girls and the FBI agents.

"It's okay. Everything's okay," she yelled.

Claude reappeared in the doorway.

"What the hell is going on?" he shouted.

"Stand down, everyone," Agent Reese ordered loudly, and with swift obedience guns were holstered and business was resumed.

Claude ran to Nellie's side while the woman in the ripped jeans ran up behind the girl in pink and whispered, "Chrissy, let go. It's not Julia. Remember? We talked about her twin coming. This is Nellie."

Slowly Chrissy's arms dropped from around a stiff Nellie and she backed away. But her gaze remained fixed on Nellie's face. Tears filled Chrissy's eyes and began to drip down her cheeks. The woman in the sweatshirt put an arm around her shoulder and pulled her into a side embrace.

"It's okay, Chrissy," she said. "I'm sure you and Nellie can get to know each other a little later. After she's had a chance to get situated. Would that be okay, Nellie?"

"Uh, sure," Nellie said.

"I'm Laura, by the way," the woman said, extending her hand to Nellie and then Claude. "Laura Carson. I'm Chrissy's caseworker."

Nellie stared at the girl called Chrissy.

"Do you know my sister?" Nellie asked her.

Chrissy nodded with tears still spilling undeterred over her cheeks. Laura handed her a tissue from the box on the island, but Chrissy ignored her.

"You look so much . . . ," Chrissy whispered. "I just thought maybe . . . maybe he went back . . . and got you."

"Who went back?" Laura said.

"The guy . . . the one in the coveralls. I promised I would go when the door opened. She told me . . . Julia said the door was going to open," Chrissy stated. "I never should've left her. She's so sick. She's the one . . . she's the one who should be here." A huge sob erupted from Chrissy's chest. "She's the one who has people who . . . love . . . her."

Nellie brushed her grandpa's protective arm away and stepped toward Chrissy.

"We're gonna get her back, you know," she said.

Chrissy sucked in a ragged breath and stared into Nellie's fiery eyes.

"I hope so," she whispered over the sound of a motorcycle slowing cruising past on the street outside.

"Can somebody please tell me what the holdup is with Agent Bergsman? He was supposed to be here twenty minutes ago," Agent Reese bellowed out to the buzzing crowd of FBI personnel the following morning.

"Traffic on 405, ma'am," yelled back a man from the far side of the Flanagans' dining room with a cell phone pressed to his ear. "Got an ETA of twenty minutes."

The living room had been turned into a conference room, with chairs pulled up in rows of semicircles behind the plush leather couches. A whiteboard with a schedule of events listed in bold letters with pictures of Winston Chambers III and Manuel Ramirez Santos prominently displayed at the top stood on an easel in front of the fireplace. Most of the team had already taken their seats. Some were taking advantage of the short delay to refuel with coffee and snacks ranging from trail mix to sandwich wraps to doughnuts.

Jimmy Flanagan sat in a mid-century swivel chair, flipping through an old copy of *Golf Digest*. Chrissy was situated on the couch with her knees tucked under her bottom and her head lolling over onto the padded armrest, her eyes closed. She was still dressed in her velour loungewear from the day before. Laura Carson was right beside her with phone in hand and thumbs flying.

"I hope that's not classified information you're texting out, Ms. Carson," Agent Reese said to the social worker.

"Do I look stupid?" Laura responded, only slightly raising her eyes to meet the agent's.

"I wasn't implying . . . ," Agent Reese replied. "Just my job to keep this whole operation clean."

"And it's mine to keep this girl safe," Laura said, setting the phone in her lap. "And let me repeat, in case somebody hasn't already recorded this—I am not in favor of sending her back into the situation."

"Duly noted. But as we discussed, the best chance we have of luring this slippery SOB out into the open is the girl getting outfitted back there," she said, pointing in the

The Agreements

opposite direction to a room down the hallway, "and the girl sitting next to you."

"Duly noted. But you are taking a tremendous risk that I am not comfortable with, and I want my objection written into the record."

Agent Reese turned to a woman seated at the end of the glass coffee table who was busily typing on her laptop, her eyes carefully averted from the conflict.

"You got that down, Amy?" Agent Reese asked.

"Got it, ma'am," the woman replied.

A hush suddenly fell on the room and heads swiveled toward the hallway entrance. Standing there between her grandpa and a young woman in a gray pantsuit was Nellie. Her short-cropped hair was covered in a long, black wig, and her jeans and T-shirt had been replaced with a formfitting, blue dress and high heels.

"Bring her here, MaryAnne," Agent Reese said.

"She's not too sure about the heels, boss," MaryAnne said as they approached. "Looking for some other options right now."

Nellie clunked self-consciously through the gazing eyes with Claude by her side, his hand under her elbow to keep her steady.

"Yeah, let's find her another option," Agent Reese agreed. "We need her to be mobile."

"On it, boss," MaryAnne said, bending down to remove the offensive footwear from Nellie before she disappeared back down the hallway.

"We've got some seats for you right here," the agent in charge said to the Jolicoeurs as she led them past the couch and over to the matching loveseat.

Nellie plopped down beside Claude, who tucked her protectively under his arm while she tugged at the dress's hem in an attempt to cover more of her exposed thighs. Chrissy, roused from her nap by the activity, stared in disbelief at Nellie.

"Holy shit," she whispered. "If I didn't know any better . . . you've even got her necklace."

Nellie reached up and fiddled with the silver cross as shades of pink flushed up her neck and cheeks.

"Uh, Agent Reese," Claude piped up. "I know this is your show and all, but I think I know my granddaughter better than anyone in this room. And I can tell you right now that getting her all gussied up like this might get her looking just like Julia presently looks, but she'd operate a whole lot better with a bit more fabric covering her limbs."

Agent Reese ran her hands through her hair and sighed deeply.

"Just get her one of these," Chrissy said, tugging on the sleeve of her Juicy Couture outfit. "Win loves these things. Gives them out like gold medals to girls that get on his good side."

"Johnson," Agent Reese said to a man with half a doughnut sticking out of his mouth, "get back there to MaryAnne and help her track down something like this for Nellie."

"It's gotta be Juicy," Chrissy interrupted. "Win hates knockoffs."

"On it," Johnson replied, wiping powdered sugar from his lips and hustling down the hall to do his boss's bidding.

Nellie locked eyes with Chrissy and mouthed a silent thank-you.

Just then the front door burst open.

"Ah, Agent Bergsman. Nice of you to join us," Agent Reese said to the man who entered towing another man in cuffs through the door behind him.

"Sorry about that, ma'am. Traffic on 405," the agent replied.

"So I've heard," his boss remarked. "Take a seat and let's get started. Daylight, such as it is in Seattle in January, is burning. Oh, and welcome to the party, Mr. Gomez."

Raúl Gomez stopped dead in his tracks.

The Agreements

"Gomez," Agent Bergsman said tugging on Raúl's arm. "You heard the lady. Take a seat."

But Raúl didn't budge.

His face blanched as he gaped at Nellie.

She gaped right back at him.

Chapter 46 – The Signs

Freddy and Rosie stood beside the motorcycle and sipped from the hot chocolates they had purchased from Starbucks a few minutes before. They could see the back of the Flanagan house through the trees from their vantage point on the street just around the corner and up the hill. Their helmets hung from either side of the handlebars and their backpacks lay open on the leather seat. Rosie pulled a stocking cap from a side pocket and tugged it down over her unruly hair.

"Still cold?" Freddy asked.

Rosie nodded and stamped her feet against the damp morning pavement.

"You sure we didn't leave anything in the back of the truck?" Rosie asked.

"Yeah, I'm sure," Freddy replied. "Folded the blankets just like they were when we got in last night. You were there too . . . why are you freaking out at me?"

Rosie let out a nervous breath, making her lips vibrate.

"I just don't want to have Claude figure out that we spent the night in the back of his truck because of some stupid piece of Taco Bell wrapper or something."

"Relax, would ya? Nellie said in her text that they're so busy with all the prep for this operation today, there's no time to think about anything else. And you know when we talked to Beto that Mom and Lita have totally bought our spending the night at the Alvarezes' to work on the science fair projects."

"I know . . . I know . . . and Junior is keeping them occupied with his playing-sick role."

Freddy let out a small chortle.

"Can you believe Beto even made up some fake puke for him and the kid totally fooled mom with it?"

"Junior's flair for the dramatic has finally paid off."

The two siblings sipped their warm drinks in silence, each appreciating the success of their mad scheme thus far. Freddy popped the lid off his paper cup and licked the remaining whipped cream from the bottom and around the rim of the cup. Then he crushed it, stuffed it into the designated garbage bag, and leaned back against the parked three-wheeler.

"Now what, genius?" he asked his younger sister. She was the one who had insisted on coming, the one who had said there was no way she would abandon Jewels or Nellie in their hour of need.

"Well, Nellie says they're gonna be there for a little while longer," she said, tipping her head toward the house. "So, how's about we go and do a drive-by of the spa? We've got the address Nellie sent us, right?"

"Yeah, but what good is that gonna do?"

Rosie scrunched her eyebrows and wiped the chocolate moustache off her upper lip.

"I don't know. Maybe we'll see something that might help. Or maybe we can sneak in and get a look around," she said.

"That's your brilliant plan? You and me, dressed like this . . . we're gonna just wander through the doors of some fancy spa? What are we gonna say, 'Excuse me? Do you happen to have a girl named Julia Gomez here? And could you maybe send her on out?' What if we screw up the whole operation before it even starts? Have you thought about that?"

Tears threatened at the edges of Rosie's eyes.

"You got a better idea, genius?" she spat back. "All's I know is we've only got a few hours before Mom figures out we're not where we're supposed to be and digs the truth out of Junior or Beto. She'll send the whole freakin' cavalry out looking for us, you know, and our faces will be all over the news and Facebook and the backs of milk cartons. So, if you've got a suggestion as to how we might better spend our free time, then spit it out!"

"Alright, alright. Jeez," Freddy said, backing away from his sister's wrath and taking a seat on the curb beside a thick laurel hedge. "Just seems to me like maybe we spent too much time planning how to get here and not enough planning what we would do when we did."

Rosie let her shoulders sag and shuffled to the curb to join her brother. They sat in silence for a few minutes shoulder to shoulder, their knees tucked up to their chins.

"I wish Lita was here," Rosie said. "She'd know what to do."

"You gotta know she's praying," Freddy said. "No way she'd not be praying for Jewels and Nellie and everybody."

"Yeah, well, we could use a few prayers too."

Freddy took a deep sigh and nodded. A red Mercedes drove slowly past them and the two dropped their heads, pretending to look at the map on their phone. Rosie looked up and waved with a bright, friendly smile and the car kept going.

"One thing's for sure," Freddy said. "We can't stay here. Maybe we should say a few prayers of our own."

Rosie grabbed Freddy's hands and the two bowed their heads.

"Father God," Rosie began, "we know maybe we didn't think this thing all the way through . . . but if you could help us know what to do next, we promise we'll consult with you more frequently in the future."

"We know you talk to our grandma and she says you'll talk to us too," Freddy added. "So, if you've got one of those signs or wonders or something stored up, now would be a good time for it. In Jesus's name . . ."

"Amen," they said in unison and opened their eyes.

Suddenly, a pair of goldfinches dipped and dived through the gray morning in a flash of brilliant yellow. They alit on the pegs of a bird feeder hanging from a tree branch across the street. Hungrily, the birds poked and pecked and pulled on the seeds, spilling as many or more on the ground as those that went into their bellies. The more brightly colored male flew to another branch higher up in the tree. He puffed his golden chest and flicked his head from side to side as he cheeped and tweeted and warbled. Answering cheeps and tweets and warbles rang from unseen goldfinches in trees and shrubs all around the Gomez siblings.

"Freds," Rosie whispered, not wanting to disturb the birds' song.

"Yeah," he whispered back.

"Remember how Lita always tells Jewels, 'You sing like a bird'?"

Freddy nodded. "Yeah. You think maybe the birds are trying to tell us something?"

Rosie rolled her eyes. "Not the birds, dodo brain. God. God is trying to tell us something."

"Okay, but what? You got a translation for cheep, cheep, cheep, twit, twit, twitter?"

Rosie punched him in the shoulder. "Don't be stupid," she said. "It's not what they're singing, it's what they mean. I think Jewels is calling us. Just like that bird on the branch is calling all these other birds we can't even see. I think she knows we're here somehow and she wants us to find her."

***

In the Gomez kitchen in La Verdad, Lupe and Maria sat next to each other in the chairs beside the empty table, their heads bowed in prayer. Hector had gone to meet with Pastor Valdez, saying he had to get out of the house and do something. They had all tried to go about their morning as usual, but it was not a usual morning. Besides Junior's sudden bout of stomach flu and the absence of Freddy and Rosie, who had asked to spend the night at a friend's in order to work on their science projects, the knowledge of what was about to go down at some point that day had set them both on edge and driven them into intercession.

In the midst of an extended time of silent prayer, Lupe suddenly sat up straight against the chair's wooden dowels.

"Mamá? Are you okay? Do you see something?" Maria asked.

Lupe nodded slowly, her head cocked and her eyes scanning the space above her daughter's head.

"What is it?"

"Birds."

"Birds? You see birds?"

"No. I hear them singing."

"Birds singing? Are they saying something? Is it a message? Is it a sign? What is it?"

"It is who they are singing to," Lupe replied, standing to her feet and marching to the stairs leading to the boys' bedroom.

"Come," she ordered.

Maria jumped to her feet and followed her mother to the basement. They went straight to the boys' bedroom where Junior lay sleeping in the toddler bed beside Beto and Freddy's bunk beds. Lupe sat down beside her grandson, whose back was to her, and jostled his shoulders.

The Agreements

"What are you doing?" Maria asked. "He needs his rest, Mamá. He's been so sick."

"He is not sick," Lupe said.

"But I took his temp this morning and it was sky high."

"He is not sick," Lupe repeated and shook the toddler's shoulders a bit harder.

Junior rolled over and blinked his eyes before letting them focus on his grandmother.

"Lita," he croaked out, closed his eyes, and rolled back over.

"No, mijo," Lupe said. "No more sleep. You must tell us. Where is Freddy? And Rosie?"

"With Jewels," Junior said, still half asleep. He let out a small breath and added, "And Nellie."

Maria leapt to the bed beside Lupe and flipped Junior onto his back.

"Freddy and Rosie are where? They're not at school?" she demanded. "Young man, you sit up right now and tell me what is going on here."

She yanked Junior up by his arms. He sat bolt upright and stared with wide eyes at the two women sitting on his bed. And then tears erupted from his eyes.

"I'm supposed to do my part," he said. "I promised . . . I promised Nellie. Rosie will kill me if I talk."

"Nobody is going to kill you," Maria said. "But Mommy needs to know the truth, or you will be in very, very big trouble. Do you understand me?"

Junior sucked in a breath and nodded.

"Seattle?" Lupe asked. "Are they in Seattle?"

"Yeah," Junior replied.

"Seattle! But how on earth did they get there?" Maria asked.

"On the motorcycle," Junior whispered.

"Motorcycle? Whose motorcycle?" Maria continued.

"Tío Raúl's."

Maria sprung to her feet.

"What are you going to do, mija?" Lupe said.

"I'm going to call Hector and then I am going to call the FBI," she said as she spun around and ran out the door. The sound of her feet taking the stairs two by two echoed into the bedroom.

"Lita?" Junior said while his mother's nearly hysterical conversation with his father filtered down through the air vents. "Will I go to hell for fibbing?"

"No, mijo," Lupe said, gathering him into her arms. "But you might get some punishment from your papá. Lying is never a good thing."

"Sometimes is feels like a good thing," Junior replied.

Lupe sighed and stroked her grandson's disheveled hair.

"Yes, sometimes it does."

Chapter 47 – The Cavalry

It was the oddest thing. Carlyle was sensing strongly that it was time for him to leave Julia's side. She was sitting up and singing to herself as she detangled her hair with her fingers and arranged it into a side plait. Though her eyes roamed the tightly enclosed space as if she were seeing beyond its limitations, she gave no sign that she could see him. Whatever window had been opened allowing their face-to-face interaction seemed to have closed. At least for the time being.

He was anxious to return to Nellie and see what was happening with the crazy scheme she and the Gomez children had brewed up. But when he looked for his light machine, it simply would not appear. Even with the key in his hand and a readiness in his heart to go, it was nowhere to be found. It was almost as if (dare he believe it?) the time was drawing near when he would no longer need the contrivance.

Julia shed her blanket and slowly stood to her feet. She leaned back against the cold cement wall to steady herself, closed her eyes, and took several deep breaths. Clearly, the hours of sickness had taken a toll. But when she opened her eyes, they still glowed with the otherworldly light that the trip to the quarry had seemed to impart to her, and her heart light pulsed strong and true. With small, shaky steps she inched her way over the mattress to the door and began to pound on it with what strength she had left.

Bam, bam, bam, bam, bam.

Bam, bam, bam, bam, bam.

She stopped and pressed her ear against the door, both listening for any response and resting from the energy she had exerted. Twice more she banged against the hard wood surface, but no footsteps sounded in the hallway. She lowered her forehead to the door and stood motionless, save for the rubbing of her fingers over the cross pendant at her neck.

Then, with one deep breath, she lifted her chin and began to sing straight into the door's oak grain. Sound reverberated around the small chamber like a clapper connecting with the inside of a brass church bell:

Great is Thy faithfulness, O God my Father
There is no shadow of turning with Thee
Thou changest not, Thy compassions they fail not
As Thou hast been, Thou forever will be
Great is Thy faithfulness
Great is Thy faithfulness
Morning by morning new mercies I see
All I have needed Thy hand hath provided
Great is Thy faithfulness, Lord unto me

The longer Julia sang, the stronger her voice became. As she was about to launch into the second verse of the hymn, a set of heavy footsteps pounded down the hall.

"Shut up in there," Manny yelled even before his key slid into the lock.

Julia continued to sing.

"I said, shut your trap," Manny snarled when his face showed up in the opened door.

Julia stopped singing.

The Agreements

"Hello," she said. "I was wondering if I might get some water and a bite to eat."

"Up off your death bed are ya? The boss will be glad to hear it, though I'm not sure why he even bothers with you. You haven't made him a dime since you've been here. Just trouble. That's all you've given him is trouble."

Julia smiled beatifically.

"And a shower?" she said, smoothing out the crumpled-up surface of the dark-blue dress she had been wearing for days. "I really need a shower."

Manny stared at her with a mixture of confusion and something like admiration.

"What makes you think you can ask me for anything?" he said.

Carlyle kept completely still as the two stared at each other in silence. The longer they stared, the more the determination in Julia's eyes grew until Manny stepped backward as if to avoid further scrutiny.

"Alright. Get out here now. I ain't got all day to play babysitter. The boss and I have an important appointment soon," he said, grabbing Julia by the elbow and yanking her out into the hallway. "Seems somebody has found our little friend Chrissy."

Julia stopped and her chin dropped to her chest.

Manny let out a harsh laugh.

"You didn't think she'd stay away for long, did ya?" he said, pulling her forward. "She never does. Always comes back, that one. Like a dog to its vomit." And he laughed again, seeming to enjoy Julia's dejection. "Oh, and you'll particularly like this part," he continued as they approached the bathroom that contained the lone shower stall in the whole building. "Guess who she bumped into?"

He paused before releasing her into the room.

Julia turned and looked him square in the eye, and Carlyle was glad to see her jut out her chin as she replied, "I have no idea."

"None other than your favorite Uncle. Raúl Gomez. Remember him?"

With a final cruel guffaw, he pushed Julia into the bathroom and locked the door in her face.

"You've got five minutes," he barked through the door. "So, I wouldn't waste my time pouting if I was you."

It wasn't until the water was streaming full blast over her body that Julia burst into tears. She sobbed and scrubbed and sobbed and scrubbed some more.

And Carlyle sat on the stack of towels outside the shower curtain and allowed his own tears to flow. Would this nightmare never end?

From where they were hiding behind the large green dumpster, Freddy had a sight line between two blue garbage bins to the man standing in the alley beside the spa door. He was leaning against the brick wall, one leg bent with his booted foot planted on the wall and the other dug into the black asphalt. In his right hand, a cigarette dangled next to his leg, dropping bits of ash beside his foot. In his left, he was scrolling through his phone with his thumb, stopping occasionally to view some image or another and then continuing to scroll. Beside him, the red metal door stood slightly ajar.

Rosie tugged Freddy back into the dumpster's shade.

"Is he still there?" she whispered.

"Yup."

"I've got an idea," she said, pulling him close and whispering into his ear.

Freddy jerked back after hearing her out.

"You can't do that. Mom and Dad would kill me if you got caught," he protested a bit too loudly.

The Agreements

The guard by the door stopped mid drag on his cigarette, held the smoke in his mouth, and cocked his head to the side.

Rosie and Freddy froze.

Slowly the man exhaled, blowing smoke in a long, steady stream before returning his attention to the screen in his hand.

"Jewels is just behind that door. We can't get this close and not try to find her," Rosie whispered. "I made a promise, Freds."

Freddy stared out the other end of the alley where they had parked the motorcycle. He had to think.

"Okay," he whispered at last. "One chance. That's it. If it doesn't work, we're outta here. You know the FBI and God only knows who else is gonna be here any minute."

"I know. That's why we've gotta go now," Rosie insisted.

Before Freddy could move, she threw her arms around him in a quick embrace. He patted her back twice and broke away, moving with stealth acquired in many iterations of neighborhood secret agent spy games. Rosie prayed silently for him until he disappeared behind her around the corner of the strip mall. Only then did she turn around and peek through the garbage cans to wait for her moment.

"Okay, people. Almost time to roll. We want to get into the spa before it gets too busy. Let me reiterate—our goal is not to arrest a bunch of clients but to get to Chambers and Santos. Then we clear out all the women, especially keeping our eyes out for Julia Gomez. The women are not to be put under arrest at this point but merely rounded up for questioning. If there are some johns there, cuff them and get them out of the way as quickly as possible. They are small potatoes compared to the head honchos. Everyone clear on their parts and the timing of events?" Agent Reese asked from her place beside the whiteboard in the Flanagan living room.

Heads nodded all across the room.

Claude slowly raised his hand up into the air.

"You don't have to raise your hand, Mr. Jolicoeur," she said. "Just ask the question."

"Any possible way I can be closer to the action and to Nellie?" he said.

The agent in charge set the dry-erase marker she had in her hands back onto the shelf of the board.

"My answer is the same as the last time you asked me: no. The fewer untrained civilians we have in the field—anywhere in the field—the better. You will remain here with me at command central. Understood?"

Claude crossed his arms over his chest tightly. Nellie, who was newly attired in a navy-blue Juicy Couture lounge set and blingy flip-flops, put her hand on his shoulder.

"I'll be okay, Papa," she whispered.

"Agent Reese," one of the guys remaining at the computers sitting on the dining table called out.

"Just a minute, Mack," she replied. "We're almost done here."

"Uh, ma'am, I think you're gonna wanna see this right now," Mack insisted.

Agent Reese marched around the seated participants to the table and leaned over Mack's shoulder.

"What am I looking at?" she asked.

"The alley behind the spa, ma'am," Mack said.

"Okay. Our team is in place there, true?"

"Yeah, just rolled the laundry-service truck into place. That's not the issue. Look right there," he said, pointing to the screen.

"What the . . . ?" she gasped. "Is that a kid behind the dumpster?"

"Yeah. The truck is still a ways back in the alley making routine pickups from the various businesses. You know, keeping our cover and such, but . . ."

"But what? Is that a kid or not?"

"Yes, ma'am. It is. There were a couple of them. A boy and a girl."

"Can you zoom in on her?"

The computer screen filled with the image of the back of the girl hunkered down behind the dumpster.

"We've got our eyes on 'em," Mack said. "Thought they were just some kids looking for a place to smoke or drink or something."

"What happened to the boy?" Agent Reese said.

"He took off. Thought the girl might follow, but no such luck."

"Well, get her out of there. But do it quietly. We don't want to send up any alarms at this critical juncture."

"Yes, ma'am. We're on it," Mack replied, tapping his earpiece and relaying the information to his cohorts in the van.

"Agent Reese, I've got an urgent phone call for you," another guy across the table from Mack spoke up.

"I am aware of the situation, Sid," she replied. "It's taken care of."

"No, ma'am," Sid said, holding his hand over the speaker of his phone. "It's not that. It's Maria Gomez, ma'am. Says it's an emergency. She's pretty wound up."

Rosie got up on her haunches and prepared herself for takeoff. She could see Freddy making his way toward her from the other end of the alley, stumbling and singing off-key as he moved closer and closer to the spa door. The guard dropped his cigarette, ground it underneath his boot, and came to a full, upright, locked, and loaded position.

Freddy kept staggering forward in a manner that would have caused Rosie to bust out in laughter under different circumstances. As it was, she tried to control her heart rate with several long, steady breaths and scooched closer to the opening between the blue garbage cans.

"Hey, kid," the guard barked at Freddy.

Freddy spun around in a circle, pretending to look for whoever the guard was yelling at.

"Yeah, you, kid," the guard said, taking several steps away from the door and into the middle of the alley.

Rosie left the shelter of the green dumpster and slid between the plastic receptacles.

Suddenly, up from the shadows of the alley right next to Freddy, a homeless guy in dingy clothes and a floppy green hat jumped up and started singing right along with the boy. Freddy was so startled, he froze. The man slung an arm around his shoulder like a drinking buddy and spun him around.

"Get outta here," the guard yelled, moving toward the tipsy duo. "Take your buddy and your booze and get the hell outta here."

Although she had no idea who the other "drunk" was, Rosie figured it must be an angel sent to amplify the distraction tactic. She bolted from her spot just as a hand reached for her ankle, causing her to nearly sprawl face-first onto the asphalt. Thinking it must be another alley denizen, she didn't even turn around to check but caught her balance with her hands and scrambled to the open door of the spa.

Seeing her stumble, Freddy resisted the tug of the bum and threw his hands over his head, belting his song out even louder. The supposed bum grabbed him by the arm with a vice grip, causing him to yelp in pain.

"Come on, Cheto," the unidentified homeless man slurred. "They don' wan' us here."

The Agreements

"That's right," the guard yelled louder, with his hand settled on the pistol tucked into the back of his belt. "Get outta here."

The metal door was heavy but well oiled. Rosie slipped inside the spa undetected while the guard's attention was still focused on assuring the exit of the bums.

Julia pulled on a pair of black leggings and a T-shirt she dug out of a basket of discarded clothes in the corner of the bathroom. They weren't exactly clean, but they were better than what she had been wearing for days. She bent over at the waist and flopped her wet tresses forward over her head before wrapping them in a towel and securing them in a twist. As she stood up, she swayed slightly and reached out a hand to regain her balance.

Just then the door unlocked and Manny appeared.

"Time's up," he said, stepping to one side.

Carlyle hovered in the space over Julia's head as Manny led her by the elbow out into the dimly lit hallway. Turning the corner toward her room, Carlyle nearly dropped from the sky at what he saw at the far end of the corridor. It was Ardith. She waved enthusiastically in his direction and pointed to a spot just below her at floor level, where a tiny portion of a face and one brown eyeball belonging to Rosie Gomez poked out past the wall. He waved back, resisting the urge to spin in circles at the sheer joy of seeing the familiar faces.

"Git in," Manny ordered Julia, shoving her into her closet.

Just then, a commotion echoed down the passageway from somewhere in the spa or just outside. Manny's head swiveled and his hand froze over the set of keys on his hip. Inside Julia's room, Carlyle could hear the ruckus coming from the alley and his heart leapt. Something was definitely going on.

Manny slammed the door in Julia's face and took off running toward the back entrance to the spa.

Julia dropped to her bottom on the mattress and unwound the towel from her head. She seemed lost in her own thoughts and undisturbed by whatever was happening elsewhere in the building. The news about Chrissy's capture had sucked a substantial measure of wind out of her sails. He could tell by the dimming of her heart light. But as she ran her fingers through her damp locks, she began to pray.

"Father," she said, "thanks for the shower. And the clothes. And this towel."

With each stroke she whispered another item of gratitude.

"Thanks for healing me."

He'd heard her do this before. Her way of encouraging herself. Something Lupe had taught her long ago.

Did she even realize what was transpiring around her?

"Thanks for a really great dream." She paused to gaze up, and her eyes glowed as if lit by remnants of heavenly memories of a jewel-encrusted quarry.

Did she realize that although Manny had slammed the door, he had not locked it?

"Thanks for my family," she said and began to list them one by one, starting with her dad and mom and Nellie and advancing through the Gomez clan.

As she whispered the name Rosie, the oak door slid open.

And there she was—Rosie Gomez in the flesh.

Julia's hands stopped in mid stroke.

For a split second the girls stared at each other as if trying to discern if the other was real or an apparition. Then Rosie flew across the few feet between her and her sister and engulfed her in her arms. The two fell back onto the mattress and wept and pulled back long enough to see each other's faces and then held each other close again.

Caught up in the joy of the reunion, Carlyle and Ardith hugged and danced above them in a jubilant version of some sort of polka.

Suddenly, Julia extricated herself and crawled to the door that stood slightly ajar. She stuck her head out into the hallway and checked both ways before carefully pulling it shut and leaning up against it. Rosie crawled over and sat next to her, shoulder to shoulder, knee to knee, hand in hand.

"How did you . . . ?" Julia whispered.

"Freddy," Rosie replied. "He drove Tío's motorcycle."

"From La Verdad?" Julia gasped. "Just the two of you?"

Rosie nodded. "I told you I'd come with help."

Julia held a finger to her lips.

The two watchers paused their exultant dancing and listened.

"We've got to be really quiet," she said, pulling her little sister even closer so they could continue their whispered conversation. "But you shouldn't be here. How did you find me? How did you get in? Past the guards? And the locks?"

"That was a close one," Rosie replied and then went on to describe the goings-on in the alleyway. "And when I got in, I had no idea where you were, but I peeked around the corner and saw this guy dragging you to this room. And then all of a sudden, he was running right at me. I thought I was toast."

"Oh my gosh," Julia gasped.

"So, I jumped into this big bin of laundry and hid under some towels."

"But how did you know I was here? In this building?" Julia squeezed her sister's hand. "Tell me everything."

"I will. I will. But first, are you okay?" Rosie said, scooting around and putting the back of her hand on Julia's forehead. "You feel kinda hot. Chrissy said you were really sick."

Julia's hand flew to her mouth.

"Chrissy! I thought she . . . how could you . . ."

Rosie slapped herself in the forehead.

"I should've told you first. Chrissy called us. And she's gonna help the FBI . . ."

"The FBI!"

"Yes, the FBI. They're gonna raid this place today, and Chrissy agreed to help."

"But I thought Tío Raúl got her."

"No, he got arrested, but he's gonna help. But that's not even the biggest thing," Rosie added.

"What? What could be any bigger?"

"Jewels . . ." Rosie took a deep breath and stared deep into Julia's eyes. "Nellie is with them too."

Carlyle and Ardith watched as that momentous piece of information sunk in.

"Nellie . . . alive?" Julia's words barely made it past her lips. "But . . . she . . . that's not . . . alive? That's not possible."

"Believe me! I've seen her. I've talked to her. She looks exactly like you. Except maybe her hair and stuff, but she's totally alive and she's on her way here."

Julia seemed stunned into muteness.

"She's part of the raid too," Rosie added.

Carlyle turned to Ardith.

"Today?" he asked.

"Yes, and soon, from what I gathered," Ardith confirmed.

Rosie got up on her hands and knees.

"Are you strong enough to run?" she whispered.

"She's really alive?" Julia said.

"I promise, Jewels. I've seen her. She's been living with her, uh, your grandpa in North Dakota all these years,"

The Agreements

Rosie put a hand on her sister's cheek. "And she'll do anything to see you again. Just like me. So, can you run?"

Julia stared at Rosie, who was getting to her feet.

"Is this a dream, or are you real? 'Cause I can't seem to tell anymore," she whispered.

Rosie bent down and peered into Julia's eyes.

"You are definitely not dreaming. Now, come on. Get up. We've got to get out of here," she said, grasping her sister's hands and pulling her to her feet.

"Manny," a man yelled down the corridor outside the girls' closed door, causing the girls to freeze.

"Manny, what the hell is going on down here?"

"It's Win," Julia gasped.

Winston Chambers's Italian loafers clipped down the tiled hallway toward them while another set of hustling footsteps came from the other direction.

"We're all good, Boss," Manny said.

The two men stopped just on the other side of the door.

"What was that all about?" Win demanded.

"Just a couple of drunks in the alley," Manny assured. "And they're gone now. Nothing to worry about."

The sisters and their watchers held their collective breaths as they listened to the conversation.

"Well, I don't like it," Win replied. "Especially not so close to this thing with Chrissy. Something doesn't feel right."

"I'm telling ya, Boss. It was two homeless dudes who'd already had a few too many sips. That's all."

The tapping of the tip of one of Win's shoes sent tiny shadows bouncing under the door.

"Any idea what the special surprise is Gomez mentioned was coming along with Chrissy?" the boss asked.

"Some other chick we'd be surprised to see. That's all he'd say," Manny replied.

The tapping stopped and the footsteps began to move.

"Ten minutes before we find out," Win said as the two walked away together.

Rosie squeezed Julia's hand.

"Ready?" she said.

Julia nodded.

"Do you think Rosie knows what she's doing?" Carlyle said to Ardith.

Ardith shrugged.

"We're about to find out."

Chapter 48 – The Intercession

The tension in the Gomez living room was palpable. By the look in Maria's eyes as she glared at Beto, it was apparent that she was struggling to know whether to hug him as if she'd never let him go or thrash him within an inch of his life.

"How could you . . . ?" she began.

Beto just stood in front of her with his chin resting on his chest and his fists stuffed into his pockets.

Hector, who had picked up Beto from school as soon as Maria had called, came and inserted himself between the two. He grasped both of his wife's hands in his and steered her to the couch where they sat side by side.

"Mi amor, let's focus right now on the fact that the FBI is aware of the situation and they're doing all they can to get everybody home safely. We can find out all the details of how this all came to be later," he said, letting his gaze drift up to his eldest son, who was clearly both chagrined and terrified—and whom he had already grilled for the entire ride home.

Maria yanked her hands free and jumped back to her feet.

"But you planned this? You lied to us!" she said, grabbing her eldest son by both shoulders and shaking him. "And now it's not just Jewels and Nellie in danger but Rosie and Freddy too! How could you think in any way, shape, or form that this could possibly be helpful?"

Junior, who was sitting on Lupe's lap in the recliner, hid his face in his abuelita's shoulder and began to sob.

"Mija," Lupe interjected as Hector tried to disengage his distraught wife from his equally distraught son. "Mija, let him go."

Maria snapped her head around and glared at her mother.

"I can't," she cried and pulled Beto into a fierce hug. "I can't let him go. I can't . . . I can't . . ."

She, too, began to sob, and Beto along with her.

"I'm sorry, Mami," Beto repeated over and over again between gasps for air.

Hector wrapped both arms around the two of them and let his own tears fall freely. Junior peeked out at them, slid from Lupe's lap, and ran to the group hug, where he proceeded to pry open a spot and wheedle his way into the center of the bodies.

Seconds ticked by before Lupe eased herself up from the recesses of the recliner and walked over to her family. She placed one hand on Beto's back and the other on Maria's.

"We pray," she said to the heads that were already bowed.

Claude took a long draw on his pipe while the phone rang in his ear and he waited for Elsie to pick up. Sunshine peeked through the clouds, causing the leaves to glimmer in the trees that draped along the edges of the ravine under the Flanagans' deck. He stared at the Seattle

The Agreements

skyline across Lake Washington and out to the tips of the Olympic Mountains poking above a bank of clouds on the eastern horizon. It was a stunning view and a beautiful day in the Pacific Northwest, but none of it eased the tautness in his neck and shoulders. He stepped back and closed the sliding glass door that led into the house. He needed a moment away from the buzz of command central. He needed to hear her voice.

"Claude? You there? Can you hear me?" Elsie said.

"Yeah, yeah. Sorry. My mind is in a million places today," he said, pulling the pipe from his mouth as he paced back and forth over the fabricated-wood deck.

"What's going on? I didn't expect to hear from you 'til . . . you know, until everything was over. Are you okay? Is Nellie okay?" Elsie said.

"No, sorry, yeah, we're okay. I think . . . I hope. Everything is going as planned. At least that's what they tell me. But I don't know. It's just . . . I'm so . . . I don't know . . . I'm so . . . ."

"Scared?"

Claude nodded and took another deep drag on his pipe.

"Listen, Claude," Elsie said. "Are you listening?"

"Yeah."

"You've done all you can, and the FBI is doing all they can, and Nellie is doing all she can. Now we just have to trust God is doing all he can. Which is way more than any of us can do. Right?"

"Yeah, I guess."

"Alright, I'm going to pray. And you're going to listen and agree with me. Okay?"

"Yeah, okay," Claude said as he sat on a cushioned patio chair under the roof's overhang. "Fire away."

He bowed his head and let the prayers of his friend wash over him.

***

In the back seat of the sedan parked outside Sheer Pleasure Spa, Chrissy fidgeted and bounced her legs up and down on the black leather seat. Nellie, on the other hand, sat absolutely still, staring at the back of Agent Bergsman's capped head in the driver's seat in front of her. The deeply tinted windows on the side and the back of the vehicle kept them hidden from view.

Every now and then the driver spoke to some unseen person on the other end of the listening device stuffed unobtrusively in his ear.

"Ten-four. We are advised," he said, glancing into the rearview mirror and catching Nellie's stare.

She quickly averted her eyes.

"Hey, you as nervous as I am?" Chrissy whispered.

Nellie nodded.

"I can't even believe I'm back here. Can't believe I'm doing this," Chrissy added, looking out the tinted window at the spa she had so recently escaped. "If it wasn't for Julia, I'd say to hell with it."

"Me too," Nellie said, and the girls' eyes met and the briefest of smiles passed between them.

"You know what she told me?" Chrissy asked.

Nellie shook her head.

"She said I'm a daughter of the King," Chrissy said. "What king would ever want me for a daughter? Her, maybe. But me? Hard to believe."

Nellie stared at Chrissy.

"What else did she say?" she asked.

"Crazy shit like, 'God has a plan for your life. He loves you. He wants to set you free.'"

Nellie nodded. "He does, you know. My grandpa always says God has plans to prosper us and not to harm us. To give us a future and a hope."

Chrissy turned and stared into Nellie's deep-blue eyes.

The Agreements

"You not only look just like her, you sound just like her," she whispered.

"I hope so," Nellie whispered back.

"Yes, ma'am. We are good to go here whenever you say," Bergsman's chatter interrupted the girls' moment.

"Hey, before we have to do our part, would it be okay if we prayed?" Nellie said to her blonde counterpart.

Chrissy shrugged.

"I guess so. But you'd better do it," she said. "I'm not sure God recognizes my voice…yet."

Chapter 49 – The Sting

"Raúl, you are good to go," Agent Reese said quietly into the mouthpiece of her headset from her position standing in front of the large monitor on the Flanagans' dining room table.

The screen was divided into three separate sections displaying the three strategic positions of her team. One showed the back alley of the spa from the cameras in the laundry truck where Freddy was safely in custody. Another displayed the front of the spa and the parking lot from the vantage point of the sedan carrying her agent and the two girls. The third exposed the upstairs office of Sheer Pleasure Spa via a tiny lapel camera on Raúl Gomez's flannel shirt.

"Alpha and Bravo teams be advised, the bait is about to be put out," Agent Reese continued to orchestrate her agents like a conductor with a baton. "Bravo, be ready to roll for takedown and extraction on my cue."

"Ten-four, Bravo is ready."

"Ten-four, Alpha is set."

Winston Chambers sat behind his large mahogany desk in his second-story office with his back

The Agreements

pressed against the leather of his chair, swiveling slightly from side to side. Manny stood right behind his boss, his feet shoulder width apart, his hands behind his back close to his gun.

"Heard about your buddy Rico getting snatched up by the feds," Winston said to the man seated in one of the straight-backed chairs opposite him. "How'd you escape?"

"Oh, I'd split from that guy and headed back up the coast before that all went down," Raúl replied. "He kept telling me there was more money coming, but after a while I started to wonder. Maybe you never paid him or maybe he just kept it all for himself."

"Knowing Rico, my guess is the latter," Winston smirked. "Too bad you picked the wrong guy to do business with."

"Well, I guess he sorta got what was coming to him," Raúl replied. "Besides, it looks like I might get another opportunity to cash in, so to speak."

"Is that so? You think I'm going to pay some sort of reward for picking up Chrissy? She's of no real value to me. And besides, she'll come back of her own accord if you give her a quick minute," Winston said. "The only thing I'm really wondering is how on earth you came to find her."

Raúl chuckled.

"Now that is a bit of a serendipitous story. Like I said, I've been back around these parts for a few days, and I was just minding my own business when me and my buddy see these two girls eating at our favorite diner down by the airport. I don't know Chrissy from Adam, but the girl with her I recognized right away."

Winston stopped the rhythmic swaying of his chair.

"And who would that be?"

Raúl stood up and moved to the office window that overlooked the parking lot. Manny instinctively reached for his weapon at Raúl's sudden movement, but Winston held up a hand to ease him down.

"Let's see what the man has to offer," he said to his faithful bodyguard as he stood to join Raúl at the window.

Raúl put his hand into his pocket for his phone and Manny tensed again.

"Dude, just getting my phone," Raúl said, carefully easing the phone from his pocket and showing it to Manny. He punched in a number, glancing back up at Manny between digits. "Yeah, he wants to see the girls," he said into the phone.

Winston stepped closer to the window.

"Here we go, people," Agent Reese said to the agents assembled around her and in the field. She pulled the microphone away from her mouth and spoke softly to the agent next to her. "Johnson, make sure those two stay outside. Just in case . . . ," she said, indicating Claude, who was pacing back and forth on the deck, a steady stream of smoke coming from his pipe, and Laura Carson, who stood just outside the sliding glass door. sipping a Diet Coke and staring intently at the action inside the house.

"Bring 'em out," Raúl said into his phone to his accomplice.

Agent Bergsman got out of the dark sedan and went around the front of the vehicle to the back passenger door. He opened it and reached in a hand, pulling Chrissy out beside him.

Raúl glanced at Winston, who gave no outer indication of shock or relief.

"That her?" Raúl asked.

"That's her," Winston replied. "Now who's the other one? I'm nearly dying with curiosity." He eased one hand nonchalantly into his linen slacks and set the other on the windowsill, where the only sign of his stated curiosity was a slight tapping of his fingers.

Raúl lifted the phone back to his ear.

"Bring out the other one," he said and turned to watch Chambers's reaction.

Bergsman again reached into the car with one hand while keeping a firm grip on Chrissy's arm with the other.

"**Slowly, Alpha.** Slowly. Let's set this hook," Agent Reese instructed her agent.

Two blingy flip-flops appeared, followed by two navy blue-velour-covered legs.

Winston's fingers ceased their tapping.

Nellie eased out onto the ground, partially obscured by the FBI agent.

Chambers's other hand came out of his pocket and gripped the windowsill as he leaned even closer to the glass. Nellie stepped out into the open with her chin down and then, with coached deliberateness, lifted her face until it was fully revealed to the unseen onlookers.

Winston's head snapped back as if he'd been slapped.

Agent Reese pumped a closed fist into the air.

Raúl allowed himself a small grin. "Recognize her?"

With his face still pressed close to the window, Winston Chambers made no reply.

***

"Alpha, have her play with the necklace," Agent Reese instructed Nellie's handler as her eyes played back and forth from the scene in the office and the scene in the parking lot.

Nellie lifted up her free hand and rubbed the silver pendant at her neck, flashing it in the shafts of breaking sunlight.

"I thought you said she was here," Winston barked at Manny, who stood gaping at the sight before them.

"But . . . but . . . I just saw her, Boss. Just a few minutes ago," Manny stammered. "She's in her room. I'm sure of it."

"Well, clearly you are mistaken, you idiot. Look! She's standing right there."

Manny opened his mouth to reply, but no words came out.

"I was surprised to see you'd let my niece slip away so easily," Raúl said.

Winston Chambers spun around and grabbed Raúl by the front of his shirt.

"You lying, cheating . . . This was your plan all along, wasn't it? Plant her here. Jerk me around. Pull her out."

"We've lost visual on Gomez," Mack said from his place at the computer to Agent Reese. "Audio still loud and clear though."

Raúl laughed in the face of Winston Chambers's wrath.

"No way, dude. I ain't that smart. And Jewels . . . I could care less what happens to her as long as I get a piece of the action. She's a pain in the ass. Always has been. I'd be happy as a one-legged man in a fanny-kicking contest to have her out of my hair."

A moment of tense silence rang over the audio feed.

"Get downstairs and make sure you haven't misplaced anybody else," Winston hissed at his head of security.

"And visuals are back up," Mack announced.

Manny wiped off the small beads of sweat that had popped up on his upper lip as he fled from the room to do his boss's bidding.

"Nice job, Raúl," Agent Reese said. "Now get down to the money. We need to see the cash exchange hands. And Bravo team?"

"Yes, ma'am," came the reply from the laundry van in the alley.

"Stand by to engage."

"Bravo standing by."

"Remember—Santos first. Then the girls."

"Ten-four, ma'am."

"Ready to talk turkey?" Raúl said, heading back to the desk.

Chambers remained staring at the two girls in the parking lot.

"What do you want from me?" he said, turning slowly to face Raúl. "You've already got the girls. So, take 'em."

Raúl sat back in the chair and crossed his arms.

"Sure, I could do that."

"Fine," Winston said, stepping back to his place behind the desk and settling himself into his leather chair. "You found them. You keep them. Why all this . . . this show?"

"Just a courtesy. Before I did anything else."

"Like what?"

"Like calling the FBI tip line for the missing princess out there and giving them this location . . . along with some other pertinent information about you and your operations."

Winston leaned his elbows onto his desk and steepled his fingers under his chin.

"What good does that do you?"

"Just the satisfaction of being a good citizen before I dip over the border into Canada."

Winston chuckled.

"I see, I see. How very noble of you." He leaned back into his chair and assessed the man sitting across from him. "I tell you what, just to get you out of my hair and get on with my day, I will make you an offer: $500 for both of them."

Raúl shook his head and laughed. "Fifteen hundred, and not a penny less."

"You know, you are sitting in my office, in my business, and I could very easily have Manny arrange for you to . . . let's just say have a less-than-pleasant day."

Raúl lifted up his hands in mock surrender.

"Okay, okay. How about an even thousand and we call it a day? You get these two lovelies back in your flock," he said, "and I get a small reward for keeping your business your business."

"Fair enough," Winston replied, opening the safe under his desk.

Agent Reese's attention was captured by movement in the parking lot. Chrissy's hand shot up and

The Agreements

pointed at the front door of the spa. She appeared to be quite excited about something she'd seen. But the audio feed wasn't picking up her words.

"What's going on, Alpha? What's she so worked up about?" Agent Reese asked.

"Not sure, ma'am. I can't see what she's seeing," Agent Bergsman replied.

"What do you mean you can't see? See what?" the agent in charge asked.

A gust of wind whipped across the parking lot and the field agent had to release Nellie's arm to keep his ball cap from flying off. The long strands of Nellie's wig flew in front of her face and she struggled to clear them away.

"Alpha, get those girls back in the vehicle and tell me what is going on!" Agent Reese barked into her microphone.

"Sorry, ma'am. The wind just whipped up," replied the agent, stuffing the girls back into the car. Chrissy resisted, straining her head back in the direction of the spa's entrance.

"What is she looking at, agent?"

"Says she sees a guy in gray coveralls, ma'am. Says it's the guy who sprung her free."

Agent Reese and Mack both leaned closer to the monitor.

"Can somebody give me a clear shot of the spa entrance, please?" she ordered.

A camera from a light pole rotated in the direction of the spa.

"You see anybody in gray coveralls, Mack?" Agent Reese said.

"No ma'am. I don't see a thing," Mack replied.

"Agent Reese, ma'am?" the head agent from Bravo team chimed in.

"Go ahead, Bravo."

"Did you send someone in ahead of us?"

"Negative."

"We've got a guy who looks like one of the laundry guys at the back door."

"And you're sure he's not one of ours?"

"Yes, ma'am. He's a bulky dude who looks like he could sure handle himself, but I've never seen him before."

"Well, what is he doing there?"

"He's holding the back door open and waving us in."

"Somebody get him out of there and do it now!"

"Yes, ma'am . . . uh, wait a minute."

"No, Bravo, do not wait a minute. Get it done."

"It's just that . . . well . . . uh."

"Well what?"

"He, uh . . . he just disappeared."

"Okay. Good. Just have somebody follow him and make sure he doesn't come back," Agent Reese said.

"I would, ma'am, but . . . he really has . . ."

"Has what?"

"Disappeared . . . ma'am."

The Agreements

Chapter 50 – The Escape

The light spilling into the corridor from the back entrance of the spa cast a ray of gold across the tile. Rosie froze in her crouched position behind a large laundry cart. Julia was right behind her with a hand on the middle of her back. It was so warm, it felt like a hot pad cranked to high. Even the short distance they had run to reach this spot had caused Julia's breath to become raspy and shallow. Rosie knew she had to get her out, get her help.

She crept past the bin and peeked around the corner. The guard by the back door was looking away from them into the alley.

"Thought you guys only came on Thursdays," the guard said to someone beyond Rosie's sight.

"Yeah, that's the usual. But we had some mechanical issues and had to reschedule a bunch of routes. We talked to . . . let me see . . . to a guy named Manny about coming today. You wanna check with him?"

"Nah, if Manny says it's cool, then it's cool. Come on in. Got a couple of bins right around the corner."

"Hurry, get in!" Rosie whispered, running back to Julia and hoisting her into one of the large laundry bins. She threw towels over her before leaping into the other cart and burrowing under the dirty linens herself. The musty smell of towels dampened with sweat and water and who knew what caused her to gag. But she checked the impulse with no small effort and breathed as quietly as possible through her mouth.

Finding a riveted opening in the canvas, she pressed one eyeball up against it. She could see the guard walking right toward her with a guy in gray coveralls following.

"Great. Thanks. I think I can get it from here," the laundry employee said.

"Ah, I can help ya push a bin out, no problem," the guard replied.

"Alright. Suit yourself," the man in coveralls said, pulling the bin Rosie was in toward himself.

The guard walked past to the bin containing Julia.

"Jeez, this thing is heavy. You'd think there was a dead body or something in here," the guard said.

Rosie watched through her small porthole as the laundry bin rolled down the hallway, bumped over the threshold, and continued out into the daylight.

"Thanks for the help, man," the laundry guy said.

"No prob . . ." the guard began to reply and then abruptly stopped.

Rosie saw pairs of darkly clad legs run by and heard some brief scuffling. There were at least four other pairs of legs besides the ones in gray coveralls, but they walked so quietly that if Rosie hadn't seen them pass by, she wouldn't have known they were there. Her bin began to move again.

Rosie waited until the wheels beneath her came to a complete halt. She peeled back the layers of dirty laundry from her head and took a deep breath of fresh air. Then, ever so slowly, she sat up and peeked over the rim. The man in the coveralls was headed back to get the other bin with Julia in it. Just as she was about to climb out of her hiding spot, a hand gripped her arm while another covered her mouth.

"Be quiet and come with me," a woman's voice said. "My name is Vicki. I'm with the FBI. You are safe."

The woman helped Rosie out of the bin just as the man in the coveralls pulled up next to them with the other bin.

"Who's she?" he said.

"You need to get her out," Rosie whispered to Vicki.

"We will be getting all the women out as soon as we can. But right now, you need to follow me," Vicki said, pulling on Rosie's arm.

Rosie yanked herself free and ran to the bin.

"Get her, Stan," Vicki said to the man in coveralls.

Stan wrapped both arms around Rosie, who had already pulled several towels from their place.

"No, no. You've got to get her out of the bin! Jewels is really sick. She needs help now," Rosie said.

"Julia Gomez?" Vicki asked, rushing to the bin. "She's in here?"

"Yes, please get her out and get her a doctor."

Vicki ripped the dirty laundry from the bin, exposing the curled-up body underneath. Julia was not moving.

"Stan, give me a hand," Vicki said.

The two FBI agents lifted Julia's unconscious body from the bottom of the cart. Stan cradled her in his arms against his chest.

"She's burning up," he whispered.

Vicki grabbed Rosie's hand and ran toward the laundry-service truck parked just beyond the green dumpster. Stan followed close behind with his precious cargo.

The scene around the Sheer Pleasure Spa was organized chaos. At least, that's what it looked like from Carlyle and Ardith's vantage point in the very crowded laundry truck where computer screens displayed what was happening in and around the premises. Rosie sat in Freddy's lap on a bench that ran the length of one side of the truck's interior while Julia lay on the floor with towels beneath her and on top of her.

"She doesn't look so good," Ardith said to her fellow watcher.

"I know," Carlyle replied. "But, thanks to Rosie, help is on the way."

In the back alley, transport trucks were being loaded with young women as they emerged with agents from the bowels of the spa. A couple of police cars were being crammed with men in handcuffs. Carlyle scanned them as they came out but did not see Winston or Manny.

In the front parking lot, the sedan holding Nellie and Chrissy had been joined by four large SUVs and a handful of local police vehicles. Agents in Kevlar vests marked prominently with FBI in large white letters and armed with semiautomatic weapons were moving toward the front entrance of the spa. Similarly equipped teams had already entered the back of the spa and were stationed at doors and windows.

"It's almost unbearable," Ardith whispered.

"What's that?" Carlyle replied.

"To have the twins so close together and yet . . ."

"And yet not quite together?"

Ardith nodded.

"I'm hoping," Carlyle said as his attention was drawn to a sudden flurry of activity on the screens showing the front of the building.

A man was being led out of the front entrance of the spa between two agents. Close behind them was Raúl Gomez and another set of agents.

Suddenly the door of a car flung open and Chrissy jumped out.

"Win!" she yelled. "I'm sorry. I didn't mean for all this to happen."

The Agreements

"Hey, hey, hey, get back here," Agent Bergsman shouted as he raced around the vehicle toward Chrissy.

Winston Chambers looked up at her, his face devoid of any emotion.

Agent Bergsman caught up to her and wrapped both arms around her waist, lifting her off the ground.

"Let me go," she screamed.

The shattering of glass caused her to stop fighting. Every head swiveled to find the sound's source.

"What was that?" Ardith said.

"Over there," Carlyle pointed to the business next to the spa where a window on the second floor had been smashed wide open. A man stood inside the shattered space with a gun aimed at the parking lot.

"Oh my," Ardith's hand flew over her mouth. "Isn't that Manny?"

A barrage of shots rang out.

Car windows exploded.

Alarms sounded.

Raúl Gomez dropped in a heap to the ground.

Shots volleyed back.

Agent Bergsman dropped to the ground with Chrissy beneath him, reaching for his weapon as they fell.

More shots were fired.

The FBI agent slumped and rolled to the side, exposing Chrissy completely.

"Look over there!" Ardith said.

She pointed to the top of the picture, where Nellie was emerging from the sedan and running in a low crouch toward Chrissy.

"What is Nellie doing?" Rosie cried out, leaping from her place on her brother's lap, stepping over Julia, and finding a spot to peer over Agent Vicki's shoulder.

"Get back, right now," the FBI agent ordered.

"But what is she doing?" Rosie insisted even as she retreated to Freddy.

The agent did not reply.

"I think she's trying to rescue Chrissy," Carlyle said to Ardith.

FBI agents and police who were ducked behind vehicles fired a barrage back at Manny, providing cover for the man dragging Raúl to safety and another man whisking Winston Chambers into custody. Agent Bergsman lay lifeless on the asphalt.

Meanwhile, Nellie had reached Chrissy and was trying to get her to move. It was hard to tell whether the older girl was physically impaired or just terrified. Finally, Nellie rolled her over, sat her up, and hauled her to her feet. Getting behind her, she half lifted, half shoved the older girl back toward the car.

Right as Nellie was pushing Chrissy into the back seat of the car, another round of shots rang out.

Nellie spun around and fell to the ground.

Rosie screamed.

Freddy dropped his head into his hands.

Carlyle and Ardith sat in stunned silence as sirens split the air.

Chapter 51 – The Choice

Claude Jolicoeur sat in the vinyl recliner beside the hospital bed, sipping his coffee half-heartedly. Harborview Medical Center was known in the region for its excellence in treating adult and pediatric trauma cases, but not so much for its coffee. Perhaps if he had ventured beyond the machine available in the waiting room to the coffee shop on the first floor, he could have purchased a more quality product. But he didn't want to be absent from his vigil too long. Besides, he wasn't quite sure he would be able to find his way back to this room through the labyrinth of hallways.

"Mr. Jolicoeur, have you gotten any sleep?" the nurse who had just entered the room asked as she pumped liquid sanitizer from the dispenser on the wall and rubbed it into her hands.

"Oh, I've had a wink or two," Claude replied.

"I know you want to be here in case anything changes, but you won't be much use to anyone if you collapse from fatigue," she scolded, moving to Nellie's bed to check her vitals.

"Any changes?"

"Not since my last check. But she's holding her own. Quite a fighter you've got here."

"I know that's true."

The nurse replaced an IV bag, typed in some notes into the bedside computer, and then moved to the other bed in the room.

"And what about Julia?" Claude asked, allowing his hand to drift up and over the metal bed rails to stroke the hand of the granddaughter he had only met in the last hours—and who had never met him.

"Well, give me a second and I'll let you know."

It had been two days since the raid at the spa where Winston Chambers had been captured, Manny Santos killed, four men arrested, and fifteen women taken into protective custody. Raúl Gomez was still in serious condition from the shot he had taken in his upper thigh. Claude had heard he was improving. He didn't know what was going on with the FBI agent who had gone down. As for Julia and Nellie, they both still lay unconscious and fighting for their lives.

"Well, her temp is stable. Which is good. Haven't seen a big spike for a while. So that means we just might be getting ahead of this infection," the nurse said. "But she's not out of the woods yet."

"Any guess when either one of them might wake up?"

The nurse stopped and sighed.

"Not really, I'm afraid. Nellie lost a fair amount of blood, as you know, but she has really stabilized in the last six hours or so. And Julia is . . . well, she's quite a bit more fragile than her sister, but seeing all she's been through in the past few weeks, that is to be expected. We are doing all we can for them, Mr. Jolicoeur. The rest is up to them and any higher power you might believe in."

"If I didn't believe in one, I wouldn't be sitting here right now. And I'm guessing neither would these two."

"I'm with you on that," the nurse said with a wink. "I'll be back in half an hour. Anything I can get you?"

"If you've got a miracle or two stashed around here somewhere, we sure could use 'em."

The Agreements

"You and every other family on this floor," she said as she turned to leave, pulling the privacy curtain along its rails in the ceiling to shield the beds from the door.

Claude fell back into his chair and set his cup on the broad windowsill. He stared out the window at the leaden Seattle skies visible between the towering buildings that made up the medical center. Darkness was creeping into the January afternoon on a day so gloomy and wet it was a misnomer to call it a day at all.

"Sure could use a little sunshine," he muttered. "Got any left up there?"

Just then, someone softly rapped on the door.

Claude sat up on the edge of his chair.

"Who's there?"

A hand pulled the curtain back a few feet.

"It's me, Claude," Maria Gomez said, entering the room in her thick raincoat and boots. In her arms she carried an oversized envelope that was threatening to burst at the seams.

"Well, I'll be," Claude said, rising to greet her. "It's about time they let you come over."

He pulled her into a side embrace.

"Agent Reese pulled some strings to get us sprung from house arrest," Maria said. "Besides, I think her agents are getting a little tired of babysitting Freddy and Rosie."

"Where are those two, anyways? I heard they were part of this whole thing, but I haven't seen hide nor hair of them."

"They have them in a safe house. We stopped and saw them on our way here."

"Is Hector with you?"

"He is, but he asked to go see his brother for a few minutes before he came over here."

"Ah, yes, I suppose that would be good for both of them," Claude said. "Why don't you take your coat off and stay a while? Wanna put your package down?"

"Oh, this is for you and the girls," Maria said. "It's a bunch of get-well cards and a banner and stuff. Half of La Verdad has been dropping off cards and leaving messages and food and balloons. Junior, of course, is loving it. Everyone is just so excited that we've found Jewels. And, of course, now word is getting out about Nellie's heroics too. It's quite the story, you know."

Claude took hold of the envelope and filed through the top layer.

"Oh, don't I know it. I've been watching the news crews down there on the street gathering like a bunch of vultures. Haven't even thought about how we're gonna deal with all that hoorah."

Maria draped her coat on a hook behind the door and walked to the space in between the two beds. Tears filled her eyes as she gazed at the girls.

"Well, I think right now you are focused on what we all need to be focused on: these two girls. I am just so grateful . . . I mean . . . the two of them . . . both alive."

Claude nodded.

"How are they doing?" she asked.

"Holding steady, the nurse says."

"Well, that's something to be thankful for. Wait a minute," Maria said suddenly, marching back to where Claude stood. "How could I have forgotten? I am so sorry. I meant to tell you right away. There is somebody out in the waiting room who is very eager to see you. They wouldn't let her come with me into the room. Said her name wasn't on the list."

"A woman?"

"She was just checking in at the nurse's desk when I came along. Says she's a friend of yours from back home. Her name is Elsie."

Claude's head dropped back and he chuckled.

"Don't that beat all," he said, looking upward. "Guess you do have some sunshine left after all."

***

The officer assigned to Hector Gomez stopped at the door of the hospital room to confer with the officer seated in the hallway.

"This is the room," he said, turning back to Hector.

"Okay. Good thing you knew the way, 'cause I would never have found it," Hector replied.

"Part of the security set in place for guys like your brother who could attract visitors who are what you might call 'less than friendly.'"

"Yeah, I suppose that is entirely possible," Hector agreed. "Can I go in now?"

"Sure. I'm going to go grab a cup of coffee. I'll be back for you in twenty minutes. The officer here will be right outside the door, so don't even think about running off without me."

"Don't worry about it," Hector said. "I have no intention of doing anything stupid."

Hector's escort left and the other officer opened the door leading into Raúl's room without saying a word.

Raúl's eyes were closed as Hector approached his brother's bed. He stood for a moment and stared at the face that was at once familiar and strange. Not for the first time, he wondered if he actually even knew this man he called brother.

"Ya gonna stare at me all day, Kiki, or you got something to say?" Raúl said without opening an eyelid.

Hector chuckled.

"How'd you know it was me?"

"The door ain't made of lead," Raúl said, looking up at his kid brother.

"No, I suppose it's not."

An awkward moment hung between them as they silently assessed each other.

"Might as well have a chair," Raúl said.

Hector complied, stepping around the bed to the lone chair in the spartanly outfitted room.

"Has Cynthia been around?" he asked once he was seated.

"Won't hardly leave me alone," Raúl replied. "I told her to at least go get herself some decent food. So she just left a little while ago."

"She's a good woman."

"Better than I deserve."

Another quiet moment passed.

"How are the twins doing?" Raúl asked.

"They're both alive. Unconscious, but stable, from what I hear. I'm heading over to see them as soon as we're done here."

"That's good . . . that's good."

"So, how are you feeling?" Hector asked.

Raúl shrugged.

"I've been better. But I've been worse."

"That's what I heard. Your leg must be pretty sore."

"They got me doped up most of the time, so it isn't too bad just yet. They say I'll live."

"That's good news."

Raúl pressed the gadget on his bed rail in order to sit himself higher.

"Is it?" he said.

"Of course, it is, man," Hector replied.

"I wouldn't blame ya if you wanted to see me dead."

Hector sighed.

"Don't say stuff like that. You're my brother. My only brother."

Raúl leaned his head back onto his pillow and closed his eyes. A single tear slid down his face.

"I didn't mean for it all to happen," Raúl whispered. "I just wanted to . . . I don't know . . . scare you . . . make you pay."

The Agreements

Sirens blaring on the street outside reached a crescendo and then waned as they passed by.

"Rosie was never supposed to be a part of it," Raúl continued. "I let her go, ya know."

"I know. She told us."

"And Jewels . . . wanted to . . . I should have . . . she wasn't supposed to . . . to wind up with . . ." Raúl's voice constricted. "She's such a sweet kid. And now . . . now she's gotta live with . . . if she even does live . . . oh, man. Maybe I should've just died. It's what I deserve."

Hector rose to his feet and drew near to the bed. He reached out a hand and placed it on Raúl's shoulder.

"Raúl, I want you to hear me. Whatever happened to the girls is just as much my fault as it is yours."

Raúl wiped his nose with the back of his hand.

"That's not true," he said.

"No, it is. If I hadn't agreed to keep Jewels from her grandfather all those years ago, if I hadn't moved the whole family out here and asked you for a job and asked you to help us cover our tracks—if I hadn't chosen to do any of those things, none of this would be happening right now. Jewels and Nellie could have grown up safe and sound in the middle of North Dakota with a grandpa who, turns out, is a pretty great guy. And you and I . . . well, we probably would have remained contentedly disconnected from each other on opposite sides of the country."

"Well, now that just might be true," Raúl admitted.

The door to the room swung open and Hector's assigned officer entered.

"You've got about five more minutes," he said. "So, whatever you got to wrap up, get it done."

He turned and exited.

"I'm gonna go to prison," Raúl said. "My attorney went to bat for me and worked out a decent plea agreement, so I don't have to go to trial. They're taking into account my cooperation. But I'm still gonna do some time."

"Me too," Hector said.
"Nah . . . Are you messing with me?"
"Nope."
"For what?"
"Same thing as you—kidnapping."
"Seriously?"
"Yup. Even though Claude says he won't press charges. The feds are of a different mindset. Just too big of a story to let us off scot-free."
"What about Maria?"
"We're working on that. Hopefully she'll be able to stay home with the kids. Maybe have some kind of parole situation. We don't really know yet what we're going to have to do."
"No shit?"
"No shit."
A low chuckle rumbled up from Raúl and he shook his head.
"If the old man could see us now . . . he'd expect it from me. But you? He'd never believe it."
"Well, I guess, you and I aren't so different after all," Hector replied, offering his hand to his brother.
Raúl stared at it for a moment and then reached out and gripped it.
Tears and smiles mixed on both their faces.
"Hey, man, you need a good attorney?" Raúl asked.

Nellie's body tensed as the dream began.

Soft, filtered light surrounded them. Humming floated by and wrapped them in song. Julia's arms pulled Nellie closer until her head pressed into her chest. Their heartbeats synchronized.

They rested.

Content.

The Agreements

Safe.

"I've missed you so," Julia whispered.

Nellie nodded against her twin's heart.

"You know we'll never be apart again, don't you?" Julia said.

Nellie pulled back and gazed into the deeply familiar amethyst eyes. Something about her voice left her with more fear than comfort.

"What do you mean?"

A sudden pressure pushed the two even closer together, removing any distance.

Nellie gasped for air. Julia patted her back.

"It's okay. Don't be afraid. It's just time."

"Time for what?"

Another contraction pressed in on them. Julia began to ease up and away from Nellie.

"Wait! Don't go!"

Nellie grabbed Julia's leg as it slid by. Julia stopped and looked down at her.

"But we agreed," she said. "Me for my time and you for yours. You need to let go."

"But you just came back. You can't leave so soon."

Julia allowed herself to be pulled back into Nellie's embrace.

"But I agreed to go first. After we read our scroll, we signed the paperwork. Remember?"

"I remember that you signed right away," Nellie replied. "But do you remember what I did?"

"Um . . . you sort of hesitated, didn't you?"

"I did. And do you know what I was doing?"

Julia shook her head.

"I was negotiating," Nellie whispered.

"Negotiating? For what?"

"More time."

"More time? For who?"

"For you . . . for us."

"Can you do that?"

"I don't know if you can or can't, but I thought I should at least give it a shot."

"But . . . but didn't you see all the good that would happen if I went first? All the lives you would touch? And all the impact our story would have?"

The womb contracted again and Nellie kicked at the contraction, willing it to stop.

"I did see it," Nellie replied. "But I also saw all the good that could happen if you stayed."

Julia's face wrinkled in consternation.

"But I'm ready to go," she said. "I hadn't thought about staying . . . I didn't know I could."

"I'm pretty sure you can. At least, I asked if you could and I only signed the agreement because I was told you had the choice. Please stay, Jewels . . . for my sake."

Suddenly Julia's body began its journey up and away from Nellie once again.

"No, stop!" Nellie cried.

But Julia just kept slipping by.

"Jewels!"

The name erupted from Nellie's mouth.

Her eyes flew open.

Maria Gomez was holding her hand.

"It's okay, mija," Maria crooned. "You're okay. I'm going to go get your grandpa. I'll be right back."

"Claude!" Maria yelled out the door and down the hallway. "Claude, come quickly!"

One nurse scurried from behind the front desk toward Maria while another appeared from the neighboring room and hustled into the twins' room.

The Agreements

"I'm gonna need you to quiet down, ma'am," the approaching nurse said. "We've got other patients who need their rest."

"I'm sorry," Maria replied. "I just need to get Claude."

"I can help you do that," the nurse said. "I think I just saw him in the waiting area."

Just then Claude came around the corner at a trot, with Elsie close behind.

"Maria," Claude said, closing the distance between them quickly. "What's going on?"

"It's Nellie. She's waking up."

Chapter 52 – The Joy

In the midst of the flurry of activity, a sudden and all-consuming light flooded the Jolicoeur twins' hospital room. Purples and blues, reds and yellows, indigo and orange, all merged together into a white-hot ball of energy. The light was so brilliant, Carlyle put a hand up to shield his eyes. Slowly he lifted one eyelid and peered between his fingers, unable to stare directly at the light, yet equally unable to look away.

He'd seen this before.

Long ago.

Before the beginning of beginnings.

And like before, he knew there was something more beyond the light, something that might ease the deep unease he was experiencing in his inmost being. Yet, try as he might to see what the light contained, he was unable to penetrate its intense brilliance.

Just as he was about to give up and turn away, someone tapped him on the shoulder. He spun around and there, bathed in the light, was Madeline. Silently she reached out her hand. Carlyle took it and allowed her to lead him forward.

"I can't go through there," he said.

The Agreements

Madeline stopped her progress, already half-immersed in the shining.

"But don't you want to see?" she said.

"See what?"

"The joy."

"Joy? Are you serious?"

"Oh, Carlyle," she said. "Of course I'm serious. Why else would they agree?"

With a gentle tug, she pulled him forward into the light and across the time line to the year 2028.

The sign on the door read "Destined for Freedom – Laura Carson – Executive Director."

A woman dressed in a sundress and sandals knocked on the door. The full sleeve of her tattoo caught the natural light pouring in from the skylight overhead. The head of a lion adorned her shoulder, its fierce, golden eyes lifelike in their stare. Its tresses flowed all the way down her arm, and in their midst was inscribed "Freedom 1/14/14."

"Come on in," a voice came from behind the door.

"Laura," the woman said, peeking her head into the office. "The conference room is all set. You want a latte or anything before we start?"

Laura Carson pulled her blonde tresses back off her forehead and lifted up her empty coffee mug. "Thanks, Chrissy. I'm already fully caffeinated."

"Okay cool. Meet you in there," Chrissy said, backing away.

"Hey," Laura called out after her, and Chrissy returned into full view. "How's our little Liberty?"

Chrissy leaned against the doorframe.

"She's so amazing. A little cranky this week. Her daddy thinks she's getting teeth."

"At seven months? Isn't that a little early?"

"That's what I said, but he says his daughter will always be ahead of the curve."

The two women laughed.

"Well, make sure and bring her in sometime soon," Laura said. "You doing okay with being back at work?"

Chrissy dropped her chin.

Laura got up from her desk and walked over to her. She placed a hand atop the tattooed lion.

"It's a big adjustment, I know. But we'll be flexible. We've made this journey together thus far, and we will do whatever we need to do to keep you and your family healthy and connected, right?"

"I know," Chrissy said. "It's just . . . I don't know. I never thought I'd be so . . . you know, attached and stuff. Never thought I could love someone so crazy-like. Surprised?"

Laura lifted Chrissy's chin with her hand.

"From the moment I met you that day in Jimmy Flanagan's living room, I knew that underneath that pink Juicy Couture hoodie there beat a fierce and compassionate heart. So, no, it doesn't surprise me in the least."

The alert on Laura's phone rang inside her trouser pocket: "Your call is waiting, Your Majesty."

Chrissy laughed.

"Last week it was Madame President."

"Needed an upgrade," Laura said. "Let's go before everybody else thinks we're slacking off out here in Seattle."

The conference room consisted of a large, round table with eight matching chairs. Windows ran the length of the wall and looked out over a parking lot full of cars shimmering in the warm August sunshine. A large video monitor sat in the middle of the table. Faces had already begun to populate the screen in separate squares.

"Can you lower the blinds so we can see everyone a bit better?" Laura suggested, moving to take her place at the

The Agreements

table with her laptop while Chrissy moved to the windows to tug down the pleated shades. "Hey everyone, you all doing okay?"

"We're both above ground out here in the prairie," Elsie Jolicoeur was the first to speak up from her kitchen table in Grace, North Dakota, where she sat wrapped in a thick, knitted shawl. "You'd think it was October with the weather we've been getting this week."

"Hotter than the dickens out here at the moment. Maybe we can send some of this summer your direction. How's Claude feeling?" Laura asked as she swiped over her laptop screen sitting on the table in front of her.

"Much better, thanks. Wishes he could be on the call, but I didn't think you'd all want to listen to his barking," Elsie replied.

"Tell him to take it easy. Bronchitis is nothing to mess with at his age," Laura advised.

"That's what I say, but he says, 'What age?' Thinks he's still a spring chicken," Elsie said. "More like an ancient rooster. But he's my ancient rooster and I think I'll keep him."

"Tell him we're praying for quick healing," Maria Gomez piped up from her chair beside her computer nook in La Verdad, Washington.

"That's right. We need that old fella to keep us all in line," Hector said, pointing into the camera from his spot next to his wife.

"Well, Hector, I will certainly let him know," Elsie replied.

"Hey, when are you guys headed to Quantico, Maria? Isn't Rosie's graduation ceremony coming up real soon?" Chrissy asked as she took a seat beside the table.

"We're driving to Seattle tomorrow. Fly out to Virginia on Wednesday. Can you believe she's already done? Seems like we just celebrated her getting into the FBI academy and now she's graduating," Maria said.

"She's been selected to receive the Director's Leadership Award. Did ya hear that?" Hector added, tugging his shirt over his expanded girth.

"I think maybe you might have mentioned that," Laura said.

"Yeah, like about a hundred times," Chrissy added.

"Just wanted to make sure," Hector replied.

"Do you guys know where her first field office will be yet?" Elsie asked.

"Chicago," Maria said. "That's where the center for Violent Crimes Against Children is located now. She's been assigned to the Human Trafficking Task Force in the Midwest region."

"So cool," Chrissy said.

Another square lit up on the video screen, revealing the top of someone's head. Then quickly a face popped up.

"Hey guys," Nellie said, settling back into a mound of pillows on her hotel room bed, the black and neon green of her Kawasaki team jersey a stark contrast against the white linens. She patted down the errant strands shooting out from her short, dark mane. "Sorry we're late. Eric made me stay up late binging that stupid show of his."

"If it's so stupid, why'd you watch?" Eric's voice came from somewhere off camera.

Nellie rolled her eyes and stuck out her tongue.

The group laughed at her antics.

"How'd the school assembly in Bellingham go yesterday?" Hector asked.

"Packed gymnasium. The kids were super attentive and receptive. Of course, first they want to hear all about motocross racing and how's Eric's arm and will my husband ever race again…blah, blah, blah. You'd think he was the one who'd won more races than anyone in his class."

"Hey, I can hear you, ya know," Eric yelled.

"And will he be ready for the circuit this spring, do you think?" Hector asked.

The Agreements

"Oh, yeah. He'll be fine. It's not his first broken bone," Nellie replied.

"We are well aware of that," Elsie said. "As are his parents, who I ran into down at the post office yesterday. And they told me that if I spoke to him any time soon, I was to reiterate what they have been saying. Be fully healed before you jump back on the bike. Do you hear me young man?"

"Yes, ma'am. I hear you," Eric yelled back.

"Hey, Chrissy, how's your book doing?" Nellie asked.

"Not on the New York Times Bestseller list," Chrissy replied.

"Not yet," Laura added.

"It is selling well at all my speaking engagements," Chrissy said. "And the publisher says they are committed to a second printing."

"That's awesome," Eric said as he joined Nellie on the bed, his matching jersey blending in with hers.

"Well, your story is so powerful that's not hard to believe," Maria said. "We are all so proud of you. Without you, I'm not sure this whole thing would even have started."

"And without you and your family, I wouldn't have that story," Chrissy replied.

Quiet settled over the team for a moment.

"Speaking of our beginnings," Laura cleared her throat and looked down at her computer screen. "We are coming up on our ten-year anniversary next spring. You all are making your plane reservations to be at the grand opening of our newest *Destiny Home* in Brooklyn, aren't you? Maria, your sister Carmen and her team are getting totally geared up and ready to go."

"She's so excited to finally be a part of all this, she won't allow us not to be there," Maria said.

"And your mom? How are you guys doing without her?" Laura asked.

"We're not eating nearly as well," Hector remarked. "Although you'd never know that, judging by my waistline."

"We definitely miss her around here and for more than just her cooking. But it was time for her to go back to Brooklyn and be with the rest of la familia," Maria said. "And Carmen has given her a position at the new location. Did she tell you that?"

Laura and Chrissy looked at one another and shook their heads.

"Head Prayer Warrior," Hector said, and everyone on the call let out murmurs of agreement.

"What about the rest of your kids?" Chrissy asked. "Will they be able to make it?"

"Freddy and his wife and baby are coming with us for sure," Maria replied. "Not so sure about Junior yet. He's got so much going on at school. Just got elected president of his senior class and will probably be on tour with the choir about the time we'll be headed out east."

"Wow, the kid is getting a life," Eric remarked.

"Sure is. And it's a good thing he can drive himself around these days cuz he's tiring us out with all his activities," Hector said.

"And Beto?" Laura asked softly. "Any word from him?"

Maria shook her head.

"He did get in touch with Freddy about a month ago. Said he was working somewhere in Texas," Hector said. "We think he's doing a little better… not totally sure."

"Well, at least he's in communication again. That's something," Elsie said.

"Yup, we're still believing in total restoration for him," Hector replied.

"And we are standing with you on that," Laura said.

"Appreciate that more than you know," Maria said, grabbing her husband's hand. Hector turned and gave her a quick kiss on the cheek.

The Agreements

"You okay, mi amor?" he said quietly.

Maria nodded and mustered a small smile.

"Now tell us more about the new place in Brooklyn," Hector said, returning his attention to the group on the screen.

"The remodel is right on target. It's so beautiful, guys. You're just gonna be amazed," Laura reported.

"You should see the piano that was just donated for the music room," Chrissy jumped in. "It's a baby grand! And it's gorgeous."

"Very cool," Nellie said.

"Did Jewels have something to do with that?" Hector asked.

"Oh, you know it," Laura replied. "She's got a gift for touching people's hearts."

"And getting into their pocketbooks," Eric chimed in.

"Where is my sis, anyway?" Nellie asked.

"I'm right here," Julia said, sweeping into the conference room. "Sorry I'm late. Just got done recording an interview for NPR."

"Who would ever have believed this?" Maria said with a smile. "We could barely get her to sing a solo in front of our tiny church at Christmas, and now she does podcasts and speaks at conferences. Not to mention interviews on national television."

"I'd say it's a miracle, all right," Hector agreed.

"Oh, amen," Nellie said.

"Knock it off, guys," Julia said, setting her laptop tote onto the table and pulling out the chair that was vacant between Laura and Chrissy. "A person is allowed to grow and change, aren't they?"

"We're just teasing, mija," Hector said. "Of course, you are. And we are all super proud of you."

Julia settled herself into her seat and leaned over to Laura. She whispered something in her ear and Laura nodded.

"What's going on there, you two?" Nellie asked.

"Yeah, you gonna share with the class?" Eric added.

"Yes, we will," Laura said. "In just a minute. But first, I've been putting together some things for a small book of my own…well, of *our* own, about the story behind *Destined for Freedom*. I want to be able to give it out at the ceremony in Brooklyn."

"That sounds great," Elsie said. "Would love to hear about it."

"Well, I've got a lot of work to do still but I thought you all would like to see some of the stats about what we as a group have accomplished," the executive director said as she slid a document full of statistics from her computer onto the shared video screen where everyone could see them, "In our nine-and-a-half year history thus far, we have helped 442 people transition out of captivity in the sex trade to functioning, productive lives. We have conducted 352 seminars in schools, churches, and community centers, educating people about sex trafficking in their own towns and neighborhoods. We have partnered with local law enforcement and city officials at eight Super Bowls, six Final Four tournaments, and nineteen music festival sites to raise awareness and put safeguards in place for victims. We have raised funds for and set up *Destiny Homes* in Bismarck, Minneapolis, Seattle, and in the near future, Brooklyn, New York."

Laura sat back in her chair and let the statistics sink in.

"I don't know that I say this often enough, but I am incredibly proud of the work we have done together. And I feel very fortunate to be connected to this remarkable extended family," Laura said, "this family that decided to take the traumatic events of their own personal lives and turn them into something so life-giving for so many. It is a joy… an indescribable joy every time I see another soul rescued. Another life turned around. Another destiny restored. So, thank you for choosing to give back. And thank you for choosing me... as part of the team."

"Oh, dear Laura, we could not have done it without you," Elsie said. "You have been the captain at the helm of this thing. We would've sunk a long time ago without your expertise."

"That's for sure," Hector said.

"Agreed," Maria added.

Laura waved off the compliments and wiped the moisture from her eyes.

"Well, thanks. I appreciate that," she said, "but that's not why I called this meeting together. There is an urgent item of business that we need to discuss."

"Sounds serious," Hector said, scooting his chair closer to the Gomez laptop.

"It is. Serious but good. And rather delicate," Laura said. She scrolled through a list of emails with her finger, finally stopping on one highlighted in yellow. "I received a communication earlier this week from Sophia Van Horton."

"*The* Sophia Van Horton?" Maria asked.

"Who's Sophia Van Horton?" Eric said.

"I think she's some New York billionaire or billionairess or whatever you call a super-rich lady," Nellie replied. "Am I right?"

"Yes, she is a very wealthy woman who lives in Manhattan," Laura replied.

"What does she want with us?" Elsie commented. "Does she have a pile of cash to give away?"

"Um, well, this is the sort of delicate part," the executive director cleared her throat. "Elsie, I know Claude isn't quite up to snuff, but I really would love for him to be part of this conversation. We've made this entire journey as a team... as a family. And this is a decision I'm not willing to make without complete agreement from everyone. Do you think you might be able to take your laptop to him? Or is he sleeping?"

Elsie sat to attention. "I will find out," she said, shedding her shawl and lifting up her computer before beginning her journey through the kitchen and up the stairs.

Maria and Hector whispered back and forth between themselves.

Nellie and Eric adjusted the pillows behind them.

Chrissy scribbled a note and passed it to Julia, who read it and gave her a nod.

"Must be a big deal if you sent the missus up here," Claude Jolicoeur's gravelly voice pierced the lull in the meeting.

"Hi, Papa," Nellie blew a kiss across the miles.

"Hi, Papa," Julia echoed. "How are you doing?"

"Feeling better already," Claude said as Elsie propped him up, climbed onto the bed next to him and reached over to button the top button of his striped pajamas. "Although I sure am hankering for a nice draw on my pipe."

"Papa!" Nellie interjected. "That's the last thing you need right now."

Claude shrugged sheepishly.

"Don't worry, Nellie. He'll not be puffing on that thing anytime soon. Now, let's get busy doing what we need to do. I won't have my patient unnecessarily worn out," nurse Elsie directed.

"Yes, ma'am," Laura said. "Chrissy, can you get this email ready to share on the big screen please?"

"Ready whenever you are," Chrissy replied.

"Okay, so here's the deal. Sophia Van Horton emailed me concerning a, and I quote, "sizable contribution should we choose to accept it." I was, of course, immediately intrigued. She gave me a time to call and a personal number to reach her and we conversed at length last Friday. The gist of the matter is that she is the executor to her brother's estate. He passed away about ten days ago. They have been estranged for quite a number of years since the passing of their father."

The Agreements

"Wasn't her father the guy who was killed in 9/11 going back into the tower to rescue his employees?" Hector interjected.

Nellie froze.

Eric took her hand.

"Yes, that is true. Her father owned a large financial services business located in the north tower. He managed to assist quite a number of his employees as well as others from the building before its collapse. But he himself.... well, you know the story. Sophia and her husband stepped into his position and have spent several decades rebuilding the family business. Quite successfully, I might add. Her brother went... let's just say, a different direction."

"Okay, so who's her brother?" Maria asked.

"We'll get to that. But let me say this first. Ms. Van Horton told me her brother had recently reached out to her, having had what she called 'a radical spiritual experience of some sort.' Due to this experience he had made some changes to his will that he was insistent she be made aware of and equally insistent that she carry out. For reasons that will become apparent to you, he has made *Destined for Freedom* a beneficiary of his estate."

The group gasped at this announcement.

"And while he was not as wealthy as his sister," Laura continued, "he still had a significant nest egg."

She nodded to Chrissy, who sent the written correspondence she had queued up to the larger screen.

"Take a look for yourself," Laura said, and sat back in her chair, her fingers steepled on her lips.

"Winston Chambers?" Hector spat out.

Claude began to cough violently.

"Sophia Van Horton's brother is Winston Chambers?" Eric echoed.

Laura held her hands up, palms out, to stop the fury.

Elsie patted her husband's back and reached for a glass of water.

"Yes, Winston Chambers is, or rather was, her brother," she said. "But please, please, take a moment and read what he has written before you throw the baby out with the bath water."

Hector and Maria put on their reading glasses.

Eric and Nellie leaned closer to the screen.

Claude sipped from the glass Elsie had and took a breath.

"Read it aloud will ya, honey?" he croaked.

Elsie opened the document wider on her screen then reached over to her bedside table for her reading glasses.

"Okay, well, it says here, 'I, Winston Chambers, being of sound mind for maybe the first time in decades, do hereby bequeath a sizable part of my estate to the family of Julia Jolicoeur and Nellie Jolicoeur-Nelson and the non-profit organization they have established. Having this conviction, that they have taken the thing that I meant for evil against them and turned it for good for many who have fallen victim to those who would prey upon the innocent and needy for their own gain. It is my desire to make reparations, though I recognize that nothing can take away the trauma they have sustained due to my greed and corrupt practices. I ask for your forgiveness, knowing full well I do not deserve it. I have chosen you to receive this financial gift, not because you are the only family I grievously harmed, but because you are the only one I know of who has committed themselves to wholeheartedly trying to right the wrongs and bring freedom to as many individuals as possible. I therefore believe that you are best suited to wisely and justly utilize the sum of $22 million...'"

"Twenty-two million dollars?" Nellie gasped.

The three women around the conference table nodded.

"Holy macaroni," Eric added, while Hector let out a long, low whistle.

"That's what it says," Elsie continued. "$22 million dollars to continue the work you have begun with *Destined*

The Agreements

for Freedom and *Destiny Homes*. I have also set aside a lump sum to be distributed directly to Chrissy Lombardi as well as a few other individuals, which my sister will arrange directly with them. The aggressive neurological disease I am facing will most likely prevent me from ever seeing the outside of the prison walls that have been 'home' for these past years. But, by the grace of God in sending your daughter/sister Julia to me, I am no longer afraid. In fact, I am looking forward to the freedom of life beyond this planet and the opportunity to observe from a higher perspective what I can only hope will be bountiful and effective usage of the funds which my father wisely set aside in an account I could not squander. If, perhaps, it is too much for you to accept this gift knowing its source, I do understand. My sister is fully capable of redistributing the funds to other needy organizations. But it is my sincere hope that you can find it within your hearts to receive this small token of my heartfelt attempt to right the wrong I have done to you all. With the greatest of regrets for the hurt I have caused, but standing in the forgiveness of Christ, Winston Chambers.'"

Absolute quiet ruled the space between them all.

Laura Carson waited and watched as the family members each scanned and re-read the document. "I think perhaps now you can see why I wanted all of you on this call without any of the newer staff members present," she said.

Claude struggled to sit up straighter, inducing a coughing jag.

When he recovered his breath he said, "What does he mean 'by the grace of God in sending Julia'? Feels like I'm missing something here."

Laura looked to Julia. "You want to tell them, or should I?"

Julia shifted in her seat and adjusted her white cardigan. "Jewels, what the heck did you do?" Nellie asked.

"Yeah, out with it," Eric urged.

Chrissy put her hand atop Julia's and gave it a squeeze.

"Um, well, a few months ago, I had a dream," Julia began. "And I saw a bunch of men sitting in a row with chains around their feet and hands."

"Serious?" Nellie said.

"Yes, serious. Why?"

"I'll tell you later. Just keep going." Nellie said.

"So, all the men's heads were bowed and I couldn't see their faces as I walked by them. Then one looked up at me."

"And?" Hector prodded.

"And it was Winston Chambers. And he was shriveled up like an old man, but I knew it was him. He didn't say anything to me, but I could feel what he wanted to say. And I woke up."

Another quiet moment passed.

"And then what?" Claude asked.

"And then, I called Lita," Julia said.

"That was a good idea," Maria said. "She's always so good with understanding dreams. What did she say?"

"She said I should pray about it and the Lord would tell me what to do."

"Was he asking you to forgive him?" Nellie said.

Julia nodded.

"So did you talk to him or something?" Elsie asked.

"I did," Julia confessed. "I talked to him face to face."

"You went to the prison?" Eric said.

"Yes. I felt like it was what God was asking me to do."

"I did go with her to Walla Walla," Laura interjected. "But she did all the talking."

"What did you say, mija?" Hector asked.

"I told him that I forgave him. And that, while I did not like any of the things that happened to me or Nellie or Chrissy or anyone else, that we, as a family, were seeing how God was turning it all around for our good."

"What did he say to that?" Claude said.

Julia paused for a moment.

The Agreements

"He started to cry," she said quietly. "And he asked me to tell him something good... anything good that could have possibly come from all his greed. So, I did. He was pretty sick by then already... and weak... so we only stayed for a little while. But as we were leaving, the prison chaplain stopped us and thanked us for coming. He said Winston had been asking to speak with him more and more the sicker he got and that me showing up was nothing short of a miracle."

The group gathered on the screen did not move or speak.

"Jewels, from now on, I am going to make sure that everybody knows that you are the brave one between the two of us," Nellie said.

Julia shook her head and pulled her hands into her lap.

"Good job," Chrissy whispered.

"Okay," Laura said. "Now that we have that out in the open, we still need to make a decision about accepting Sophia's...or rather Winston's offer. I do need total agreement and Ms. Van Horton would like to hear from us before the end of the month."

"I don't need a bunch of time to think about it," Claude said.

"Okay, but let's not be hasty, Claude," Laura cautioned.

"Oh, I ain't thinking about rejecting his offer," Claude said. "Who cares where the money comes from? Money is a neutral entity. Only thing that makes it good or evil is how it's used. My vote is we accept the offer and start using it for good ASAP."

"I second that vote," Elsie chimed in.

"Me too," Hector said.

"Me three," added Maria.

The young couple in the hotel room in Bellingham remained quiet.

"My vote is whatever Nel's vote is," said Eric.

Nellie laid her head back atop her pillow and stared at the ceiling.

"Like I said, you don't have to decide right now," Laura said.

Nellie wiped away the tears that had begun to stream down her face and shook her head.

"No, I'm…." she hesitated, swallowing the lump in her throat. "I'm not gonna change my mind a day from now or a week from now."

Chrissy whispered to Julia, "You did your best."

"Alright. Well, that's it, then. We will not move forward without complete agreement. And if Nellie isn't for this then…" Laura began.

"I didn't say I'm not for it," Nellie jumped in. "I said I've already made up my mind. If Jewels can forgive that guy, then I'm gonna work on that too. Let's take the money and run with it."

Elsie clapped her hands. "That's the spirit!"

"Amen," added Claude.

"We're with ya," Hector said, while Maria simply nodded, too emotional to talk.

"Wonderful. I will speak to Sophia tomorrow," Laura added with a smile that could light up half of King County.

The group took a collective long sigh.

"Who would ever have believed that Winston Chambers would have such a change of heart?" Hector said.

"Well, look at your own brother, Raúl and the man he's become," Maria added quietly. "Look at all the men he's helped inside the prisons by leading Bible studies and giving his testimony."

"That's true," Eric said. "Like Jewels said, every man needs room to grow up."

"Says the man who rides motorcycles for a living," Nellie said, leaning into the camera.

"Look who's talking," Eric said, yanking her back.

"Okay, you two," Elsie said. "No fighting."

The Agreements

"No worries," Eric said holding up his hands in surrender. Then he leaned over to Nellie and whispered in her ear. Nellie whispered something back.

"What are you two up to?" Claude said.

"Oh, Eric just wants me to tell you guys that I won't be riding the circuit this winter down south," Nellie said.

Laura and Chrissy exchanged a surprised look.

Claude gasped and began coughing again. Elsie pounded his back.

Hector and Maria leaned into the camera so quickly they bumped heads.

"Is your bike broken down?" Hector asked.

"My bike's fine. Freddy has it purring like a kitten," Nellie said.

"Are you sick?" Elsie asked.

"Not exactly," Eric said, putting his arm around his wife's shoulder.

"The doctor said riding might be too risky for the baby," Nellie said.

Exultant screams erupted all over the screen.

Maria's hands flew up to her face and she began to weep.

Elsie grabbed a tissue and blew her nose.

Chrissy bopped Julia on the arm. "Did you know about this?"

Julia smiled and nodded.

"How could you keep this from us?" Laura added.

"Oh, you who have a just dropped a $22-million-dollar-donation bomb on people have very little room to criticize," Julia said with a laugh. "Besides, I thought it was about time we had a day filled with nothing but good surprises."

Epilogue

In a place outside of time, where destinies were fulfilled, dreams accomplished and races finished, an agreement facilitator strolled along a path that bordered the upper rim of a huge amphitheater. His navy livery was immaculately pressed, such that the pleats fairly cut through the atmosphere as he moved. The light bouncing off the rows of gemstones that lined his shoulders sent vibrant shafts of color out to his left and his right.

Beside an entrance to the amphitheater, an usher stood, directing a constant stream of people to open places down the rows of seating that opened onto an enormous circular viewing space at the bottom.

"Ah, Carlyle," the usher said. "Back for more?"

"Keeps me going," Carlyle replied. "I can't always be in the field observing, so coming here is the next best thing."

"Lots of encouraging and miraculous things happening, judging by the cheers and roars I've been hearing. Anyone in particular you're here to see?"

Carlyle scanned the crowd. Millions of souls chatted and sang and watched without any sense of chaos or confusion. Across the way, about halfway down the stands, he spotted them.

The Agreements

"Over there," he said. "Just below the row of teal and green."

The usher smiled at the two women who Carlyle indicated. One was garbed in the richest of blues and purples, while the other's robes radiated stunning reds and oranges. At times though, when they linked arms and leaned forward, or threw back their heads and laughed, the colors they emitted swirled together, making it difficult to discern if they were two or just one.

"The Jolicoeur twins," the usher said. "They've been quite enthusiastic... again."

"Yes, they sent me a message that I should join them. Not exactly sure why but with those two, it's always a good bet it will be something interesting."

"No doubt about it. Go and enjoy, my friend."

The two shook hands and Carlyle traversed the airspace in a blink and landed beside Julia and Nellie.

"Carlyle!" they said in unison, rising to greet him with warm hugs.

"We're so glad you could join us," Julia said.

"It's just about to happen," Nellie said.

"And what exactly would 'it' be this time?" Carlyle asked.

"Oh, you'll see," Julia said.

Far below them in the expansive opening, a panorama of the earthly realm spread out in crystal clear detail.

"What year are we at?" Carlyle asked.

"January 1, 2105," Nellie replied.

"Ten years after your final graduation?" Carlyle said.

"To the day," Nellie acknowledged.

"Ten years and one day after mine," Julia added.

"Ah, yes. We must not forget, you did indeed go first," Carlyle said. "And where are we focused?"

Nellie pointed to a city along the east coast of the United States. "Boston Children's Hospital."

"And who are we focused on?" Carlyle asked.

"Hanna Jolicoeur Smythe," Julia replied. "My great-great granddaughter…well, Nellie's great-great granddaughter."

Carlyle was aware that Julia had never married nor had children of her own.

"Technically that is true, but not in matters of the heart," he commented. "It seems to me that you two managed to share those children and grandchildren quite beautifully."

"Well, it was the least I could do after convincing her to stay," Nellie said.

"You didn't convince me," Julia replied. "I chose to stay."

"Okay, ladies, let's focus on the event at hand which is… what exactly?"

"Hanna is about to take her first step," Nellie said.

"Her first? And she's how old now?"

"She just turned five," Julia said.

"Five? Years?" Carlyle asked.

The twins nodded with huge smiles lighting both their faces.

Carlyle was a bit perplexed, not being familiar with this particular offspring.

"She's about to do it," Nellie said. "Let's go join in the moment."

The sisters each took one of Carlyle's hands and the trio left the realm of eternity and entered the earthly scene – a therapy room in the research wing of Boston Children's Hospital. Along one wall, a team of five researchers stood chatting quietly back and forth. A sense of excitement exuded from their corporate heart lights. In the room's center, a three-foot-wide mat ran for about four yards. It looked firm but spongy, with lines of some sort of electrical wiring running the entire length in parallel lines every two or three centimeters.

The Agreements

"Rose looks so beautiful," Nellie commented as the three took up their place behind a young woman.

"Takes after her great-grandmother I'd day," Carlyle said.

"If you want to see a family resemblance, look at little Hanna," Julia said. "Her face looks just like you, Nel, right before you'd snapped down the lid of your visor at the start of a race."

Carlyle laughed. "Bingo! You've got that right."

"Well, that's not all bad, is it?" Nellie replied.

"Shh...she's getting up," Julia said.

Hanna eased herself up off a stool and stood. She was small for her age, with spindly legs that looked as if they had never been used. Her head wobbled slightly from its place atop her curved spine. Her feet were clad in bright pink tennis shoes that glowed with some sort of inner vibration. The special mat she stood on was emitting a frequency so high Carlyle doubted any of the humans in the room could hear it. Hanna's mother, Rose, stood to the side of her daughter with all of her fingertips tapping nervously along her thighs.

"Okay sweetie, nice and easy. There's no hurry," Rose coached her daughter.

Hanna looked at her and smiled. Then she let her gaze wander to the space right around her mother.

"What is it?" her mother asked.

"Visitors," Hanna replied. "I like visitors."

"The doctors?" Rose asked.

Hanna shook her head.

"Do you think she knows we're here?" Julia asked.

"Could be," Carlyle replied. "Some kids are pretty good seers."

In front of Hanna, a therapist reached out her hand.

"All right girl, here we go. Today's the day," the therapist said. "You've got this."

Hanna turned her attention back to the task at hand and scrunched her face in concentration. Her right leg began to vibrate as she lifted it ever so slightly on the surface of the mat. The toe of her sneakers caught, hindering her progress. But just as it seemed she might topple forward into the arms of her therapist, she found her balance, balled her hands into fists, and willed her foot up and forward.

Exultant accolades erupted from both the earthly and heavenly rooting section.

"She did it!" Nellie shouted. "She took a step!"

"And she's taking another!" Julia added.

With each step, the little girl's spine straightened and her head steadied.

Carlyle clapped his hands and smiled, enjoying the energy of the Jolicoeurs as they whooped and hollered.

"Wasn't that amazing?" Julia said when the great-great granddaughter of her heart had completed her short journey.

"Isn't she something?" Nellie added. "She's got so much spunk."

"For sure," Julia added. "I don't think anything is gonna get in the way of her accomplishing everything on her scroll."

"Reminds me of a few girls I once observed," Carlyle said, grinning at the shining countenances of his former charges. He didn't know if they would ever fully appreciate how much their lives had radically altered his understanding of the wondrous partnership between the Designer and the human race. He had learned to never underestimate what they could overcome and accomplish together.

Once they had agreed.

Acknowledgments

Thanks are due to so many. To the One who endured the cross for the joy set before Him, the Lord Jesus Christ, I give my adoration and praise. He is Worthy. To my husband who supports my writing habit and lives out his own passions, I give my thanks and undying love. To my children who have all flown the coop yet still find ways to bolster my sometimes-flagging enthusiasm for the creative journey, I give my appreciation. I love watching you fly. To my parents who instilled in me the love of reading, I am indebted beyond what I can repay. To my dear friends Wendy Marie, Amanda, Cheri, Nita and Danielle who volunteered to read early drafts of this story, I give kudos for bravery and thanks for gentle but sure suggestions for improvements. To my mystical mentors Nancy and Shannon, who first planted this seed of pondering our pre-existent agreements in my soul, I give recognition for your extraordinary lives and love. Keep running before us. To my Table-mates who prayed and encouraged week after week after long week, I owe you and promise to return the favor. To my Mexican-American family of in-laws who have embraced me as their own, I give gratitude for your inclusive hearts and wonderful storytelling skills. To Julie McKnight for her awesome cover design, I applaud both your skills and your heart. To my editors Hannah Comerford and Lori Baxter at The Scribe Source, I give sincere thanks for your guidance, correction and professionalism. To Livia Mae for proofing my Spanglish, muchas gracias mija. Any foibles, fumbles or errors I own as mine alone.

About the Book

It was December of 2017 and I was gazing out at the Rocky Mountains through the tall windows of the conference center I was sitting in with my husband. I'm not sure if I was distracted by the stunning view or if the 8,500-foot elevation was affecting my cognitive processes, but I was having a hard time concentrating on the speaker's words. Of course, the depth and mysteries of Nancy Coen's words alone sometimes have that affect on my brain. But then she said something that I caught. She said, "You have all read the scroll of your life before you arrived here on the planet and agreed to everything written on it."

I'm not sure I heard anything else the rest of that day because I was so taken aback by that statement. Was that true? And what if it was? Ramification and ripples zipped through my mind and I debated the points with myself long after we left the conference grounds in Colorado and returned to the oxygen rich air of our home just outside of Seattle.

In some ways I was appalled by the thought. How could that take into account the depth of human suffering throughout all of history? Who in their right mind would agree to live in and through those things? But in other ways, I was inspired. How bodacious is the human spirit? Could it be that we humans – made in the image of our Creator – are even more like Him than I imagined? Afterall, scripture says that the Lord Jesus Christ was slain before the foundations of the world (Revelation 13:8). In Hebrews 12:2 it says that He endured the cross, scorning its shame for the joy set before Him. So, He knew what He was getting into before He took on human flesh. And He did it anyway because He saw the end from the beginning and He decided the price to be paid was worth it. Scripture also says that as He is, so are we in this world. (I John 4:17b)

Setting this all before the Lord in prayer, I felt the stirrings of a story. It pestered me and plagued my thoughts until at last I sat down and began to write. As with my previous book, I had no outline or story arc in mind. I just stepped out and wrote what came to me from this place of pondering a mystery. The difficulties and pain of the characters who emerged on the pages disturbed me and many times, knowing what was unfolding, I stopped and refused to continue. I didn't want to write the traumas and losses and abuses because in doing so I had to go there in my mind – in my heart. But eventually, I sucked it up reminding myself, "This is just a work of fiction. Real people are living in much worse situations than anything I can imagine. The least I can do is tell a story that might inspire someone to carry on in the midst of whatever it is they are suffering."

There were a number of times when after listening to a news report or reading a headline about yet another wave of atrocities or yet another tragic circumstance I fell into a sort of existential crisis and stopped writing. One such time I was taking a walk with my brother and we were chatting about what was going on in our lives. He asked me about what I was writing. I hesitated to tell him. When I asked what he thought about the premise that we have seen our lives before we were born and agreed to them, I believe his exact reply was, "Oh, hell no." I had to laugh. I understood that response. But then we began to talk about people we admire – people of influence – and what they endured in their lives that shaped their characters and informed their destinies. I think he began to at least entertain the possibility.

My motivation for writing *The Agreements* began very selfishly. I simply wanted to push a thought out to an extreme and see if it still held – see if it changed the way I viewed myself and my neighbor – see if it encouraged me to identify less as a victim and more as an overcomer – see if it emboldened me to be more like Jesus.

I am hoping that perhaps those desires to explore will extend to my readers as well.

If you are angered, offended or confused by the premise of this book, I beg your forgiveness. It is not my intention to minimize anyone's suffering or capriciously intimate that you should just get over something because this is 'what you signed up for'. Not at all. My hope is that perhaps in some small way I might cause you, like me, to ponder a possibility. One that stirs each of us to seek out the treasures in darkness and the riches stored in secret places that we might know that He is the Lord, the God of Israel, the One who calls us by name. (Isaiah 45:3) And one that prompts us to look for the heart light in every soul knowing that we are all mined from the same quarry of His heart. (Isaiah 51:1)

Shalom.

Something Delicious – Algo Delicioso

My mother-in-law Josephine Valdez Cerna (1925-2014) was an amazing lady. In the character of Lupe Hernandez, I have slipped in some of my fondest memories of Josie. She was forever feeding people and insisting, "You have to eat something, mija." Her prayers were powerful and continuous covering all of her twelve children, their spouses, her grandchildren, great-grandchildren and many, many others. She had the ability to know what was going on in people's lives and love them anyway. I greatly miss her keen sense of humor and quick laughter. But I see glimpses of her in different family members and recognize her voice in my heart at times when I most need to hear it.

One of the small things we all miss are her homemade tortillas – which she made daily in impressive quantities when her children were growing. She didn't have a bread drawer. She had a tortilla drawer. Oh, to be able to raid that today and stuff a fresh tortilla with the beans cooking on her stovetop, a sprinkling of cheese and her canned salsa. I pass on to you this recipe that I wrangled out of her one day as I watched her work. She couldn't tell me exact quantities – she just felt them. I am the one who needed to measure what she threw into the bowl. So what follows is what I wrote down from that day in her kitchen.

Te amo Mamá.

Josie's Tortilla Recipe

2 cups unsifted flour
1 tsp salt or less
1 tsp baking powder
Less than ¼ cup vegetable oil
¾ cup lukewarm water

Put flour in a mixing bowl. Add salt and baking powder. Mix.

Put water in center and add oil. Gradually mix dry ingredients with water and oil.

Form a ball and knead thoroughly until smooth. Form into a ball again and let stand for 10 minutes. Knead again and form into a ball again. With small amount of oil, grease the dough ball. Let it stand again for 10-15 minutes.

Divide dough into small balls of about 2" in diameter.

At this point they will be ready to roll out. Or you can wait for another 5 minutes before rolling the small balls out.

You can use a little bit of flour so the balls will not stick to the surface of the rolling pin. Roll them out thinner than you would roll out pie crust. Smooth over a hot griddle and cook. Keep turning each over now and then until bubbles start to puff up the tortilla.

Recommended Reading

Limitless: Living the Life of and Overcomer
by Nancy Coen
Revelation Partners in association with Nancy Coen Media (2019)

Beyond Human: Fully Identified in the New Creation
by Justin Abraham
Seraph Creative (2016)

In Our Backyard: Human Trafficking in America and What We Can Do to Stop It
by Nita Belles
Baker Books (2015)

Girls Like Us: Fighting for a World Where Girls Are Not for Sale
by Rachel Lloyd
HarperCollings (2011)

Stay in Touch

www.facebook.com/wendyjocerna

I'd love to hear from you.
Just be gentle…please.